WITCHLORE

"You loved her," Bastian says. I stare at him. He doesn't say it incredulously or jeeringly, just factually. There's something about it that's comforting. That it's not an opinion. The sky is blue, life sucks, I loved and still love Elizabeth.

"It should have been me," I say, voice harsh as I stare at a couple of swans swimming together. A pair. Inseparable. "I wish it had been. I'd do anything to change what happened..."

For E, who is magic.

First published in the UK in 2025 by Usborne Publishing Limited, Usborne House, 83-85 Saffron Hill, London EC1N 8RT, England, usborne.com.

Usborne Verlag, Usborne Publishing Limited, Prüfeninger Str. 20, 93049 Regensburg, Deutschland VK Nr. 17560

Text copyright © Emma Hinds, 2025

Author photo © Emma Hinds, 2025

The right of Emma Hinds to be identified as the author of this work has been asserted by her in accordance with the Copyright, Designs and Patents Act, 1988.

The name Usborne and the Balloon logo are Trade Marks of Usborne Publishing Limited.

All rights reserved. No part of this publication may be reproduced, stored in a retrieval system or transmitted in any form or by any means, electronic, mechanical, photocopying, recording or otherwise without the prior permission of the publisher.

This is a work of fiction. The characters, incidents, and dialogues are products of the author's imagination and are not to be construed as real. Any resemblance to actual events or persons, living or dead, is entirely coincidental.

A CIP catalogue record for this book is available from the British Library.

JFMAMJJA OND/25   ISBN 9781835409589   9914/1

Printed and bound using 100% renewable energy at CPI Group (UK) Ltd, Croydon, CR0 4YY.

WITCHLORE

EMMA HINDS

Content note:

WITCHLORE is a work of fiction but it deals with many real issues including suicidal ideation and self harm.

Prologue

The day she dies is beautiful. It's May, the summer holidays have just started, and the air over the fields is hazy and still, smelling of wild garlic. The light is so golden, it has that intense quality of a lazy afternoon first thing in the morning. She laughs as she tugs my hand, pulling me through the shaded trees towards the cave.

"I'm not sure." I lag behind, staring at the mine gully suspiciously. The ground beneath our feet is hard and dry but the air coming off the ancient grey stone around us is chilled. With the small hole of the cave a black mark in the green and grey stone, weathered smooth and moss covered, it feels as if all the lush, whispering green trees above us are egging us on towards a secret.

"Please, just try." Elizabeth cups my face and kisses my lips. She tastes like coconut lip balm. "For me."

I can never refuse her, tasting so sweet and smelling like suncream and sweat. Her blond hair is like the shimmer off a puddle or the ocean, catching every particle of light as she moves her head.

"Okay."

"Great!" She smiles that perfect smile, the one that shows off the slight asymmetric nature of her teeth. "Don't worry. No one's going to see at this time in the morning."

There is nothing inside the cave but a thick black darkness that swallows us. It stinks of wet things, of the mulch under leaves, of the inside of a tree. Reluctantly, I press my right hand against the damp stone, its coldness seeping into my skin, making me shiver.

"Are you ready?"

I should say no, tell her that I can feel something wrong coming towards me, that there is danger lurking under the wet moss, but I don't. She is too excited, too certain, so I only nod. She grins, the bright light outside of the cave only catching one half of her face, an absurd half smile.

"Let's do it," she says. I can't help my admiration when she holds her hands up in the preparatory triangle, taking a deep breath as her beautiful opal ring begins to glow. She flexes her hands. Watching her do witchcraft is always breathtaking; the way power radiates from her and the air around her smells like toasted almonds. Other witches make me feel inferior with their magic, and watching them only increases my resentment towards them, but not with Elizabeth. I never hate her for possessing the skill I lack. Her hands are so fluid as they move through the spell shapes, polished nails catching the pearly glow of her ring.

Then she starts to chant and something is terribly wrong. The coldness from the stone wall is strengthening like ice in my blood, spreading from my fingertips down into my veins, creeping towards my heart.

"Elizabeth," I gasp, and my breath is cold against my own lips. I try to pull my hand away from the stone but it's like it's glued there and the harder I pull, the more I feel it: the stretching, gnawing feeling that I associate with a shift. "Elizabeth, stop—"

She looks at me with such excitement and I realize she doesn't know the danger yet, she thinks this is proof that her spell is working. I've lost my voice, it's been frozen out of me, so I can't tell her that something awful is happening, something neither of us can control or stop, something worse than a shapeshift, more violent and more powerful. I can't do anything and I can't save her from it. The last thing I see before the rushing coldness hits my heart is her eyes; one blue in the light outside the cave, one blackened by shadows. Then light explodes from my chest and I am gone.

Chapter One

Four months later

I stare at the red, healing lines on my right wrist.

"Ouch," I hiss, as I carefully spread on the antiseptic cream and rewrap my arm. "Ouch, ouch, ouch—"

"How is it?" Beryl asks. She's standing at the door of the bathroom holding Mr Pebbles in her arms. Mr Pebbles is not a cat. He's a demon. He hisses at me and leaps down to stalk along the edge of the bathtub, glaring at me with yellow eyes. He has no fur, which I find suspicious in a cat, and a habit of trying to urinate on everything I own, which is frankly just disgusting.

"The same," I say. It's been four months and it still looks awful. In the first two months, I could not stop scratching it, so now it has that slightly gnarly look – as if it is deliberately taking its time to pull back together.

"You screamed in the night," Beryl says, pulling at the crystal on a ribbon around her neck. "I tried to get in. Did you lock your door?"

"I was fine." I live in a halfway house for young adult witches with "problems" run by Beryl, who is nice but also as sharp as a bowl of marbles. She's about sixty, with long grey hair that she wears braided in a crown or loose with feathers in it. She loves a tunic and making her own deodorant and looks, to my mind, like the typical midlife white British witch. She's also kind enough and makes an excellent cup of tea, but since this is a halfway house she is not the only one who lives here, so of course I keep my door locked. People like me don't do well in shared environments with unlocked doors. Mr Pebbles hisses. I almost hiss back.

"You're not meant to do that." Beryl frowns and takes my other wrist, turning it over, a daily self-harm check. When she sees the skin is cut-free she drops it with a sniff. "Your counsellor said no closed doors."

My counsellor at the hospital, Counsellor Cooper, is the one who recommended Beryl's as a good alternative to going back into student accommodation. Given my "challenges". I could technically leave whenever I want, but it's better than my parents' house, which was floated as the other possible option for my mental-health recuperation. If their house was a healthy place for mentally scarred shapeshifters I wouldn't be in the habit of dodging all their emails. Besides, Beryl's is convenient for college, even if there is a lot more chat about celebrating the inner goddess and processing trauma through mime than I prefer.

"If you wanted to get in, you could have," I say. I eye the lapis lazuli ring on her middle finger with dislike. I've had quite enough of witches and their damned rings. "But Mr Pebbles pisses on my bed when I don't lock it."

"Hmm." Beryl twists her fingers in a crooked sequence and

the blue stone in her ring glows. Mr Pebbles is suddenly out in the hall, licking his bum, a glow of dark blue magic settling around his ears. I look away in disgust. As a witch's cat, Mr Pebbles is used to being moved by witchcraft. After the summer I've had, it makes the hair on the back of my neck stand on end.

"You said her name again. In the night."

I pause. I am trying very hard, every minute of every day, to not say her name aloud. I should be allowed to scream it in my dreams.

"So?"

"The counsellor said, didn't she, that dreams could be connected to—" Beryl gestures at my body. "—all of that?"

Counsellor Cooper is right. Apparently shapeshifting, especially changing sex when you have absolutely no control over your ability, can be a bit traumatic. This is ironic because my shift is the least traumatic thing to happen to me this summer.

"It's fine," I say.

"How is all this?" she asks, looking me up and down as if deliberately seeking out my broader chest even though she didn't even know me in my old form. She frowns. "I thought the counsellor suggested you...adjust your clothing to something more masculine? To help you get used to the new form?"

"It's not new, it's been four months, and what's feminine about a T-shirt and jeans?"

I look down. Being a shapeshifter, I'm drawn to the same clothes over and over, as a way to reassure the witches around me that I'm the same person under all this different skin.

"Nothing, but..." Beryl gestures towards my ears. I reach up and touch the hoops. They're white gold. They were Elizabeth's and I am never, ever going to take them off.

"Boys can wear earrings and, besides, I'm not a boy," I say, picking up my backpack from the floor of the bathroom. When I told Beryl I was non-binary she thought I was talking about computers. "I'm going to be late."

"Have a good first day back at college, Lando," she says. My stomach lurches. I think a good day might be too much to ask for. I'll settle for a not-terrible one.

I brush past her and head to the front door, past the conservatory where a witch from a local coven is leading a light-and-healing celebration. Eight witches, all between the ages of sixteen and twenty-one, sitting blissfully in the golden September morning light, their rings glowing with inner peace. Beryl thinks it's best I do any morning meditation on my own. She says it's because group stuff won't suit my rehabilitation plan, but I'm not the only one in here after a suicide attempt. I am the only shapeshifter, though. They're nice enough, the other witches recovering from eating disorders or drug addiction or depressive episodes, they're fine to share a kitchen and bathroom with and no one's particularly rude, but I imagine the idea of having a shapeshifter in their morning ceremonies makes the witches twitchy. Especially when the shifter in question accidentally killed a witch over the summer.

When I arrived, there was one witch who wouldn't stay in a house with a shapeshifter. I said to Beryl that it was a pretty bigoted response, but she just sighed and said sternly, "We don't judge here, we try to deal in facts rather than feelings. The facts are that a shapeshifter with no magical control is not less threatening. It makes you unpredictable and, since you are twenty times more powerful than everyone living here, that unpredictability is dangerous."

I got the message, loud and clear: *We do judge here, just the same as everywhere else.*

I press my key fob against the electronic door, trying to ignore the sensation that I am checking myself out of a prison. Beryl's halfway house is in an old red-brick Victorian building in Chorlton, which unfortunately has the look of a haunted hospital, from the twisted wrought-iron gate to the tiny slit windows on the fifth floor. When I first arrived a few months ago, I imagined someone was going to lock me in an attic in a straitjacket and feed me gruel. In reality, it's a leaky old municipal building that's been shoddily converted into a facility for young people. The double glazing is terrible, the bathrooms have no windows, and when someone cooks onions the smell gets into every nook and cranny.

I walk the ten minutes down the road to Chorlton tram station and put my headphones on, just like all the other students waiting for the next tram. No one looks twice at me. It's only when I'm at college that witches know to stare. *Freak. Abnormal. Shifter.*

I let myself settle into the fantasy of another life, just for a moment. Right now, I could be on my way to the Manchester

University library, ready to meet some mates for a study session and get coffee together. If only.

I see a witch further down the tram platform. She's a bit older than me, dressed for a corporate city job. She's trying to balance a coffee cup on one of those tilted seats they put on the platform, more a bum rest than an actual bench. In frustration, she spreads her fingers wide and twists them into a spell, her jade ring glowing softly green. The cup sticks to the surface. Around her, several people give her a suspicious glare, stepping away slightly. She is holding the spell with her ring hand, her fingers trembling from the exertion while she fumbles in her bag for something. *Not going to be fast enough,* I think and, sure enough, the spell fades, the cup falls, and the people either side of her jump back in annoyance as coffee splatters over them.

"Fucking witches," a man in a suit mutters, trying to brush coffee flecks off his white shirt.

"Maybe invest in a Thermos, love," an older woman says, handing the blushing witch a pack of tissues.

"If I was a witch, I'd change my nails every two seconds," a schoolgirl standing next to me says. She's in the middle of sharing a morning Egg McMuffin with her friend, both of them leaning indolently against the wall in their blazers.

"Get a manicure, it lasts longer." Her friend shoots the witch a stunningly disparaging look for her age. "Nothing they do lasts. If it doesn't last, what's the point?"

I watch the embarrassed witch, her ring still haunted by a residual glow as she throws the remnant of her coffee in the bin. She looks up, clearly feeling me watching, and for a second she frowns and my stomach lurches. I duck my head and cough, looking away, wondering if I'm imagining suspicion in her eyes. You never know what a witch will do with someone they suspect could be a shapeshifter. I remember when my father taught me about magic and witches when I was about five years old.

"Witches are like musicians," he says. "Their rings are their instruments, magic is their music."

"So their rings help them make magic?" I stare at my father's bare fingers, always one moment away from shimmering with white magic. "If a human had a witch's ring, like—" I think of the humans I know. There aren't many. "—Donald the postman, could he do their magic?"

"If a person took a maestro's violin, could they make noise? Certainly. If they studied, might they learn to make music? Possibly. Could they make music like the maestro who has practised since they were born, has lived for nothing but music, who has dreamed in music as their first language, whose musical culture going back generations has baked it into their soul? I do not think so. That is what witches are like. Magic is the air witches long to breathe, their only connection to an ancient, greater past, when they were leaders. Gods. Now they are mediocre."

Father doesn't look sad about it. He looks pleased. Father is rarely pleased.

"But...there are powerful witches?" I ask hesitantly.

"There are surprises, prodigies, there always will be."

He shrugs. "But the magic inside them is smaller than it used to be. Much smaller than ours."

"So we don't make music like they do?"

"No, Orlando." He smiles at me, magic glittering across his face as it changes, a father of a thousand faces. "We are the bird, we are the river, we are the tempest, we are our own music, all the time, always singing. We are magic. They can never have it, they can never take it away from us, and for this, they will always hate us. They will never trust us. Remember that."

When the tram arrives, the two schoolgirls take seats near the embarrassed witch and, two stops later, they are asking her if she has a crystal ball at home or if she dances with the devil. The witch is answering, explaining paganism, and I feel a strange thrum of envy. For better or worse, witches can be themselves in this world. Maybe my father was right and they think more power is the answer to all their problems. I am the proof that is categorically not true. I am a shapeshifter who is learning witchlore and witchcraft, and in May, my girlfriend died and everyone thinks it was my fault. All I have are problems.

Chapter Two

If you ask someone to imagine a witchcraft college, they'll spout off about turrets and gargoyles. In reality, Demdike College is on the other side of a metal door with the word "cock" graffitied on it in the Northern Quarter of Manchester. It's a Merlin Foundation college, one of many around the UK, and some of them, yes, might have pretty spires and arches but this one is housed in an old mill building near the Port Street Beer House with metal window and door shutters that are magnets for the Manchester street artists. The sign over the door is small, easily missed, and has the words *Demdike College* printed in Comic Sans over a vague silhouette of a goddess symbol. It's pretty tacky, but witches seem to love any marketing that makes them indistinguishable from a yoga studio.

My parents are the ones who insisted I go here rather than a normal university, where, god forbid, I could study creative writing or sociology and maybe actually have a good time. Or rather, they told me if I didn't come, they'd cut me off. With a choice between being homeless or coming to Demdike, I chose

Demdike. Besides, anything is better than living under their roof. Just like the various Bible colleges in Manchester, Demdike only offers a degree in faith-based studies, four-year courses in witchlore. It's generally for witches who come from covens and families who care about keeping the faith and craft alive, and witches who are actually good at doing witchcraft. Once every fifty years or so, they might get a shapeshifter come through. Unfortunately, for the last two years, that shapeshifter has been me.

It's the first Monday in September and all the schools and colleges are going back, so obviously, the wet end-of-August weather has given way to glorious sunshine that bounces off the red brick and street art in vibrant primary colours. Despite my heaviness at having to face it all again, Manchester in the autumn sunshine – with its gothic facades, industrial edge and yellowing leaves of the ginkgo trees blowing in the fresh breeze – lightens my step a little. I get lost in listening to music and smiling at hipsters walking their miniature dachshunds along the bustling streets. I stop in at my favourite coffee shop, Ezra's, to shore myself up with some caffeine. When I pay, I rest a library book I need to return on French witchlore against the counter. When I move over to wait for my takeaway, a hipster with a goatee who's also waiting snorts at me.

"You know science exists now, right?" he asks, nodding to my textbook.

I glare at him. I want to say, *Yeah, and I'm a shapeshifter, put that in your science and smoke it,* but, just to be a dick, say, "That's discriminatory against my beliefs, you know. I feel oppressed."

He rolls his eyes and looks at the witch working behind the counter who has just used a small spell, twisting her fingers over his cappuccino with a softly glowing peridot ring to produce some latte art of a cat.

"Can you remake that for me, please?" he says. "The proper way."

She catches my eye as she tips the coffee out. Sometimes it's just not worth the effort.

I pick up my coffee, smiling at the flawless latte leaf before it fades into bubbles, and stepping out onto Faraday Street. It's nice and quiet today. Sometimes, there are antiwitchcraft protestors outside college, mostly conspiracy theorists who, along with thinking the world is flat and 4G transmits viruses, think witches are an arm of the shadow government. They're convinced we herald the end of the world and are sitting on a vast stock of power we will one day use to destroy everyone, choosing to ignore the fact that those types of spells and the grimoires that held them were lost long ago or are hidden away by the Merlin Foundation. The ancient times, when witchcraft was on the lips of every monarch in Europe, when witches cast horoscopes for kings and brewed tonics for princes, have gone. Cursing and condemnatory magic has been lost, grimoires burned and witches executed, old practices falling to the wayside. Spells dedicated to chaos have disappeared into the mists of time, and most modern employers look at witches with their little domestic spells that never last more than a few hours and consider them just part of a bizarre belief system and a source of a few helpful tricks for the office party. Besides, today most witches wouldn't have the power to sustain bigger spells even if they came across them. A shapeshifter would, but that's part of the reason why I've only ever had one witch friend, and why she's dead.

"Is this Demdike College?"

I look up as I reach the front door. There is a tall, dark-haired guy standing on the pavement holding a takeaway coffee. He's dressed like every other handsome student in Manchester, his denim jacket just the right level of distressed vintage, but he's got a monster of a sapphire ring on his middle finger. It's a dead giveaway. He's either got a really weird fashion sense, or he's a witch.

"Yes, this is it." I look pointedly at the clearly ineffective sign.

"Right." He shifts his backpack on his shoulder. "I wasn't sure."

"Okay." I don't know why he is talking to me. I look him over for clues as to whether maybe I know him. I take in his light brown skin, curly black hair, greenish brown eyes, the kind of casual stance with a straight back that comes to guys who know they're impeccably good-looking. I've definitely never seen him before. I'd remember that dimple in his cheek when he smiles and he is still smiling at me, which is very weird. "You're starting first year?"

"Third year transfer. Witchlore and Witchcraft."

"Ah. Me too. Not the transfer bit, but everything else."

I don't have any words of welcome for this new person, so I just stare at his cup. Train station coffee is gross.

"Ezra's," I say abruptly.

"What?" He frowns.

"Ezra's." I point at his coffee cup and then to mine and then across the street. "The best coffee in the city."

"Oh. Thank you." *Still* smiling.

"You're welcome." I find myself smiling back, even though I don't want to, not a bit, and it's at that exact moment that Carl Lord slams his shoulder into me from behind, pushing me out of the way to open the front door of college.

"Watch it, shifter," he snaps.

"Watch yourself, dickface," I say back. *Here we go,* I think dismally.

"Heard about your 'attempt'." Carl mimes slashing his wrists and I hate that I blush. "Couldn't even get that right, could you?"

"Work it up your arse," I say.

"You wish."

Carl Lord is the great gay gatekeeper. He's handsome in that harsh, brutalist way; skin shockingly white, vivid blond thatch of hair, he looks like he should be on a Soviet poster for farming from the 1930s. He's from Salford and he calls everyone "mate" and is built like a semi-professional footballer. This has made him the Most Popular Queer in college and he hates my living guts.

"He's jealous of you," Elizabeth used to say. *"You're a shifter. You're full of magic."*

If it's true that Carl's jealous of magic I can't even control, he hides it under a crapload of disdain. Some of my father's words of warning pop into my head again: *They will always hate us. They will never trust us. Remember that.*

Carl holds the door open and looks me up and down with

some of that classic witch distrust. "I heard you're a lad again." He shakes his head in disgust as he lingers. There's no point in telling him that I'm not a lad or a girl because he has never cared. He looks at the new guy. "Coming in, mate?"

"Um, yeah, sure." The new guy looks between us, completely confused, but I let him walk ahead of me into the rickety old lift. There's no way I'm climbing into a potential deathtrap with Carl Lord. I wait until Carl has pulled the brass grille across them both and the lift has jerked upward before stomping up the stone steps. It's a spiral sandstone staircase with classrooms and small department libraries on every floor, but of course, the room designated as a student common room, with a grubby kitchenette and a temperamental microwave, is on the top floor.

With each step, I think of the reasons I shouldn't have come back. It's strange having everyone know my business when, for two years, hardly anyone knew my name. I was just the shapeshifter. Now they all know who my girlfriend was and about my "fragile" mental health. (Counsellor Cooper's term, not mine.)

"I'm not ashamed," Elizabeth says, her fingers tangling with mine as we lie on her bed. Her mum is out at work. I fiddle with her ring, a beautiful opal that, whenever I touch it, sends magical sparks down my spine. "I'm just not ready to come out to everyone yet."

Counsellor Cooper says flashbacks are normal, but I think

there's nothing normal about living in two moments simultaneously, especially when one of them leaves you feeling like you are drowning on air. I bend over at the waist on the fifth floor and put my hands on my knees, forcing myself to breathe deeply. I close my eyes and try not to see the moment she died. It's like trying not to blink. There she is, golden hair spread out around her, coughing up blood as the spell out of her ring dims down to nothing. *Don't leave me, Orla.*

It's an ironic set of last words, really. After all, she was the one leaving me.

I climb the last flight of stairs and push open the door to the common room, which makes it sound fancier and more austere than it is. It's the useless top floor of the building, all exposed crumbling brick and precarious hanging light bulbs. There are tables spread out with various pieces of second-hand furniture around them, all of them wonky and uncomfortable and smelling of must. The threadbare velvet sofas by the giant floor-to-ceiling windows that look out over Manchester are considered the best seats, having the most stuffing left in them.

Since it's the first day back at college, it's busier than usual, with newly matriculated first years all reading through their welcome packs, second and third years marking their territory and fourth years looking world-weary. Carl's already lounging across one of the best sofas as if he owns it, twisting his fingers in a sharp cutting motion so that his pink tourmaline ring glows and his hair changes from black to blue and back again. His mates are laughing appreciatively. I don't look at him, but I feel his eyes, the eyes of everyone on me. It was like this the last time I shifted; I've only done it twice since starting college, so it's still a novelty. Even when I wear the same boots, the same coat, presenting a uniform for people to navigate, their eyes still pillage me, seeking out all the ways I am different. I find a grotty table in a dark corner that has a chair with the seat nearly worn through and avoid looking at anyone at all. It doesn't stop the whispers.

"Didn't even go to the funeral…"

"Do you think they were really sleeping together?"

"I didn't know they were lesbians…"

I sigh heavily and pull out my headphones again. I don't turn any music on, I just enjoy the way they muffle the theories and questions buzzing around me. Part of me wants to tell everyone that I didn't go to the funeral because I was banned by Elizabeth's parents. Her mum threatened to curse me to hell and back and looked like she'd sell her soul for the power to do it. As for the sleeping-together stuff, well, that's no one's business.

I pull my summer work for my spellcrafting class out of my bag and look down at the various hand positions on the paper. I can get on fine in my lore classes, they're all essay based and are my highest marks, but witchcraft is an absolute nightmare. I try my hardest to pick modules that are all written coursework, history and theory courses, but everyone enrolled on the Witchlore and Witchcraft degree is required to take at least one practical craft course a term. This term, it's Twelfth-Century Witchcraft, and the tutor will probably despair of me as much as every other craft tutor I've ever had.

Taking a deep breath, knowing it will come to nothing, I move my hands in the correct motion, telling myself over and over what my parents and every shifter teacher I've ever had has told me since I was about five years old: *Shapeshifters don't need rings. Use your shifting power, direct it to your hands, craft the spell...* It's supposed to be easy, innate, lifting off my skin like mist, travelling through my fingers just like it does for my parents, beautiful and terrible all at once. Nothing happens. What should bring light and magic out of me is just weird hand movements, like I'm doing a daft shadow-puppet theatre. I can see some girls at another table looking at me and smirking. It's been two years and I'm still the weird shapeshifter who can't control their powers. At least one thing is the same about this year.

"Hi again."

Someone sits down beside me. I look up. It's the new guy. He's smiling at me. Again. I slowly remove my headphones and stare at him.

"It's Orla, right?"

"I go by Lando." I cover my work with my arms. I don't want him to see how I'm still practising first-year transitions. He frowns.

"I thought it was Orla." He looks over his shoulder towards the group all lounging on the sofas. They're competing, moving their hands rapidly, racing to be the first one to cast a small breeze to make wind chimes sing. Carl laughs when it glows pink, a corresponding colour to his ring, proving it's him. I look at the new guy. I can't understand why he's over here instead of over there.

"That was a nickname my friend gave me last year."

I can hear her voice in my ear. *Don't leave me, Orla.*

"Shapeshifters change their names every time they shift gender?" His voice is eager and not at all scornful, but I don't owe him an answer. Some witches are like this at first, approaching a shapeshifter with excitement, but it always curdles and I don't want to be the odd thing in the window of the curiosity shop that new people stare at.

"I don't change gender." I glare at him. This particular glare has always been enough to push everyone away. I can imagine exactly what he'll say to the others when he swans back over to the sofas. *Crazy shapeshifters, no wonder they're so messed up in the head.* He doesn't move.

"I'm sorry," he says quietly. "I shouldn't have...that was crappy of me."

Literally no one at this school has ever said that to me. His apology leaves me speechless. He sticks out his hand with the ring on.

"I'm Bastian," he says. "He/him."

I don't take it. I don't like touching witches' rings any more, not after Elizabeth.

"Orlando," I say. Everyone knows my pronouns.

"You're a shapeshifter and your parents named you *Orlando*?" He sounds amused. "Is that an homage or a dig?"

"And you're a witch named after one of the classic pieces of German fantasy literature so I think you can shut up," I snap.

I think this will surely be enough to send him running, but he smiles slowly.

"Most people think it's short for Sebastian." He fiddles with his ring.

"Yeah, well, I read a lot," I mutter. There's very little else to do when you grow up with no friends.

"So your parents were fond of twentieth-century queer literature, were they?" he asks.

There are plenty of queer witches (after all, they don't have the reputation of dancing together naked under the moonlight for nothing) and there's even a non-binary witch tutoring practical brews here at college, but they're twenty-five and they're not a shifter so they don't get shit for it like I do. So I hesitate. I check Bastian for the usual signs, piercings or rainbow stickers or undercuts, and don't find any. He might be closeted, but a closeted boy is probably the last thing I need after what happened last year.

"Why? Are you fond of queer literature?" I stare at him steadily.

"Yeah." He shrugs. So, not closeted. Just tall and handsome and sitting with me.

"I don't know what my parents are fond of."

"I'm sorry." He looks genuinely sad about it. "They said you were..."

An orphan. Nobody at college ever asks what happened to them or where they are so I never have to tell the truth. It's easier to have no parents than explain the parents I do have. The locked doors, the emotional blackmail, the appalling and weirdly affirming realization that even a hospital-mandated halfway house for mentally unstable teenagers would be better than living with them again.

"Did you hurt your wrist?" he asks.

"No, it's a fashion statement."

"Shapeshifters can't heal themselves?"

"No, I'm not Wolverine." I scowl at him and put my bandaged wrist under the table, out of sight. His eyes follow it.

"I could heal it for you, if you like." He lifts his hand and twists it, the stone of his ring catching the light. I stiffen. All witches can heal with brews (bubble, bubble, toil and trouble and all that) and anyone can make a healing tonic or two with ginger and lemon. But a talented few witches can heal with stones. Rings are inherited, passed down generations with different magical properties attached to them. A healing stone is a rare ring, however, so rare that most modern witches would prefer to take a broken bone to the hospital than trust in the volatility of an ancient stone. If he's confident in his ability, he must be more naturally talented than most of the witches I've met.

I examine his ring. It's a very traditional chunky piece, clearly ancient, yellow gold in a square setting that has lost the sharpness of its edges and runes graven into the sides of it. The sapphire itself is oval and a dusty blue, not cut like a modern gemstone but smooth, like sea glass. It looks so comfortable on his finger, as if eager to perform witchcraft for him. I stare down at my bare fingers. I've been trying to learn witchcraft my entire life and I still can't do the basics. I can't even control my shifting.

I have a sudden flash of memory, my father standing over me as I cried, his face impassive as his body filled with light, the hair on his arms growing long and then disappearing, the disgust in his eyes still the same. *A shapeshifter who cannot control her powers is less than a witch, less than nothing. We are made to be the strongest, not the weakest.* I don't know what I was made to be, but I knew I couldn't make him happy and it was my fault. Always my fault.

"No, thanks," I say. I would be a naive prat to let a strange witch use their ring on me. He has sexy eyes but he might be a secret douchebag. So many people are.

"Another time, then," he says.

"Can't *wait.*"

I am deliberately sarcastic but Bastian doesn't seem to care. He grins broadly and nods, pulling a library book out of his bag and opening it.

"What are you doing?" I ask.

"I have this reading to do before my Early Medieval Brewing class in ten minutes." He frowns. "Did you want to talk about something else?"

"No, I mean, what are you doing—" I gesture to his body, sitting opposite mine, and then to the various spaces at other tables around the room, implying the obvious question: *What the hell are you doing sitting with me?*

"Do you want me to go?"

"I don't..." I go to pull my hair back from my face, that familiar smoothing motion of scooping long curls back into a ponytail only to find the shortness of my new curls. The back of my head and neck suddenly feels very exposed. "Sit wherever you want."

"Okay." He turns back to his book. "I'll sit here."

I watch him for a minute, wondering if this is some kind of ploy and he's going to start asking me if it's really my fault that my girlfriend is dead, but he doesn't. He seems to be underlining something with a pencil. I wait. He turns the page.

"Fine," I say.

After all, what does it matter to me if some new guy wastes his time with the weird shapeshifter? I have a sudden urge to tell him my version of things; it rises in my throat until I can taste the words on my lips: *It didn't happen like they say.* But I don't speak. No one believes me, after all, and neither will he. By lunchtime, he'll have heard their version and he'll never sit with me again. That's just what happens.

Chapter Three

I think I expected every second of college this year to be an absolute ball-ache, but it turns out even gossips and bullies have new schedules to manage, reading lists to update and summer holidays to boast about. Against my expectations, I survive the first day back with no additional drama. And then the next. I'm starting to think I might actually get away with skulking through this year without too much notice, then as I'm leaving my first class on Wednesday (the History of Pre-Roman Necromancy) Kira Tavi steps across my path.

"Hi," I say uneasily. She's always very put together and that makes me uncomfortable. She has a kind of preppy vibe that I feel must be painfully high maintenance. Today, it's an orange jumper with a sharp white shirt underneath and the collar peeking over the top, matching orange glasses that complement her brown skin and her black hair pulled neatly back. "Do you need something?"

Despite being in college together for the last two years, this is the first conversation we've had. That wouldn't be weird – she's in the year above me, we don't have loads of classes together, and there are plenty of twats in this place who treat me like a piece of wall – but Kira Tavi was Elizabeth's best friend. She was the only person who knew about our relationship. She didn't out us, but she never so much as looked at me, so it's not hard to infer her disapproval. Consequently, I barely know her but here's what I do know. She's got a girl-gang group of friends who tend to be very into female empowerment, so I'm only on their radar when I'm in a form that they like. She's not just studious, she does extracurriculars, like leading summer camps at the Moroccan witch community centre. She also spearheads "peer mentoring", which seems like a recipe for a superiority complex.

"I've been assigned to be your peer mentor," she says, looking at her nails. I notice she's got one of those cool rainbow manicures that I would love to get. I stuff my bitten-to-the-quick nails in my jeans pocket.

"What?"

"I'm your peer mentor," she says impatiently. "Professor Wallace asked me to mentor you."

I look up at the dusty brick ceiling above us. Beryl and Professor Wallace, the head of college, are in the same coven and Beryl is chatty. *Witches and their covens,* I think darkly. After all, Elizabeth and Kira had been part of the same network of covens since they were babies and that's why Kira thinks she can look at me this way. As if she already knows all of my worst secrets.

"Thanks, but I already have a counsellor."

"It's compulsory in third year."

I stare at Kira. She has this slightly pitying smile on her face. I hate her for it.

"No."

"No?" Kira stops looking at her nails.

"I don't want one, no offence," I say. I do mean that. It's not just perfect Kira, or the fact that she looks at me sometimes like she's remembering everything Elizabeth ever told her about me. It's that there isn't anyone in this whole damn place I would consider being mentored by.

"None taken." Kira shifts and has a martyred expression. "But Professor Wallace really wants you to reintegrate, to adjust to college without Elizabeth."

I wince. Most people accompany Elizabeth's name with a hushed tone, something that denotes the fact she's dead. Not Kira. She says her name like she's simply relocated somewhere else and might pop up at any moment.

"Let's talk. It will only take five minutes," Kira says, jerking her head to an empty tutorial room next door. I sigh and follow her inside, since this doesn't seem like the kind of thing Kira is just going to let go and the last thing I want to do is escalate the situation to a sit-down with Professor Wallace. Also, there's a part of me that thinks it would somehow be rude to Elizabeth to just walk away from her best friend without a word.

The tutorial room was clearly once a broom cupboard when the building was still a factory and somehow still smells of cotton dust. It has two chairs and a bookshelf so I sit down on one.

"So as your peer mentor I'm going to be checking on you

regularly to make sure you're all right," she says, standing in front of the other chair.

I lean back into the leather behind me. It creaks.

"I've been given some information about you—"

She's opening her bag, one of those "feminist army" tote bags that everyone has, and pulling out a folder and an honest-to-god fountain pen. I watch her unscrew its lid and open the folder, pulling out a big brown envelope that has my name on: ORLANDO SOUTHERNS. I wonder if Kira has a label maker.

"How did you get that?" I demand. I wonder what Professor Wallace has told her and if I can yell at Beryl about it later.

"Your guardians emailed Professor Wallace." She pauses. "Did they not tell you?"

So it's not Beryl I have to yell at for the breach of privacy. I notice, too, that Professor Wallace didn't feel it was appropriate to inform Kira that I have living parents, not guardians. I press the nail of my index finger through my jean hole into the soft skin of my thigh. The pain helps.

"It's nothing embarrassing," Kira says, in what I imagine she thinks is a comforting tone. "It's just some information about your situation."

"You mean my girlfriend dying?" I snap.

"Elizabeth's death," Kira corrects. Her tone is still soft but I feel the reproach in it: *Not just your girlfriend.* "And your...hiccup over the summer."

A hiccup would be not finding a summer job or getting off with someone at a festival and contracting chlamydia. What happened to me was not a hiccup. A shitshow would be more appropriate.

"So!" Kira says neatly, pulling a piece of paper out of the folder. "I have a list of questions."

"Of course you do," I mutter.

"Hmm?" Kira gives me an arch stare that would be perfect for a librarian.

"Nothing." I scratch my nail against my thigh.

"First is..." Kira frowns down at her list. "Are you overwhelmed with the desire to take your own life today?"

"Jesus!" I glare at Kira.

"Just a yes or no is fine."

"I'm not answering that."

Kira gives me a long stare then makes a note on her page.

"Okay, next question," she says. "On a scale of one to ten, how well are you sleeping, one being not sleeping at all to ten being sleeping eight hours a night?"

"You sleep *eight hours* a night?" I stare at her.

"Yeah, of course, it's recommended." Kira frowns. Elizabeth never mentioned that Kira had absolutely no sense of humour. "On a scale of one to ten?"

"Three."

No point in lying. It's also roughly the amount of hours I sleep every night, thanks to the nightmares.

"Three," she repeats. "Is that because of, like, nightmares?"

I get a weird twinge of anxiety, like the feeling of someone running a finger down the back of my neck. I glare at her ring, at the wide, intricate silver setting, delicate filigree surrounding an orange stone. Some witches have rings that give them hints of empath powers. Old stones that might have once been the kind of conduit that could help a witch read minds are mostly now reduced to intuiting when someone is a bit sad. I've overheard Kira telling people that hers is an Amazigh ring from her Moroccan ancestors. The Tavi witches have been in Manchester since the 1800s, but I've never heard that their powers included telepathy. For most of my life, I've barely worried about the rings of witches. As my father always used to say, *What does a shifter have to fear from a conduit when we have magic at our fingertips?* But that was all before the summer and Elizabeth's ring. Before the cave and the spell.

"None of your business," I say.

"Okay!" Kira is not even slightly deterred. She's moving onto the next question. "How optimistic do you feel about life today on a scale of one to ten, one being not optimistic at all and ten being incredibly optimistic?"

"Really?" I huff out a bitter laugh. "You expect me to answer that?"

"One to ten?" Kira prompts.

"How optimistic do you feel?" I demand. "Your so-called best friend died four months ago, how optimistic are you?"

She glares at me. I have the tingling, regretful feeling of crossing a line.

"She *was* my best friend," Kira says. "And I'm asking the questions."

"Then ask them," I say tersely.

"Fine." Kira's voice is equally terse as she turns the page.

"Do you have any career plans or options you'd like to discuss with me?"

"I suppose you already know what you want to do," I say.

"Yeah. I'm going to be a counsellor."

"Shocker."

Elizabeth told me Kira's dad is a psychiatrist and her mum is an SEN specialist for witches. She gives me a curt look. I'm a little victorious to see I've broken her smiley demeanour.

"What about you?" she says, shifting where she's sitting. "You could get a job at GCHQ, go into—"

"Don't say espionage," I snap.

"—politics," she says slowly. I glare at her. Witches can be anything openly in the world nowadays. Being a shapeshifter is completely different. The general population have no idea we exist unless they work in certain arms of the government where shapeshifters are known and prized. It's what my parents did for years and years; it's what they expect me to do too. What I want has never mattered. Kira flushes, like she's embarrassed, but presses on.

"Well, what do you want to do?" she demands.

I've been asked this question kindly only once before. I remember, with a sudden lurch of my stomach, how it felt when Elizabeth would lay her head down on my chest and tell me her plans for the future. Like Kira, she wanted to follow her parents into their version of witch family business and become an academic. When she had spoken about it, painting a glossy, confident picture of the future with her words, it had felt like anything was possible.

"Nothing," I say. My words feel rotten in my mouth as I slump back in the creaky chair.

"Nothing?" Kira repeats.

"I have a job," I say. "At Unicorn Grocery in Chorlton. I'm all set for a career."

I can't say more. I can barely breathe. It's like I can still feel her, Elizabeth, pressing down on my sternum but now she's a dead weight, literally.

"Okay, well..." Kira gives me a long look, as if she's expecting me to speak. When I don't, she sighs heavily. "Do you have any questions for me?"

"No."

She closes her folder. She's going to leave and I'm going to be left alone here, with the weight of my dead girlfriend pressing down on me. I need to do something, anything to distract myself, and my mind is racing, trying to find something concrete. Weirdly, the face of the guy from the first day of term suddenly pops into my head.

"Yes."

"Really?" Kira perks right up. "Great! Go ahead!"

"Who's the new transfer?" I ask.

"The new transfer?"

"Yeah, bloke, sapphire ring, I think he's called Bastian?"

I watch her pull a different page out of her folder. The inside cover of the folder is coated in doodles, notes. With a pang, I see some of them have speech bubbles written in Elizabeth's handwriting.

"Bastian Chevret." Kira runs her finger down the page. "He's transferred from a college in London. That's all I know."

"Bastian Chevret," I repeat his name quietly. "Thanks."

Kira nods and puts the file away, then hesitates.

"I have one last question for you."

"Fine," I sigh.

"Are you okay? Are you...feeling dysphoric and stuff?"

I stare at Kira. I can't believe she has the balls to ask me this question, to even use this word in front of me.

"That's on your peer mentoring questionnaire?"

"No." She looks bashful for a moment then squares her shoulders and looks me in the eye. "She – Elizabeth – told me you sometimes felt that way. After shifts. That you told her you did."

I stare at her. Those words are unaccountably painful. Before Elizabeth, there was no one I could talk to about my shifts. How, with every change, my parents pushed me to dress in the gender they felt was most appropriate to my form, how all of those past experiences had alienated me from myself, left me trapped under other people's expectations, unable to breathe. Talking to her made it hurt less. Now it hurts more, knowing she told someone else. I stand up.

"You'll have to get your counselling degree before I answer you, and also" – I glare down at her – "I will never fucking answer that question."

I march to the toilet and splash some water on my face. I stare at myself in the mirror, trying to breathe normally and get that weighted feeling off my chest. Even after a few months, this face doesn't look like mine yet. None of my body does and there is absolutely nothing I can do to change it. My face is heart-shaped and babyish, which definitely makes a male form seem more effeminate. My hair is a light strawberry gold and sort of wispy, the same with my eyebrows. My eyes are a kind of muddy green and my white skin is a little sallow. I don't yet know if it's because I'm unhealthy or this is just what this new skin is like. I touch Elizabeth's earrings; the familiarity of them helps. I wipe away tears I didn't realize had fallen. I sit on the loo and look at my phone. As always, I open the last messages between Elizabeth and me.

> Come over today.
>
> > Is your mum working?
>
> Yeah. I've got an idea.
>
> > Okay. Give me a hint?
>
> Later.

I hate that our last messages aren't something to do with love. I flick back through my photos. I don't have many with Elizabeth – she was the one who took the selfies and I reckon her mum has probably found and deleted every single one. The ones I do have are either in her bedroom or outside in the garden of her parents' house in Alderley Edge, taken lying down on her massive trampoline that had been there since her childhood. I pause on one where the afternoon light is making her face glow so she looks sort of heavenly. I'm in my second form that she knew me in; my hair is dark and curly and long, my cheekbones higher, my eyes dark green, my mouth pouty, and my face round and cherubic but I'm wearing her earrings. I look at the picture of us and have a weird thought: *Would Elizabeth still fancy me in my new form?* It's pathetic, but right now I worry she wouldn't. Because she's not here to tell me otherwise.

College doesn't have a canteen or anything like that, just the frankly dangerous microwave and kettle in the upstairs common room and an outside space next to the car park where people can sit and smoke and eat takeaway on the wooden picnic tables. The surprising September sun has persisted into lunchtime and a few students are going so far as to roll up their T-shirt sleeves and lie on the patch of grass. People have pulled out sunglasses and I think someone's got a bottle of cider and there's a general air of lingering summertime, coconut-scented vape smoke in the air. I find an empty picnic table and pull out my lunch. That's when I notice it. It's down by the back stairs, leaning against the wall of college, slightly grubbed by the weather: a giant photograph surrounded by cheap bunches of flowers and balloons and grotty neon teddy bears. A picture of Elizabeth. It's the photo from her social media, where her hair is at its longest so she looks like Rapunzel. I watch as someone, a second year I've never spoken to, walks forward and produces a tacky bunch of carnations from their backpack. They set them down and then twist their fingers in a sequence I recognize as one from a first-year craft module that helps flowers bloom. A first-year spell I still can't do. I turn my back to the entire charade. I'm about to put my headphones on and listen to the next chapter of *Carrie* (to maybe get some ideas) when someone sits down opposite me on the slightly damp bench.

"Hi there," Bastian says. He's got the same open, pleasant face, the same distressed denim jacket. I'm not sure what I expected to change in two days.

"Hi."

I watch him take a box of salad out of his leather satchel and set it down on the table. I watch him take out a reusable bamboo fork and open the salad. I watch him spear a leaf and eat it. Then I watch him notice me staring.

"You all right?" he asks, glancing between me and my sandwich. "Not eating?"

"No, I am."

"Okay." He crunches down on his salad leaves and pulls out a book. It's a copy of *Brideshead Revisited*. I snort with laughter. He looks up at me. "What?"

"Bit on the nose, isn't it?"

"What is?" He looks at the book cover. "You got a problem with Evelyn Waugh?"

"No, I just mean, like, you're a Londoner, you're queer and you're reading *Brideshead Revisited*?"

"What makes you think I'm a Londoner?" He wipes salad dressing off his chin. I notice he doesn't say he's not queer.

I don't feel like admitting I asked my peer mentor to fact-check him, so I just say, "You're not from the north, that's for sure."

"Yeah, not like you." He smiles. "Proper northern brogue."

"Ta very much."

"I'm from Cornwall." He digs his fork into his salad. Now he's said it, I can hear it, the slight roll in his accent that makes me think of the sea. "I just went to college in London."

"Nowhere closer?"

He pauses, the bite on the end of his fork midway between the salad and his mouth.

"My parents thought London would be good for us," he says quietly. It's weird when you just know that someone has been through something shitty. Maybe there's some kind of sonar for broken people, but I can hear it in his voice.

"What's it like, London?" I ask. I don't know why I'm trying to be nice to him. Just because he's sad about something doesn't mean I have to be.

"Never been?"

I shake my head. I don't want to say I've never been anywhere.

"Seen it on TV, though," I say. "Seemed…loud."

"It is loud, and busy. Fun, though, and the libraries are good," he says, eating again.

"That's your thing, then?" I ask. "Libraries?"

"Yeah, basically." He smiles. I can't work out if he's a nerd who happens to be a very handsome man or if he's a very handsome man who pretends to be a nerd for the humblebrag cred. If he's the second, then he's probably a twat. If he's the first, then he's the last thing I need. However, I do wonder, as I slide the pickles out of my sandwich, if it's not so bad to talk to him a bit. I'm about to ask him what his favourite book is, the question is literally forming on the edge of my tongue, when something drops onto the table between us. I stare at it. It's a suicide hotline pamphlet with all of the people's eyes crossed out, crude doodles of various self-inflicted deaths scribbled around them. I look up. Carl Lord is grinning down at me. His ring isn't glowing. He's clearly taken the time to bring this in from home, like a serial killer.

"Just in case you get too depressed, shifter," he says loudly, jerking his head towards Elizabeth's photo. No one laughs. I'm aware of a siren somewhere in the city, of someone parking their car over the road, slamming the door shut. It's like everyone is waiting for me to speak.

"Piss off," I mutter, grabbing the pamphlet and scrunching it into my fist. I don't look at Bastian.

"Aw, feeling guilty, shifter?" Carl laughs. "Well, you should, shouldn't you? You're the reason your girlfriend's dead, mate!"

I don't mean to blush, but I do, and I curse myself for it, as the best way to deal with Carl is to ignore him and then think of vengeful acts later. I accidentally catch Bastian's eye. He is frowning. He's working it out, I can tell, and now he'll never talk to me again. That's worse than Carl somehow, and I berate myself for letting my guard down, even for a second, for being so bloody stupid to ever think I could have a normal conversation with someone in this hellhole. A bleak question from my days in the hospital comes back to me: *What's the fucking point?* Avoiding Bastian's curious gaze and Carl's sneer, I grab my sandwich and leave.

Chapter Four

I walk down to the canal and keep walking. I follow the pathway away from the city and into Ancoats, walking under bridges that smell like piss, covered in graffiti, and over locks that are full and swirling. Further down in Keepers Quay where the riverboats moor up, there's an amazing bakery on the edge of the water. It's a great place to stand and smell delicious things, fresh sourdough and recently made croissants, and sit on the stone benches and watch as the swans flock around the green-and-red patent houseboats, their white bodies vibrant against the dark water. It helps today to be there and watch them swim in pairs, so graceful, and not think about Bastian's puzzled expression, Carl's poisonous delight. My mind unhelpfully lingers on the words spread across the front of that bloody pamphlet – depressed...manic...lonely...suicidal ideation – then I'm suddenly back in the bathroom in May. *My breath so hard and fast, the splash of my blood on the white rug under the sink. A leafy pattern, and the drops of blood are tiny rosebuds, perfect circles, becoming rivers—*

"Hey."

I look up, blinking, pulling myself back to the bench and the canal. Bastian is standing there, holding two cups of coffee from Ezra's.

"Are you following me?" I ask.

"Yeah." He looks down at the cups. "I didn't know if you were vegan so I just got one with oat milk and one with no milk. What do you want?"

I stare at him for a long moment, waiting to see if there's some clue in his face to what he's thinking and why he followed me, but there's nothing. Just an expectant anxiety that he might have bought the wrong coffee. *Well,* I think, *might as well get a free coffee.*

"Oat milk," I say. He hands me the cup with a smile. It's annoyingly cute. Then he slides his satchel off his shoulders and sits down on the bench beside me. We both stare at the water for a long minute, at a Canada goose who is shitting on the top of a fire-engine red narrowboat, its feathers ruffling against the potted petunias on the roof.

"You didn't have to bring me pity coffee," I mutter, sipping it anyway.

"It's not a pity coffee, it's just regular coffee. Do they sell pity coffee?"

He leans back with his eyes closed, face tilted towards the sunshine. His dark eyelashes are ridiculously long, the lucky bastard. Mine used to be like that, in my last form. Now they're gingery and practically invisible.

"So that guy, Carl," says Bastian.

"Yeah."

"He's a twat."

I sip my coffee. I could tell him that Carl Lord has always been a twat. That when I first came to college, I was the youngest in my year by two years because of homeschooling, and I had a male form. Carl wanted to be my friend and I thought we were. It was a nice surprise, different from what my parents had told me to expect – that no one would like me or want to be friends with a shifter. But I realized quickly that Carl didn't have friends, only people he used. I could tell Bastian about how, for the first eight months of college, Carl took me on a roller coaster of his affections, telling me he was my friend but also trying to aggressively slobber over me whenever we were alone. I could tell him that when I shapeshifted into a female form before the summer term in first year, Carl took it as a rejection and the teasing and goading has pretty much never stopped. I could tell him that being the toxic masculine gay leader has made Carl Lord the worst kind of bully and predator, who has monopolized a queer community that could have sheltered me and instead made it unsafe for me. But what good would that do? Bastian is exactly the kind of person who will fit into Carl Lord's pack of super-attractive, super-popular queer witches. There's no point in me telling him what he's destined to find out for himself, very soon.

"So that…" Bastian nods at my arm in its bandage. "You did that yourself?"

Lying will be completely ineffectual. I sip my coffee all the same, trying to hold onto the moment when he thinks I'm a tiny bit less pathetic than he will do in a minute.

"Yeah, in May," I say, like the time that has passed makes it less painful. It doesn't.

"Ah." He looks awkward. Everyone always looks so awkward. Who knew that attempting suicide would be such a conversation killer? I half expect him to stand up and walk away now that my status as a nutter is solidly confirmed, but he doesn't. He just sips his coffee and keeps frowning.

"And the memorial they've got up there," he asks. "That was…"

"Elizabeth," I say. "My girlfriend."

"Elizabeth," he repeats. "She died?"

"Yeah." I swallow the coffee, wincing at the bitterness, praying he doesn't ask how. Thankfully, he doesn't.

"Your relationship was a secret, right?"

I don't ask how he knows that. The gossip has been all over college, all over the covens of Manchester. The spin on the sordid story usually casts me as a jilted lover, a weirdo who lost control of their magic out of jealousy, and Elizabeth, the sweet, popular bi-curious girl who suffered the consequences. I drink my coffee and inhale the canal air, the scent of fresh cinnamon rolls from the bakery and the damp, earthy smell of the water. I think about Elizabeth. She had always been on my radar, this beautiful girl, seen from afar, who was studious and lovely. Then, at the beginning of second year, we had the same module, History of Tudor Witchcraft, and we sat next to one another.

"It was her laugh," I say quietly.

"What?" Bastian asks. I look at him to see if he's scornful, but he just seems interested. So I speak, partly out of a need to correct whatever horrible tale he's absorbed and partly just to remind myself of the truth.

"Her laugh did it for me. We had to sit next to each other in a class and I made a joke about Anne Boleyn—"

"What joke?" he interrupts.

"Just a silly music joke."

"Tell me."

"Why?" I stare at him.

"I like silly jokes, indulge me."

"It was cringey, we were doing this thing about how King Henry was trying to persuade Anne Boleyn to be his mistress and I said..." I flush. "If he liked it, he should have put a ring on it."

Bastian stares at me.

"Did you do that old dance? With the—" He flips his hand back and forth. "—hand thing?"

"Yeah."

"So she laughed?"

"Yeah." At the time, it had seemed miraculous. Her laugh was the opposite of her, brash and bawdy rather than tittering and girly. I loved it first, before I loved her.

"Huh," Bastian says thoughtfully. "That is funny."

I wonder if he always announces things he finds funny rather than laughing at them.

"And was that it, then?" he asks. "She was blown away by your quirky personality?"

"No, we became friends first." I smile, remembering the notes we'd pass in class at the beginning and how we escalated to messages, to secret meet-ups, each step a milestone to me of a closeness I'd never had with a friend before. I didn't even care that we never hung out with her friends, or sometimes she'd pretend we'd never spoken. I took every second of her attention as an unforeseen miracle, but soon they had piled up and my life was saturated with Elizabeth's brightness. "Yeah, she was popular but, like, she wasn't stuck up. She was nice to me, and she had this laugh and I just…"

"Caught feelings?" Bastian says ruefully.

"Yeah." I sigh. "Then we kissed this one time, randomly, and it…snowballed."

We'd both been the only two in the college library at the end of a cold December day, preparing for the practical presentation at the end of my module that would be seventy per cent of my grade. I'd been trying to make magic come out of my fingers to no avail for hours and finally, feeling like I was the worst person ever, I'd slammed my head into the desk so I wouldn't cry. She'd looked at me, leaned across the table, and pressed her lips against mine. At first, it was soft, sort of comforting, but then I realized it might be my only chance to kiss the girl I had been low-key obsessed with for months so I went for it. When I did, she made this delicious little gasping sound and her opal ring glowed with a creamy light. That was that.

From then on, I kissed her whenever I could, catching the train to Alderley Edge and walking to her house to "study". She didn't live in student accommodation, since her family home was only a quick train journey from the city, and while both her parents were at work, we watched movies, ate ice cream, had dreamy daytime sex and listened to music sitting on her trampoline in the big back garden that looked out on the woods. She was too scared of being outed to go on real dates in the city or to stay overnight at the student accommodation in Ancoats with me, but it didn't stop the five months between December and May being the most perfect time of my life.

I realize my cheeks are wet. I brush tears hastily away with the back of my sleeve and look down, hoping he hasn't noticed.

"But...you didn't kill her?" Bastian asks hesitantly. It's weird, because even though the police and the coroner are satisfied it was a brain bleed from the fall, even though legally, I absolutely didn't kill her, my parents, Elizabeth's parents, the college, all the other students, even sometimes myself are absolutely sure that I did. But the truth? Well, as always with me, it's more bloody complicated than it looks.

"No."

"So why do they say—"

"Because I was there," I say sharply, and I tell the truth, mainly because not saying it is a knot in my throat that I can't undo. "When she died. I don't know, we were in this cave, she wanted to do this spell that she said would boost my magic, so I'd actually be able to cast a spell for a change..." He doesn't even look a little bit surprised. Of course, he'll have already heard from our classmates how inept I am at both shifting and witchcraft.

"She didn't, like, explain, and then she started doing the spell and I..." I take a shuddering breath, remembering the feeling of light and magic roaring agonizingly through my bones. "I shifted, my magic was weirdly intense, it pushed her, she fell and when I came round…"

"It was too late?" Bastian finishes for me softly. I nod. "So your shift, it was, like…a magical discharge thing?"

I nod again. Everyone afterwards used these words: Elizabeth's parents, Professor Wallace, Beryl, Counsellor Cooper. They say it in a certain way, though. It's not neutral. It still leaves the blame properly at my feet. After all, only shapeshifters who carry magic inside us, able to break free from our skin without any conduit, are capable of this kind of thing. I was the one who discharged the magic. If I hadn't done that, if I had better control, if I was a better student and a better person, she'd be alive, a beloved girlfriend and daughter.

"You loved her," Bastian says. I stare at him. He doesn't say it incredulously or jeeringly, just factually. There's something about it that's comforting. That it's not an opinion. The sky is blue, life is shit, I loved and still love Elizabeth.

"It should have been me," I say, voice harsh as I stare at a couple of swans swimming together. A pair. Inseparable. "I wish it had been. I'd do anything to change what happened, not that it matters."

Counsellor Cooper says that suicidal thoughts aren't to be feared. When we fear them, we make them stronger. That, actually, suicidal thoughts are a part of us warning the rest of us that we're really hurting inside. I feel like I didn't need the warning. I feel like I've been bleeding inside since Elizabeth died and soon, I'll bleed out with it. Silently and gradually, I'll just stop existing, drowned in my own blood.

"But you know there are spells to resurrect the dead, right?"

I stare at him. For the first time, I wonder if I've got a completely wrong read on Bastian Chevret. I had him penned as a hot geek, the type who reads the classics and watches vintage horror movies and eventually goes out with some eco-warrior witch and starts a blog about their perfect polyamorous explorations as they backpack ethically through Europe. Maybe it's because I've read too many Stephen King novels, but now I wonder if Bastian Chevret is more of a conspiracy theorist, Dr Frankenstein wannabe.

"Are you taking the piss?"

"No." He looks puzzled by the notion that he would be. "There's this grimoire—"

"Don't twat about with me," I say. "I might be shit at witchcraft and shapeshifting but I do actually listen in lectures. I know there's no existing grimoire with resurrection spells in it and if there ever was, it would be locked away somewhere! Even if it *wasn't*, what would be the point of resurrecting someone for two minutes? No witchcraft is permanent any more—"

"It's not a witch's grimoire, it's a shapeshifter's grimoire. It's a permanent spell." He says it so casually, like this isn't something out of a history book, extinct as the dodo.

"If there was a shifter book about resurrection, I'd know."

"Would you?" Bastian raises his eyebrows. "Because you're the authority on shapeshifter stuff, right? What with not being able to control your own powers and everything?"

I shoot him a filthy look because it's a low blow and completely correct.

"We could find it, you know," he says. "The book. I mean, we don't need to find it, I know where it is. We could…use it."

"And do what? Resurrect my girlfriend?"

"Isn't it worth trying?" he says.

I stare at him, wondering: *Where the hell did this person come from?* That, however, isn't the question that comes out of my mouth.

"Why would you even want to do this?"

"I'm interested in the book, and I want to work for the Merlin Foundation one day." Bastian takes off his jacket. I can see a string of necklaces over his T-shirt. Some look like traditional Cornish charms, snake bone necklaces to increase power or dried rowan berries for protection, but some seem to be from cultures less familiar to me. I think I spy an Obeah fetish necklace similar to something I've seen in my textbooks referencing Afro-Creole magic. All of them together speak to one thing: he's clearly part of a family that values old magic, maybe a coven that reveres it. Most UK covens today don't bother with charms and poppets or other ancient magical practices, no longer having the power to sustain them. They give healing balms to their kids instead of Calpol, celebrate their religious and cultural holidays with food and gatherings, and prepare their children for lives lived blended with the human world. Then there are the more isolated, secretive covens. It's generally suspected that these witches are more powerful than the average, that they hoard ancient spells and talents, just like Bastian's many charms and tokens. The only thing my father ever said about witches from ancient covens was: *They are the only witches worth our time. Of course, they would rip the magic out of our blood if they could.*

"Oh, I get it," I say. "You're in one of *those* covens, right? Like a Shipton coven? You're a *The Witch Will Rise* person, aren't you?"

"I don't have a coven right now." He tangles his fingers in one of the charms, a small, polished bone dipped in silver with what looks like a Vodou symbol carved into the metal. "But, yeah, I've got a professional interest. I need my dissertation next year to get the Merlin Foundation's attention. Rediscovering a resurrection spell would be the perfect subject. Successfully performing a resurrection spell would be even better."

"You think *you* can do a permanent resurrection spell?"

The look he gives me is cold. It is pretty impolite for a shapeshifter to question a witch's magic, but he's been pretty impolite about my abilities so I think we're even.

"I think I've got game, yeah," he says. "And even documenting an attempt would get their attention, maybe get me a job offer at one of their research centres when I've graduated."

Most witches find jobs in the wider world that blend in, keeping a separation between their professional life and their faith practices. Others will only work in witch-owned businesses. There are a plethora of witch-led meditation studios, talisman shops and forest apothecaries; Beryl, for example, owns a crystal shop in Chorlton and sells blessed topaz and speciality blended fertility teas that smell like an old lady's knicker drawer. Then there is the Merlin Foundation, the political group that protects all magic users and magical creatures. It's got some long, boring history about how it started by repealing the 1736 Act Against Witchcraft. They're involved in government, all witchlore educational institutions are accredited by them, and most shapeshifters in some way either work for them or consult for them. It's basically the only place where shifters and witches work together. They don't generally recruit; instead they handpick from covens and, like everything in witch culture, family is important. I've never met a witch before who had the balls to think they could just capture their attention. Bastian only looks back at me expectantly. I start to think he might be in earnest.

"Seriously? You want to resurrect my girlfriend so the Merlin Foundation recruits you?" I say.

"Yeah," he says, without a moment of doubt. "Why not?"

Looking at Bastian, everything about him now makes sense: the intelligence that isn't quite geekiness, the beauty that isn't quite sexy; it's academic drive, I see it now. I'm looking at a person who wants magical prowess and nothing else. That is probably the last thing I need.

"You're twisted." I stand up and put my coffee cup in the recycling bin. "We're done."

"Wait, here—" He picks up my phone from where it's sitting on the bench, holds it in front of my face to unlock it, and before I can stop him, is tapping something onto the screen. "That's my number. If you change your mind."

He hands it back. I stare down at the new contact. BBB.

"BBB?" I frown.

"Bastian Balthazar—"

"Bux." I nod. "The name of the kid in *The NeverEnding Story.*"

"Classic piece of German fantasy literature." He smiles suddenly. "Message me."

For a second, it's enticing, then I remember what he wants.

"No," I say. I walk away from him, thinking about how Bastian Chevret must have a few screws loose, because who else but a deeply warped person offers to resurrect the girlfriend of someone they've just met?

When I return to college, I see none other than Carl Lord outside the door, kissing a pretty first year. *Poor sod,* I think. It doesn't bother me, seeing Carl with someone else (other than vague disgust) but the look on this tragic first year's face – the excitement, the gratitude – brings the past back to me. I used to look at Elizabeth like that and suddenly I am heavy with everything that's been taken.

One thought crystallizes in my head: at least with Bastian's plan, I wouldn't be standing here, so weighed down by all the broken things. At least I would be moving, I would be *doing* something. Which is better than what I am right now, bloody useless and utterly helpless. Even if he is weird, what does it matter? Everything worth losing I've already lost. I pull out my phone and send a message to BBB: I'm in.

Chapter Five

> I'm in.

Cool. Meet me next Monday at the
John Rylands Library at 4.30 p.m.

> Why?

Meet me there and find out.

I nearly back out. I lie awake in the middle of the night between nightmares and write Bastian messages saying I've changed my mind. But on Monday morning I get up and go to work at the vegan supermarket, since I don't have a class at college until Wednesday. (Counsellor Cooper suggested I get a part-time job before college started to stop me wallowing, and I've decided to stay on.) Suddenly, it's four o'clock and I'm finishing at work, catching a tram into town. I shove my apron into my tote bag and run from St Peter's Square to the John Rylands Library.

It's one of the most beautiful buildings in Manchester, in my opinion, particularly in a slightly pinkish afternoon light like today. It's a lump of dark red brick that over the years has shaded with industrial soot to a deep aubergine shade, almost black on grey days, with spires that look like stalagmites. Some people say it looks like a purple armchair, with its stacked, square shape, but I've always thought there's something almost organic about it, as if it grew like coral out of the earth rather than being built in the nineteenth century.

Bastian is standing outside the entrance. He's still annoyingly handsome in all black with a velvet waistcoat, and it looks like he's washed his hair. The shiny curls catch the dying light. There's something about him, reminding me of a debonair time-travelling librarian, that makes me feel very shabby, in my same old jeans and boots. I stop in front of him and he smiles, tugging at something by my armpit.

"Is that an apron?" he asks. "Are you a baker?"

"I work at a vegan supermarket in Chorlton." I blush and stuff the apron back into my bag. "Why am I here?"

"It's a library, why do you think we're here?" He smirks. He really is very self-satisfied.

"The grimoire's in here?"

"Yep." He holds out his phone. It's a John Rylands webpage that has a picture of an old book open on it.

"But the John Rylands isn't a lending library." I fold my arms and look at him sharply. Bastian grins.

"We're a solution-orientated team here, Orlando," he says.

"Lando, I go by Lando."

"Yeah, but it's still your name, right?" He tilts his head to one side. I imagine he does this because he thinks it makes him look cute, and it does, but it also makes him look like a cocky wanker.

"Do you want me to give you the statistics about trans teenagers and depression and chosen names?" I demand.

"Yeah, sure, go for it." He shrugs. He's got me there. Usually people just mumble apologies and move on. I grimace.

"I don't know them," I say sulkily. "But they're really bad."

"You don't know them?" Bastian grins some more. "You're clearly a very bad gay, then, aren't you?"

I can't help myself. I snort with laughter.

"Are you going to tell me how we're getting the book?" I ask.

"Live a little."

"I don't want to live at all," I quip back and then realize, too late, that super-dark suicidal jokes aren't funny to anyone but me.

"Good thing this is a life-threatening spell we're after, then!" He walks backward towards the door, arms spread wide in an annoying gesture of invitation that makes me want to slap him with my rolled-up apron. *Smug dick,* I think, but I follow him through the glass doors into the gift shop. Inside, he leans a hand on the desk and smiles flirtatiously at the student with glasses behind it. "Can you tell me where the origins of witchcraft exhibition is?"

"Upstairs," she says, handing us both leaflets. "First floor before you go up to the main library."

"Thanks so much." Bastian winks at her and she actually simpers. I wonder where he got that kind of instinct from. How does he just know how to be charming, and who to charm and when? I've had a male body multiple times in my life and sometimes it's even been the kind of body that gets admiring looks, but I've never had this kind of confidence, to know without hesitation that because I'm handsome, I'll be wanted.

"We're here for an exhibition on witchcraft?" I ask, as we turn the corner and climb the white marble stairs up into the old building.

"Yes." Bastian gives me a sidelong look. "What's the problem?"

"Nothing, it's just a bit ironic," I say as we reach the top of the stairs and turn down the dark corridor that is the start of the old library, a combination of beautiful heavy wood, carved grey stone and strategically placed spotlights. "Don't we know our origins?"

"I thought you were shitty at witchcraft," he says drily. "Maybe you can learn something."

"Are you always such an arse or is it just for me?"

"Are you always so defensive or is it just for me?" he returns.

"I'm not defensive!"

"They said defensively." Bastian turns left into a room that's lined floor to ceiling with books, items in glass display cases running down the centre of the room.

"At least you don't misgender when you're being insulting," I mutter, staring at a rusted metal scold's bridle in a display case.

"I would never." He says it lightly, but I can tell he means it.

We walk unhurriedly around the exhibition. The first mounted informational panel has an illustration of Stonehenge on it and witches standing with their hands raised to the sky. EARLY PRE-ROMAN WITCHES PRACTISED PAGANISM AND WERE OFTEN VILLAGE LEADERS, HEALERS AND EVEN HONOURED BY COMMUNITIES FOR THEIR POWERS. I feel weirdly detached. Shapeshifters were there at the very beginning too, before Christianity, when the world was wild and magical and humans lived under the protection of witches and shapeshifters. We even shared magic back then and lived in covens together, shapeshifters and witches, intermarrying and raising families. Nowadays it's something witches will say about bad luck, *Oh, you must have had a shapeshifter in your family once upon a time,* as if we are a lingering curse. There's a reason Elizabeth was terrified to tell anyone about me and it's not just because she was scared of coming out to her mother. I glance at Bastian and wonder if he might think the same things other people at college did: *Who would date a shifter? Did she have a death wish?*

"Learning anything?" Bastian says blandly. I shrug and move on. He follows me. We stare together at a painting of a witch burning. I'm suddenly uneasy. My mother's voice from the past pops into my head: *A witch will never trust a shifter. We used our skills to avoid their fate. They never forget it.* This is the historical moment I've had to write at least three five-thousand-word essays on in college so far: the Great Cull, the seventeenth century witch trials. Shifters avoided all of the worst prejudice against witches in those terrible days in the past by disappearing into the background and that's where we have stayed. Witches refused to accept us back into covens, so now we live long lives in small families where children are rare, tolerated in society because of our value to the Merlin Foundation and the government, but the trust between us has never rekindled. When I look at Bastian, staring at the painting, I wonder if any of his ancestors died this way, on a pyre or under a pressing stone. It suddenly feels very weird for me to be here, with a witch, staring at this picture of all the reasons we should hate each other.

"You know, most witches wouldn't want to look at this with a shifter," I say, attempting a light, disinterested tone to test him. Bastian gives me a withering look.

"Please," he mutters.

"Please what?"

"Look, I know most witches still carry prejudice from all this, but those witches are idiots." His voice is shockingly matter-of-fact. "Witches and shapeshifters lived together on this island for hundreds of years before it happened."

"But it did happen." I look almost apologetically up at the screaming witch.

"Shifters used their skills to survive and I don't see anything wrong with that. Besides, there are shapeshifters working at the Merlin Foundation. Or so I've heard. I'd have to get used to it."

"So, what? You're getting used to it now?"

He gives me a strange sideways look.

"I love how you just assume you're the only shifter I've met," he says.

It's a declaration that shocks me more than it should. There's no one else at college like me. I'm the only person who has to stare at their books and blush whenever a teacher mentions the witch trials, weathering the muttered snide comments of other students. *Traitors.* But Bastian isn't like that. Bastian has met other shapeshifters; he doesn't look at me and put all of history on my back. He might be insufferable but at least he's not prejudiced.

I nod and we move on. I can almost pretend we are just two friends walking through a museum, rather than two strangers looking for a grimoire. Then Bastian stops in front of the display case. "Here it is."

I stare at the book. It's old and open on two pages that are full of spells, pentagrams and other symbols. The little sign on the glass says: THE WITCHLORE OF BODIES. THIS ANCIENT GRIMOIRE WAS LEFT IN THE CARE OF THE JOHN RYLANDS COLLECTION AS PART OF A LEGACY IN 1951.

"It's inside the display case," I say, my hands beginning to moisten with sweat.

"Yep." Bastian is running his fingers around the edge of the display case, looking for something.

"Wait, you want to *steal* a book from the exhibition?" I stare at him.

"No, obviously not." Bastian looks affronted at the notion. He sets his leather satchel down on the floor and pulls out an equally old-looking book. "We're going to *borrow* it and replace it temporarily with a fake."

"Give me it." I snatch it out of his hands and stare between the book I'm holding and the book in the case. They definitely look the same. "Did you make this?"

"Yeah. I just found a book that's of a similar age and redid the pages and the illustrations by copying from the photographs online."

"Wow," I mutter. I open the first two pages and see that the illustrations perfectly match the ones of the book in the display case. Then I turn the page. "You've only done the first two pages!"

"Yeah, well, it's only going to be open on that one, isn't it?" Bastian says.

"And you don't reckon someone will notice when they open it up to check and most of the pages are *blank*?" I hiss, slamming the book shut.

"Why would they check?" Bastian frowns. "Look, it's in this exhibition for the next six months, it's already been set up, they won't check unless they think something has happened and they won't think something happened if we don't make it a big deal."

"Don't you think book stealing is a big deal? Especially if it's an ancient grimoire with a resurrection spell?"

"Not book stealing, book swapping," Bastian says emphatically, taking the fake back from me.

"And how are you going to swap them?" I demand.

Bastian holds up his middle finger with the massive sapphire on, inadvertently (or perhaps deliberately) giving me the finger. "Or did you forget that we can do witchcraft?"

"*You* can do witchcraft; I can't do shit."

"Exactly, which is why you're the lookout," Bastian says calmly. He pulls out a small notebook and sets it down on the floor. Then he stands, widening his stance, holding his hands in a triangle shape with the fingertips and the thumbs meeting. My heart jolts. This was how Elizabeth stood in the cave on the day of her death.

"What are you even going to do?" I ask suddenly. I realize that Bastian hasn't actually done any witchcraft around me yet. Maybe that's why he's been so easy to talk to.

"An unlocking spell," he says, nodding at the small padlock. "I'll just lift the lid off the case and switch them."

"Seriously?" I stare at his hands. Most unlocking spells are ancient, only relevant for the kind of traditional locks from hundreds of years ago. "Do you even have enough power?"

He gives me such a sharp look that I regret it instantly. It's definitely rude for me, a shifter, supposedly full of power, to question a witch, and I cringe at my clumsiness. His ring is already shining, the light of it pulsing slightly in that uncanny, mesmerizing way, as if the magic inside Bastian is desperate to be released. I can feel it, even from here; it makes the hair on my arms stand up like in a lightning storm. It reminds me of Elizabeth's last breath, and suddenly I really don't want him to do any witchcraft.

"Why can't we just use the pages that are online?" I ask desperately. He sighs and drops his hands, turning to look at me. The feeling of coming bewitchment in the room suddenly halts and I hate myself because I'm relieved.

"Because it's incomplete, the spell won't work," he says.

"How do you know?"

"I just do." Bastian's voice is level but he's clenching his fists in annoyance.

"And I'm supposed to just trust you? I barely know you!"

I stare at the grimoire in its case. There are real potential consequences here and it is scaring me that I don't know what they are. I know I'd do anything to get Elizabeth back but doing this, right now, seems impossible.

"Okay, Lando, let's put it this way. I'm borrowing this book," Bastian says firmly, turning back towards the lock and taking up his stance, hands held ready. The air around us prickles.

"You can help me or you can piss off."

I watch as he twists his fingers from the triangle into the diamond, the basic steps of a classic spell – a complicated twisting motion first, the Tangle of Loki, followed by a blinded Hare's Run – and his ring begins to glow with that strange, unearthly blue light. My throat tightens. He's not messing around. I can tell from the strength of his fingers and the quickness of his twists that he's good at this, maybe good enough to pull this off. *No going back now.*

"Christ," I mutter.

I go to stand at the doorway, peering down the dark corridor. It's empty. It's not a surprise really; it's the last ten minutes of the day, and soon the museum will be closing. There's a tingle in the air, the same kind of feeling you get when someone who hates you stares at you for a long time, and I look back at Bastian. His fingers are still moving through the sequence, repeating it, his eyes fixed on the grimoire. When Elizabeth started her last spell the air was tight and cold. With Bastian, the air feels hot and a bit dangerous, like standing next to a bonfire, and there's a smell on the air that's different to Elizabeth's magic. No longer toasted almonds but something deeper, woodier, like logs spitting in a roaring fireplace. It's the kind of power I have never sensed before, not from a witch. I realize he might actually be in with a shot at the Merlin Foundation. The glass case is beginning to glow, burning red at the edges. That's when I hear footsteps.

"Someone's coming," I say, my voice dropping to a stage whisper.

"Distract them."

"With what?" I exclaim.

"Well, if you were a real shifter, I might say shift into someone distracting—"

"You're a wanker," I snap, and I spin around to stare at the student who had been sitting behind the desk now marching towards me with her lanyard swinging.

"The library is closing in ten minutes, it's time to go," she says, all of the simper she had for Bastian lost when she looks at me.

"Yeah, I'll be down in a second." I swallow. I have no idea what will happen to us if she sees the spellwork. It's all well and good to be told to be distracting, but I'm not a handsome bloke like Bastian is. I'm not a bloke at all and to her I probably look like I'm up to trouble. *Be distracting!*

"Um, I don't know if this is a problem or anything," I gabble, sticking my hands in my pockets to stop them shaking. "But I saw that someone spilled a drink upstairs in the main library—"

Her eyebrows shoot up.

"Not water, something nasty," I add quickly, imagining a librarian's worst nightmare. "Something purple and sticky."

"What? There are signs." She shoots me an accusatory glare. "Was it you?"

"No, no, I'd never bring a sticky drink into the library," I say. "I love libraries, I only ever bring in water, I swear."

"Christ alive," she mutters, then glares at me, clearly the prime suspect. "You need to leave, okay?"

"Yeah, yeah, sure, on my way out." I watch her as she walks

away along the corridor, her skirt swinging.

"I'm done," a voice whispers, and I jump. Bastian's standing right behind me, his breath warm on my neck, and I glare at him.

"Don't do that!" I hiss at him, stepping back, alarmed at his closeness. I look down at his satchel. "You switched it?"

"Yeah." He nods. I push past him and stare at the book in the glass display case. It looks absolutely identical and I have no idea how he managed it.

"Wow, it looks dead real," I say. Still, a part of me wants to tell him to put the real grimoire back, now.

"I know." Bastian pulls my arm. "Come on, we need to leave."

He drags me down the stairs. The heaviness of his satchel against my elbow is the thump of a literal priceless object and I panic wildly that we're damaging it, that by carrying it out we will accidentally turn it to dust. The shop is empty, an employee is putting chairs up on tables and someone else is wiping down the coffee machine, and outside, the late afternoon sun is blossoming in a golden blaze over Deansgate. Bastian is smiling at people and saying polite things to the staff and a part of me wants to stop, to call out to them and to turn us both in, tell them I'm not a criminal I just made a mistake, but my mouth won't work. The automatic doors open and we step out into the cold.

"I can't believe we did that—" I mutter as the doors slide close behind us. "What if we get caught? There must be cameras…"

"Only in the corridor and they'll just see your distracting alter ego," he says as we walk down Deansgate. "Lando

Southerns, defender of books from sticky liquids."

"I'm not in the mood for jokes right now." I try not to look over my shoulder, waiting for a yell or running footsteps or sirens.

"Then keep walking." We march down the road, my heart thundering as I try to embody someone who has not committed larceny. I can't stop imagining the footage of me directing a staff member to an imaginary clean-up, of us rushing out of the library with surreptitious looks, Bastian's bag hanging at his side. *Won't they check? What if they clean the inside of the cases?* Someone knocks into me, rushing past, and it's such a jolt I'm suddenly convinced I've been caught. I wheel back away from them with a cry, stumbling over the edge of the kerb.

"Lando, whoa, be careful!" Bastian grabs my arm to pull me out of traffic.

"Why are we doing this?" I gasp out. It's absurd, I don't even know this person and I just made myself an accomplice to a crime. "Why are we even doing this?"

A car horn honks loudly behind me, the sound assaulting my ears, making me jump out of my skin. Bastian keeps a firm grip on my arm, his fingers digging in painfully.

"To resurrect your dead girlfriend," Bastian says urgently. "Remember that?"

I stop. Suddenly I can't breathe. Most of the time, I know Elizabeth is dead and it's fine. Or not fine at all, but possible to endure, as long as I never forget it. Because then, when I remember it, when I realize that she's really not here and now I'm walking around Manchester with a complete stranger talking about resurrecting her, it thoroughly takes the air out of me and it's agonizing. I bend over and press my hands to my knees, thoughts churning: *Elizabeth is dead, Jesus Christ, Elizabeth is really dead and it's my fault.* I hear Counsellor Cooper's words in my head: *Breathe deeply and slowly.* How can four words seem so impossible?

"Lando?" Bastian stops beside me, one hand on my back. "Lando, what's the matter?"

I wish I could tell him. But I can't breathe.

Chapter Six

"You're having a panic attack," Bastian says bluntly above me as cars roar past and people sidestep me.

"No...shit..." I gasp out, staring at my boots as they whizz round and round in red circles, smelling an upturned mushed takeaway that's been spilled a few paces away, ground into the pavement by passing pedestrians. I'm trying to remember everything Counsellor Cooper told me about panic attacks but the only thing I can think of is that she told me they typically go in cycles of ten minutes, and right now ten minutes seems like an impossibly long time. *Breathe, for fuck's sake.*

"Do you want me to help you?" Bastian bends down to stare into my face and I nod at him viciously, hating him for making me ask. Bastian grabs my arm, pulling it around his waist and then putting his arm around my shoulders, holding me upright and starting to walk us in long steady strides down into Spinningfields, the rising skyscrapers glaring down at me with their glistening points and sharp, unkind edges. "Come on, I live around here. Breathe in time with our steps, okay? Concentrate on the out breath, not the in breath."

He's speaking in this clipped, commanding voice that makes me think he was probably the captain of his school newspaper or maybe the orienteering club. How do men like him always have this prime minister/sergeant major mode of existence that kicks in? Where do they get it from? Is it all private school or is some of it just cisgender masculine magic? I don't have any of the answers, but wondering about it does help my breathing slow down as we stop outside a glass door with neat green lollipop hedges in pots outside of it. I think he's lost or he's going to ask for directions or something, but Bastian leans forward and types a code into the console and the door buzzes. He manoeuvres us through it sideways, since his arm is still clamped across my shoulders.

"You don't live here," I mutter, looking at the brushed chrome letter boxes and the concierge desk with an orchid on it. Everything around us is gold finishes and mirrors and marble and makes my chest feel even tighter.

"Yeah, I do, so?" He presses the gold button next to the lift and the doors open. It looks tiny. Suddenly, all I can see are the walls of the cave, closing around me as I shift and I hear Elizabeth's scream.

"You do *not* live here," I say, sliding out from under his arm and ignoring the dizziness I feel when I'm not being steadied by him.

"Will you just get in the bloody lift?" Bastian demands, slamming a hand against the doors as they close. The woman in the neat black uniform at the concierge desk is trying not to stare at us.

"No, I'm claustrophobic," I lie, staring at the small space. "We'll do the stairs."

"You can barely breathe and you want to climb twenty flights of stairs?" Bastian demands.

"Twenty?" I gasp, pressing a hand against the wall, feeling so sick suddenly. "You live in the penthouse?"

"Get in." Bastian reaches out and grabs my arm. I'm too weak to stop him and I stumble inside. The doors close on me with a soft chime. Immediately, my skin itches and I glare at him but when we lurch upwards, I feel too nauseous to even yell at him. I just gulp heavily and bend over. I'm surprised when I feel Bastian's hand rubbing up and down my back.

"It's okay, take slow breaths," he says quietly. "In and out... In...and out..."

I listen to the inane lift music and do what he says. I'm a little bit annoyed when it starts to work.

"In...and out..." Bastian intones softly above me, stroking my back in time with his words. I realize this is the first time I've been touched like this since Elizabeth died. "In...and out..."

The familiar touch is comforting. I need to put a stop to it. I pull away and stand up, avoiding his eyes and coughing.

"You're like a meditation app," I say, hating my voice for shaking. "Did you go on one of those world tours of waterfalls to find inner peace? A spiritual gap yah?"

I try not to stare at how weird my new ears look in the mirror. It's always like this when I shift. For months after, I catch myself and realize there are still parts of me I wouldn't recognize in a line-up.

"You just make stuff up about me, don't you?" Bastian says, giving me a sideways look.

"Is any of it wrong?" I snap.

"Most of it," he says calmly. I scowl at him. It's really unfair that I've been vulnerable and messy in front of him and he's just the same: unruffled and sardonic.

"Well, I'm not wrong about this," I say flatly. "You're rich."

"I'm not rich, my dad is rich."

"That's something only rich people say," I snort.

"What else do rich people say?" Bastian shoots me a kind of fond, frustrated look.

"I don't know, stuff about ponies?"

I'm surprised when Bastian laughs.

"Come on," he says, and he puts a hand on my back as the door opens. I try not to jump. "Let's go and get you something to drink."

Bastian puts his key in a door that is just on the other side of the lift as it opens. My jaw almost drops. I know that there's a bar in Spinningfields where you can sit at the top of a skyscraper in a garden that looks over the city, but I never thought that people could *live* in places like this. It's an open-plan kitchen and living room, the kind with a sunken fire pit in the middle and a kitchen so shiny that it looks like it's from the future. The windows are floor to ceiling, a panoramic view of the skyscrapers, canals, cranes and train tracks spilling out towards the green fields in the south. Right now, the sunset is blazing and making the industrial chrome shimmer in every direction. I have a sudden flash of memory of my parents' cluttered living room in their crumbling Georgian red-brick semi-detached. My parents have lived for nearly three hundred years between them, they have a Blitz-spirit attitude and prefer hoarding rather than spending, so this is completely out of my comfort zone.

"This looks like something out of a TV show about teenage billionaires who live in Dubai," I say.

"I'd watch it," says Bastian. He walks me towards the sofa while he goes to the kitchen. As soon as I sit down, I can breathe easier. "Water okay?"

"Yep." I watch as he puts a glass under a button in the fridge and chilled water comes out. I see there are a few things pinned on it with magnets that look like marbles, including a picture of a handsome-looking couple and something that looks like a shopping list. I don't think this is the kind of household where they pin up sentimental finger paintings with LIVE, LAUGH, LOVE magnets. I peek around for other telling family photographs, hoping for an embarrassing childhood picture of Bastian to make me feel better about my humiliating vulnerability, but I'm surprised to see there are none. There's a lot of art: carved wooden statues by the doors; huge, expensive canvases of brightly coloured abstracted human forms mixed with some symbology I think I can identify as Haitian-Vodou inspired; a giant collage piece of tiny landscape photographs that delicately make up a Jamaican flag. It's all beautifully curated, but as I look around, I keep feeling like something is slightly off.

Then it hits me. I can't see any of the accoutrement I would expect to find in a typical witch home. I'm by no means an expert, but based on my experience living in a multi-person multicultural witch accommodation, even when a witch only has a room of their own they'll stuff it to the gills with magical decor. I'd definitely expect more than some vague symbols hidden in the art. I peer around the corner, wondering where the talismans of heritage magic are hiding – do they have it all shoved in a cupboard?

I open my mouth to ask but a door opens somewhere in the flat and a voice calls out, "Bastian? Is that you?"

A man walks into the living room, tall, dark, curly hair with a receding hairline and much darker skin than Bastian, but I can instantly see the resemblance. This must be Bastian's father. He's wearing stylish black jeans and designer trainers, a white T-shirt that looks like it costs more than anything I have on and an artfully distressed leather jacket.

"Oh. You didn't tell me you were bringing a...friend over," he says, looking up from his phone. He has an accent; I think it's Canadian but it has a cadence I don't recognize. French, maybe, and the way he pauses tells me that Bastian is definitely gay. I flush at the idea that I'm being framed as his son's hook-up. I hide my face in my water glass.

"Dad, this is Lando. They're on my course at college." Bastian's tone has dropped below freezing. "Lando, this is my father, Eric Chevret."

"Hi." I raise my hand awkwardly.

"Hello." His dad gives me a hard, steady look and then looks at his son. "Not another Merlin Foundation wannabe, I hope."

"Dad." Bastian frowns. I don't know what to say. I scan Eric's hands for rings, for any sign of charms around his neck or on bracelets around his wrists. There's nothing but a sleek watch. It's baffling. If someone had asked me to draw a picture of Bastian's dad, based on my limited knowledge, this would not be what I expected. Bastian's magical prowess and beliefs don't come from nowhere. I'd imagined that, like most witches, he had learned them from his family and coven. Eric Chevret does not look like the kind of man who is part of a coven; he doesn't even look like a witch.

"I work in a vegan supermarket," I say blankly.

"Wonderful," Eric says absently. "Perhaps you can encourage Bastian to look at more practical future options."

"You mean like running a bloody *tech start-up?*" Bastian speaks the last three words like they are the equivalent of drinking toilet water. Eric merely sighs, as if he has heard it a million times and gives me a wan smile.

"You'll forgive me, I'm on the way out. I have a dinner meeting in London." He turns to Bastian. "Behave."

"You too," Bastian says. His tone is so flat and cold that I want to blush with the awkwardness, but I try not to. Eric is walking to the door of the flat, looking at his phone again as he opens the front door and presses the button for the lift.

"It was nice to meet you, Landen," he says.

"Lando," Bastian corrects fiercely, but his dad has stepped into the lift and the doors have closed with a musical ding.

"Christ," I mutter to myself, thinking that if father–son relations got any colder, we would have to relocate to the Arctic.

"What does that mean?" Bastian snaps.

"Nothing, I just—"

"Wondered why he's such an asshole?" Bastian slams his own glass down on the marble countertop. I try not to flinch.

"No, I just...you know, you're clearly so..." I gesture to his necklaces and see his jaw tighten, but I can't seem to stop speaking. "I guess I expected your dad to be like you."

"Right, because you know exactly who I am. Having a *tech bro* dad who couldn't give a shit about witchcraft doesn't conveniently fit into the elitist witch home you've imagined for me, does it?"

Bastian's voice is so harsh, so visceral, so familiar that I respond without thinking.

"What did he do?" I blurt out. Bastian stares at me coldly.

"I don't know why I should tell you."

"You don't have to." I swallow hard and look at the setting sun, descending like a wilting orange marigold below the dazzling line of the skyscraper in front of us, casting Bastian in shadow. I decide to give him a bit of honesty because I get the uncomfortable feeling I'm one fuck-up away from being thrown out. "But...I do get hating your parents."

"I don't hate my dad."

"I didn't say you did." On the edges of the room, the sunset dances brightly but we're sat in the shadow. "I just said...I get it."

There's a long pause. I hold my breath, wondering if I've made it worse.

"He didn't do anything," Bastian says quietly.

"Is it just you and him?"

I nod to the only photo in the flat, stuck on the fridge. The woman, who I assume is his mother, is smiling and looks to be only about twenty. She's got milky skin with a spattering of freckles and auburn hair and she's leaning against a much younger version of Eric. His dark hair is thicker and his eyes are livelier than the man I just met. Bastian grimaces and looks away from it.

"I don't know why he even put it there." Bastian shakes his head, whipping the photo off the fridge. I almost expect him to throw it in the bin but he just walks over from the kitchen and sits on the sofa beside me with a heavy sigh, holding the photo in his hand.

"They look happy," I say tentatively. They both look joyful and adventurous and young, the epitome of classy witches in their twenties, with their large rings on their clasped hands. Eric's is chunky, with symbology carved into it that matches some of the symbols hidden in the art on the walls. Bastian's mum's ring is more Celtic, with a knotted band, like Bastian's ring.

"Yeah, they were then," Bastian snorts derisively. "They're witchlore researchers, or they were. They met travelling. Dad's Canadian, his side of the family are all Jamaican-Canadian and Haitian-Canadian. He grew up in Quebec."

"He speaks French?"

"Québécois," Bastian corrects. "Pépé, my dad's dad, he speaks Haitian Creole but Dad didn't learn it." I want to ask him if he speaks any of these languages, but he goes on. "Mum is Cornish. She wanted to raise her family there, in her coven." Very briefly, he touches a finger against his mum's face. His own expression has contorted into something very complicated. "They were both so into ancient witchcraft. Then he changed."

Bastian's face darkens. I can tell something happened, something bad, but I absolutely cannot ask about it. I wait for Bastian to go on.

"Everything broke apart. He started working late, changed careers, went into one flashy business venture after another. He stopped coming to coven meetings, stopped practising the craft. He started saying witchlore was just a quirk of his upbringing, that it had no bearing on our lives. Witchcraft is everything to Mum." From the way his mouth twists with scorn I can tell this was one of the most painful ways his dad changed. "So she left him. Asked for a divorce. Who could blame her, really?"

"Where is she now?"

"She's still a researcher for the Boscastle Witchcraft Museum. I think she's in Cuba or something."

The way he says it tells me it's still sore.

"And…do you see the rest of your family?"

"Not since the divorce." His voice is very clipped. "I call my nan down in Cornwall but she's very low tech. She doesn't always answer. I keep up with my cousins and Pépé and Grandma Olive in Quebec online, but we used to go over every year, sometimes twice a year, and now…" He shakes his head and looks angrily around the flat. "But why shouldn't they be mad at him? It's like he's severed off half of himself! I wouldn't speak to him either but I have to live with him, so…"

Bastian trails off. As I wait, unsure what to say, I realize something. Bastian might have grandparents and cousins and a whole world I don't know about, but right now, he's just as isolated as I am. My thoughts are interrupted by the sound of a door opening and something clicking towards me. Then a furry face appears by my knee. It's a grey French bulldog with the most plaintive amber eyes I've ever seen.

"Oh my god, you have a *dog*?" I instantly begin ruffling its adorable little ears and it pants happily. "Why didn't you say?"

"This is René."

"René?" I laugh, as René jumps up on the sofa next to me, putting his front paws on my thighs.

"My mum likes philosophy," Bastian says. René trots along the long sofa and climbs up on Bastian's lap, licking his face. Bastian smiles and it's the most genuine smile I've seen on his face so far.

"So like…René Descartes?" René trots back down the sofa to me, as if he wishes we were sitting closer together so he could lick us both at the same time.

"Yeah." Bastian smiles fondly. All the tension has gone from the room like air let out of a balloon. "Look, shall we…pretend that my dad isn't an arse and just look at the book?"

I'm very relieved. I don't want to sit with this uncomfortable feeling that I've misjudged him and made assumptions about what his life must be like. After all, the flat might be gorgeous but it must be lonely with only René for company and the people he loves halfway around the world. It's odd to have had him pinned in my mind as one kind of person and now be seeing him differently. I don't know if I really want to.

"Yes," I say. "Let's do it."

Chapter Seven

Bastian smiles gratefully, reaches into his satchel and pulls out the grimoire, setting it on the coffee table, and we both scoot closer together so that René is happily squashed between us. The book is astonishing close up, the cover embossed with what seems like years and years of markings and the leather worn down and soft at the spine. I tentatively open the pages, inhaling that musty, sweet antique scent.

"Wow, this is dated from the 1700s," Bastian murmurs, on the first page. We flick through it. The handwriting is hard to understand, sometimes faded, sometimes entirely indecipherable and sometimes it's just diagrams and reams of numbers that could be astrological information, I'm not sure.

"This is all spells?" I ask.

"No, not just, look—" Bastian points to a part that looks like it's written in French. "This is a recipe for soap."

"Why?"

"Lots of witches throughout history used grimoires like journals, you know?" Bastian says, flipping the pages back to the beginning. "Recipes, gramarye, spells, family trees, shopping lists…"

"Shopping lists?"

"Uh-huh." Bastian frowns and runs his finger down the page. "I read one from the 1500s that included a list of what type of buttons she wanted to buy."

"So what family had this one?"

"No one knows. Sometimes family names are inscribed in the leather, but not this one."

"How can that be possible?" I stare at all of this history, so rare and wonderful, and the authors of it all lost to the sands of time.

"I guess you go back far enough in history, one life looks very much like another," Bastian muses, turning the page.

"So we're all boring in death?" I say, stroking René's ears.

"You're a morbid person, you know that?"

"I do, yes." It is one thing I know to be definitely true. "But then how can you know it's a shapeshifter grimoire?"

"Lucky guess." Bastian's voice is evasive. I wonder if I should press him, but does it matter how he came to his "lucky guess"? After all, I'm just here for the results. On the other hand, does blindly trusting him make me the careless idiot my parents always thought I was? "Here it is."

I'm distracted from my conflicting thoughts by my first look at the resurrection spell. The page is etched with complicated symbology and text, and Bastian's face takes on an eager quality as he looks it over.

"So this is all normal, all expected gramarye."

"Is it?" I say drily, looking at the complicated notations that look like music, indicating hand movements and hints of ancient languages that I can only understand about two per cent of. Gramarye, the act of writing or creating spells, is one of my worst subjects. This is what comes from only taking one practical witchcraft module a semester. Bastian is glaring at the page, tracing his fingers over every word, as if expecting something to jump out at him.

"If this is all of it, why didn't it...?" he mutters.

"Why didn't it what?"

He turns the page. The next doesn't look like the others. It's completely dark, as if it's been dipped in blood.

"Is it a replacement page?" He turns it and then, seeing only blank pages after it, says, "Fuck."

"So it's incomplete? We can't do the spell?" I ask. Bastian doesn't answer. He looks thoroughly pissed off, biting his bottom lip. I feel a confusing mix of things: relief, then creeping disappointment. This has been a scary, thrilling day but at least it's been different. Now it'll just be more of the same: days at college, nights at Beryl's, the rest of my life spent missing Elizabeth.

"Maybe it's not a replacement page," I say, trying to find something to hold onto. "Maybe they dipped it in a different colour to hide it, maybe there's a way we can...I don't know, lift the dye off it?"

I touch it and, oddly, it's *warm*. When my fingers meet the dry, slightly textured surface, the red dye shimmers. It wiggles, as if hundreds of woodlice are trapped underneath it. Bastian sucks in a breath of surprise. I withdraw my hand sharply.

"Whoa," I say shakily. I wasn't expecting *that*.

"Yeah, whoa." Bastian hesitates and then touches it too.

Nothing happens. "Why would it work for you and not for me?"

I frown. I have no idea, but having such an old book in my hands makes me think of my father's own collection, of the ancient tomes smelling sweetly of dust, some locked with spells so intense only he can unravel them. I remember him standing over one, pressing a bloody fingerprint into the cover.

"Could it be blood locked?" I ask hesitantly. I'm sure Bastian's thought of it already, but it doesn't hurt to ask. "Shapeshifters in the past sometimes used blood locks."

"Really?" He looks up at me, eyes bright with excitement again. "Witches haven't used them for hundreds of years, but shapeshifters still can?"

"Yeah." I'm weirdly nervous. This would definitely fall into the category of a secret my father would hate me to repeat. I even imagine the angry furrow of his brows.

"It's a good idea." He's immediately rifling in his bag and pulling out a penknife. "Try it."

I look between the sharp edge of the pale knife and the deep red of the page. I swallow in trepidation. Gingerly, I take the penknife. I try not to remember the bathroom, focusing hard instead on the feeling of a French bulldog panting beside me. Mouth dry, I dig the knife into the bulbous pad of my finger, gritting my teeth against the sting. I wipe my bloody finger over the ancient page. I hold my breath as my fingerprint sinks into an ocean of blood, losing itself. Then, the wriggling begins again, intensifying, splitting like curdled milk.

"It's working." Bastian's eyes are wide with astonishment. "*Whoa.*"

Unlike the notations I've seen in college, the words are written in script that circles the page in a strange pattern, too small to even make out. When I look closer, it seems like the page shifts, or the words do, impossible to catch. "Wait, is it seeping through?"

I hastily flick the page and we watch, captivated, as more words, not spells, spill out across the pages. It's as if the words are water: they're soaking through from the spell all the way to the back page and then spreading out in a weird, unsettling revelation.

"It's a diary section," Bastian says. "I told you, some grimoires are like journals."

We flip back through so many different diary entries to where it starts and I read the first entry.

December 31st, 1878. Today is my seventeenth birthday. Father has given me the care of the family grimoire. I have decided to use this book to mark my most important moments, to tell the tale of my shifts...

"They were a shapeshifter!" I say. There's something about the handwriting that's appealing to me. "You were right!"

I look at Bastian's face and it is split in a wide, enthusiastic smile.

"No, you were right," he says. "Now let's look at this spell properly."

He flicks back to the resurrection spell page, the tiny writing formed out of blood. Bastian reaches underneath the coffee table to the shelf covered in magazines and pulls out a magnifying glass. I wonder who on earth just has a magnifying glass lying around in their house, like Sherlock Holmes?

"These words are in Latin, I'm pretty sure," Bastian mutters.

"Okay. Read it."

"You think I read Latin?" Bastian looks at me in amusement.

"I mean, yeah, you're rich and cultured and you're named after a fantasy character—"

"Yeah, and I have access to the internet." Bastian pulls out his phone. "Let's look at this..."

He pulls out a notebook and begins to write things down, muttering to himself as I suck the tip of my finger to get rid of the blood, my tongue full of its metallic taste.

"Okay, I've got it."

He shows me the words he's written down in his notebook and I read them aloud:

"In Boggart Hole Clough the demon's name

Kilgrimol bones underneath the waves

Hair of the Black Shuck that stalks holy ground

Earth from the grave of the lost love

Blood of the shifter.

Hand on the stone of the wizard.

"That makes no sense," I say.

"Yeah, well, maybe my translation isn't perfect." Bastian scowls. "Also, it's an ingredients list, it's not poetry. This is the secret of the resurrection spell, that it needs tokens and ingredients to work and then" - he points to a tiny fleck of a notation between the fifth and sixth line - "an instruction for the spellcrafting."

"So the ingredients are…" I squint as I look at it again. "The name of a boggart, a bone from Kilgrimol, hair from the Black Shuck and dirt from Elizabeth's grave?"

"And your blood," Bastian says. "Don't worry, we only need *some* blood, not all of it. Looking at the equations here, like maybe a pint and a half?"

"A pint and a half?" It's an astonishing amount of blood for a spell. I learned about this kind of thing in some of my Roman history modules where they used slave blood for spells, but the slaves always died. I look down at my arm and wonder how many pints I have in me. Then I think of the bathroom, of Elizabeth in the cave, and the hair at the back of my neck stands up. I try to push it away but the elation I felt when the blood lock unlocked is rapidly twisting into anxiety.

"The rest is all spellwork, but…"

"Bastian…" He looks up at me as I swallow the taste of my own blood in my mouth. "This isn't a normal spell, is it?"

"It's a resurrection spell," he says slowly. "I mean, what did you expect?"

I immediately feel foolish. Of course it's dangerous. I might not be the best at witchcraft but I know that ancient spells like this, something crafted for permanence, requires a heavy sacrifice. It's not like Bastian has lied to me.

"What happens if someone finds out we've done it?"

"Lando, if we do it right, *everyone's* going to know we've done it. Then you get your girlfriend back and I get the career I want." Bastian looks at me, narrowing his eyes, as if he's trying to figure out what's truly bothering me. "Are you worried we'll get in trouble? Or worried they'll be able to undo it? They won't, and the worst they can do is take the grimoire away to the Merlin Foundation and tell us off for being bad, reckless students, but who cares? We'll have what we want."

Elizabeth, I think. I nod and Bastian, satisfied, looks back to the book.

"So the first places it mentions, Boggart Hole...*Clough* and Kilgrimol, do you know them? Are they local?"

"They're both in the north-west." I wonder if it was written by a shapeshifter from the north. "Boggart Hole Clough is a wood near the city – it's got ravines and gullies in it, that's what clough means – and Kilgrimol is a drowned village near Blackpool."

"How far away from the city is Boggart Hole Clough?"

"It's out near Failsworth, we could get the tram out..." I check my phone. "It'd be, like, forty-five minutes?"

"Okay." Bastian jots some words down in his notebook. "Boggarts like half-moons, so this weekend is good. How's Friday night for you?"

I stop stroking René's ear and stare at Bastian. He's really hard to read sometimes.

"Wait, you're taking this list literally? We're going to the park to find a boggart?"

"Yeah, of course I am, how else will we complete the spell?" Now he's looking at me like I'm mad, and all I can think is: *Who is this person who talks about boggarts like he meets one every day?* Obviously, I know that magical creatures exist, but they mostly prefer rural settings where they can stay hidden from humans – kelpies off the coast in Scotland, piskies on Bodmin

Moor. Witches in those places strive to live in balance with the magical creatures in nature around them but here, in the city, I would never expect to find them. In fact, the closest most witches come to meeting a hidden magical creature is meeting me.

I wonder how many other spells Bastian has done, how many strange magical creatures he's encountered. I nod.

"Friday, then?"

"Yeah. You should take this home with you." He stands up and hands the grimoire to me. "I've got what I need right now and we should take it further away from—"

"The scene of the crime?"

"My dad." Bastian stuffs his hands into his pockets. "It will be safer with you than with me."

I nod and we awkwardly wait for the lift to come up.

"So is this the kind of thing you usually do? Weird and dangerous spells?" I say, trying to make conversation.

"Why? What have you heard?" He frowns.

"Nothing." I step into the lift. I can't imagine doing a magical scavenger hunt across the north-west of England is going to be much fun if every conversation we have is such hard work, but Bastian doesn't seem to be the type of guy for small talk.

"Bring cheese on Friday," he says, in lieu of goodbye.

I'm so baffled by this that all I can say to the closing doors is, "What kind?"

Obviously, I don't get an answer.

* * *

When I get back to Beryl's and I've kicked Mr Pebbles off my bed and locked the door and Beryl has yelled through the locked door at me about how I'm not allowed to have my doors locked, I climb onto my bed and open the grimoire. I stroke my fingers over the embossed title on the leather: *The Witchlore of Bodies.* I've got a shoebox under the bed filled with old notebooks that will be a perfect hiding place, but I'm interested in this shifter from the past. I flip past all the spells and evidence of hundreds of years of different authors to the diary bit. The part that starts in 1878, when the shifter was given care of their family grimoire. I settle against the pillows, reading the words from an entry at the beginning:

> Mother and Father say that now I am seventeen it is my responsibility to settle in my resting form, to choose a gender and abide in it. That it is the safest path to protect myself.
>
> I do not understand how they can fathom remaining in one traditional form when everything is changing so rapidly, when Mrs Wollstonecraft's words are lighting the world afire. We are none of us safe in this life, there are so many dangers. Surely now is the time to challenge our ideas of what a woman or man can be? My ideas for my future are so much more vast than what my parents could ever imagine.

I press a hand against the words on the page, marvelling at the grainy feel of it under my fingertips. It has existed for so long, this story of the past, but the pressure they're describing, I feel it so keenly. Instantly, I have a memory of my mother, telling me to put a dress on even when I didn't want to. *No matter how you shift, you are a girl. You were born female. This is your resting form.* I didn't have the words to tell her then, but at six years old I knew that, even if I could control my shifting, even if I learned everything she so desperately wanted me to, I still wouldn't feel like a girl. When I finally did have the words for it and the bravery to tell them, I was ten and they called me ridiculous. Reckless. *Do you not see how gender is safety for shapeshifters, the one way we can fit in?*

For the first time in my life, staring down at the words of another shapeshifter who feels like me, I realize how lonely I have felt being the one who questions it all. The one who can't control their shifting, who can't make themselves safe, no matter how much I try. I have felt lonely for so long that until Elizabeth came into my life, I didn't realize that I even was lonely. I just thought I was alone. Then Elizabeth was there, changing my perspective, and now she's gone and I don't want to go backward. I want her back.

When I have tucked the grimoire safely in the box under my bed and have turned out the light, staring up into the darkness, my mind is full of what getting Elizabeth back might actually mean. Will she know that she's been gone? Will her soul or something have been absorbed into nature, like many of the witch covens believe? If that's the case, will her soul come back endowed with some kind of special knowledge from being dead? Will she even want me still, if she's all wise and in touch with nature? What if she comes back from the dead and changes her mind about me, about us? The thought makes my heart race and my hands sweat, so I pull my pillow over my head and try to do one of the breathing exercises I learned in hospital to get myself to sleep.

I am sitting at a writing desk, holding an old pen in my hand as I scrawl across the page. I look out of the beautiful bay window onto long, flat lawns covered in snow, and it drifts down outside the window.

"Dearest?" a voice calls behind me. I turn to see a man coming through the door, wearing a tuxedo and a proud look. I know he is my father and I feel warmth rising inside me. "Are you ready? We're getting started downstairs."

"Yes, I am ready."

He holds out my tuxedo jacket for me and I pull it on. He brushes the shoulders and assesses me so fondly.

"There now. What a fine young gentleman."

I try to smile back, wanting to make him proud as we walk down the stairs. The great tree is decorated with candles and dried oranges; my mother and our tenants are there, all raising their glasses to the new year.

Strangely, in the corner, by the beautiful Christmas tree, is a young girl. She has hair the colour of spun silk and I feel as if I know her. She's dressed queerly, wearing trousers like a man, and I think to myself: You don't belong here. *She turns her face towards me and blood mats one side of her golden head. It's Elizabeth, I realize, her face pale in death. I desperately reach out, trying to catch her, but she's falling away and the world is darkening. The Christmas tree is gone, the candlelight disappeared, I am scrabbling over the rough surface of a cave floor to get to her.*

"Don't leave me, Orla," she rasps out.

I jerk awake, gasping, staring at my dark ceiling that, for some reason, has had glow-in-the-dark stars stuck on it. They're old, so they only have a faint greenish tinge around them. I try to breathe slowly, Elizabeth's dead face in the light of the Christmas tree fading with every exhale. It is normal for me to dream of her; there hasn't been a night since her death when I haven't, except for those foggy first days sedated in the hospital. What's strange is everything else that happened in the dream, the loving parents who aren't mine, the grand house in the snow with servants in black-and-white uniforms and the guests in Victorian dresses. Perhaps I dreamed about the shapeshifter who wrote in the grimoire. It's odd, to have imagined my way into their life.

I reach under my bed and pull out the grimoire. I set it down on the pillow beside me, wanting to keep it close and check it doesn't glow or emit magic, but it simply sits there, with that leathery scent of pennies, near my face. The smell is calming, familiar, like a hint of a memory I can't quite catch. I place my hand on it, its binding uncannily warm under my fingertips. In the dark, it almost feels like a live animal, as if it could be awake too and whispering a thousand unknown words into my dreams. I shiver, wondering as I drift back towards sleep if I should be more afraid.

Chapter Eight

I know I shouldn't take *The Witchlore of Bodies* with me on Friday night. But I do. I feel better when it's close to me, when I can reach into my bag and touch its leather cover, which never seems to be cold, whatever the temperature. I sit on the tram, reading it as I ignore the group of fourteen-year-old lads further down the train taking turns throwing empty cans of Coke past my head.

There's something about the way the words on the page sound in my head that's comfortably familiar, like listening to my own voice:

> I'm going to the protest today. I want to support the women. Father says that if I care so much about suffrage for women then I should settle into a female form, but why should only women care that women are under-represented? So I shall go to the demonstration and I shall stand with the women in a female form beside them. I enjoy the female form and the male. Why should I choose a path when I am made of both?

I stare at those words for a long time. I've never considered that there must be non-binary people so far back in history. It's kind of a surprise to see my own thoughts and feelings echoed in such an old book, and from a shapeshifter too. It's like a hand has sprung out of the past, dived into my chest and squeezed my heart to keep it pumping. I take a couple of deep breaths and notice that a small tear has dripped down onto the page. I brush my thumb over it, worried that it's going to ruin the ink, but it only blurs the date. Then I frown. It's dated July 1906. I do some maths; I hope it doesn't take me until I'm in my forties to feel as confident in my own difference. But I don't have any time to consider how long the next thirty years or so could feel because the tram is stopping at Booth Hall Road and I need to walk to get to the woods. Where there might be a boggart. I try not to think too much about the potential danger and instead reassure myself by repeating the same calming platitudes over and over: *It won't be there, Bastian's wrong, a boggart in the city is just ridiculous.*

I tuck the book carefully deep down into my backpack and trudge along in the darkening evening, through the quiet suburban backstreets with red-brick houses and cars parked on the pavement. Bastian is standing under a street light near the edge of the woods reading his book, the green lawn of the Boggart Hole Clough Park spread out behind him. He's wearing dark colours again. I wonder if it's a calculated choice so he blends into the shaded woods or if he simply has a bit of a goth streak (which would frankly explain a lot). However, it feels weird to open a conversation with an interrogation of his fashion choices so instead, I say, "I brought cheese."

A dog walker passing us stares at me with a ludicrous expression and I wince with embarrassment, my cheeks flaring with humiliation as I castigate myself: *Normal people say hello, you plonker.* I stare at Bastian, biting my tongue to stop more awkwardness spilling out, desperate for him to say something, *anything.*

"Good." He's putting his book away and, mercifully, seems like he wants this to be all business. The fire in my cheeks dies down. Bastian jerks his head towards the entrance to the woods. "Let's go."

"Why did I bring cheese?" I fall into step beside him. We stride along the tarmac path that cuts through the fields, the new trees in their plastic sleeves rustling their turning leaves on either side. The grass has been cut recently and the smell of it, combined with the rain we've had today, is pungently sweet in my nostrils.

"Because boggarts love cheese, obviously." Bastian is easily clambering over the chained fence at the entrance to the woods, the last light of the day entirely lost in the thick press of the trees.

"I don't think that's obvious," I say, struggling to follow him, the rip on my jeans catching on the wire.

"Do you not know where boggarts come from?" Bastian watches impassively as I tumble over the fence and fall into a mush of churned-up mud and leaves.

"I'd assumed it was, like, hell, or something." I brush dirt off my hands. Since I am nearly ninety-five per cent sure there absolutely won't be a boggart hanging out in a Manchester park,

I've not really looked into their provenance. "Am I wrong?"

"Yeah, you are, actually." We start walking into the darkness of the woods, both of us holding up our phone lights. It's nearly nine and there are no dog walkers in here, the distant sounds of kids circling their bikes around the football nets getting lost in the dense bushes and bark. "I guess you didn't take any modules on magical creatures?"

I get one of those horrible pangs of grief that threatens to strangle me because I wasn't thinking about her and that was stupid of me, really stupid, because the remembering pain is so much worse than the knowing-it-all-the-time pain. They were her favourite modules.

"Elizabeth liked all that kind of stuff, she wanted to teach witchlore at a college one day."

"Ah." There's a long, awkward pause and I can think of nothing to say to make it better. "Do you want me to tell you about boggarts?"

"Yes, please."

"Boggarts aren't demons, not really," Bastian says, guiding us down the wood-chipped path. I hear rustles on either side and hope to god it's just squirrels. "They're silkies, that's what my mum calls them, but they have other names, like brownies in Scotland."

I frown, trying to think of everything Elizabeth ever mentioned about silkies. There are so many different types of magical creatures – some that might have gone extinct and some that witches know still exist. I've never really been the kind of person to memorize them. Some parents buy their kids those cardboard baby books with flaps of cute boggarts and gnomes on them. My parents were not those kinds of parents.

"That little goblin that keeps fires lit and all of that?" I say, dragging that fact up from memory.

"Yes, well, sort of, they're not goblins, they're little domestic creatures that are connected to the land." Bastian's voice gets quieter the deeper we walk into the woods. "When they are fed and kept happy, they help keep the land safe and look after domestic dwellings."

"Yeah, but that's not what boggarts are today." I remember everything that Elizabeth told me. "I mean, boggarts now are mean and make nests and collect the bones of kids—"

"Yes, because when a brownie or a silkie isn't looked after properly they become a boggart," Bastian explains. "They become resentful and nasty and if you name them, then they can never leave."

"So that's why people say never name a boggart." It's an idiom that pops up with witches all the time, a way of saying you did something that led to an unlucky series of events: *and then I named the boggart.* I give him a sideways glance.

"And you really believe we're going to find one?"

"We'd better, otherwise the spell will be a dud."

"And we'll just be weirdos wandering around a forest with cheese."

"Exactly," Bastian says. I check quickly to see if he's making fun of me, but it doesn't look like it, despite me being the most awkward person on the planet. I quirk my lips into a tentative smile.

"But if it *is* here..." *It won't be,* I tell myself. "We don't just have to find it, we have to get its name?"

"Yep." Bastian doesn't sound bothered at all. Does *anything* ever faze him?

"So how are we going to do that?" I press him.

"Show me the cheese."

I dig into my bag and hand it to him. He stares at the net of round cheeses that he's holding.

"These are Babybels," he says, shaking them slightly.

"Yeah, it's cheese."

"Are you eight?"

I flush and snatch them back.

"You asked for cheese!" I protest.

"It's not even cheese, those are *vegan* Babybels—"

"Like the boggart will care! What did you bring?" I snatch at his satchel, opening it up and then stepping back, overwhelmed by the smell coming from it. "Christ, that is rough."

I cover my mouth with my hand. It smells like a pair of really old football socks died.

"It's blue cheese," Bastian says stiffly, pulling out a package wrapped in beige cloth. It smells rank but it looks very posh. "It's what my dad had in the fridge."

"It's so nasty!" I cough. "I'd definitely rather eat a vegan Babybel."

"Well, let's see which one the boggart likes best." Bastian starts unwrapping it and then crumbling bits of it and dropping them onto the forest floor. "Come on, leave a trail."

I follow his lead and start unwrapping Babybels and breaking them into pieces that I drop behind me as Bastian steps off the path and starts to make another one through the dense trees, stamping down stinging nettles, the wet leaves slipping past my cheek and twigs catching on the shoulders of my coat. I think of the lucky dog or squirrel that is going to be feasting on my Babybels later.

"Lights off," Bastian mutters. "Don't want to scare it."

Now that we're off the path and there's no open sky above us, no moonlight or starlight, I'm very aware of the crunch of branches under my feet and the sound of Bastian's breathing beside me in the dark. Unhelpful questions chase around my mind: *What am I doing here with this person? What kind of impulsive prat am I that I'm doing this?* Even if there's no boggart to be found, willingly taking a stroll in a dark wood with a strange man is hardly peak decision-making for someone like me.

"So your dad's into stinky cheese?" I ask, mainly to stop the worries in my head that I am, like Counsellor Cooper says, "behaving recklessly with my own existence".

"Yeah."

"Maybe that's why your mum left," I quip. Bastian whips his head around to stare at me as I wince. Elizabeth used to say my mouth works faster than my brain. Classic case in point.

"That...was incredibly insensitive," he says, stopping. My face reddens. I don't know what it is about him that makes me so awkward I spew inappropriate nonsense, but it's definitely becoming a pattern.

"Oh, come on, it was just a joke," I say weakly, so distracted by my own thoughtlessness that I trip over a tree root and step in a dog poo, an entirely deserved karmic turn.

"Do you feel better when people say that afterwards?" Bastian demands.

"No, sorry," I mutter. I feel like I'm being told off by a teacher and I'm suddenly sweaty with humiliation. *Twat.* I repeat inside my head, *I am a total twat.*

"Are you?" Bastian turns and starts to walk away and I have to jog to catch up. I've never been good in social situations (thank you, homeschooling) but I've got worse since May. I wonder if there's any point in apologizing. How would I even phrase it? *Sorry, my parents kept me locked up and I've only ever had one real friend. I'm pretty much socially illiterate.* Then I think that he's the one who can cast the spells and he's the one helping me with this step towards getting Elizabeth back. Also, he's been kind to me, in a superior sort of way, and it's none of my business why his mum left his dad. At least he talks to me and he wasn't a total arse about the panic attacks.

"Yeah, I am," I say. "Really."

Bastian sighs heavily and I wonder if he's the kind of person who holds a grudge or needs to give a lecture before he accepts an apology. I steel myself for whatever is coming next.

"It wasn't the cheese," he says softly. "It was because of my brother."

My stomach lurches painfully because I know that regretful, wistful tone. I know that whatever he's sharing with me now is a secret, a painful one, and I know how hard this can be to do.

"I didn't know you have a brother."

I don't want to ask what happened, but I want him to know it's okay to tell me and I have absolutely no idea how to communicate that.

"I don't." I look at his face. It's shadowed but his lips are pulled into a tight line. "I mean, I don't have one any more. Or I do, he's just..." Bastian sighs and tilts his head back. "He died."

It's absolutely not what I expected. I don't want to say any of the things people said to me when Elizabeth died. Instead, I say the first thing that pops out of my mouth.

"Oh, crap. Really?" I wince at my continued lack of tact but Bastian doesn't seem to mind this time, or he doesn't notice.

"Yeah," Bastian says, his voice suddenly distant. "Two years ago."

"And your mum...?" I ask hesitantly.

"She and Dad were less and less happy anyway, before he died. My brother tried to shield me from it, I think, but he was only a year older so he couldn't hide the way she was holding it together for us." Bastian sighs. "But then...when he was gone...it was too much. They both raised us to love exploring witchcraft, but after everything happened, Dad actively hated it. It's like Mum was leaning into witchcraft to cope with the tragedy and Dad leaned the other way. They fought about it all the time."

"What did you do?" I ask.

"Tried to ignore them," Bastian says with a bitter smile. "Mum did her best but Dad became someone I didn't want to know. He doesn't even wear his *ring* any more." Bastian's voice is full of disgust. I feel a flutter of disquiet.

"So you really don't like people who don't do witchcraft?" I ask, trying not to sound as nervous as I feel.

"No, it's not like that, I don't hate you because you can't do witchcraft, it's different," he says fervently. "You don't know what my family was like before it happened, witchlore and witchcraft was who we *were*. Then after, Dad said…if magic can't save someone, what's the point of it?"

Bastian's voice breaks and I understand these are the words that have embedded their thorny edges into his heart. I know how it feels to live with words like that.

"And your mum just left you?" I'm definitely not the authority on family, but even I can see that's an unkind thing to do to your grieving son. "Seems…harsh."

"I'm an adult. She has to work, especially with the divorce. She did what she had to do."

He's still walking with purpose but there's something raw in his voice that reminds me of the times Elizabeth would talk about how worried she was that her mum, who dreamed of her little girl getting married in a Barbie-and-Ken style event, would find out she was queer and in a relationship with a shapeshifter.

"Did you want to go with her?" I ask. Bastian's face twitches.

"I need to finish college," he says quietly. I take that as a yes, and that he had absolutely no say in the matter.

"And you chose to move to Manchester?"

"I wanted a change. At least now Dad's never around," Bastian says bitterly. "He's in London all the time. He only comes to Manchester for meetings and to make sure I'm not dead."

Now there's a parental dynamic that's more up my street.

I can hear the loneliness in his voice and I understand it, being alone in a city without a family, feeling like you don't have an anchor, a place to return to.

"What was his name?" I ask abruptly.

"Excuse me?" Bastian almost trips over a small bush.

"What was your brother's name?" I repeat.

There is a shaft of moonlight that falls across his face and he looks the most shocked I've ever seen him.

"Shasta," he says.

"*The Horse and His Boy.*" I nod, recognizing the reference to the CS Lewis novel.

"Yeah." He shoots me such a surprisingly fond look that I blush and look away.

"What was Elizabeth's full name?" he asks. "No one's told me."

"Elizabeth Toppings." I smile, because I always thought it was a cute name, making her sound like she should run a tea room in the nineteenth century.

"Everyone talks about her at college when you're not around," he says.

"They do?" I turn to stare at him. He nods.

"They all talk about how sweet and kind she was, good student, perfect friend. It all seems kind of fake. I still don't have any idea what she was really like as a person."

"Oh. Um." It's suddenly too much to imagine everything I could tell him about Elizabeth, so much pressure that my mind is drawing a horrifying blank. I end up blurting out the first things that come to me. "She liked trampolining, she had one in her garden. She always took the pickles out of burgers. She loved Christmas movies..." I feel uncomfortable, realizing that while I loved her so much, the closeted nature of our relationship meant that all the practical things I knew about her revolved around activities we could do in her parents' house in secret or takeaway we ordered. I can tell Bastian what was in her to-be-read pile, but I can't tell him what she was like at a party. I try to focus on facts. "Her best friend was Kira Tavi, from college, and her mum leads an Artemis coven in Alderley Edge. Her parents are both academics."

"An Artemis coven?" Bastian repeats with a frown. "That's a fertility coven."

"Yeah." It was one of the reasons Elizabeth was so nervous to come out as gay to her mum, who had always envisioned a particular future for her.

"You do know that most fertility covens would be against this spell we're trying to do? That they think that only female-born women can give life?"

"Oh. Yeah." I try to sound as if I've considered all of this but the truth is, I hadn't even thought about it. I've been so focused on the idea that of course Elizabeth's parents would be happy to have her back that I didn't consider how her mum's beliefs might come into play. But surely having your only child back trumps everything else?

As if he's reading my mind, Bastian asks, "I know we're still a long way off from this being a reality, but have you thought about how she might react to her daughter being resurrected this way?"

Nope, I think. *Not even a little bit.*

"Well, it's like you said, we're a long way off that." I try to keep my voice light and my face neutral but Bastian looks like he isn't buying it. I sigh. "Honestly, I think she would do anything to get Elizabeth back and if it's something that involves risking my life, so much the better."

Bastian opens his mouth, probably to ask more about Elizabeth's mother, but then he closes it, his head snapping up, face watchful, nostrils flaring.

"What?" I ask, feeling trepidation creep along my skin.

"Did you hear something?" he asks, looking over his shoulder.

I turn. Behind us, in the thick darkness, something moves.

Chapter Nine

I stare between the trees, my eyes struggling to make shapes form in the sudden blackness. It's like the moment that you wake from a nightmare and, suddenly, everything in your room seems strange and alien. You stare at the unknown monstrous form of your coat on the back of your door and dare it to move, frozen in fear, until you lurch awake and realize it's all in your head. I stand, hearing my own rapid breath, waiting to wake up, for the trees to become trees again, but they don't. A slithering shape made of darkest night is following us, just on the furthest edge of my vision, and I can hear a snuffling, horribly intimate wet munching.

"It's eating the cheese," Bastian whispers.

"Holy crap, it's real," I whisper, my voice coming out much more panicky than I expected, but I'm equally as surprised when Bastian, in a similar tone, whispers back.

"It fucking is!"

I realize that, for all his talk, a part of him didn't expect it to be here and having a real-life magical creature within ten paces of us is a complete shift in reality.

"What do we do now?" I say, hoping to god he actually has a plan, and cursing myself for not doing some bloody preparation. *Ninety-five per cent,* I chide myself. *It's the five per cent that'll kill you.*

"We make a deal." Bastian holds his cheese out but I also see him getting his penknife out of his pocket.

"How?" The slithering shape is crawling closer. I can't see hands or eyes or limbs; I can only sense its malevolence and the overwhelming feeling that I should be running very fast in the other direction. I feel like I'm confronting a bear or a puma. I know literally nothing about how to survive this encounter and am instantly furious with myself. *What kind of numpty walks into this situation willingly with someone they barely know?* The answer is obvious. It's me.

"Stand very still," Bastian whispers. "Unwrap a Babybel and hold it flat in your hand so it can smell it, like you're feeding a horse."

"But it's not a horse!" My whisper is getting hysterical as the liquid sound of a vast, wet mouth chewing gets closer and closer.

"Do not panic," Bastian hisses. "Do *not* panic."

I hold the Babybel flat on my outstretched palm like a small moon. *I'm doing this for Elizabeth,* I tell myself. *It's all for Elizabeth.* The chewing sound stops. I listen to a heavy, rattling breath and imagine a wheezing animal with sharp teeth. I do not want it to get any closer to my fingers. I tell myself to not panic and to stand still but I realize I can't do anything else. My knees have locked. I'm stuck.

"Show yourself to us," Bastian says in a commanding voice. There is a low hiss in response and the darkness slithers back a few paces. I can't help but exhale with heavy relief when its shadows retreat from my boots. "We have offerings."

Bastian breaks off a piece of his cheese and throws it towards the shadow. There is a horrible snap and I imagine a great jaw closing, a thousand pointy teeth wetly masticating. Then suddenly, it speaks. Its voice is uncanny and sets every hair on my body on end.

"You smell of human flesh and cow, surrender both to my claws now." It sounds like a sick child. A high, young voice that's somehow phlegmatic, full of gravel and damp. I swallow down the disgust in my throat, the overwhelming feeling that I want to turn away and never hear it speak again.

"It speaks in rhyme?" I manage to squeak out.

"Yes, all boggarts rhyme, give it the cheese."

I shakily throw the Babybel towards the shadows, a ridiculous parody of throwing treats for a dog. There is a flash of something silver, maybe eyes or maybe teeth, and I stumble back from it, my heart thundering. Then it laughs, a nasty high-pitched giggle so lonely and sharp that it hurts my ears.

"You feed me but I smell your fear, what prompts such cowards to draw this near?"

"We want your name," Bastian says.

The laughing stops. In a gust of wind, the shadow snaps close, close enough that a pair of ghoulish white eyes stare unblinking at us. We both gasp and I don't mean to, but my hand clasps around Bastian's clenched fist. I have no idea what a boggart should look like but this is probably going to give me nightmares for the rest of my life.

"Then name me, child, face your fear, and you will always have me near," it whispers. We both take a slow step backward and Bastian unclenches his hand, gripping mine. His palm is sweaty.

"We have come to bargain." Bastian's voice is shockingly level. "We want your name."

"Come to bargain with what, little child?" the boggart croons towards Bastian. Their faces are horribly close; I can see saliva dripping onto Bastian's shoes. He leans his head back but seems determined not to move his feet. *"I see your fear in your eyes and smile."*

Bastian's breath hitches and I realize that he's gone mute with terror. Out of nowhere, I'm speaking instead.

"Hey, don't talk to him like that, you're not eating him," I blurt out. It was the wrong thing to do. Now those bulbous white eyes are focused on me.

"What of you, then, little skin changer?" it whispers. *"I've eaten children but none stranger."*

With trembling fingers, I throw another Babybel a few paces back. The boggart lurches away, hastily devouring the cheese with those slick, wet sounds. Bastian has my hand in a vice grip. I'm not even sure he's breathing properly; he looks scared silent, his eyes wide and still. *Oh, shit,* I think. *This is a deer-in-headlights moment.* I have no idea what to do so, of course, I keep babbling.

"Do you spend all your time thinking up rhymes?" I improvise, shoving my fear right down inside me, just like I did when the police took me to the station after Elizabeth's death. "You think you'd be better at it. You know poetry has evolved beyond rhyming couplets."

"Your fire is nothing compared to my ire, I shall light your skin up like a pyre."

The boggart twists its head a sickening 180 degrees with a crunch. I taste a surge of bile in the back of my throat. *Do not fucking panic,* I tell myself angrily.

"By the pricking of my thumbs, something wicked this way comes," I say shakily. "See? I can do it too. Tell us your bloody name!"

This senseless antagonism, this infuriating backchat, it's been there my entire life. The boggart is my mother, my father, the twenty tutors I had, the shifting specialist I hated. *Sarcasm will not make you better at what any shifter infant can do, Orlando*, was what he always said to me. Maybe he's right but it will help you distract a boggart. I look at Bastian desperately, because I know this stalling is only going to get us so far, and luckily, it looks like he is back with me, breathing fast and hard but eyes more focused than before.

"We've come to bargain," Bastian repeats, stepping forward and breaking off more cheese. "We want your name."

"Then offer me something, small witch, say what you come to bargain with."

"I have a dog," Bastian says.

"You are not going to give it René to eat!" I exclaim, jerking on Bastian's hand, which, for some reason, has ended up holding mine again.

"Obviously not!" Bastian snaps at me. "Just shut up, Lando."

Somehow, him being annoyed at me feels good, a hint of normality in this otherwise utterly bizarre encounter.

"I have a dog and I'll walk it here at least once a week," Bastian goes on. "I'll bring you an offering to protect the wood. Once a week, an intentional offering for you of whatever you want—"

"I want the curdled milk of goats to soothe the rage inside my throat."

"You want a weekly offering of goat's cheese?" I can't help but blurt out as I stare at the hunched shadows. Like everything in life, it gets a little less terrifying the longer I look at it. I still don't want to take my eyes off it, though.

"Lando, don't—" Bastian hisses.

"Seriously, it's the most bougie boggart on the planet."

Bastian sighs and drops my hand. He raises his knife and, in a quick moment, has pulled it across his palm and sprayed blood down on the mulch of wet leaves. I jump back, a thickening in my throat. Inside my mind, I see the bathroom, those sharp rosy drops of blood, tiny flowers scattered under my feet. I swallow copper-tasting saliva. *I'm not there,* I tell myself sternly. *Stay here, you have to stay here or you might not get out alive.*

"I swear on my blood I will bring you goat's cheese once a week and if I cannot bring it, someone else will bring it in my stead," Bastian says clearly. "For this offering, will you give me your name?"

The shadows still for a moment, as if whatever hidden horror lives inside is considering its words carefully. We wait. Panic builds inside me, nudging its way to a slow crescendo that makes me want to scream, to run, to cry but I can do none of those things. I'm planted to the spot, waiting to see if a magical creature will accept an offering of goat's cheese. It's utterly absurd, it's practically laughable, except that my throat is locked tight with pure, rigid fear. For a second, I absently wonder if it will kill us and lick our bones clean, like they do in the stories, and then hate my brain for doing that to me.

"*The name is not for you, but for your friend, the one who will need it, in the end,*" the boggart whispers. A tingling begins behind my knees. Bastian turns to look at me.

"What does that mean?" I ask. I hate that my voice shakes. The boggart circles us, creeping over wet leaves, the shadows whipping around us. The air chills with the rapid movement, suddenly cold enough to see my breath. There's a smell too, the sweet decomposing mulch of dead leaves and mud, like the earth underneath a heavy rock. *Run,* a part of me screams, but it's like that dream when your mouth opens to scream but nothing comes out. All I can do is stand, desperate and shaking, in the middle of a storm of rotting.

"*I speak in riddles, it is my curse; but what was done to you was worse.*" Its whispers chase me. I turn my head this way and that, trying to catch hold of those pallid roving eyes.

"You know nothing about me!" I shout. Bastian's hand grips my elbow. "Give me your name!"

I turn my head and it's right in front of me, it's *right* in front of me, so close that I can see the tree roots that make up its face, the rotted mushrooms that form its skin, the lank trails of dead leaves that make up its hair. It's like a little child, if they had disintegrated into the forest floor, half-alive and slowly mouldering. A red mouth speaks, teeth sharp and grey like pebbles. All my jokes are gone, every comeback, every witty retort has vanished from my mind. Quietness descends, like the moment when Elizabeth stopped breathing, nothing but unbearable, ringing silence.

"*What dwells beneath your anger?*" The boggart's musty words smell like death and cheese. I try not to choke as it leans close, wet, spoiled leaves catching my face and leaving a slick residue. "*My name is this: Elander.*"

Light explodes from my every pore and I feel that familiar wrenching, agonizing *pull* in my bones that precedes a shift. *No, no, I can't shift,* I think, horrified. *Not here, not now!* I want to push Bastian back; I want to make sure he's safe, but I can't move because it's coming now. Shifts are unstoppable. I throw my head back, screaming, and give in to the roaring light and pain inside me. Suddenly, I'm not there any more.

I'm arm in arm with my sisters, our flags caught in the high breeze, our dresses dusty from the dry ground around the clough, listening to a speaker as he cries aloud the need for the right to organize and the right of free people everywhere. The sun is high in the sky and bright. There are thousands of us, nearly thirty thousand, many suffragettes and ordinary folk, come to hear about the cause as the speaker's voice travels over the flat space between the hill and the ravine. Then suddenly, over the hill comes a shout, a brawling bustle and like ants over jam they spread. A surly gang of protestors, screaming their insults to the skies and shouldering women out of the way, not caring who they knock down, trying to get to the centre, to the speaker and the woman beside him. I know if they reach them, they will be done for.

"Run!" I scream at them.

I see them pushing their way through the crowd, hemmed in on all sides, and I sigh with small relief when I see her scrambling over the hill. Mrs Pankhurst's daughter is safe. Then I link arms with my sisters and turn to face the oncoming tide of fists and kicks, standing between these violent men and the daughter of the mother of the movement. As the sun beats down, I look up to the high clouds and think that perhaps this is a good cause to die for.

Chapter Ten

"Lando! Lando, wake up!"

I jerk back into reality. The bright sunshine above the protestors is gone, and the heat of the bodies pressed beside me, facing down the enemy, is replaced with a chilled damp, the pain in my body, and fear, liquid and nauseous in my mouth. I can make out a worried face and hear a shrieking all around me, but I don't know what's happened, only that it is still happening and it is terrifying. The shrieking is the vilest kind of childish scream, vibrating agonizingly in my eardrums.

"Get BACK!" someone screams and there is a flash of violent blue light. In it, I see the silhouette of a witch, their hands held together above their head in a hand sequence I don't recognize – clenched fists crossed over one another at the wrist – blue light pulsing out of their ring, so blinding I wince and turn away, so harsh it pushes the shrieking boggart back from us. The air is thick with the smell of magic, of burning, as if the forest has been set alight with us inside.

My heart is thundering. My whole life, people have witnessed my shifts, sudden and uncontrollable, and seen me as scary. I've never seen witches do magic as powerful as shapeshifters, and for a breathless second, I panic that this person might not truly be in control, that he might be able to hurt me. Then there's an unexpected thrilling familiarity, a surprising recognition and a singular, rogue thought: *He's a bit like me.* He's got hold of my hand, urgently pulling me to my feet, forcing me to move.

"Run, Lando!" he screams. The spell has pushed the boggart away but I can hear screeching getting closer, coming back for a second pass. So I run haphazardly in the darkness, staggering over uneven ground and slipping on dead leaves and gasping as something shrieks and whirls behind us, following us.

"What happened?" I yell at Bastian as he drags me on.

"You shifted and the boggart freaked out!" Bastian jumps over a log and I follow, nearly toppling over. "It's gone mental!"

"Why?"

"Well, maybe it doesn't like having sudden bursts of ridiculously bright light shot at it!" Bastian yells.

"You did it too!"

I dodge a tree and drop Bastian's hand, the boggart whistling and gnashing its teeth behind us. I am just one trip, one tree root, one false step away from those horrible teeth plunging into me, dragging me back to whatever hole or grave beneath the earth it lives in. I can almost feel it, the cold dirt covering me, the sharp pain of stinging incisors ripping into my flesh, and I can smell it, that mouldering dusty smell, getting closer and closer.

"Watch out!"

Bastian tackles me and we thud painfully to the ground, tree roots digging into my spine, and then we're rolling down one of the clough's ravines. We're tumbling and my head is hitting stones and then, suddenly, we stop.

"Don't get up, don't move, they can't see very far," Bastian hisses. "Try not to make a noise."

We lie there, Bastian pressing down on top of me, both of us listening intently to every sound above us. My heart is pounding sickeningly, like it's separated and migrated around my body, clamouring in my throat and my legs and arms, so loudly I think the boggart must hear it. Yet, as we lie there, our breath hot and fast against each other's faces, all we can hear is a slow munching far away. I fumble against Bastian's leg and reach down to check my pocket.

"I must have dropped the Babybels," I whisper. Bastian stares down at me.

"Saved by vegan Babybels," he whispers back, smiling wryly. It gives me tingles from my elbows to my wrists. It's different than before. I want to match his tone with something light, but my heart won't slow down and every part of my body hurts. My clothes all fit weirdly again and I'm suddenly very conscious of it.

"No, *you* saved us." I wriggle out from under him, aware of the awkwardness of it, my new boobs brushing against him, but he doesn't seem to notice.

"Not just me," he says. "Thanks for, y'know, distracting it."

"I do seem to be very distracting."

I only mean it in the sense that it's really all I've been good for so far (if this was a tabletop game the value of my character would be extremely fucking low), but I hear my own words and blush, violently.

"I didn't mean it like that..." I mumble, but then that's so much *worse* because now I've put the idea in his head! *Stop it, you absolute muppet,* I chide myself, but luckily, Bastian doesn't seem to notice my internal agony.

"Come on," he says, and we crawl away on our bellies, nothing but rasping breath and the squelch of leaves between us. As we do, I wonder why he did it, why he threw himself at me to save me from the boggart, but that leads my mind down uncomfortable paths that give me butterflies. Except I can't have butterflies for anyone but Elizabeth so I guess they're the rubbish version of butterflies. Mosquitoes.

I know we are far enough away when I can no longer hear it, the mulching sound, and I start to think maybe I even imagined it, but my knees are soaked through with wet mud and Bastian's ring still has a slight unearthly glow. He really did that exceptionally powerful spell. We really saw a boggart. It happened.

"You look different," Bastian says, standing up and turning on his phone light to look at me.

"Yeah, well, I shifted," I say uncomfortably. I reach up to pat my face. It's rounder, my hair is coarser than it was before and falling over my shoulders; my jeans fit differently, too baggy at the waist and way too tight on the bum. I wince.

"Everyone said you couldn't control it." Bastian shook his head. "I didn't think it would be so...violent."

"Just be glad you're not dead," I snap, thinking of Elizabeth.

"Yeah, but I wonder why," Bastian says, completely undeterred. "Why did you have such a big magical discharge then that you *killed* someone? I mean, I'm obviously fine—"

"Can we not talk about it?" I glare at him, grimacing and rubbing my elbow. I bashed it in the roll.

"I'm not trying to be a prat," Bastian says. "I'm just saying that maybe...it had more to do with the spell she was casting than to do with you. Maybe it wasn't your fault."

I stare at him for a long minute. It seems like maybe the kindest and the cruellest thing to say to me right now. I don't know what to do with it, this possibility of hope and forgiveness and relief from the guilt that's eating away at my heart.

"Its name is Elander." I jerk my head back up the ravine towards where the boggart was. "Can we go now?"

"Sure." Bastian nods and pulls out his phone, opening maps. "We can get back on the path down here. Come on."

"Okay...whoa." I stumble against him and Bastian grabs my elbow. It feels weird now to think of holding his hand, but up there, facing the boggart, it had felt totally normal. I flush and mumble, "Different legs," but I can't stop myself from leaning on him.

"So," I say as we stagger through the dark. "About the spell you used on the boggart."

"Oh." Bastian doesn't speak for a few steps. "I thought you were out of it. To be honest, for a second, I thought you were dead."

"No, I saw it." I think about how to bring it up in a way that isn't accusatory. "That was pretty powerful witchcraft."

"Not really, it's just something my mum taught me." His voice is light but forced, and I know he's trying to make it less of a big deal, but he can't stop me from remembering the hand position, the wide stance of his legs, the force of the spell that caused his hair to ruffle and mine too. I imagine that I can hear my father's voice in my head: *Powerful witches are the only witches worth our time.* I may not be able to perform magic but I'm not an idiot, I know that a spell with that kind of elemental force, enough control of light to deter a magical creature, is not something to be shrugged off.

"What's the name of that hand position?" I ask.

"*Golow Taranis,*" he says, and his accent becomes more pronounced. "It's Cornish."

"I've never heard of it."

"It's...quite old." His voice is becoming more strained as he speaks. "It's not dangerous or anything, just a deterrent. My old coven in Cornwall teaches it."

There's a hint there, something to question. It's telling that he says the coven teaches it, not practises it. Perhaps it's a spell that's been passed down as part of their Cornish witchlore and Bastian is just the rare individual who can actually perform it. A prodigy, as my father would say. Or it could be that he's grown up in one of those isolated covens that my mother always said still live in the sixteenth century. *The things they would do to hoard power,* she used to say, with a shake of the head. *Useful, though,* my father always added. Glancing sideways at Bastian, I have the nasty sensation that he is probably the kind of witch my parents would be impressed by. Which means I should get as far away from him as possible.

"Which coven is that?" I ask, attempting to sound casual.

"*Arlodhes an lynn,*" he says in Cornish. I stare at him, and he looks slightly abashed. "Lady of the Lake. Ninianne in English, or…Nimue."

"Are you kidding?"

"No."

It's the worst possible answer. The Nimue coven definitely fall into the category my mother described: powerful, secretive and in it for life. They rarely educate outside their coven yet here Bastian is, hanging out with a shifter. An outcast. The breakdown of his parents' marriage must have been more than devastating. For his father to turn away from magic, to discard his ring, no wonder Bastian treats him like a traitor. I also realize I'm doing this with a lone Nimue witch with potentially threatening magic and no one to check him but me.

"So you know that you can't do that kind of spell at college, right?" I say nervously. "I'm not judging—"

"Sort of sounds like you are," Bastian says sharply.

"Of course I'm not, you just saw me shift," I say, trying not to match his tone. "They kick people out for doing ancient witchcraft unsupervised. Believe me, I know."

Professor Wallace was very clear with me after Elizabeth's death about what the consequences of me "attempting similar levels of magic in the future within college" would be. Forgetting entirely, it seemed, that I can't do magic at all.

"Well, I'm not going to tell them." Bastian gives me a steady look. "Are you?"

"No," I say. "But I don't love you doing that kind of spellcraft around me without asking first."

"Prejudiced much?"

"No, the last time any witch did ancient witchcraft, a spell of that strength around me, she *died,*" I say with emphasis. "Just ask next time."

"Well, I would have if you had been conscious," he says crossly. "But you weren't. Because you shifted, which might not be *Golow Taranis* but was a fucking huge magical moment, and it's not like you asked my permission to do that—"

"I didn't even ask my own permission to do that!" I snap at him. "Do you think I like having uncontrollable magic? You don't think I would have chosen literally any other time to shift form than when we were knee-deep in boggart negotiations?"

"Okay, fine!" Bastian nearly stumbles and we both list sideways, trying to keep our balance. "Fine. Just…forget it even happened."

I give Bastian a long look and wonder, for a moment, exactly what kind of person I have got myself tangled up with. In my life, I've seen more wild, raw magic than most witches. I remember the one time my father powered his study with his magic during a blackout, his hands glowing with pulsing light while he read and worked, so intense it spilled out from the door and down the stairs. Witches are different. Before Elizabeth and the cave, I had never seen a witch channel so much power in their ring. Now, when I look at Bastian, I don't just see a smart, studious young man. I see the witch who stood over me, pulsing blue light out of his ring with a spell I've never seen before. I am not sure if I like it. I wonder, suddenly, what it will look and feel like if we do get to the resurrection spell, if I have to watch Bastian use my own blood to bring Elizabeth back to life. I get a horrible shiver down my back and can't stop from shuddering. Bastian looks at me.

"What?" he asks.

"Do you think the spell will work?"

"I don't know." He sounds like he might have been thinking about it too. "It's a good sign that we could get the boggart's name. Hopefully, it means the other parts of the spell aren't out of date."

"But the actual resurrection," I begin, trying to put words to some of the anxiety that is flooding my mind with all kinds of images and terrors. "Do you know exactly how it works? Like, will she appear where we are or, I don't know, go back inside her body? Christ, will we have to dig her up?"

"I honestly don't know," Bastian says, and he doesn't sound nearly as worried as I feel. "We can only go by what old accounts of resurrection spells teach us and they're pretty diverse. Some of the ancient stories imply people walk out of the coffins, some that a new body is built by magic; that seems most likely with everything I've looked at in the spell—"

"Okay, okay." I try to breathe through my dizziness that I don't think is coming just from the sudden tumble down a ravine. "But she could...she could be a different person? Like, look a different way?"

"Maybe, it depends if the magic rebuilds a replica of her old self or not," he says. "But we're very far away from all of these things."

"Right," I say faintly. I have several horrible images in my mind. One is of Elizabeth's hand, thrust through freshly ground earth, zombie-style. Another is of a person standing in front of me, made of magic, looking nothing like Elizabeth but with her eyes, not recognizing me, all love between us lost beyond the grave. Is that what I want? I wonder. To have Elizabeth back, even if she doesn't love me? But even if she stopped, at least no one could blame me for her death any more. I don't know right now if that's enough, and I feel the painful weight of guilt shift nauseously in my belly.

"It was weird, your shift," Bastian says, jerking me out of my reverie. "I've always heard that shifters change fluidly, but yours was all in one burst and then you just...stayed unconscious. Do you remember anything about it?"

"No," I lie, thinking about what I did see, the strange dream of the past that I don't understand. My head is a bit dizzy and I'm horribly thirsty, like I always am after a shift. But Bastian is looking at me with an interrogatory glance and I feel I have to say something, so I lie. "I had a weird moment when I came back round. I thought you were a suffragette."

"A suffragette?" He laughs. "That's odd, although...I guess sort of fitting for the setting."

"Why?" I look around at the dark trees and green slopes.

"Because there was a suffragette gathering here, ages ago. Emmeline Pankhurst's daughter was here and she was chased away by anti-suffragette protestors. I read about it when I was doing my boggart research." Bastian gives me a sharp look. "But you knew that."

"Yeah. Of course I did."

I did not. My mind starts running. I try not to breathe too heavily or suspiciously with the racing of my pulse. Panic is swirling inside me, because nothing makes sense. How can I possibly explain that when I shifted I had a vision or dream of the past? That it felt so real, like I had lived it? As we walk along the path, I recall those rowdy voices and the sweaty press of women's bodies all around me. For a split second, when I look up and catch the moon peeking brightly out from behind a cloud, I can imagine it is the burning sun, roaring down on me in the middle of July. I do not know what is wrong with me.

"It makes sense your mind would imagine something associative," Bastian says. "Brains are strange that way."

"Yeah."

I can't be comforted by this. Brains might be strange but mine is clearly competing in the Mystifying Olympics. It's not just that I'm possibly having weird hallucinations of the past, it's the whole thing. Hanging out with this kind of witch, trusting him with my life and putting myself in harm's way to protect him too. Is this what Counsellor Cooper would call reckless endangerment?

"Hey." Bastian puts a hand on my shoulder and I jump, so tangled in my thoughts I've forgotten he's here. He withdraws his hand slowly, like I'm a dog that might bite. "I just...wanted to encourage you. We're one step closer to the spell."

I nod mechanically and try to push all my fears and worries down. This is all that matters, after all, not the hallucinations or Bastian's magic or shapeshifting for the first time since Elizabeth's death. This is all that matters: I am one step closer to getting her back.

Chapter Eleven

It's a long walk back to the tram stop. We stumble along, my legs feeling like they're turning to lead, me leaning on Bastian.

"Oi oi!" someone yells as we stagger past the chippy. There are two white blokes standing in the doorway smoking. One of them is holding an empty pint glass from the pub next door. "Had one too many, has she?"

"Yeah, mate!" Bastian calls back in a jovial, laddish voice that sounds nothing like him, but his hand tightens across my shoulders. "Getting her to the station now!"

He hurries me on faster. I'm not surprised, and I'm not mad at him for playing straight. It definitely seems safer. We walk past them, my legs still wobbling and unpredictable, my steps sloppy. I trip over a kerb and Bastian has to steady me. "Shit."

"So it all feels completely different?" Bastian asks, holding my elbow tightly as I straighten up. I hate these questions; I've always hated them, because this is supposed to be as easy for me as growing, as breathing. Instead it's violent and broken and produces frowns rather than smiles.

"How would you feel if you suddenly grew tits?" I demand.

"Weird, I reckon." He says it so calmly that it takes all the indignation out of me.

"Yeah." I'm too tired to brush him off with sarcasm. "I don't usually…"

"Don't usually what?" He slows his steps down until I've got back into a heavy, limping rhythm, definitely looking like a drunk.

"I don't usually shift so often," I admit. "Before this summer, my last shift was the summer of first year."

That had been the shift after Carl Lord's consistent attempts to jump me in annoying places. At least my hair becoming long and curly, my waist narrowing, my boobs suddenly appearing had been enough to deter him.

"How many times have you shifted?" he asks.

"Um…it's hard to say but…maybe twelve? Since I started college this will be my third."

"That isn't usual for shifters, is it?"

"No," I say flatly. "For most shifters, it's like changing a coat or putting on pyjamas. They have a resting form they return to. It's natural."

Which makes me unnatural. Or at least, that's how it's always been told to me. I try not to think about it as I continue to stagger towards the luminescent glow of the tram stop. Bastian walks quietly beside me.

"I don't know how you do it, anyway," he says eventually. "If I had to change form like you do, I'd not cope. I'd be massively dysphoric."

"Well, I'm not coping and I am massively dysphoric," I say automatically and then wince, wishing I hadn't. I don't want him to pity me.

"Touché," he says. Then he gives me a steady, sidelong glance, his left hand held out towards me like he's indicating on a bike, as if he wants to leave it there for me to grab in case of emergency. "There's something I don't get."

"What?"

"Well, shifters don't age like humans or witches, right?" Bastian says thoughtfully. I nod. It's another reason witches don't like us very much. We can outlive them by double. "You get old but your forms, once they've reached adulthood, they don't have to get old."

"Yeah."

"So why not look young for ever? Why not be whatever gender or no gender and just embrace the intersectionality of it?" Bastian asks. "It seems like all shifters should be as flexible with gender as you are."

"That's hilarious, please tell every shifter you ever meet that."

"Why is it such a big deal?" Bastian presses.

I sigh and pause to give my sore muscles a rest, leaning my head against the wall. It's the question that's haunted me my entire life and I still don't have an adequate answer, unless you count: *Because this is the way we are, Lando.* They told me I could be like the shifters who settle into one form and never change again, who age their form as naturally as they want, who follow the obvious paths of humanity and when their body wears out, because our bodies do eventually wear out of their ability to shift and pump blood and breathe, die in a manner that reflects a human death. They told me I could follow in the family business, go into espionage or security, shifting between forms but maintaining a key, solid gender identity at home, as if playing dress up in my skin should be enough to fulfil the part of me that has always wanted more. *Align with your resting form, Orlando!* a voice yells at me from the past. *Don't give them a reason to hate you!*

"Because shifters still live in this world, with all the prejudice and bullshit that comes with it," I say, staring up at the lamp-post light that is casting a dim sepia gleam over us. "We're not like witches, we're hidden, concealing our powers from humans to stay safe and managing our magic so witches don't hate us more. Conforming to a gender binary is a type of safety, another tool we can use to hide our difference. At least that's always how it's been taught to me. Not conforming to a gender binary is seen as needlessly reckless. They don't believe that actually being non-binary is who I am. They think it's a *choice.*"

I can't help the bitterness in my voice on that final word, one that my parents have thrown in my face all my life. There is a long pause and Bastian doesn't seem to know what to say.

"I don't hate you," he says finally. "I think you're...brave."

I stare at him. In the glimmer of the street light his handsomeness is curiously transformed, the gruesome glow making him too tall, too sharp, too crow-like. Somehow, it makes me like him more.

We walk down the ramp onto the empty platform. A fox

runs across the opposite platform like it's late for the tram, a flash of burnished fur and neat black paws, and then hops off, disappearing into the bushes. Two pinpricks of light appear in the distance that remind me nastily of the eyes of the boggart and I shiver. The tram rattles in, casting a mechanical yellow shine over us both, and suddenly, looking at Bastian in the normality of fluorescent lights, I see how scruffy he looks. Denim jacket muddy, T-shirt torn, hair full of twigs. I can't imagine I look much better.

"Are you sure you want to do this still?" I ask uncertainly, because it seems like the polite inquiry after you've nearly been killed by a boggart.

"Yes," Bastian says quickly. He leans past me and presses the button. We both climb on board and find seats. I'm surprised that when I pick two seats by the window, he slides into the one next to me rather than finding another set, further down. He sighs and leans his head back, eyes closing.

"Sleepy?" I ask.

"Not to be dramatic but my hand really hurts," he mutters, and I look down at his cut hand. It's filthy, smeared with mud and blood. "And I have to stock up on a lifetime's supply of goat's cheese when I get home."

I smirk to myself, imagining how that online shop is going to go.

"There's this great cheesemonger in Didsbury," I say. "You could probably set up a standing order."

"Christ," Bastian groans. "I suppose I could just get an actual goat and make it myself."

"And where would the goat live?"

"In the flat, of course, can't you tell it's remarkably goat friendly?"

"And what about René?"

"I've been thinking about getting René a mate to play with."

"Most people choose another dog."

"I don't want René to be one of those racist dogs who only has dog friends, Lando, come on."

I laugh and my laugh turns to choking because I'm so thirsty. Bastian reaches into his satchel and pulls out a reusable bottle of water, handing it to me easily. I'm too dry to cough out a thank you and by the time I've glugged down half of it, Bastian's eyes are drooping and his breath has evened out into a doze. I don't blame him really. It was a lot of magic he did and I would be feeling sleepy myself, if I didn't have so much to think through. I roll my sore wrists in circles and finally turn my mind fully to my shift.

What does it mean that I had a vision of a suffragette meeting in Boggart Hole Clough, the site of a famous gathering? Why are the stories in an old diary infecting my mind? I've heard of ancient witches who have visions – some have old rings that once held the gift of foresight – but I don't know of any shifters who do. Also, if it was a vision, why did it feel so real? Why can I still feel the brush of the long dress around my ankles and the bake of the sun on the back of my neck? For a wild second, I pull out my phone. I've even selected the contact marked MOTHER and hovered my thumb over the CALL button before I come to my senses. If I want answers about shifters, I will literally go anywhere else in the world to get them. The tram slows down, pulling into St Peter's Square, the closest stop to Bastian's flat. I nudge his shoulder. He jerks awake.

"Shas!" he gasps out. My chest tightens. I know that feeling; I recognize that desperate tone. *He's been dreaming about his dead brother.*

"It's your stop," I say. I know that the last thing I want after I've dreamed about Elizabeth is to be asked about it.

"Oh." He looks around a little blearily. "Well. Goodnight, then."

"Yeah."

I can tell he's still struggling to pull himself out of his nightmare and I don't add anything else as he gets off the tram. I watch him walk down the platform in the dark as the tram pulls away into the night, taking me out of the city. I wonder what his dreams are like and if they are as bad as mine.

When I get home to Beryl's, I do what I always do after a shift. I stand naked in front of the long mirror that hangs on the back of my door and look at my reflection, trying to learn myself in this new form, stretching and flexing every muscle to feel its limits. People always think shifters will change themselves into miraculously strong or brilliantly slim forms, but they forget that shifters can't change what they don't have. I've never been a very athletic person, easily running to fat. My last form was taller so I was leaner, but this one is shorter. I'm still pudgy and soft all over, but rounder in the face and hips and fuller in the chest. My eyebrows are bushy and my hair is dark and coarse all over, and shoulder length from my head, in curls that I can see will easily go to frizz with a little humidity. My eyes are dark brown, and as I look at my wide hips and wobbly thighs, taking in my round nostrils and pointed Cupid's bow, I feel like I always do after a shift, like I've borrowed someone else's flesh.

I've never had this happen before, shifting so abruptly. Aside from the incident in the cave with Elizabeth, throughout my childhood I used to always feel a shift coming on, the same way you feel vomit coming. I've absolutely never had a vision while shifting. Just thinking about it makes the hair all over my new skin rise up, an uncanny sensation flooding my body. I try to tell myself it doesn't mean anything – I read a story in the book, I had a strange dream, so naturally, my shift followed my thoughts. But shifts are not supposed to follow whims, they're supposed to follow will, they're supposed to be inside my control. *Magic is to be directed, Orlando!* my mother used to shout at me. *Directed by will!* Shivering, I climb into bed and tell myself the same thing I tell myself every time I shift, over and over, until I fall asleep: *I am more than my body, I am more than a label, I am Orlando, I am Orlando, I am Orlando...*

Chapter Twelve

When Counsellor Cooper told me I should get a part-time job after the hospital, I don't think she anticipated I would have to explain shapeshifting to the management at the local vegan supermarket. Beryl takes one look at my new form when I come into the kitchen to make tea the next morning and makes a call.

"This is what happens when shifters don't learn to control themselves," Beryl says darkly, eyeing my waist and hips and longer hair. "Chaos."

I'm meant to be working in the afternoon, and I spend the entire morning on the phone to Counsellor Cooper, answering questions on a GAD-7 questionnaire to check my risk of harm and enduring a very thorough investigation of my mental well-being. By the time it's done, a package has been delivered by hand courier addressed to me.

"From your parents, is my guess," Beryl says. She's right. When I open it, a familiar heavy necklace falls into my hands. I instantly recoil from it, the silver chain as thick as a rope and the huge black opal stone the size of a quail's egg. I remember the weight of it from my childhood, the magic oppressive, making it difficult to breathe. Counsellor Cooper must have called them and asked them to send it. I glare at it with dislike.

"Fuck them," I mutter, weighing it in my hand.

"What is it?" Beryl asks, nosing over my shoulder. "Ah. A shifter shroud spell. Just what you need."

I turn the package upside down, shaking it, but nothing falls out. There's no note. They must have paid a fortune to have someone personally courier the shroud to Chorlton. They always told me I had to be ridiculously careful with enchanted objects like this, yet they were willing to send it with no note. Then I wonder why I'm surprised. Why would they need to write a note, really? All of their words still rattle around my mind as I look at the shroud, their voices roaring back: *You will wear this until you can transform properly! I do not care if it hurts you!*

"No," I say, feeling sick as I push the shroud into Beryl's hand. I hate the way the metal feels against my skin, sticky and weighted.

"It's up to you," Beryl sighs, holding the shroud in between her fingers where it hangs, ominously. "But it's this or you find a new job. Or you pull a sickie until you can change back."

I give her a deadly look. We both know I can't change back and neither can I casually explain shapeshifters to my very human manager. I sigh heavily. I could quit, I suppose, but I like having my own money. I like saving and thinking that one day I'll not need theirs and never again have to live under their roof or be forced to wear painful shrouds against my will.

"Fine," I say, bracing myself as Beryl drops the shroud over my head. The black opal is heavy with its own ancient enchantment and all it needs is a bit of magic, provided by Beryl's twisting fingers, before I feel the magic of the shroud settle uncomfortably over my skin like a heavy suncream. When I look in the mirror, my reflection is the same as yesterday afternoon; same fey, slightly gingery hair, same pinched face with dull green eyes, same male form again.

"Remember, shrouds can only be worn for six hours maximum or you can have medical problems, overheating, trouble breathing," Beryl says, dusting off her hands, cinnamon- and orange peel-scented magic sprinkling off her fingers. Mr Pebbles stands up on his wrinkly hind legs, batting at the blue sparks.

"Yeah, I fucking remember," I snap, slamming my way into my bedroom. I hate that even though they're miles away, my parents are managing to impose the same solutions they always did. No matter where I go, their message is still nastily the same: My body is not my own.

Work is uncomfortable; I feel lethargic and slow wearing the shroud of my old form, and sweaty too, like wearing a duffel coat on a hot day. I hate the idea of going back to Beryl's and facing all of her questions about how my day was under the shroud, and it's just when I'm considering taking myself for a long, lonely walk around the lake to avoid it that a message arrives from BBB.

> Some college people are getting together for a drink in the Northern Quarter tonight. See you there?

I stare at the message. I want to tell him of course he won't see me there, that these are the types of things I haven't been invited to since my first year, when I was still basking in the questionable radiance of Carl Lord. I could lie to him and tell him I have to work, but the grocery closes by early evening and he could easily look it up online and catch me in a lie. While I'm hesitating, another message arrives.

Would be good to see a familiar face.
I'll buy you a drink.

No one has ever offered that to me. Not even Elizabeth, because we never really went out of her house. Yet here Bastian is, wanting my company after saving me from a boggart, still barely knowing me. It's nice to be invited, I think, and Counsellor Cooper did say I needed to make an effort to socialize with my peers. Besides, isn't anything better than Beryl's hovering concern right now?

What time?

Seven.

See you then.

Despite my mind running a hundred miles an hour through all the ways I could potentially embarrass myself in front of my classmates, I'm grateful to be on the tram up into town, the shroud tucked away in my bag, the cool air on my real skin. I'm still getting used to a female form again, the way men's eyes slide towards me as I travel, and I'm grateful that I've worn my big flannel shirt over a vest top. I know people from college will be full of comments when they see my familiar clothes are encasing a different body, so I make sure I've got my headphones on when I approach the outside seating in Stevenson Square near college.

The pedestrian area is full of Saturday night revellers crowded into the clusters of metal seating outside different bars and restaurants on either side of the ginkgo trees: gaggles of girls in heels and short skirts out on the lash; groups of lads shoved shoulder to shoulder on long Oktoberfest-style tables, necking pints; couples having a night at the craft brew bar with friends, a pug or a French bulldog sitting happily at their feet. All of these bodies and people, set to this shabby industrial Mancunian backdrop of red brick and bold political street art, it has a festive, anticipatory feeling, as if the buzz of the city centre is electric and infectious. I find myself lengthening my stride, standing straighter, actually getting excited. But then I spot them, witches from college who have pushed together a bunch of small metal tables into a cluster. There's more of them than I expected, about fifteen, chatting in small groups. And then they spot me. They look at me like I'm a street performer or a climate-change activist who's tied themselves to the front door of Boots. No one looks at me like I'm still myself. More than one set of eyes is drawn instantly to my chest and I cross my arms, thinking I'm going to have to pull out my old binders from under my bed, when Bastian stands up from a table on the end of the group, smiling at me.

"Lando! Here!" He's raising his hand in that weirdly formal gesture of greeting that is somehow absurdly endearing. I'm grateful to squeeze my way through the watching witches and settle down in a metal chair beside him, the drops of rain still lingering on it from the day seeping into the back of my jeans.

"Hey, I got you an IPA, I hope that's okay," he says, sliding one of the two glasses towards me.

"Yeah, it's great."

I'm not really much of a beer drinker, or any kind of drinker, since I've never had any friends to do it with. I take a sip. It's sour and foamy and honestly reminds me a little of the taste of cardboard, but he bought it for me and that's nice.

"Did you come from work?" He frowns, eyeing my apron poking out of my tote bag. "How did you manage that?"

He gestures to my different face.

"Oh, nothing, a shifter shroud spell," I say, sipping my drink. Bastian's eyes light up.

"Really?" He looks so eager. "Do you have it with you? Can I see?"

I hesitate. I imagine my parents bellowing at me, screaming at me not to share secrets with witches, but Bastian did save me from being eaten by a boggart yesterday. Carefully, I reach down and withdraw the shroud from my bag, holding it in my hands under the table, trying not to wince. The pull of the spell, still connected to me, is hot and prickly against my skin. Bastian's eyes widen.

"Bloody hell, I've seen drawings in books but I never thought I'd see one in real life. It's so heavy," he says, feeling the weight of it in his hand. I'm kind of relieved not to be holding it. "Is it enchanted right now?"

"Yes, Beryl started it for me."

"Who's Beryl?"

I grimace, thinking the only way to say this is to say it in a big rush, to just get it out. If he decides he thinks it's weird it won't change the fact we need to do the spell together. Besides, there's a good chance Carl Lord has been making nasty jokes about my living situation behind my back and he already knows.

"She's in charge of the shared house I live in. It's kind of like a halfway house."

"Halfway from what to what?" Bastian frowns.

"Halfway from the hospital to...normality, I guess," I say, keeping my eyes on the shroud in his hands, then taking it back and carefully putting it into my bag. I wait for him to ask more, but he doesn't.

"Hey, I got you this." He drops something into my lap. I jump and stare at it, rolling the small blue glass tub between my fingers. "It's a muscle salve. You said you were sore last night."

I undo the lid and take a hesitant sniff. It smells like arnica and eucalyptus.

"Did you make this yourself?"

"My ring's good for healing," Bastian says modestly, twisting his ring on his finger and confirming my suspicion from when I first met him. I suddenly imagine him making a brew in his fancy kitchen, stirring a pot, the blue of his magic glowing softly, doing all of that for me. The thought makes a warmth spread through me. I dip a finger into the salve and rub some over my wrists. Oddly, wrists and elbows and knees and ankles are the joints that hurt the longest after a shift. "I can't believe you made this for me."

"Yeah, well, consider me the Healer in this particular raiding party." Bastian grins.

"Is that a D&D reference?" Of course he plays Dungeons & Dragons, he's got Dungeon Master written all over him.

"Well, what do you call strangers who team up on a quest?" Bastian demands.

"In *The Lord of the Rings* they're the fellowship."

"'The Nine Walkers shall be set against the Nine Riders that are evil,'" Bastian quotes, and I smile widely.

"Nerd."

"I'm not a nerd."

"Quoting Elrond is very nerdy." I laugh.

"Not nerdier than *knowing* it's an Elrond quote." Bastian smirks. "I guess you're my companion, then. If you're okay with that?"

I feel weirdly okay with it. I find myself smiling. Out of the corner of my eye, I see Kira and her friends deep in conversation, their eyes flicking over to me and Bastian. I try not to pay them any attention, because the evening September sun is setting, bouncing gorgeous rosy light off the three-storey Victorian Fred Aldous building, making it glow like a cherry, and the orange umbrellas advertising Aperol spritz seem summery and Mediterranean. It's still warm enough outside not to need a jacket, but the air smells of the turning leaves and it mingles with the tart taste of hops on my tongue. A nice guy is making jokes with me and for a moment, things feel okay. Then someone knocks against my chair and there's beer spilling down my back.

"Shit!" I quickly pull off my plaid shirt, forgetting for a moment that I'm actually trying to hide my new boobs.

"Christ, shifter, what happened to you?" Carl Lord laughs, pushing past us so our table lurches and Bastian has to clamp his hand over our glasses to stop them spilling. Carl squashes in beside his mates, lounging back in his chair. His ring is giving off a telltale pink glow. Now I know that there was a little bit of magical mischief in that accident. "Get boobier overnight or did you shift and murder someone else?"

Everyone in his group laughs. He slings his arm around who I can only presume is the latest boyfriend. It's the same first year I saw him kissing last week, blond and doe-eyed and looking like he's on cloud nine. I feel a cringe of embarrassment for him.

"Leave it," Bastian says to Carl. His voice is level and steady but it travels and a momentary hush descends among the drinking witches. Everyone else around us, the rest of the Northern Quarter, continues laughing and basking in the very last dregs of summer, but the witches watch Bastian. The sapphire in his ring glows. I instantly remember what he did to the boggart, and while imagining him blasting Carl across the square with an unearthly gust of bright light is deliciously vindicating, I clamp my hand on top of his. I'm relieved when Bastian doesn't pull away. Carl merely glances at our hands, smiles tightly and laughs.

"Oh, mate, I get it, you're new and she's a shifter and that.

You think she needs your pity!" Carl's laugh rings in my ears. "Thing is, she doesn't need your pity. She just wants to get laid!"

"And you don't want to shag that!" one of Carl's other friends pipes up, tapping his glass against Carl's. "It's like a black widow spider, it kills who it mates with!"

That produces uproarious laughter from Carl Lord.

"Don't be sexist." Kira scowls. I feel like that's less about me and more about my form. I'm a "girl" again so now she can defend me. I shoot her an angry glare and she looks away, eyebrows drawn tightly together as she sips her Aperol spritz.

"Can you leave us alone?" Bastian asks, and once again, his voice travels. Kira and her friends all stare. There aren't many people in college who stand up to Carl. Mostly, the technique is to roll eyes and ignore him. "We're having a conversation."

"Yeah, we're all having conversations." Carl smiles. "No need to get mardy, it's just chat, isn't it? Just banter."

"Yeah, I don't need your banter, actually." Bastian's voice is getting sharper by the second.

"You say that now," Carl sneers, giving me a sudden, vicious look. "Come and find me, mate, when she screws you over. She's nothing but a cock-tease."

I stand up abruptly and glare at him.

"I'm not a she," I say.

"That's all right." Carl gives me a cruel, predatory glance that immediately tells me I've done the wrong thing by engaging. "'Murderer' isn't a gendered term, is it?"

That gets a laugh, a genuine one. Bastian tries to grab my arm, but I brush him away. As I push past Carl's group I catch a glimpse of him moving his fingers rapidly under the table and more drinks fall, directional splashes of cold beer that soak me, made colder and more intentional by witchcraft. Everyone on this square sees a poor clumsy sod, rushing home to dry off after an accident, not someone fleeing the scene of some well-placed magical bullying. Carl's always been good at taking advantage of the fact his spells aren't powerful enough to last. Leaves no evidence.

I walk fast, out of the square and down Hilton Street, past college and the tall industrial mill buildings down to the wide paved walkway beside the canal. I ignore the Canada geese strutting around and the lads on either side listening to music and smoking vapes. I sit myself down right on the stone edge, dangling my feet towards the murky water. I breathe in hard as I press my palms into my eye sockets, smelling eucalyptus on my skin and that particular cold pondweed smell of city water. One word chants in my head: *murderer, murderer, murderer.* I shake my head and roll my shoulders, just like Counsellor Cooper taught me when I find myself overwhelmed with anxiety (*physically moving our bodies can help us release tension*), but it's like I'm trying to dislodge the physical feeling that my bones are calcifying.

"Hey."

I look over my shoulder. Bastian is standing there, holding my wet plaid shirt. I sniff, wiping away any rogue tears quickly with the back of my hand, and he sits down beside me, gently draping my shirt over my shoulders. It's a sweet gesture and for a second, tears threaten to overwhelm me, so I stare down into the water beneath my boots, concentrating on the shadowy bodies of fish I see there.

"I don't know why I bothered coming," I mumble, when I'm finally sure I can speak without howling.

"I honestly didn't know he was going to be here." Bastian frowns. "Kira invited me."

"Yeah. Well. She doesn't think much of me either."

"I thought she was Elizabeth's best friend."

"She was. She was the only one Elizabeth told about us, but we never talked, and she definitely wants nothing to do with me now." Bastian gives me a questioning look and I reluctantly carry on speaking. "She blames me for her death, I think."

"Or maybe she's just grieving," he says reasonably. "Here."

He puts his hands in the preparatory triangle.

"Oh, you don't need to—" I begin.

"It's no problem," he says, and his sapphire ring glows. His hands move in a sweeping motion, the left over the right with the fingers spread wide and then twisting around until his left faces his chest and his right touches my shirt – a Neptune's Rise into a Logi's Spear, a combination I've not seen before. The shirt begins to dry, the splash marks steaming away, the smell of his magic, today lighter and softer like the smell of burning paper, catching in my nostrils.

"Whoa," I whisper, as Bastian's ring continues to glow. On the other side of the canal, the lads start clapping.

"Nice shiny ring!" one of them calls.

"Witches have such cool tricks, man," another says.

"Naw, mate," a third says, unimpressed. "Just science dressed up, innit?"

This makes Bastian smirk and he stops, dropping his hand

to rest on the edge of the canal.

"Another Nimue spell?" I ask. He shakes his head.

"Pépé taught me," he says. His right hand is near my thigh and I can feel the heat off it, the power of the witchcraft he just did like it was nothing at all. All these historical family spells he's sharing with me with absolutely no fear of retribution from judgemental parents. There's an envy bubbling up inside me that I can't quite push down.

"You just do what you want, don't you?" I say. If he catches the jealous edge to my voice he doesn't show it, just shrugging casually.

"Witchcraft is bigger than we think it is," he says. "Most British witches seem content making themselves smaller to fit in or stay out of trouble, but I won't be that way."

"Most witches don't have the kind of power you have."

"You have it too. I've seen your shifts, you're full of magic," he says, fixing his eyes on me. They're so eager, like he's expecting me to be the same as him, and all I can imagine is the furious voice of my father scolding me.

"Yeah, and witches hate me for it," I say, thinking of what everyone said after Elizabeth's death. *Magical discharge. No control. Shapeshifters need to be vigilant.* "Even if I could control it, I'd still need to think about safety."

"You think I don't?" His voice is harsh all of a sudden. "You said it yesterday: this is still the world with all its shitty prejudice and no amount of witchcraft makes *me* safe in it."

I think about the way he hurried me past the two drunks last night: the tension in his shoulders, being the young black man escorting a seemingly drunk white girl home. It's like he sees my remembrance in my face, and he nods firmly.

"So I'm not going to shrink my power down, waiting until I get into the Merlin Foundation or to find another coven or until someone tells me it's safe to be myself, the world isn't *safe.*" His voice is thick and bleak as he looks down the canal. "Witchcraft might not fix it, but it's something, at least. It's power."

I feel the uncomfortable tingle of having misjudged someone's motives. Bastian isn't showing off his power because he's too comfortable or unaware, but because like me, he feels the pressure of being unwanted by the world, of not fitting in. Since he's been so truthful, I feel the urge to at least match his honesty.

"Every witch I've ever met says I'm too powerful, I'm too much, I'm not safe," I say. "Not safe to be anyone's friend, to study with anyone, to be trusted."

To be loved by anyone, I add silently, kicking my Doc Martens against the wall of the canal. When I've got control of my grief, soaring through my chest like a bird with feathers made of sorrow, I go on.

"Maybe if I could actually shift it would be different, but my power doesn't make me feel safer," I admit, not letting my voice rise above a whisper, too ashamed to speak loudly. "Mostly, I just feel…fucking lonely."

Bastian doesn't say anything for a while. I wonder if I spoke too quietly for him to hear. A goose flaps its wings and slides into the water, gently paddling upstream. Then he speaks.

"We could study together," he says.

He doesn't phrase it like a question, but a statement. It's funny, because in it I hear something different. *You don't have to be alone* is what I hear. I've not felt that in a while now, like someone believes I'm safe to be around. That someone wants my company. Bastian might treat witchcraft differently to any witch I've ever met, but he's here and he's not afraid of me.

"Yeah, okay," I say.

Chapter Thirteen

Over the next two weeks, I find myself reading the diary in *The Witchlore of Bodies* whenever I have a spare minute. It's becoming an old friend. It feels miraculous to read the story of someone like me, and they are so honest about their feelings, the agonies of their life and the terror of not being accepted. Seeing it down on paper makes me feel less alone. Bastian and I also start studying together. He mercifully doesn't question the way I try to avoid being inside college apart from classes, and we meet up to write essays in coffee shops or book the music rooms in the Manchester Central Library so he can practise witchcraft and I can practise pointless hand waving. I love working in there, the anonymity of being just one of thousands of students and visitors in the city sitting in the beautiful panelled circular reading room with its dynamic domed ceiling and the way the smallest movement of someone's chair echoes all the way around the stone. It's nicer, however, to have someone to sit beside, to watch my laptop while I go to the loo, to share crisps with and guard the rare, coveted plug sockets with. In my weekly call with Counsellor

Cooper, she even says that it seems my mood is improving. I think it might be. I tell myself over and over that it's not real, it's not *friendship,* it's just companionship. It's still better than being alone all the time.

"We need to make a plan for the next stage of the spell," Bastian says on Thursday, when we are in one of the small music rooms. It's toasty warm, despite the cooling autumnal air outside, because Bastian's been trying to teach me his grandfather's Haitian heating spell. The power of his has left him sweaty, standing in just his T-shirt.

"Okay." I fruitlessly move my hands into a few forms. Nothing happens.

"You need to lift your thumb up higher on the Logi's Spear," he says, lifting the edge of his baggy T-shirt to wipe his sweaty forehead. I'm grateful for this, that he offers correction on my form even if it yields no results, unlike everyone else, who just makes me feel useless. "The bone from Kilgrimol, you said it's near Blackpool. I looked it up and it's on the coast, a town called...Lytham?"

"Yeah, I know it," I say lightly, trying not to sound like I *really* know it. I perform the movement again with my thumb more rigid and Bastian nods approvingly.

"I thought we could go on Sunday."

"I have to work on Sunday." I pause. "But I have a whole weekend off next week, we could go then. Or you could go on your own, I guess."

Part of me wants him to say that's exactly what he'll do, and then I don't have to reckon with going back to those familiar beaches and that long open sky. Another part of me likes that I have someone to do things with now, to study with, to go places with. Yes, the boggart was terrifying, but there are no boggarts that I know of in Lytham.

"Next Saturday is great," he says. "I'd like to try and get to the final stage by Samhain, or we'll have to wait until the winter solstice."

Samhain is six weeks away. It seems impossible to me that Bastian will still want to hang out with me in six weeks, but the thought that maybe he will makes my cheeks flush.

"Sounds good," I say.

On the Friday before we're due to go to Lytham, the last day of September, I actually find myself getting excited about our trip.

"I'll drive us tomorrow," Bastian says.

"I didn't know you drive."

"Yep, passed last summer." Bastian pulls on his satchel as we prepare to leave the library after a day's studying.

"And you're good at it?" I follow him down the wide marble stairs, past the snowy white sculpture of the Reading Girl. "Like, you didn't reverse into a bollard or kill any hedgehogs during your lessons?"

"No and no. I did, however, run over my driving instructor's foot on my first lesson."

"That does not fill me with confidence."

Bastian grins and I realize I like this, the ease with which we can joke with one another, the way it's almost becoming normal now. We've reached the bottom of the stairs, the blue light from the stained-glass windows reflecting weakly on the floor, when Kira Tavi steps into my path. Today she's dressed in a dark green long-sleeved jumpsuit that, to my mind, makes her look like a classy astronaut.

"Hiya," she says, shooting Bastian a curious look before turning back to me. "Can I speak to you? Alone?"

"I'll wait out front," Bastian says. I nod and follow Kira under the arches into the library café, bustling with old people having a coffee, babies sucking on orange-juice cartons and students having a snack and watching TV on their phones before heading upstairs. She's set up on one of the white plastic booth tables with her laptop out and a coffee and sandwich beside it. I wonder, suddenly, if she's been waiting for me. After all, she usually studies with her little crew of high achievers in the college library.

"Join me," she says, gesturing to the blue bench opposite her in a way that makes me feel like this is a job interview and I've walked into her office. I sit down warily on the edge of the cushioned plastic. I don't slide all the way in opposite her and don't take off my bag. I already get the sense I might want to make a quick escape.

"I've got a tram to catch," I say. Kira nods and folds her hands. She's changed her manicure. Now it's all autumnal browns and yellows, very seasonal.

"Just a quick catch-up, that's all." She smiles. It doesn't quite reach her eyes. "How's it going in your new form?"

"It's fine." I look at her blankly. "Is this a peer mentoring thing?"

I was under the impression those meetings would be taking place in college. I didn't realize I'd signed up to be randomly accosted anywhere in Manchester and asked about my deepest secrets.

"No, I just..." Kira tilts her head to the side in a way I find instantly patronizing. "How's it going with Bastian?"

I frown. This is definitely not a peer mentoring question. This almost feels like a friend question. Which would make a lot more sense if Kira and I were, in any way, friends.

"Why are you asking that?"

"Oh, nothing, nothing at all," she babbles, in a way that makes me aware that it is definitely *something*. "It's just...maybe be careful around him."

"*What?*"

"Well, it's just, he's new and you're...you." I flinch at that, all the old catcalls rising in my memory: *Abnormal. Shifter. Freak.* "And you never know what people's motives are."

I feel a red-hot flare of anger rising up inside of me and a flush filling my cheeks. The unmitigated gall of her astounds me. It's the kind of rage that makes my hands shake and my throat tight and irritating tears prickle at the corners of my eyes.

"You're wondering what possible reason someone like him could have for hanging around with a weirdo *shifter* like me," I start, my voice trembling as I try to keep it under control in a public place. "It couldn't be that he just *likes* me, could it?"

"I'm not saying that at all!" Kira's eyes widen. "I'm worried about you, we don't know anything about him—"

"And knowing something about a person makes them better,

does it? Makes them safer?" I lean forward as all my resentment against everyone in college who has ever made my life hell pours out on Kira Tavi. "I've known nearly everyone in college for two years and my girlfriend died and *still* no one even cares that it happened to me! Instead, they just act like it's all my fault! So you can fucking *shove* your fake concern up your ruddy *arse*!"

I stand up, struggling to pull the other strap of my rucksack on, my emotions so high they are making my hands move awkwardly, as if my rage has given them some kind of jitters. There are two middle-aged women having tea and scones at the next table, subtly gawking at us as they spread jam. I have a feeling that I have not been as quiet as I could have been. I need to get out of here, now, because the last thing I want to do is cry in front of an audience.

"It didn't just happen to you," Kira says. Her eyes are shimmering slightly but her voice is clear. An impending sense of dread rises inside of me. I imagine this is what Pandora felt like, this sense that I've started something I'm not ready for.

"I was the one who was there, Kira," I say, thinking that if I can cut her off at the knees with this then she'll stop talking and she can't say the devastating things that I can see building in her glassy eyes. "Don't tell me how it happened."

"I'm not going to. What I meant was that you talk about what happened like it only happened to you." Kira's voice hasn't changed volume, but her south-Manchester tone is so sharp it could cut me. "She had parents who loved her, parents who are getting a divorce now. She had a coven, a family of witches bigger than you imagine; there are loads of people who were completely devastated by this. She might have been your girlfriend, but she wasn't just yours, Lando."

It's too much to bear, so I turn and walk away from her, my heart racing, hoping she doesn't follow me, and my cheeks burning as I bustle past the scone ladies watching me flee. I'm practically panting as I go through the circular doors, jogging down the marble steps to see Bastian leaning against one of the library pillars, watching the rain hammer down against the stone flags of St Peter's Square.

"Are you okay?" he asks, frowning. I nod, struggling to catch my breath. My face is damp from the rain mist and I stare out at passing businessmen hurrying through the downpour with umbrellas. Rain like this always clears the square; bustling tour groups, usually standing in front of the war memorial and the statue of Mrs Pankhurst, are huddled for shelter under the cover of the library's portico front, the rain practically falling in sheets between the columns. It's too many bodies and a small space and right now, I'd rather be out there, in the dreadful weather, than inside with Kira Tavi.

"I've got a tram to catch," I say to Bastian, pulling my hood up and preparing to run across the sheets of water covering the square and the tram tracks.

"Wait." Bastian grabs my arm to stop me, moving closer so he isn't overheard. He smells like rain and sweat and damp wool. "Are you sure you're okay?"

No, not at all, I answer in my head. *It's not just my fault she's dead, it's my fault dozens of people are devastated.*

"Yep," I say. Even if Kira was trying to tell me something

truthful, that maybe Bastian isn't everything he seems, even if it's somehow all a big lie, what does it matter? The point of all this is to get Elizabeth back and then maybe everything that Kira said won't be so damaging. Her parents will be healed, her friends will be comforted and I won't have to bear the weight of the guilt of all those things, because if she hadn't been with me, she would never have died in the first place. When Bastian continues to look at me, I add, "I just need to get on with this. The spell."

His frown clears and a particularly knowing look crosses his face.

"We are," he says. "Lytham next and then we'll be two ingredients down."

"Two down," I repeat, the words a spell in themselves, pushing me on, back to Elizabeth. *Two down.* We step out into the rain. Together.

Chapter Fourteen

"What is that?" I ask on Saturday, staring down at the car that's parked up on the pavement outside Beryl's.

"It's a Mini Cooper," he says. It's a *vintage* Mini, it's blue and rusted and the longer I look at it, the smaller and less reliable it looks.

"No," I say, stepping back and shaking my head. I'd expected that Bastian would be borrowing his dad's car, something sleek and silver with a new car smell and a P plate on the front.

"No what?"

"No, I'm not getting in that deathtrap!" I exclaim, bending down to look in the tattered interior. "Couldn't your dad buy you a car that *won't* crumple like a soup can on impact?"

I see from the taut look on his face that I've said completely the wrong thing.

"It's Mum's," he says.

"Ah." Once again, my verbal diarrhoea has got the better of me. Out of respect to his totally understandable sentimentality, I gingerly open the door. "Well. It's cute. In a kind of deadly way."

Bastian smiles gratefully.

"I'm a very safe driver. Only one minor correction on my test." Bastian raises an eyebrow at me and then folds himself into the driver's seat. It's quite comical really, because he's so tall.

"You look like a clown getting into a clown car," I say.

"I'm not sure you're in the position to be calling someone a clown." Bastian looks significantly at my rainbow jumper and the ridiculous jeans I embroidered myself. I feel so much better about my form now I'm wearing a binder again.

"Hey, this is the queer joy on display." I spread my arms wide and do a spin. When I look at him again, he's smiling and it's almost fond. I try, very hard, to feel nothing.

"Queer sarcasm, more like," Bastian says with a laugh, leaning over and throwing open the passenger door. "Come on."

I reluctantly climb in beside him, putting my backpack down in the footwell. I buckle myself in and instantly wish for one of those massive harnesses that descends down over your shoulders on The Smiler roller coaster at Alton Towers. I brace myself as Bastian puts it in gear with a crunch and we shudder towards the motorway, following the signs for Blackpool.

The rain that has been pouring in Manchester since Thursday, alternating between horrendous downpour and bone-chilling drizzle, has stopped for a rare moment. As we bomb up the M60, everything is damp and shiny, a glittering Saturday, the light reflecting off puddles in the road. High above the Trafford Centre and the M60 bridge and spinning out over the far hills of north Manchester, the sun is low and the clouds scattered and misty, as ragged as an old pair of trousers.

It's all so fresh and beautiful and I'm going on an adventure, so suddenly I'm filled with an unusual inexplicable delight at the world.

"So are we driving straight to the town?" I ask.

"Yep, we need to head to the beach at Lytham St Annes." My stomach contracts and I try to nod in an inconspicuous way. "It's one of the beaches there where they reckon Kilgrimol sunk."

I nod. I remember the legend that was told to me, growing up staring at the wide Irish Sea every morning. I remember the tolling bell that would drift, forgotten, off the sea on moonless nights, the sunken church steeple still making its haunted music. Bastian keeps talking, explaining, because of course he has no way to know that we're driving towards my hometown. *Why should I tell him?* I think to myself. *It's not any of his business.*

"Apparently it was swallowed up by the sea but still makes its presence known. People hear bells and singing and find bones, all the classic haunted underwater town stuff."

I nod like this is fascinating and pull out my phone, surreptitiously beginning to check my emails, searching for any from SouthernsConsulting@gmail.com. I see one, sent two weeks ago, with the subject heading: Paris in October. I breathe a sigh of relief. They won't be there.

"And we need to find a bone?" I say, tucking my phone away. "What, do we just pick up one of those sandcastle-making kits and start shovelling?"

"I've been thinking about it, I have a plan in mind," Bastian says, ignoring the person who is honking their horn violently behind him as he drives at sixty in the middle lane.

"What?"

"I've got it under control, don't worry," he says with a grin. I smile back tightly and try to relax my shoulders. *My parents are in Paris,* I tell myself. *They won't be there. No one needs to know.* It doesn't quite work so I take out *The Witchlore of Bodies* and pick up again on the part I reached the night before. Bastian looks at me in horror.

"You brought it with you?"

"Yeah, I'm reading the diary, it's interesting."

"It's an ancient magical grimoire and you've just been carrying it around?" Bastian swears as he swerves the car, tearing his eyes away from the grimoire and fixing them back on the road.

"It's fine, I keep it wrapped in a plastic bag."

"You're meant to be keeping it safe!"

"It is safe with me!" I can't explain to Bastian why I feel itchy whenever I consider leaving the grimoire under my bed, but I know that if I had left it behind today, I would have been worrying about it at the back of my mind. "I live in a house full of witches, Bastian. This way I make sure no one nicks it."

His jaw is ticking and his lips are pursed in anger. I can tell I'm not getting him on board so I decide to change tactic.

"Look, what if we need it for something to do with the spell? Doesn't it feel right that we have the grimoire with us when we're finding the essential components? I mean, isn't that what everyone says you should do with complicated gramarye? You wouldn't go shopping without the recipe, would you?"

"I suppose."

This is what we're all taught in class and I can see Bastian is swayed by it. I don't tell him the truth; that to me, doing this without the grimoire feels wrong, as if I'm leaving someone important out of a conversation.

"And look, it's really interesting reading too. This is from the First World War, listen—" I shuffle the book on my lap and read aloud:

"Father wants me to shift into a female form now that war has broken out, but I don't know how I could stand to lie to the lads here who are joining up. Lots of them are my friends, I saw them grow up, some of them marched with us and supported Mrs Pankhurst's cause. I can't let them go alone. There are terrible things happening in the world and it is my job to do my part, to speak up, to help where I can help. If I do not, what is there?"

"So they weren't into traditional gender stuff?" Bastian muses. "That seems unusual for the time period and for everything you've told me about shapeshifting culture."

"Yeah, it is." The thought of it makes me happy. "I get the impression they liked to shun shifter expectations."

"Kind of like you." Bastian grins. It's not a sarcastic smile or a wry smirk. It's genuine. I want to bat it off, to say something funny, but the words stick in my throat. I flush, even though I don't want to, and fix my gaze out of the window so I don't have to look at that smile any more.

"Thanks," I say quietly. I open my phone and find my photos of Elizabeth. I stare into her face and think about how good it will be when I have her back and how this tiny, fluttery feeling I have when Bastian compliments me will fade, it'll become nothing, when she's back in my arms.

As soon as we get out of the car and smell the salty air, I realize this was a bad idea. The sound of wheeling gulls immediately takes me back to my childhood: tuning into the sound of their mournful voices to ignore whatever recriminations my parents were shouting at me, shame curdling inside.

Stop it, I tell myself. *They're in Paris.*

If Bastian notices me withdrawing into myself, he doesn't say anything as he pays for parking and I follow him mutely into my childhood town.

"So this is Lytham St Annes," Bastian says, as we walk down the high street and past NatWest, the small pretty houses with their pointed roofs and the traditional shopfronts – the greengrocer, the fishmonger – with their green Victorian awnings on either side. "Seems like every other seaside town."

"Seems like it." I keep my voice light, attempting to hide the truth that I am holding my breath, hoping we don't run into anyone who could recognize me. Then, with a jolt, I realize that no one ever recognizes me. A sharp bitter wind is blowing off the sea and down the high street, pressing against us. In the off-season, it has that sleepy, neglected feeling, as if the closed-up pastel-coloured beach huts are props for a show that hasn't started yet. All the seaside accoutrement that usually hang from awnings, the aqua blue and hot pink inflatables and bodyboards in primary colours, are gone, and the residents and shoppers are dressed in heavy coats with umbrellas hanging on their arms. Some of them glance at us a little suspiciously, all eyes fixing on Bastian's face and then darting over my eccentric clothes that scream "gay as hell" at the top of their lungs. We're attracting a lot of "you're not from around here" kind of looks and it makes me want to run back to Manchester. Bastian's shoulders are so tense they're practically up by his ears. He catches my nervous gaze, his gait deliberately slowing down.

"You okay?" I ask quietly.

"I grew up in rural Cornwall," he says with a tight smile. "This is nothing."

"Okay." I nod, trying to ignore a couple who have walked past us and turned their heads back to stare. Bastian's back is rigid but he doesn't acknowledge them, glancing curiously down the road.

"I wonder if anything interesting happened here," Bastian muses, his casual tone hiding any discomfort he feels.

"You mean apart from the drowned town?"

"Let's get a coffee," Bastian says, jerking his head towards a tiny place that sells typical seaside tat, watercolour paintings of buckets and spades and candles that are supposed to smell like sea salt. Maybe he wants to get away from prying eyes or is just as freezing as I am. Perhaps a hot drink will thaw some of the coldness that seems to be infecting my blood, that old feeling of numbing my emotions to get through something. Not even my old navy wool peacoat, an item that used to belong to my father and was purchased in the thirties, is keeping out the chill.

"Oat latte?" Bastian asks me.

"Yes, please." I watch him through the window as he enters the coffee shop, trying to distract myself from thoughts of the past by examining him. I have that weird moment when you look at someone you sort of know and observe them from the outside, see them as a stranger again; more than a stranger, see them as *strange.* There's an oddness to everyone, even gorgeous people like Bastian. I notice the length of his neck, how his eyes are a little uneven, a scar I hadn't noticed on the back of his hand. Yet all of it makes him charming. I watch how the initially unsure barista is clearly falling in love with him by the second. I stare at him and wonder how he does it. It's sort of like Elizabeth, who was always kind, even when she was just buying coffee. Then I feel weird, looking at Bastian and thinking about Elizabeth.

"Here you go," Bastian says, handing me a coffee. I'm grateful as the warmth of the paper cup seeps into my fingertips. "There was an old photograph in there. Did you know there was a military hospital here during the First World War?"

"No."

I did. My parents bought their house here in the eighties but before that, my father lived in St Annes as a child in the early 1900s, when they still wore long bathing suits and people favoured those Victorian changing huts striped in red and white and looking like miniature circus tents. He's 113 now, late middle-aged for a shapeshifter, and even though I don't want to, I think about the town as he would have known it: bicycles and old-fashioned cars, milk floats and horses. In a way, his words made that St Annes more alive to me than the one I grew up in, the one I mostly saw through a window, passing me by.

I need to get out of here, I think. *Right now.*

"Let's get on with it," I say, leading the way to the only part of my hometown I really know. The sea.

We stand on North Beach at St Annes, staring out at the Irish Sea, whipped into a cold foam. I had hoped that being by the ocean would help snap me out of my growing unease, but the beach is deserted, the sand is gritty and stinging and it's that kind of fierce diagonal rain that is soaking through the back of my trousers. It's miserable and I feel like I am shrinking back into my childhood self: frantically escaping my parents' house, running down here, lungs aching with despair to scream at the uncaring ocean. It was the only thing wide enough to absorb my fury. Today it's particularly melancholic with Bastian standing in front of it, a solo figure against all that grey. He stopped in the town and bought a bag of crab bait. Bastian has his fingers spread, doing some kind of witchcraft, but his hands keep trembling and he has to stop, shaking them out, the feeling of him making magic, of heat around him, failing and chilling down with every attempt.

"Selkies?" I say, looking at the piles of bait in disgust. "That's your plan? Selkies."

"Well, yeah, it's a drowned village and we need a bone from it." Bastian launches another handful into the crashing white waves. "And they're seals, they like fish. The spell is like a lure: when they eat it they'll be drawn to us."

"How do you know?"

"I read it in a book. It's like the boggart, we'll get it on board."

"It's absolutely nothing like a boggart," I snap at him, folding my arms and holding my body close against the driving rain. Boggarts are nasty little buggers and selkies are majestic. As I look at the water, I think about all the times I've seen them here. All the times they've seen me. The past and the present are jumbling uncomfortably together inside my head.

"How would you even know?" Bastian snaps back. I don't want to tell him but I'm cold and annoyed and he has such a manner of an insufferable know-it-all man that the words are tumbling out of my mouth before I can stop them.

"I know this isn't even the best weather for them! They like things flat and glassy and, if possible, misty and frosty, so they can dip and sing without being noticed, and I know they absolutely would never be taken in by a lure or a witch trying to manipulate them!"

It's abruptly really frustrating that he can be so smart and not know all of this, and suddenly I'm pissed off at myself too. This is the second time I've gone into something simply trusting Bastian's plan and why? Because he's confident and erudite? What's so wrong with me that I don't think I could bring something valuable?

"And how the fuck do you know that?" Bastian demands.

"Because I grew up there!" I point down the beach in the direction of Lytham, to the semi-detached house on the front that was my home and my prison for sixteen years. "I grew up by the sea. I've seen selkies swim on this beach since I was young. Yeah, I've never read a book about it, but I *know* you don't just fling pitiful handfuls of crab bait into the bloody ocean to get their attention! They're dangerous and wise and they are NOT like fucking seals!"

Bastian stares at me. His hair is damp with rain and his denim jacket is turning from a faded acid wash to a dark damp blue. He looks taut with the cold and very, very irritated.

"You didn't tell me," he says. "That's pretty unhelpful of you."

A familiar despair, the crush of criticism, washes over me, and my body just does what it always does: turns tearfulness into anger.

"You want to talk about unhelpful?" I stamp my feet to try to keep the warmth in them. "You told me not to worry, that you had it under control. You didn't give me a *chance* to give you any input and my past is *my* business! I don't have to tell you anything!"

"Yes, you fucking do!" Bastian exclaims angrily. "I don't give a shit about your past, but you have to tell me how to deal with selkies so we can get this spell done so you can get your bloody girlfriend back!"

For Elizabeth, I think. This is why we're doing everything, for Elizabeth, but even knowing that, a part of me wants to get back in the car and drive away and not be on this beach that I've been on thousands of times before. I don't want to stand here in my memories, with Bastian and his questions. I've worked for the last two years to keep all of this here, away from my Manchester life. But then I think about how much I wanted to bring Elizabeth to the beach. I never mentioned it to her – I worried she'd think my upbringing was weird – but I fantasized about how it would be to have a day at the seaside with her, sleeping in the dunes, playing in the sea, getting sunburned and eating fish and chips out of paper, doing something lovely to erase all the ingrained tragedy. All of it culminates in one piercing conclusion: *I would do anything to get her back.* So I pull my coat off and drag my jumper over my head.

"What are you doing?" Bastian asks as I unlace my boots and stand on the sand, my toes curling against the chill of it.

"I'm doing what you want, I'm being helpful!" My teeth chatter as I walk down to the ocean, the skin on my arms pimpling against the frigid wind. "You're trying to manipulate a creature that has lived for hundreds of years. It's not going to work. We have to get their attention."

"You're going in?" Bastian exclaims, running alongside me. The water is freezing and my socks are instantly soaked. "Tell me what you're doing!"

"Stay here, it isn't safe for you." I stumble into the shallow waves, already feeling the pull of the tide, ready to drag me out and under. I'm going to let it.

"How do you get their attention?" Bastian yells after me.

"You get drowned!" I call back, and with that, I dive under a big wave.

Chapter Fifteen

It's icy, it's dragging, it's everything I remember from the first time I was saved by the selkies. It was right before college: I was alone, I slipped beneath the waves and was tumbling until a slick oiled body righted me. I'd felt them before, when I'd been allowed to swim in the sea in my childhood, their wide tails and their cool bodies flush against me and, occasionally, their coal-grey heads popping up beside me, gun-black eyes blinking. They were good companions for a lonely childhood and when the moment came, they saved me. I know just how to bring them to me again. All I have to do is let go. Stop swimming. Stop trying to push myself back up to the surface, let the weight of my jeans drag me under and close my eyes against the salt and the sound of waves churning. I only have one thought in my mind: it's Elizabeth, jumping on her trampoline, her golden hair flying in the air, the sunlight catching it and making it shine like a halo. If the selkies don't reach me in time, I think it's a pretty good last thought to have. I don't mean to, but a quiet, desperate voice that I haven't heard since the bathroom slips into my consciousness:

Maybe there's a better way to get to Elizabeth.

I feel something against me as I sink under the tide, a sleek body sliding against mine. I force my eyes open, catching that curious, coal-dark glare in swirling brown and grey water. I stare at them, knowing they must choose to save me. The eagerness of my own thoughts shocks me: *Please.*

Then it's sudden. I'm being pulled up and I break the surface, gasping with the air pushing into my lungs and the cold wind whipping my face. I kick to keep my head above the water, rolling with the waves crashing in a stormy symphony around me. A seal head looks at me, its inky eyes watching me struggle.

"*Hello, fellow skin changer.*" Selkie voices aren't melodious, the way people imagine mermaids to be: they're rough, like dried coral. "*Why do you come to our waters?*"

"I need a bone from Kilgrimol," I say, gasping as a wave tries to pull me under. I swallow a mouthful of salt water, rough and stinging, and cough brutally.

"*You risk your life for this?*"

"It's for a spell, to bring someone back."

"*Someone you love?*"

"Loved, love, yes." I struggle to keep my head above water. My legs are tired. I should have stripped my jeans off. "Can you help me?"

The selkie gives me a long, steady look. Seals usually look happy, adorable, but selkie eyes have a depth in them, as black as the deep ocean floor.

"*I will do this if you swear to be careful with your life. This is the second time we have pulled you from the tides. There will not be a third.*"

I gulp back salt water and tears – I can't tell which is which out here – and everything is becoming grey; the frothing, slate ocean, the bitter cold wind and the sky pressing down on me.

"I...I promise to try," I say. I don't blink as I look into its eyes. I feel like it's examining me entirely, seeing everything I've done since we were last together. Maybe selkies can do that; I'm not sure. They have ancient power inside them, their magic unyielding and mesmerizing and wildly unpredictable. It could very well decide to let me drown.

"That is sufficient." It swims closer, bigger and stronger than a grey seal, and I wrap my arms around it, clinging to the barnacles that adorn its back, a sturdy body that has swum in these waters longer than time can tell. *"We must dive for it. Our magic will help you, but your breath may fail."*

"Let's do it!" I shout as a wave tries to tug me away from it. I heave my shoulders above the water, taking one last deep gasp of air before we plummet beneath the waves. Selkies are fast and deadly. Swimming with one is like the descent of a diving hawk. It's so fast it's almost nauseating. I barely feel the water passing me, rather that there is immense pressure around me, increasing by the second, and freezing, deep coldness squeezing my face and arms and legs. The deeper we go, the tighter the air in my chest becomes and the sharper the pain in my head, as if someone has put a vice around it and is pinching, slowly. Still, I hold on for dear life, just a little further, because if I let go now I will absolutely drown here, deep beneath the waves.

The abyss below the crashing waves is quiet, eerie, becoming nothing but grey shapes and sudden looming rocks, silver bodies of fleeting fish and wondrous broad, ragged tails of other selkies. Then suddenly, tombstones. Time-worn gravestones from bygone ages, the drowned town of Kilgrimol, its churchyard turned from a grassy hill to a watery, sandy grave. I see a bone sticking out of the ashy sand, white as dried cuttlefish, catching the little light that pierces this low under the sea. I flail my hands for it, telling the selkie we must stop, and with a flash of teeth, it has the bone in its mouth. Then, with a wide swish of its great tail that has my hands scrabbling to hold on, we are surfacing. The journey upward seems agonizingly long, the bubble of air in my lungs shrinking painfully until I feel as if it is just the tightest squeeze behind my eyes – a little bit further, just a little bit – my eyes are closing, my grip slipping – then we break the surface and there is air again. I'm gasping, I'm wide-mouthed and so desperate to gulp down wind and salty air that I swallow mouthfuls of a wave and choke violently, my chest screaming with pain.

"*It is done,*" the selkie says. "*Remember your promise.*"

Blinking stinging salt out of my squinting eyes, I can see Bastian standing knee-deep in the waves, shouting words that I can't hear. The selkie bobs beside me with the bone in its mouth. Absurdly, I think of René. My legs are so tired and I still need to try and get back to shore, but the hardest part is done surely. I'm nearly there.

"Thank you." I cough, leaning forward to take the bone from its teeth. It feels like a shell, smooth and weathered, and as soon as I touch it, light explodes from inside me. I disappear into a world that isn't mine, a memory that isn't mine, with only one thought to hold onto: *Not again.*

I am in pain. The wound in my thigh is on fire and I can't move. All I can see is the nurse above me, telling me that I'll be all right, that I'm going into surgery. I look down and see the remnants of my green uniform as they cut it off me.

"Come in from Ypres," the nurse is saying. "Another batch, just as bad as the last."

"Gas?" someone asks. I look up into the face of a red-headed doctor in a white coat, his face serious.

"Bayonet wound to the thigh and then shrapnel wounds."

I can remember getting it, slipping in the mud of no man's land, the stinging pain that had me falling before anyone could help me and then the explosion. I was drowning in mud, and now it's like the bright hospital lights are burning me. I can smell the sea, hear English voices.

"Calm down," the doctor says. "You're in the military hospital in St Annes. You're home."

"Count backwards from ten." Someone fits a mask over my face and then all I can see are red circles, a deep pool dragging me down into nothing.

Chapter Sixteen

"Lando, fucking hell, not again!"

Someone is pumping up and down on my ribs. My chest is sore and aching, different and yet familiar. No boobs and my jeans don't fit right. Even before I wake up, I know what's happened. I've shifted again. There is an inexplicable warm whooshing feeling in my chest, surging up my windpipe. I cough out salt water, turning my head to throw up a bit, feeling harsh sand prickling against my eyelids and catching the corners of my lips. A hand is rubbing my back and there's a faint blue glow around me, a telltale smell on the air that makes me think someone has lit a barbecue in the dunes. I realize Bastian must have put some magic into his CPR and I sit up groggily. He's kneeling next to me, also soaked to the skin, and glaring furiously.

"What in the pissing hell do you think you're doing?" Bastian yells.

"I'm fine," I cough out. I feel like my insides are waterlogged, like the sponge of my lungs has absorbed the entire ocean.

"You drowned!" Bastian glares at me. "I saw the light, I saw you go frigid, I saw you go under and then I pulled you out and you weren't bloody *breathing—*"

"It was a shift, I couldn't help it."

"This isn't a normal shift—"

"What the hell do you know about shifting?" I demand between gasps, the cold rain stinging my face and my muscles trembling uncontrollably. He's right, none of this is normal, but I don't want to tell him that. I don't want to see the look on his face when I admit that I'm not just shapeshifting but having *visions* about a past I know nothing about.

"I've read books!" Bastian yells. "You can't just walk into the sea and try to drown yourself!"

I hate that he's shouting at me; I can feel shocked tears welling up, but I push them down. I got the bone, that's all that matters.

"Where is it?" I scramble, patting my clothes, and look up. Bastian is holding it in his hand.

"The selkie brought you closer to shore, it was caught under your T-shirt." He drops it on the sand beside me with a wet, emphatic *thunk* of rebuke. "Great plan, Lando, really well thought out!"

"I got it, didn't I?" I hold up the bone, my teeth chattering. "My plan worked, so why are you being so fucking mean?"

"Because you're so fucking reckless!" Bastian is shaking too. The sun has started to set behind the town and the beach is entirely shaded and freezing cold. His face is pinched and livid, his hair sticking to his forehead like seaweed.

"Yeah, I'm reckless, I'm suicidal!" I stagger to my feet, wobbly again, and instantly sink back down to my knees, words spilling out of my mouth. "None of this should be a surprise to you. We started this whole thing on the premise that it's dangerous and I'm not afraid to do anything to get Elizabeth back!"

"I don't want you to die, is that so much to ask?" Bastian explodes. I feel breathless at his words and it's not the weight of my sodden binder, cold and pressed against my chest.

"You don't want me to die, or you don't want me to die before the spell is over?" I sneer. "Don't act like this is some incredibly selfless act on your part!"

"Oh my god, you're SO ridiculous!" Bastian yells to the sky and I think I might hate him. I don't know why, but in a lifetime of being called ridiculous for being too emotional, for being non-binary, for being myself, this is the one that tips me over the edge.

"I'm ridiculous? OF COURSE I'm ridiculous!" I scream at him, my words snatched away on the howling wind, managing to launch to my feet, swaying. "My fucking girlfriend DIED!"

"You're not the only one with problems!" Bastian screams back. We stare at one another, both violently shaking in the cold. The edge of the waves is lapping around Bastian's wet trainers. He shakes his head and starts twisting his fingers, his blue sapphire ring glowing, casting uncanny reflections against the wet sand.

"What the hell are you doing?" I stammer out, my teeth chattering.

"The heating spell," he grunts. "So you don't die of hypothermia."

"I don't need your bloody help!" I snap, but I immediately crumble back down onto the sand. His fingers are shaking and the light around his ring is stuttering, dimming. He grits his teeth and growls in annoyance as he presses his shaking fingertips in the Logi's Spear position against my wet top. It heats up slightly, so now it is sopping wet and warm rather than just sopping wet, but then Bastian shakes out his trembling hands in frustration.

"Shit, I don't have enough power. I'm too tired from dragging you out of the sea and the goddamned spell I used to unblock your airway." He runs a shaking hand through his hair. The heating spell is no match for the cold wind off the Irish Sea and I'm still shivering, starting to feel tired and sleepy with it. I list towards him and he swears again.

"Come on." I let him pull me upwards and immediately stagger. My legs are wooden and completely out of my control. Bastian quickly pulls my wet arm over his shoulder, half dragging me back up to where my coat, jumper and boots are.

"We need to get you somewhere to get warm." Bastian shivers, pulling on his denim jacket and throwing my coat over my shoulders as I stuff my sodden socks with sand stuck to them back in my boots. "You said you grew up around here?"

"I'm not going there, let's just drive back—" I stutter.

"Lando, I'm worried you're going into shock. You almost *drowned*," he says, crouching beside me and pressing icy cold fingertips to my pulse. "I could get us a hotel but it will take too long so it's this or A&E. What's it going to be?"

I see his logic. Just the idea of getting back to the car seems impossible and the house I grew up in is less than five minutes away. I think longingly of getting out of the wind and my wet hair is starting to freeze my brain. *They're in Paris,* I tell myself. *The house will be empty.* I nod wearily, and Bastian lets out a huff of relief before throwing my backpack over one shoulder and dragging me slowly back towards the car.

The vintage Mini doesn't have proper heating, just a hot-air blower that I press my frigid fingers against as I give Bastian curt directions along the seafront to my parents' house. We pull into the driveway of the semi-detached Georgian-style red-brick, separated from the wide expanse of the sky of East Beach by a neatly kept green and a long, flat road. He comes round to open my door, carefully helping me out of the car like I'm particularly frail, which isn't very flattering, but I'm grateful because my feet are so cold they've sort of gone numb.

"Come in," I mutter, fumbling as I put my key in the door. I nearly fall through it when it opens abruptly. I stare at the woman on the other side, perfect blond hair waved in that classic 1920s style, her eyebrows flawless and frowning, always frowning. She looks at me with no recognition for a moment, until she takes in my coat, my boots, my earrings and the key in my hand.

"Orlando," she says. Her voice is just the same: melodious, with a clipped London accent reminiscent of her class and the time that she grew up in, utterly different from mine, which adapted to the north-east brogue of the postman and milkman.

"Mother. You're supposed to be in Paris," I say. Her frown deepens.

"Your father is in Paris. I am due to join him tonight, my taxi will be here in ten minutes. I put it all in the email."

The accusation that I never read her emails beyond the subject line hangs in the air between us. Behind her legs, I see the small suitcase she always takes, an old-fashioned one without wheels and made of leather embossed with SOUTHERNS on the side. She's looking me up and down with a critical eye.

"What have you done now?" she asks sharply.

"Nothing," I say automatically, and feel Bastian gripping my arm tightly. I look at him as he frowns between me and my mother, clearly trying to make sense of our unusually hostile dynamic. I don't really want to hang around long enough for him to figure it out. "Let's...let's just get back in the car."

"Are you kidding?" he hisses at me as I lean even more of my weight against him. "You drowned!"

"Shh!" I hiss back, but my mother simply raises one arched brow and sighs with a slight slump of her normally rigid shoulders.

"Again?" she says to me. I don't answer. With a click of her teeth, she opens the door wider, which Bastian takes as an invitation before I can even protest and manoeuvres me over the threshold. When she closes the door behind us and the whistling wind is shut out, I am suddenly filled with a sense of urgent claustrophobia. I've not been in a space with just my mother since I left for college. Part of me hoped I never would be again. Both of my parents still prefer to dress in post-wartime garb – a lot of tweed, wool and linen – and tonight, in wide-legged palazzo trousers and suiting, she is frustratingly glamorous. She looks me up and down in my scruffy clothes and steps closer. I try not to flinch back. Then she lifts a delicate hand and pinches my wrist. I know she's only taking my pulse but I can't help it, I stiffen and hold my breath, fighting every instinct honed in childhood to snatch my arm back and run straight up to my bedroom.

"Well, you are not dying," she says blandly, her frown smoothing away as she drops my arm and looks at Bastian. "You are?"

"Bastian Chevret," he says.

"We go to college together," I say. Mother's eyes narrow slightly and I know that she's thinking about Elizabeth, the last person who I had a college acquaintance with.

"Chevret," she repeats softly. "A French name, *non*?"

As she speaks, a glittery white sheen of magic flutters over her features. Her hair shifts from blond to dark, her eyes from blue to brown. The scent of her magic that comes off her in waves is overwhelmingly familiar, pungent lilies, the smell of the worst moments of my childhood. I am glad Bastian's standing next to me, stinking of salt and ocean. Bastian, I notice, has gone slack-jawed and wide-eyed, instinctively looking at her hands, expecting to see a ring and movement, and finding none, he looks even more impressed. I glare at her for this ridiculous overt display of exactly how shapeshifters should be able to manage their power, to fluidly alter their bodies at will. *Making me look bad, as usual.*

"Yes, Haitian, my dad grew up in Quebec," he says eagerly. *He can't take his eyes off her,* I think with disgust. "You know French?"

"I was there during the war," she says smoothly. I could roll my eyes at this veiled boasting; everyone knows that the main thing shapeshifters were utilized for in the war was spying, and it's clearly worked. Bastian is looking at her – the flawless skin, the high cheekbones, everything about her that doesn't look a day over fifty-five when, really, she's over a hundred – with such awe. Then he looks at me, and I know he's trying to work out what makes me so completely shit at all this. Mother smiles, as if she sees his exact train of thought. Her perfect eyes rest on me.

"Still refusing to settle in a form, I see, Orlando," she says, then clicks her teeth when she touches my wet hair. I can't help but stiffen under her touch. She sighs heavily, as if my turning up looking like a drowned rat is a deliberate fashion choice designed to irritate her, and spreads her fingers in the triangle position. Panic surges through me, tasting like tannin on the back of my tongue. The jerk of adrenaline thunders painfully in my jaw and is accompanied by a singular, all-encompassing thought: *Fuck, no.* I stagger backwards, bumping into Bastian, my heart racing as I try to get away from the magic inside her, the ominous white light gathering in her palms. She has an expression of such powerful disappointment that I have to look down at my soggy boots. "It was only going to be a drying spell," she says.

"I'll just change and sit by the fire," I mumble. The awkwardness stretches. She always makes me feel this way, ungainly and clownish, naive and overly sensitive next to her implacable veneer of smoothness. Mother looks at Bastian.

"Forgive my daughter," she says with the politest of smiles. The one she uses to humiliate me. "She's always been uncomfortable with magic. If you could credit it."

"*They*," I say forcefully. "And I wonder why."

She simply looks at me, as if I am the puzzle piece that refuses to fit and she didn't cover me with the anger of her unmet expectations every day of my childhood.

"Your father was disappointed that we needed to send you the shroud," she says softly. "There is a new tutor in Paris, up and coming, in fact. He would be more than happy to—"

"No," I say firmly. No more tutors or specialists or tortures they call "techniques". I won't go back. "I'm working it out. On my own."

We stare at one another. I can feel Bastian starting to fidget, because she is always the one who brings an air of etiquette to every situation and my bluntness, my rudeness, is like a social burr in the cogs of this exchange. This is what she does, turning even the most brash of witches into bumbling courtiers, cordially offering her back phrases they would never normally use – "Oh, thank you ever so much" and "Quite kind of you to offer" – and then every cruelty she gives me, every delicately crafted embarrassment can only be met with pleasantries. I won't do it any more. I refuse to say thank you, even if they raised me that it was the only correct thing to do. This was a house that esteemed politeness, all the way until the front door closed. Then, behind it, there was nothing but frosty recriminations. Finally, she blinks, and I know it's over. This is how battles are won here, with a protest of silence.

"So I see." Her eyes slide to Bastian and then back to me. There is a barely perceptible lift of the corner of her mouth, the edge of a sneer. "Another witch."

It's so rude, so unnecessary, and yet Bastian says nothing, because why would he? She's an enchanting shapeshifter, she can get away with anything, but I know that comment wasn't for him. I remember the look on her face the one time she came to the hospital after my suicide attempt, when Counsellor Cooper explained about Elizabeth. The utter disdain, bordering on disgust. I won't take the bait. Instead I look at the clock in the hallway.

"You should meet your taxi," I say. "You know they get the house number wrong."

She gives me a steady look, as if to tell me I will not be the one to dismiss her.

"Get warmed up," she says softly. "There's kindling for the fire. There is food in the house. Your things are under the stairs. We turned your bedroom into a reading room but the sheets in the guest bedroom are clean. Please set the alarm when you are done, the code is the same."

She pulls on a brown trench coat and a wide-brimmed hat. She looks like a movie star, but then she always did. She nods to Bastian. "Good evening, *Monsieur Chevret.*"

"Nice to meet you," he mumbles, helping me shuffle to the side as she picks up her suitcase and opens the door. I think she's going to leave without saying another word to me but she turns, shimmering, as her eyes turn back to blue, to look at me.

"Read your emails, Orlando," she says finally. "It is not too much to ask."

Then she is stepping out into the darkness, holding her hat to her head as she walks down the driveway to the waiting taxi. It's only when I've seen her get into the car, when I know that I'm safe from any final recriminations and I begin to feel the tiniest bit of blessed relief, that I let the door slam in response.

CHAPTER SEVENTEEN

Just for good measure, I give the front door an angry kick – *hateful woman, just the worst person in the world* – but I've not actually got enough energy for it and Bastian catches me before I sway into the wall.

"Where's the fire?" he asks.

"This way."

With my arm still pulled around his shoulder, we awkwardly walk through the door to the living room. My parents haven't updated their style since the thirties: art deco wallpaper in fern green and gold, dark wood panelling, furniture with faded William Morris patterns and small mahogany drinks tables with carved spiral legs. All of it has a hint of the magical, the bizarre, to it; it's dusty and overstuffed with trinkets from the century of travel – enchanted Venetian masks and crystal charms in velvet boxes – scattered everywhere. The TV is the only modern appliance in here and stands out like a sore thumb. When I was growing up, all of it made me feel as if I were living in a museum designed to make me feel bad about myself. Now, compared to Bastian's sleek flat it looks comically cluttered, perhaps even chintzy or, worse, embarrassingly outdated and colonial. I grimace.

Bastian has already moved to feed kindling and rolled-up newspaper into the fire and it roars into red and gold life. I awkwardly crumple down on the Turkish rug in front of it, happy to bathe myself in its warmth, even though my skin is so cold it actually feels like it's burning in the heat. Bastian slumps down beside me, reaching into the brass coal bucket to feed the fire with the brass tongs. I feel suddenly sleepy, like I might not be able to get back up, and know I should get out of my wet clothes.

"I'm going to change," I say. "Do you need dry clothes?"

"No, I'll just take my jeans off." Bastian is still shaking. He reaches for a tartan blanket that's spread over the back of the sofa. "I'll build the fire up."

"Thanks." I stumble into the hall to the cupboard under the stairs, kneeling down and dragging out one of the boxes marked ORLANDO. I pull out a hoodie, a pair of surf shorts and ski socks. Standing in the hall, I wrench my boots off my cold, stiff feet and drag down my tight, frozen jeans. I rip off my sodden T-shirt and struggle out of my cold binder, taking a second to recognize the strangeness of this male body all over again. First, the longer, goatish legs with the fiery red hair on my thighs and in a furry trail from my belly button. Then the narrow hips and shoulders, the extra bit of height and the broadness of the backs of these new hands. I pull on the dry clothes and catch sight of myself in the hall mirror. My jaw is large and square, my nose broad, my eyebrows red; my hair is that deep ginger that's closer to brown than blond, shorter and tufty. My skin has a very pink, ruddy quality to it, the kind that sunburns in winter. I can already tell I'll have to shave my face. I cautiously pull the sleeve of the hoodie down to cover the scars on my wrist. Wearily, I move back into the lounge.

Bastian is sitting by the fire and feeding kindling into a strong, crackling flame. He's got a blanket spread around his shoulders and one across his lap. His wet jeans are on the back of a chair and his ankles and shins are visible, tucked underneath him, flecked with fluffy hair. I look away.

"So," Bastian says quietly. "You're not an orphan?"

"No, I'm not," I say.

"What's the story there?"

"There's no story." I reach for the extra blanket, a dense Tibetan thing with red stripes that's folded under the sofa, and shake it out, wrapping it around my shoulders before standing up. "I'm going to make tea."

I move through to the kitchen, turning on the light. They've changed a few things since I was last here, finally getting rid of the hideous avocado-green fridge and the yellowed Laura Ashley wallpaper, but the ancient Aga and the grimy brown filter-coffee machine that's about forty years old are the same. Even so, I'm disorientated; it takes me a minute to find the teabags. Luckily, there's some milk left in the fridge. I try not to feel anything when I notice familiar little things. Father's kukicha blend that he has every morning, the woody smell of it drifting across the kitchen flagstones. Mother's collection of teacups from around the world stored up on hooks, French glass and Chinese jade hanging in neat rows. I fill two cups from the willow-patterned set and return to the lounge, finding Bastian standing up, looking around the room, taking in the travel souvenirs, photographs, ancient books and priceless witchlore artefacts that mark every part of my parents' lives together. I very deliberately do not look at his boxers, striped blue. I hand him a tea and sit down, wishing he would cover up. *Why do I care?* I ask myself fiercely, glaring into the fire. *I love Elizabeth.*

"This house is fascinating," he murmurs, sipping his tea reflectively. I glance at him nervously.

"It's less of a house, more an antiques shop with too much stock," I say.

"A *magical* antiques shop." Bastian's eyes gleam as he gazes around. "Is that really a collection of shrouds over there?"

"Yes." I glare at it, the ostentatious curiosity case mounted on the wall, polished wood and miniature filigree gold clasps, the eight or nine shroud necklaces twinkling innocuously behind the glass, hanging on little hooks against black satin. If anything, it's the item in this house I despise the most.

"The gemstones are incredible," Bastian says reverently. "Are they all enchanted?"

"No, thank god," I mutter into my tea. When Bastian looks at me questioningly, I feel like I have to say something and the truth might at least shut him up. "They scoured the world, looking for shrouds of different strengths to use on me. Some of them have worse impacts than others. That one" – I point to the giant onyx stone on a leather braided necklace – "made me have seizures. It hurt more than shifting."

Bastian says nothing. I wonder what he's thinking as he frowns and looks around. Maybe he's wondering how anyone can grow up around this much witchlore, this much culture, and be unhappy. But then he didn't spend days under the onyx shroud, having so many fits his nose bled.

"There are no photos of you," Bastian says.

"Yeah, no surprise there." I sip the tea and wince. It tastes weird with the residue of salt and sand in my mouth.

"You can't say there's no story here. Everything here is a story," Bastian says flatly. "You have a mum. You have a house. I presume you have a dad in Paris and yet you let everyone think you're an orphan."

"I am. Technically."

"What?"

"I'm adopted," I say. "My biological parents are dead, or so I'm told. Besides, I didn't *let* people think anything, they made assumptions without asking. It's not my job to correct that."

"Yeah, but why?" Bastian presses. "She seems like she cares, so did you fall out or...?"

He lets the sentence hang. I sigh and stare into the fire. He was honest with me about his crappy parents. It only seems fair I return the favour.

"She impressed you, didn't she?" I say quietly. "So poised, so full of magic? It's fine if she did, she's very impressive."

"Yeah," Bastian admits. "I've never... Your shifts are just so different. Hers are so fluid."

"Yes, they are." I try to keep my tone as level as possible. "She's impressive and she's only impressed by people who can use their skill in the same way she can. So imagine how she felt when the shifter baby they longed for, the shifter baby they adopted, turned out to be an utter dud. If she seems like she cares, it's because she cares about me getting better."

"Well, that's good."

"No, not getting healthier. Getting better at shapeshifting, whatever the cost," I say sharply. "It's all she has ever cared about."

I set my tea down on the carpet and rub my ankles. They're sore but not as sore as they were when I did my shift at Boggart Hole Clough. I wonder if changing more frequently makes it actually less painful on my joints. I've never shifted so quickly in my life, so I don't know.

"You don't understand shapeshifters," I say, with a shake of my head. "You don't understand how they feel about witchcraft."

"Oh, you think I didn't notice your mum's barely veiled disdain for witches?" he says scornfully. "Or how you flinched from her magic? I'm not asking to be inducted into the secrets of shapeshifter society, I'm just interested in you."

I sigh and stare at a photo of my parents in front of the Leaning Tower of Pisa from the 1950s, the photograph grainy and black-and-white. They look just as they do now, as if a child has had no impact on them. I try to find words for the quiet, steady detachment of their lives from mine, for the years of pain and disappointment.

"*We are magic. They can never have it, they can never take it away from us, and for this, they will always hate us. They will never trust us. Remember that,*" I recite. "Shifters are taught really young that our only value is our magic. Our ability to shift is what keeps us safe: safe from humans, safe from witches. As long as we're magically powerful then we can hold onto our place in society. Witches will tolerate us because we're useful and humans in government will want to utilize our skills. Without our powers, we're nothing."

"Okay," Bastian says with a frown. "And because you can't do magic, your parents...?"

I stare into the fire. I don't want to have to look at him when I explain this: my mother's frustration, my father's furious disappointment.

"They wanted a child who would fit in, but I knew early on that I was never going to fit. It hurt them, I think, that they couldn't have natural children. Shifter families are so small anyway, children are important. That's all they wanted from me, really, all they asked for. That I would be a good shifter child."

"And...you're not that?"

I shake my head painfully. It feels like there's a lump in my throat that won't go down.

"Most shifter children start shifting early, they've usually settled on a resting form by the time they're five or six but I... well, I didn't."

"What did you do?"

"I wouldn't shift. I couldn't perform any magic either. I've never been able to. They were so disappointed I wasn't like *them.*" I can't stop the derision leaking into my voice. "They'd hire shifter nannies and tutors, anyone who might get me onto a normal shifting schedule."

"So you were homeschooled?"

"Yeah, but…worse." I stare at the window. "They tried all sorts of things to make me normal. The shrouds were just the tip of the iceberg, but whatever they did, I just couldn't shift at will. There was a time where I didn't shift for years, I was nine but I looked about seven still. God, that was the worst. They wouldn't let me outside, sometimes for months and months. This…" I stare around the lounge, remembering long days with my face pressed against the window. *Come away, Orlando! Until you can shift to look appropriate and without causing suspicion, you can't play outside!* "This was like a prison. For them too. They were stuck with me as much as I was stuck with them."

"I don't think it's the same." Bastian looks doubtful. "They were your parents. They had a responsibility."

"They think their responsibility is to keep me safe as a shapeshifter, no matter what. Pain and discomfort, they just think that's necessary for learning, for the greater good."

"And what's the greater good?" Bastian looks a little disgusted.

"Learning to control my shapeshifting and my magic." I shrug. "They think a shifter who can't do witchcraft, who can't access the truth inside themselves, is like a bird with a broken wing, vulnerable to predators."

"To witches, they mean."

I nod.

"That's…dark," Bastian says. His voice is very bleak and he looks at me with a slightly shocked expression. "You do know what they did is dark, right?"

I want to say, *Of course I fucking know, I lived it,* but there's a part of me that still, inexplicably, rises up and wants to say, *It wasn't that bad, you don't understand.* So I say nothing. Bastian waits for a moment and then shakes his head.

"If they're so worried about keeping you safe, how come they let you go to college?"

"Ha, that was intervention." I shake my head. "I told my A-level tutor I wanted to go to Manchester Uni and study a non-witch course, like creative writing. My parents were horrified and enrolled me in Demdike as soon as they could. They were disgusted by the idea that I was going to...surrender to it. Stop trying to shift, stop trying to do magic. Live as a human."

"Wow." Bastian takes a glug of tea. "How did that go?"

"There was no point in fighting it." I remember how desolate it felt that day, being told that what I saw as my chance to get out, to maybe be normal, had been snatched away. It was the first time the selkies had saved my life, when I recklessly went for a swim with a foolish idea I might even be able to swim to Ireland to get away from them. My parents saw it as a suicide attempt and perhaps it was, but at least the result of it was that they took my request to live away from them in Manchester seriously. "I asked to live in student accommodation. They said yes. My shifts had started to be the right age for some reason." I glare at the rain against the windows, remembering the long rainy days shut inside. "I realized that if I went to Demdike, I would still be getting out of here, at least."

"They didn't bring you home? After..." Bastian looks at my wrist.

"They haven't abandoned me entirely. They pay the rent at Beryl's, they get updates from my counsellor and from Professor Wallace. That's the closest to mental health care my parents can manage." I smile wryly. "But not because they're mean or want to punish me, they just don't care enough. They don't care that I'm queer, they don't care that I tried to kill myself, all they want is for me to be like them."

It feels good to say the truth. I realize I haven't told anyone that before, not even Elizabeth. She just thought we had a bad relationship, filled with animosity. The truth is simpler and more brutal, yet I've never said it aloud until now: my parents don't love me enough to care about me. Not the real me, anyway. We're just three people who endured these horrible years of a shared existence that wasn't satisfying for anyone. That's what I tell myself. What I'm not telling myself is that if there was a returns policy on orphans, they would have sent me back long ago. Or that sometimes, their lack of love, the punishments and treatments for my own good, felt like it was twisting into loathing.

"I feel like I'm supposed to say that's not true but I don't think my dad cares about me either," Bastian says after a long pause. "All he cares about is pushing on, forgetting the past at any expense, even when it costs him his wife, his relationships with his family. He says he can still be proud of his heritage without magic, but he can't see how hurtful that is to Pépé and Grandma Olive. It feels like he's chopped away a whole part of himself and he doesn't care that he's cutting me out of his life, too. That he's leaving me alone, no coven, nothing."

"You could join a coven here, in the north," I say, trying to be positive but immediately feeling how paltry it is. Like if someone were to say to me, *You can just get another girlfriend,* about Elizabeth.

"I'm only in college here for one more year and what's the point?" Bastian snorts. "People always leave."

I can't disagree with that. Bastian stares into the fire, his voice becoming more reflective.

"In films, grief always brings people together, doesn't it? When parents lose a child it makes them so protective of the kid that's left. It's sort of romantic, right? I guess a part of me thought it would happen to us too. But it's nothing like that. It's...grief made us all strangers who just happened to live together."

"I get that," I say softly, because I really do. Bastian has given words to the worst part of my childhood – that the people I lived with weren't my parents. I didn't love them; I just felt supremely awkward around them because they never seemed to know what do to with me. The best emotion my parents ever displayed to me was indifference.

Bastian shakes his head slowly.

"There are some people who shouldn't have been parents."

I'm surprised but I give him an appreciative look. His face is calm, reflective. He doesn't think I'm weird for being unwanted – he feels unwanted too. I know I should feel sorry for him but I don't. Right now, I'm just glad that he gets it. Right now, I'm grateful that I'm not alone. We both sit as the fire crackles, staring into its flames. I sigh heavily and stretch my neck from one side to the other and then roll my head. My skull feels heavier than before, as if I've gained a few centimetres, and my nose feels different too. Then I catch Bastian watching me, an amused expression on his face.

"What?" I ask warily.

"You're in a male form again," he says softly.

"How can you be sure?" I demand, lifting my eyebrow.

"This." Bastian's gentle finger touches my Adam's apple and it's like an electric shock. I feel it echoing through me in ways it shouldn't, and I jump back, immediately shooting my arms behind me to stop myself falling. *No, absolutely not,* I scold myself internally. *I won't feel those things.*

"One thing to learn about shifters," I say, making my voice as hard as possible as I glare at him. "It's always best not to assume."

"Okay." He's frowning and his eyes look a little hurt, a little confused, but I don't care. I don't want these feelings and if pushing him away a bit stops them, then so be it. I watch him feed newspaper into the fire and the blaze grows stronger, the warmth of the outside of my skin matching the strange lurching feeling in the middle of my cold chest. I won't touch him again, not if that's going to happen; I think I would rather never be touched again. Instead, I drain my teacup.

"I'm hungry," Bastian says. "You?"

"Not really. I'm never that hungry after shifting, just thirsty," I say. "But feel free to raid the kitchen."

"Okay." Bastian leaves the room. I can hear him opening and shutting cupboards and while he does, I pull out my phone and send a message to Beryl, letting her know I'm not coming back tonight. Then I get *The Witchlore of Bodies* out of my bag (thank god for my ingenious decision to wrap it in plastic, as my bag is utterly rain-soaked) and flip the pages, trying to find the place I left off. I have a theory that I want to test about what I saw in my vision in the water. A heavy thunder begins inside my ribcage as I read the words:

> Father is unhappy. He has aged so much since I came back from Ypres. Mother comes to the hospital to care for me, but I do not know if I will ever walk the same way again. He wants me to promise that I will shift into a female form and not go back to the front. I don't know how to explain that I have friends who are dying there, left to rot in the fields of Belgium and France. I don't know how to explain that while it feels abhorrent to turn my back on them, there is nothing I want to do more. When I dream, I relive the moment after the explosion, the rain of mud, entombing me under the earth. I never want to go back there and yet, out there is the only place where I feel like I make sense any more.

I feel dizzy as I look at the shapeshifter's words, like I might be about to have a panic attack, but maybe that's because I can still taste the chloroform they used to put me to sleep in the hospital for my wounded leg. Except none of it was me, they're not my memories, so what are they doing in my head? There are no names or places in the diary, but could it be that the shifter in the book really did end up at a hospital here in St Annes? Though...why would I be having visions of their memories, and only when I shift? None of it makes sense.

Suddenly, I wish Elizabeth was here. She was the first person I could talk to about being a shifter. I never told her the stuff I told Bastian, the stuff he called dark, but just being able to trust someone enough to admit it was complicated was very meaningful. I'd never had anyone in whom I could confide how hard it was to live in my body, without them throwing it back in my face. She was always kind, always sympathetic. I know she would listen if I told her about these dreams or visions, the way my mind is full of memories that aren't mine. She might even have an idea of why it's happening, or at least, she'd want to find out. I smile a little to myself as I imagine her diving head first into the library. She loved a magical mystery. That's what took us to the cave, after all, her desperation to help me do magic. I feel a swell of familiar guilt all over again. *Does it matter why it's happening?* I ask myself angrily. *Isn't it all worth it if I get her back?*

Chapter Eighteen

"Hey, I wanted to ask you something." Bastian sits back down beside me, his hand in a big bag of Hula Hoops and putting a packet of Bourbons between us. Despite still feeling gross from the shift, I rip the packet open and go to town on the biscuits. With my mouth full of chocolate, I sigh. It helps a bit.

"Okay," I say through biscuit crumbs.

"This thing with you and Carl," he says.

"Such a wanker." I roll my eyes while pulling apart a bourbon to lick out the middle.

"That's...so nasty." Bastian stares at me with reluctant fascination. "Why don't you just eat it?"

"I like it this way." I shrug. "What do you want to ask about Carl? If you want to know what terrible thing made him such a bully, I don't know, I think he probably came out of the womb twisted."

"What's the deal with the two of you?" Bastian frowns. "He seems to really hate you and it's not that he's a homophobe—"

"No, he is definitely not a homophobe," I mutter. Bastian

looks at me sharply and I know I've said the wrong thing. He's frowning. He's working it out. I stuff a biscuit in my mouth.

"Did he...try something with you?" Bastian asks. I'd always thought that if someone asked me about this they'd sound incredulous, they'd be mocking, they'd instantly dismiss the notion that someone like Carl Lord would try to hit on me and I wouldn't want it. Bastian doesn't sound like that. He sounds concerned. When I look at his face, it's intent; he's concentrating on me very carefully. I just know that he's not going to judge me. I brush oily chocolate residue off my lips and nod.

"We were friends at the beginning of college. He...well, he kept trying to kiss me."

"What?" Bastian's voice is dangerous suddenly.

"It wasn't that bad," I say hastily. "It was just...like, he would find a way for us to be alone and then he would, you know, push me against walls and stuff..."

My tongue feels heavy. I've never put so many words to this. With Elizabeth, I gave her a pretty standard explanation and her response was to roll her eyes and say, "Ugh, yeah, he's so vile!" I felt justified but also, perhaps, a little dismissed. Maybe I should have explained, like I'm doing now.

"That sounds really bad," Bastian says, clenching his fists on his blanket. "Did you tell anyone? Get him to stop?"

"No." I feel the curdling edges of rebuke against myself and urge myself to explain why. "He would always make it a joke. He made me feel like I had misread the situation and he didn't want me so much after all. It was a special kind of hell, being his friend, but I'd never had a proper friend before so I didn't know."

"Yeah." Bastian's voice is short, like he's holding all his anger back. "That is not what friends do."

"I got that when I shifted into a female form in the spring of first year. Suddenly, he didn't want to know me, and that's when the teasing started, the jokes about me being a shifter, all of that."

I don't want to use the word "bullying", but it is the only accurate one. Although it's so embarrassing to be bullied at my age. Surely all of this was supposed to be left behind with secondary school? Was I just an idiot for hoping that the one upside of being homeschooled was that I skipped that particular ritual humiliation?

"When I was in a female form, he completely lost interest, thank god," I say with a wry smirk. "Carl doesn't like boobs."

"This is why he called you—"

"A cock-tease? Yeah," I admit, feeling revulsion inside me. Towards him but also, a little bit, towards myself. "I would always push him off or squirm away and he'd say I was playing hard to get and then when I shifted—"

"He thought you'd cock-blocked him?" Bastian sounds incredulous. "How is this guy still allowed at college?"

"I didn't tell anyone, except Elizabeth," I say painfully, wondering if it's my fault. "And he's a bully. People expect him to be a dick to me, especially because I'm a shifter."

"Surely they don't expect him to sexually harass you." Bastian scowls. Those words give me pause. *Is that what happened?* I wonder. There's a little voice inside of me that answers firmly, *Yes, it is.*

"Witches think shifters are naturally duplicitous," I say, thinking back to my parents, how they hid me from the world. It wasn't just because they were ashamed of me, they didn't trust the world to treat me fairly. "He never bullies me about anything but being a shapeshifter. He plays into everyone's prejudice and they don't even realize it's about something else. Besides, he's not some rapey incel guy. He's gay. They don't want to believe that about him."

"I believe you," Bastian says fiercely. "Just because he's gay doesn't mean he can't also be a creep."

My heart thumps quietly. He's so sincere that it's hard not to trust him, but all I can do is nod. Bastian crunches some more crisps and as I look at the orange flames licking the air, I wonder why it's a complete stranger who's the first person to tell me that what Carl did was so wrong.

"Can I ask you something else?" Bastian asks in between licking salt off his fingers.

"Okay," I say warily. I really don't want him to ask more about Carl, about the terrible crush of confusing emotions that lived inside of me that year, a ferocious need to protect the first friendship I ever had battling against a horrified growing urgency to reveal just how awful he truly was. Always overshadowed by his snide voice in my head, scaring me into silence: *Who's going to believe you, shifter?*

"Why aren't you good at witchcraft? Really?"

"What do you mean?"

"Well, you're full of magic," Bastian says earnestly. "I've seen you shift your form twice; you clearly have more power inside you than I could ever dream of. I understand that you can't control your shifts, but surely spells should work for you."

The last person to be this interested in my shifting was Elizabeth. I wonder what she would think about me sitting in my parents' living room with a guy in his boxers. Instantly, I feel guilty and eat another biscuit.

"Just born dysfunctional, I guess."

"It doesn't make sense," Bastian insists thoughtfully. "Something must be stopping it."

"Yeah, me," I say sharply. "Don't you think my parents tried everything to get it out of me? Different routines and spells and...punishments."

I take a deep breath and try to forget how it felt to be shut away inside this house, knowing I couldn't go out unless I learned to do something I didn't understand.

"That's not what I mean," Bastian says. "I think your parents were wrong; I don't think it's you. If they gave magic according to effort, you'd be Merlin."

"Thanks." I snort with laughter.

"So it can't be you, can it?" he says emphatically. "You know spells, you've studied witchlore and witchcraft, you're capable of shapeshifting and you do it with seriously incredible amounts of power. It's something else that's stopping you."

This is dangerously close to the train of thought that took me to the cave with Elizabeth. I won't go there again.

"I don't know," I say, looking away from the beautiful sapphire ring on his finger. "I try, I really do. I can sense it in other people, I can smell magic in the air around me and sometimes taste it. I just...can't do it."

"Wait, you can smell witchcraft?" Bastian frowns.

"No, not spells, but a witch's own magic, like yours smells like a bonfire and Elizabeth's..."

I stop speaking, suddenly assaulted by the memory of the smell of almonds.

"That's unusual. Is it a shapeshifter thing?" Bastian asks, frowning.

"No, I think it's a me thing," I say. "I just got really good at paying attention to magic since I can't do it."

The first magic I learned to sense this way was my parents'. Better than hearing creaks on the stairs, sniffing for whiffs of their magic on the air taught me how to scent them out, avoid them if I needed to, hide if necessary. But I can't explain that to Bastian, it makes me sound like a paranoid loser.

"Or you're even more powerful than you realize," Bastian says softly. There's a fervent glow in his brown eyes when he says that and I look away, uncomfortable. Elizabeth looked at me that way, as if I would be able to do something amazing. Then she died. I fumble under the coffee table for the TV controller.

"Want to watch something?"

"Sure."

I turn on the TV and let the sudden burst of noise and colour distract me from darker thoughts.

"Up here," I say, leading the way along the corridor when it's finally time to turn in. He's eaten all the crisps and I've eaten all the biscuits. My father has the snacking tastes of a twelve-year-old child from the sixties and I feel weirdly delighted that he will be deprived upon his return.

"Um, is this...okay?" Bastian asks, sounding nervous for the first time, and I wonder why. It can't be sharing a bedroom with me; not someone like Bastian, who looks like he goes to the kind of parties where people sleep on top of each other like a pile of drunk hamsters.

"It's fine, it's massive," I say, opening the door. The guest room is sparse: yellowing blue-and-white striped wallpaper, a threadbare rug over cold floorboards and a severe iron-framed king-sized bed. I think I see Bastian's shoulders droop in relief. I guess my parents are partly using the room as storage, judging by the paintings and photographs leaning against the walls, waiting to be hung properly, and the stacked piles of vintage hatboxes.

"Hey, who did this one?" he asks, pointing at a small canvas leaning against the bottom of the wardrobe. I recognize it from my younger years, a painting I did of myself as a selkie. I'm honestly surprised they haven't tossed it out for the binmen.

"Oh, yeah, me, when I was about fourteen and a right goth." I can't help but smile at the drastic use of black paint and wild brushstrokes. "I wanted to be a selkie."

"Really? That's adorable." Bastian grins. Something flutters inside me. I wonder if he's being sarcastic but it doesn't sound like it. Could he genuinely find me adorable?

"Here." I open the wardrobe, reaching into the wicker basket inside that I know holds spare pyjamas. I hand him a soft baggy blue T-shirt. "Don't sleep in your dirty T-shirt."

"Okay." Bastian pulls off his damp T-shirt and I look away. No one needs to see all that perfectly sculpted skin, but I can't help noticing, out of the corner of my eye, a broad scar, a mangled mess of puckered skin across his chest and shoulder, climbing up to his neck. It looks like it would feel textured and bumpy under my fingers. *Don't think about touching Bastian's chest!* I tell myself firmly. Once I'm assured that he's climbed into the other side of the bed, I turn around. He's on his phone, frowning.

"Do you have a spare charger?" he asks. "I'm on two per cent."

"Use mine, I'm on eighty." I pull it out of my bag before plugging it in. "Give me your phone."

I ignore how warm his hands are as I plug his phone in. I can see the photo on his home screen. It's him and a man who looks a lot like a young Eric Chevret, but with glasses and longer, curlier hair. It must be his brother, Shasta. Bastian's smile in the photo is so broad, so genuine, he looks like a totally different person. It's almost too personal, as if it's something I shouldn't see. I set the phone down on the nightstand and climb into the bed, too nervous to take my hoodie off in front of him but too warm to sleep comfortably in it. He turns out the small lamp on his side of the bed and we are plunged into mutual darkness, the only light the amber glow of the street lamp through the wispy, veil-like curtains.

"Night," he whispers.

"Night," I whisper back. I lie in the dark as the bed moves and he rolls over onto his side. I wait for his breath to even out before carefully stripping off my hoodie and dropping it out of the duvet, trying not to pull the edges or wake him. I don't have the privacy to do my post-shift routine of looking at myself naked, so I just sort of awkwardly run my hands up and down my body, trying to learn its new shapes and textures.

"Are you okay?" Bastian whispers suddenly. "You're fidgeting."

"I'm fine." I stop moving, flushing with embarrassment, wondering if he thought I was wanking or something awful. I bury my red face in the pillow and instead concentrate on telling myself what I always tell myself. *I am more than my body, I am more than a label, I am Orlando, I am Orlando, I am Orlando...* Then my mind drifts into dreams.

"How is he?" I ask, pressing on the wheels of my wheelchair as my mother guides me to his bedside.

"Fading," she whispers. I look down at him in the bed, his aged face. Like most shifters, he has aged appropriately. Unlike me, who lives my youth over and over again. Now his time is coming and nothing has prepared me for this, not even seeing my friends lose their limbs and lives in the mud of Ypres.

"My dearest child," he whispers, reaching for my hand. The skin on his knuckles is so soft, so friable. It has spent a century changing, stretching and shrinking and now it is nearly over. His cloudy eyes feast on my face and then drift to my wheelchair. Dribbles of tears leak from the corners of his eye, seeking the creases in the folded skin.

"My poor darling, my precious one," he whispers. "Promise me you will not go back."

I close my eyes, fighting back the grief inside me. On the inside of my eyelids, I see the stretchers, the miles of churned earth, the hollow-eyed men squatting in the mud. I cannot lie to him.

"If I can, if I am able, then I must." I squeeze his hand, my tongue too heavy to ask for absolution, my heart screaming for it. He closes his tired eyes and turns his face away from me, for the first time in my life. A chasm of grief opens up inside me that nothing can fill.

"Then I hope you never walk again," he whispers.

Chapter Nineteen

"Lando? Lando, wake up. You're crying."

I jerk awake. Bastian is leaning over me, his cheekbones sharp in the blue shine from his ring. He's clearly using some kind of lighting spell to enhance its glow and the air smells lightly toasty. *Elizabeth*, I think and I shuffle back, instantly anxious. I'm quickly aware of how close he is and that I'm topless, and I immediately yank the duvet up to cover my naked chest.

"I'm fine, I'm fine," I sniffle, wiping my eyes as I lean against the headboard. "It's just a dream."

Was it just a dream? It felt so real, so unbearably painful to see that man, the man I felt sure was my father. How could I feel the emotions of the person who wrote the diary in *The Witchlore of Bodies*? If my own father was dying, I'd probably feel a bit relieved. Bastian closes his fist so the spell ends. I instantly feel a little bit calmer.

"Sorry, I shouldn't have used magic around you without asking," he says quietly. "Especially in this house."

I'm distantly touched that he has been noticing.

"It's fine," I say, kicking my legs out from under the duvet and pulling my knees in close to hug to my body. "I'm fine."

"You're not fine," he says. "It was the same as when you were in the water."

"What do you mean?"

"It wasn't a dream; you were all rigid and muttering and you glowed a bit."

"I glowed?" I stare at him. Bastian taps something on his phone screen.

"Yeah, I thought you were going to shift or something." He holds his phone out to me and I see myself, or my new form that I need to get used to, juddering and jerking in the bed, emitting a white glow that usually only comes with a shift.

"You filmed me?" I exclaim. "That's so weird!"

"I thought you'd want to see it." Bastian frowns.

"Well, I don't want to see a video of my nightmares, thanks so much, Bastian!" I push the phone away and rub my hands against my cheeks. I can feel rough stubble growing there already.

"It's not a nightmare," Bastian says flatly. "I get nightmares. I know it's not a nightmare."

I close my eyes and lean my head back against the wall, trying to do the mental grounding exercise that Counsellor Cooper taught me to do right after my suicide attempt to help with overwhelming thoughts. *Name something you can hear.* I hear Bastian shuffling, the bed dipping under his weight. *Name something you can taste.* I can taste my own spit, that nasty sour taste when I've just woken up. *Name something you can smell.*

I can smell the dirty scent of skin still covered in salt and sand, dusty and grubby, but I can also smell something herby and clean and pleasant. I think it might be Bastian's deodorant.

"Are you okay?" he asks.

When I open my eyes, Bastian is lying sideways on the bed on top of the duvet, propped up on an elbow, looking at me. I suddenly appreciate the sweetness of him giving me space, of putting physical distance between us. He looks weary. I wonder if he's been kept awake by nightmares.

"What are yours about?" I ask. He sighs and flops onto his back, staring straight up at the ceiling. For a moment, I think he won't answer and we'll spend the rest of the night like this, sleeping on the bed at perpendicular angles.

"Shasta." Bastian's voice is so small.

"How did he die?"

"Car accident." I remember my careless comment about the car and think, *I am such a stupid twat.*

"I'm sorry."

"It's okay. It was two years ago."

I don't see how it's possible that it is okay. I wonder if I'll feel that way two years on from Elizabeth's death. I can't imagine living even two more months without Elizabeth. *You've lived nearly five months without her,* a reasonable voice in my head says, one that sounds exactly like Counsellor Cooper. I push it away.

"What about your dreams?" he asks. I don't want to tell him about the visions so I tell him the truth about my nightmares.

"They're about Elizabeth. Her dying. In my arms."

Don't leave me, Orla, she whispers.

"Was there...was it quick?"

There's something about the darkness and the sound of the ocean out of the window that dares me to be honest.

"Yeah, it was quick," I whisper down at my hands. They look so different now, wider across the backs and hairier than they were when I tried to wipe the blood out of Elizabeth's mouth. "She'd hit her head. It was too quick for me to stop but it felt like it took for ever. Those final seconds."

I focus on my breathing, telling myself this is just one of these moments when I feel like I am holding Elizabeth in my arms. It's not really happening. It's just a memory. *Then why does it hurt so fucking much?* I wonder angrily. I think Bastian's fallen asleep but then he speaks.

"It's okay, you know."

"What is?"

"If, for a millisecond, when it was happening, when she was dying, you wished it would just be over. It doesn't mean you wanted her to die. It just means you wanted it to stop hurting. For her pain to stop. It doesn't mean you loved her less. If anything, it means you loved her more. Trust me."

I feel choked, like I'm drowning all over again. I don't know why I should trust him but there's a flatness in his voice that I recognize. It's haunted and truthful. I suddenly know that Bastian witnessed Shasta's death. I want to ask him about it, if he ever feels resentment towards Shasta for leaving him alone. I want to ask if he wanted to die too, when his brother was gone, but I can't. I sit there and swallow down my tears until I trust myself not to burst out sobbing all over him.

"Thanks for saying that," I whisper. I reach my foot down and poke his arm with my socked toes. I'm surprised when he gently takes hold of my foot, squeezing it.

"You're welcome," he says. We don't say anything else. He doesn't move to get back in the bed and I don't ask him to stop touching my foot. All I do is turn my head to the side and drift back to sleep. *Another witch,* my mother's voice whispers inside my mind.

Chapter Twenty

I wake up to an empty bed. I can hear the sound of the coffee machine in the kitchen. I sit up and check my phone. There's no message from Beryl. I check my email. There's one from my mother. Nothing in the subject, just a link to a Parisian hotel in the body. It's the first time she's ever done that. Usually, I have no idea where they're staying; even telling me a city is more precision than I'm used to. Was it seeing me with Bastian that prompted this change? A change that, if I squint hard enough in the right direction, *could* be interpreted as some bizarre variant of parental connection? I stare at it for a long time and then glance at the painting of the selkie that they kept. I don't know what to make of any of it.

"Good morning."

I look up to see Bastian pushing open the door to the bedroom with his foot, carrying two cups of coffee. He's still wearing the T-shirt he slept in but he's put on his jeans from yesterday. I anxiously pull my hoodie back on, covering my bare chest. Blushing furiously, aware that he might have seen the scars on my bare arm, I pop my head out of it and quickly grab the coffee from him. "You managed to make the machine work, then."

"That thing is a beast." Bastian shakes his head, leaning against the door and sipping his coffee as I pull my knees up inside my hoodie, like I used to do when I was little. Bastian smiles broadly over the top of his coffee cup. "You look good."

I feel like my heart stops for a second.

"What, like a boy?" I ask sarcastically, giving him a glare.

"No." Bastian looks entirely bemused. "Like you. You just look like you, with your hoodie...I don't know, it's cute."

My cheeks heat up and I get that buzzy, mosquito/butterfly feeling in my stomach. *Cute. Adorable.* Would he keep saying these things if he didn't mean them? Elizabeth's face surges to the front of my mind and I feel so guilty I have to look away from him.

"Shall we get going after our coffee?" I ask.

"Yeah," he says, sitting down on the edge of the bed beside me. The way he moves on so easily makes me think that I've imagined it. He didn't mean to call me cute in that way, just that it's a cute hoodie. *Of course he doesn't feel that way about me.* That chiding thought is immediately chased by the thought, *Why would I care if he does?*

"I have something to ask you," Bastian says.

"Okay."

"Are you sure you want to keep going with the spell?"

"Why would you ask me that?" I frown, sipping my coffee.

"Because you nearly died last night, and I need to know you're not going to pull that kind of thing with the Black Shuck.

It's too dangerous. We can't muck about."

"What is it, anyway?" I try to remember the words from the spell: *hair of the Black Shuck that stalks holy ground.* "Some kind of werewolf?"

I say that half as a joke and then I realize that I don't actually know if werewolves are extinct. *Elizabeth would know,* I think.

"It's a hellhound."

"Oh." My stomach clenches. "A real hellhound? That's... much worse than a boggart."

Hellhounds are not magical creatures, not really, not in the sense that selkies or boggarts are, that exist in our world alongside us. Hellhounds are made of magic and exist in other dimensions. Historically, ancient witches used spells to pull them through to lay curses on people or places. And now we're going to try and pull one through to give it a haircut.

"Yes, it is, and I need to know you're not going to do something...unexpected."

I can tell he is holding back and I remember the things we yelled at one another on the beach last night: *You're so fucking reckless!* He seems to be following my train of thought, because he leans closer before going on, his voice earnest.

"You were right, yesterday. I fucked up by not telling you about my selkie plan beforehand. I should have, because we're a team, Lando. We have to act like it."

"We do?" I look at him a little sceptically. I appreciate the apology and everything, but I'm not going to say so if he's just going to dump on all the ways I'm a bad teammate.

"Both of us." He nods. "We'll plan everything to do with the

Black Shuck together and…I know you can't control your shapeshifting but you can't just go off and decide you're going to throw yourself into danger when we're facing down a hellhound. There's too much at stake and you're too valuable. Okay?"

I remember the deal I made with the selkie to value my own life. The first taste of coffee in my mouth has mingled with the salt residue around my lips into something bitter. Does Bastian value me because he needs me for the spell, or because he values *me*? Either way, he saved my life twice, but faced with a literal hellhound, he might not be able to do it again.

"Okay. I can…be more careful," I say. "I don't know why I keep shifting but I can try and pay more attention to it. Maybe, I dunno, warn you. There's not much more I can do than that."

"You don't need to do anything more. Like I said, I know you can't control it." His voice is incredibly reassuring. "I just want us to be on the same page."

"We are."

He smiles at me. It's distracting so I cough into my coffee and try to change the subject.

"So when will we do it?"

"I need to research what stage of the moon cycle is best," Bastian says. "But once we know that, as soon as we can."

"And then after the Black Shuck, we'll be ready to do the spell?"

"Yeah, we need to get some earth from Elizabeth's grave, but that's it." Bastian shrugs, drinking his coffee. There's something about the way that he says this, the casualness with which he throws out Elizabeth's name, that feels like cold water poured on my head. All the sweetness I've felt towards him suddenly sours. He never even met her and yet he can talk about her grave so effortlessly, as if she's just an ingredient on the list. It's unreasonable, I know, because Bastian owes Elizabeth nothing, but it stings just the same and some of the old resentment I felt towards him slides up inside me, slippery and insidious.

"I'm going to have a shower," I say shortly. "My hair is full of sand."

"Cool," Bastian says. "I'll go in after you."

As I clamber out of bed, I get a whiff of the scent of him, salty and sweaty. Despite all my visceral annoyance, I can't help myself. It's biological, utterly unhelpful, but I automatically wonder what it would smell like if I were to stand in the circle of his arms, held completely safe. *Don't think about that, you idiot*, I snap at myself, not daring to even look at him as I rush to the sanctuary of the bathroom.

I turn on the shower and am relieved to climb under it. I wash away sand and dirt and salt and try not to think about the scars I saw on Bastian's chest. Yet I can't get his words out of my head: *You look good.*

The drive home is painless. We talk about nothing and everything and I learn things I never expected to about him. I learn that Bastian likes to sing along to songs while he drives, that he doesn't have a great voice but his enthusiasm is infectious. Soon, we're both screaming lyrics to cheesy pop songs at one another as we bomb down the motorway. I learn that his favourite book is *Babel-17* (which I obviously tease him about for being a sci-fi nerd) and, when we stop at a service station, I learn that he loves pickled onion Monster Munch more than any reasonable person should. I learn that his childhood in Cornwall was outwardly idyllic but inwardly full of complexity, a combination of finding magical acceptance and growth in his coven while also struggling with being the only non-white family in their town. When they moved so Shasta could start college, he tells me how initially bewildering and then quickly affirming life in London was. He describes the gigs he and Shasta attended, their adventures in the city and a New Year's Eve party gone hilariously awry. Bastian is suddenly alive with storytelling, animated, sometimes forgetting to hold onto the wheel as he gestures wildly, forcing me to screech and lean across him to grab the wheel as he is caught up in recollections about his brother.

"It's good to talk about him," Bastian says quietly, indicating to change lanes.

"Tell me something about him that people don't always know," I ask. "Like...what did he order in a coffee shop?"

"What?" Bastian laughs and looks at me.

"It's a way of getting a sense of a person." I smile. "When someone dies, we always talk about the big stuff, right? Their achievements and who their family were, but we don't talk about how many sugars they had in a brew." After Elizabeth's death, I unconsciously began making my tea the way she liked it, much too sweet, just to feel close to her. I shake off that thought and try to lighten my tone. "You know, a person who always orders a hot chocolate is a very different person to a Frappuccino drinker."

"Not much different." Bastian smiles. "He didn't like coffee. He thought I was weird that I liked it so much. He'd always get a cup of tea."

"Builder's?"

"White, no sugar."

"See?" I nod. "That's a steady, reasonable person right there. I feel like I know him so much better already."

Bastian smiles at me widely and I can't help but admire him, accidentally catching his eye for a second. I've never noticed until now what a beautiful colour his eyes are, hazel but much more green than brown today. *Like his brother's,* I realize, thinking of the photograph on his phone.

"What does my coffee order tell you about me?"

"Black Americano and a Samuel Delany book?" I snort. "That you secretly wish your life was a Kubrick movie."

Bastian laughs so hard we almost swerve into the wrong lane. I grin. I'd forgotten, I think, that I can be funny. Not just funny to make fun of, but actually funny. Not even Elizabeth found me this funny. I'm struck by that same feeling I had last night. *I feel safe with him.* When that thought flitters through my brain, I frown. I've been told my entire life that my magic is the thing that will make me safe, that being able to shift, that accepting a gendered form, is the only way for me to move safely in the world. Elizabeth made me feel loved and wanted, but I've never met a person who can make me feel as safe as I do being completely alone. I didn't know anyone could. I look at him with slight amazement while he sings away to the radio. *Why is it you?* I wonder, but then comes the obvious next question: *Why wasn't it her?* I don't have an answer to either.

When we arrive at Beryl's, I'm surprised when Bastian gets out of the car too and walks around to lean against it as I pull my backpack on.

"So I'll message you," he says.

"Yeah," I say, because it's obvious and it's what we've been doing for the last four weeks.

"Cool." He's looking at me sort of strangely and I can't shake the feeling that he's forgotten something. "Unless…"

"Unless?"

"Well, you're working on Saturday afternoon, right?" I nod dumbly, wondering where this is going. "I could come and meet you for a coffee or drink afterwards. To talk about the Black Shuck and stuff."

It sounds suspiciously formal, like a date, so I find myself repeating, "Just to talk about the Black Shuck and stuff?"

"Yeah," Bastian says easily, and I wonder if I'm blowing this out of proportion in my mind. After all, we get coffee and food together all the time when we're studying up in town, and talking at length about a deadly hellhound is hardly the stuff of romance.

"Okay, sounds good," I say. Bastian smiles broadly.

"I'll message you?"

"Yeah."

Bastian nods firmly and then opens his arms, stepping a bit closer and wrapping them briefly around me. I stand stiff, still, unsure what to do with my hands and weirdly cupping his elbows. He's warm and solid and smells like salt and sand and, this close, eucalyptus, which makes me think of the balm he made for me. For a millisecond, I close my eyes and breathe out and something shifts. We're closer, he's warmer, his hip bones are pressing against mine and suddenly I feel like I want…more. *No.* I step back, coughing and unable to look him in the eye.

"B-bye, then," I stutter out. I turn and run into the house, not caring how Bastian is leaning against the car with a slightly stunned expression, watching me go.

It's a Sunday so it's pretty quiet. I can hear Beryl practising her cello in the conservatory and can smell someone cooking a curry for lunch in the shared kitchen. I quickly move down to my bedroom, slipping inside. My room looks depressingly ordinary and the same, the way home always does when you've been away somewhere else for the night. I flop down on my bed, accidentally dislodging Mr Pebbles, who hisses at me and leaps away to the windowsill to savage my spider plant. I pull a pillow over my face and scream into it. Why did he have to hug me like that? To hold me just a fraction too long and then to soften, ever so slightly, so it didn't feel like hugging any more but felt like… holding. *What would Elizabeth think if she could see me now?* I don't have an answer to that question, not yet, but if we resurrect Elizabeth, there she'll be. Blond and smiling and asking questions: *Who is he?* I realize I won't have an answer to that.

I try to rehearse some options in my head.

This is Bastian, he's my...companion?

This is Bastian, he's my spell caster for this particular mission?

This is Bastian, he has nice eyes and warm arms and thinks I'm cute and adorable?

I scream some more when I think that. I'm probably just horny and desperate. My girlfriend's been dead for months and everyone hates me. Of course the first person who touches me kindly I get a little squirmy over. He's funny and charming and so very fit, after all; I shouldn't be mad at myself for not being immune to that. It just makes me normal. It doesn't mean anything. I sigh and get up from the bed, stripping off to stand in front of the mirror to do my ritual. Observing it from the outside in the cold light of a Sunday afternoon, there is something almost historical about this body. The hair is old-fashioned, the skin very pale, as if it's from a photograph. It makes me think of my visions.

The first time it happened, I thought it was just a weird confluence of occurrences, that I'd been reading about the shifter's story so it made sense that I'd had a dream or vision about it. That it's happened a second time feels spooky, like a pattern, as if it can't just be from reading the grimoire, and the additional dream still gives me a lump in my throat. The emotion had been so raw – the terror and sadness of the wounded soldier shapeshifter, facing their dying father – yet I haven't read about that moment in the grimoire. Am I having visions about the shifter that include things from the past I couldn't know? How am I doing that? Elizabeth would probably know a book I should read but I don't have anyone else I trust enough to consult. Suddenly, I'm overwhelmed by the oddness of it all.

"You can't do this," I tell myself in the mirror. "You can't get crazier. People already think you're insane, you don't need this too."

I open my wardrobe, looking for something to wear to college tomorrow. This body reads more masculine than the one I was in when term started. I sigh in heavy frustration and pull out the bag of clothes that Beryl says are "too feminine" for a boy to wear. Shifting is exhausting. As soon as I've got into a rhythm with one body, just when I've started to feel like myself, it changes. I'm tired of battling against people's expectations of how a non-binary person should dress; I'm tired of myself, endlessly catering for those people, so I pull out a frankly obnoxious pair of pink dungarees and hold them up to check the length.

Very briefly, a thought pops into my head: *What will Bastian say?* Bastian, who says I look like "me". That I look cute. I push those confusing thoughts away and get dressed, before going to make myself a cup of tea (ignoring the sideways stares from the other witches using the kitchen to make their Sunday lunch) and then returning to my room to climb into bed with *The Witchlore of Bodies.*

I love the smell of it, sort of sweet and vanilla, and the texture of the old paper under my fingers. I spend the afternoon reading. I learn the shapeshifter recovered enough to return to the front but before they could, their father died. So, to help their mother cope, they shifted into a female form to avoid going back. I realize how much that must have cost them to do, if I take what I saw in my vision to be real, their agony and fear over their need to go back to the front. When I read their grief over losing their father, I feel a lump in my throat for their seemingly endless sadness. When I read about them living with their mother and helping her with her grief, only for her to die suddenly from influenza, I feel their pain and loss at being alone and I wonder how it would be if I was so connected to my family that I felt empty without them. To have sacrificed so much of myself for them, only to lose them. I actually shed a few tears when I read about their guilt over their friends who died in the war and that their father died disappointed in them. If there are two things I understand, it's losing people and parental disappointment. Then there's a gap, between their mother's death in 1934 and an entry in 1939. I read it eagerly, wondering what they were doing in those years in between:

> I know I should be full of mourning and fear that another war has come. I will honour my father this time, even if he is not here to see it, and shift into a female form. I will not go to the front with the lads but I will do my bit from here. I have signed up to drive ambulances and I am pleased. It feels strange to say it, but I am content. I have met someone. B is the best person in the world I could know. She may be a witch, but I'm not afraid of prejudice, not from her. She is the first witch to treat me as a whole person. Is it wrong to be

so happy when so many people are suffering? In a lifetime of being a shifter alone, a shifter set apart, she makes me feel seen.

I stare at the words and I feel an inexplicable satisfaction for this shifter who lived so long ago. They found someone to love, someone who made them feel complete. A witch. Instantly, I think of Elizabeth, of how her brightness filled my life and made me brighter too. Then, without meaning to, the memory of Bastian smiling down at me in my hoodie, simply saying, "You look good," pops into my head. Feeling anxious and confused, rattled by my own thoughts, I close the book and lie down, staring at the ceiling. Maybe I need a bit of distance from Bastian, just to think about things. Clearly, the smiles and the touches and the shared laughter are having an impact.

She makes me feel seen.

It's the word, I realize, for what Bastian makes me feel. "Seen". *But if Bastian makes me feel seen, what does that make Elizabeth?* It feels like all of the questions are unanswered today, but they stay with me, little knots in my brain, waiting to be unpicked.

Chapter Twenty-One

I spend the week trying to keep a little bit of distance from Bastian. He's looked into the moon timings for the hellhound and since we can't do it before Sunday, our not-date still stands. Avoiding him is helped by the fact that he has an essay due that requires him to work with some texts that can't leave the college library, where he knows I don't want to be. I try to forget the hug that sent static electricity through my blood and focus instead on ducking Kira, who keeps sending me messages wanting to meet for coffee. I don't know how she got my number but I have no intention of having another conversation with Kira Tavi, whatever Professor Wallace mandated.

By the time the second weekend of October blows in on Saturday, the weather is so appalling I almost think of calling in sick for work. It's that kind of sideways Manchester rain where the sky presses against the chimney pots and tops of trees and the wind whips damp leaves in circles and gets up underneath my coat. Then Bastian messages, telling me to meet him at Barrio on the Beech Road after I finish work, so I wearily put on the shroud and get out of bed, at least thinking that the sweaty weight of it will keep me warm.

I've never been to Barrio, but as soon as I step inside I think I've made a terrible mistake. It's a Mexican place, moody and dark, with raw-edged wooden tables, black paint on the walls and an air of a place you go for strong drinks and spicy tacos on an intimate first date. *Which this absolutely is not,* I tell myself firmly, unwinding my scarf from my neck and looking around the steamy interior that smells like softening onions and rich, dark chocolate. I don't see Bastian anywhere and check my phone. I'm surprised when I see a message telling me he's in the garden. I frown and squeeze my way past the people drinking and laughing against the windows, fogged by the hot breath of customers, past the giant overworked coffee machine and the bartender salting margarita glasses to the rear door with the sign SECRET GARDEN on it.

I step out. The backyard is completely sheltered by an awning; black metal furniture is interspersed with oversized plants in pots and strings of hanging Edison bulbs shine yellow light. The wind howls against the plastic above and Bastian is the only one sitting at a table under the directional red glow of a heat lamp, a blanket across his lap. It's much less intimidating than the hustle and bustle of laughing people inside, but I'm suddenly awkward with the expectation of this lovely, secret space just for the two of us. *Not a date,* I remind myself.

"Come round this side, you get the best of the heat lamp," he says, shuffling over and lifting the blanket so I can slide in next to him.

"Thanks," I mumble, pulling off my peacoat and enjoying the warmth against the damp skin at the back of my neck. I look at the drink in front of me: it's pale green with a wedge of lime on the rim.

"I got you a margarita, it was two-for-one." He pushes it towards me. "I hope that's okay."

"I've never had one before," I admit, taking a sip. It's shockingly good, limey and salty and fiercely strong. "Wow!"

I lick my lips in delight and Bastian laughs.

"Go easy," he warns. "You're not much of a drinker?"

"I've not had much practice," I say, dissolving a flake of salt on the tip of my tongue.

I'm the youngest in third year and I feel it; the weighty difference in age between me and my peers and how ahead of me in life they seem.

"Fun dungarees, by the way."

His finger is playfully tracing the flower pattern on my knee. It's very distracting but, somehow, I know I don't want him to stop.

"Thanks, I painted them myself. I was bored last summer." I'm trying not to follow the shape of his fingers with my mind and keep up a conversation, but it's like trying to pat my head and rub my stomach at once. I can barely get my words out.

"That's clever. You look cute in them."

When he pulls his fingers away there's a confusing sensation inside me, part regret and part relief. I wonder if I should shuffle slightly so my knee is no longer touching his but I realize I'm pleasantly content. My mouth tastes like tequila and lime and my body is warm with the press of a handsome man against it. I realize that if I turned my head at this moment, we would practically be nose to nose. This thought produces a thrill of absolute terror and I cough, looking away.

"So, shall we talk about the Black Shuck?"

If Bastian notices my inelegant attempt to deflect his flattery, he doesn't show it. He reaches into his satchel and pulls out a heavy, musty-smelling book.

"Look what I got," Bastian says, dropping it onto the table. *Exorcisms and Conjuring Spirits and Demons: Volume One.*

"Where's *Volume Two*?" I demand. "This seems like the kind of thing where you read both volumes."

"Don't worry, this has everything we need." He flicks to a page he has bookmarked, a grand double-page spread with a woodcut print of Manchester cathedral, tall, spiky and gothic, and then, prowling around its edges, a black dog with long fangs, dripping with a dark liquid. Bulging, violent eyes. *The Black Shuck.*

"We have to summon it using a conjuring circle and trap it." Bastian flips forward to a page with a ragged drawing of a circle made of salt and blood on it. "It's not permanent—"

"Obviously," I mutter into my drink and Bastian smirks.

"But I think I can hold it in place long enough for us to get what we need. Then we release the spell, it goes back to its dimension and no one's the wiser. Pretty standard."

"Pretty standard?" I stare at him in amazement. "Done this before, have you?"

A month ago, I would have scoffed if he said yes, but since

then I have watched him deter a boggart with a preposterous spell. If he says yes, I won't be surprised.

"Sadly, no, this will be my first time." He grins.

"And what if we get caught summoning a hellhound in the city centre?"

"I honestly don't know about the legality of performing a hellhound summoning on sacred ground," Bastian says cheerfully. "But we won't get caught."

I nibble my lip anxiously. It tastes like salt. I look down at the circle of blood and try to imagine the power needed to contain this hellish creature from another dimension. I can't do it.

"You're sure it will work?" I try not to sound plaintive but I know I do.

"I'm going to do everything I can to make sure it will." Bastian places a hand briefly on top of mine and I resist the urge to turn my palm upward and grab his fingertips, taking comfort from him just like I did in the face of the boggart. "Look, we're not going in unprepared. We're going to read and do research. I'm going to do the spell but you're going to understand it too. We're a team, right?"

I take a deep breath and try to focus on remembering Bastian standing above me, blasting the boggart away with his magic. If I've seen him do that and he managed to magically resuscitate me on the beach, do I have any reason to doubt him facing the Black Shuck? Unbidden, Elizabeth's face in her last moments comes back to me. The fear, yes, but also the confusion. She never expected to fail. *That's not going to happen this time,* I reassure myself. I try to believe it.

"Right." I nod, giving myself a little shake. "So when will we do it?"

"The new moon is best for hellhounds."

"Okay. Pretend I'm a bad witch who doesn't follow the moon cycle and tell me when that is."

"Tuesday the twenty-fifth of October." He chuckles. "If it goes well and we get the hair, then we can do the ritual on Samhain."

"Got it." I try to look and sound more confident than I feel.

Bastian must notice because he says, "You could bring some vegan Babybels to make yourself feel better."

I laugh and my anxiety dissipates slightly, the tension in my shoulders dropping.

"Yeah, well, maybe I will." I nudge his shoulder playfully. "Tell me about the spell."

We drink; we talk about conjuring circles but then conjuring circles turns into talking about witchcraft in general, Bastian telling me about cool spells he and Shasta saw when they went on holiday to Haiti to visit their second cousins, and me hesitantly revealing some of the things I've seen my parents do. Soon, the book with its terrifying illustration is closed, the threat of the Black Shuck tucked away for the night and reduced to a coaster for the nachos we ordered.

"You're really good at all of this, all this serious, intense magic," I say, folding a napkin into a crane. "You're what my father would call a prodigy, I think."

"Coming from a shifter, I'll take the compliment." He smiles. "But magic doesn't have to be serious."

He gently takes the crane from my fingers.

"May I?"

I nod nervously as he sets his hand into the preparatory triangle, his ring glowing softly. Then he links his thumbs and floats his fingers and suddenly the little crane is endowed with the luminous blue glow of Bastian's magic and its tiny napkin wings flap slowly.

"Magic doesn't have to be permanent to mean something," Bastian says quietly.

"Whoa." I stare at it with a slow grin, feeling a flush in my cheeks as the crane wobbles on the air and then descends into my palm. No one has ever done this, made a spell just for me, to impress me or to bring me joy. "That's amazing."

"No, *you're* amazing."

Bastian smiles at me. It's that same grin that I've started to get used to: unguarded and affectionate. It flusters me. Being red-headed now means that when I blush, I blush all over. My words are stuck in my throat. I want to say thank you but all I can think is, *Not as amazing as you.* I try not to look at Bastian but he's still grinning, like he knows exactly what he's doing. I get that nauseating flip-flop feeling that I associate with either anxiety or kissing. I can't just be imagining this, can I? This must be real, the way he keeps touching me and I want him to and the drink he bought me and the beautiful secluded garden that seems like the perfect place for a first date? The kind of date I never got to go on with Elizabeth.

"Do you want another?" he asks, looking at our empty glasses. *Yes,* I think, *very much,* and *No, no I absolutely must not have another drink.*

"Um, no," I say, making a show of looking at my phone. "I should get back, I think."

"Okay." Bastian doesn't seem flustered by my abrupt manner, standing up and smiling at me. "I'll walk you."

"No, it's fine. I'm fine." I stand up and grab my coat, as if this one declination has pushed me over an edge and now I cannot sit in this space with him and pretend everything is normal. His smile is faltering. I know he's realizing that I'm trying to run away from him and there is a horrible churning in my guts for doing this when he's been so kind. I fumble in my pocket. "Let me pay for my drink."

"Don't worry about it." He's averting his eyes from me now, his manner becoming more withdrawn as he pulls on his own coat and follows me through the crowded bar. When we step onto the street the rain has blown itself out for a moment, the damp air and flapping awning blowing noisily around us as we stare awkwardly at one another.

"Bye, then," I say, attempting a bright tone as I turn my collar up against the chill.

"Did you not like it?" he asks abruptly, nodding towards the bar. "Was it...I don't know, too much?"

I look at him, standing in his black coat and jeans, hands stuffed into his pockets and shoulders hunched to his ears, skin catching the golden glow from inside filtered through a misted window. He's been kind to me, too kind for me to lie.

"I liked it," I say helplessly. "I just...I've never done something like this before. Elizabeth and I, we didn't..."

He frowns and I pause, shaking my head, because I'm making

myself feel worse just by speaking. Still Bastian waits, eyes fixed steadily on me, as if I'm going to say something that will push him into movement.

"Yeah, I liked it a lot," I repeat, looking at my boots. "It's just…Elizabeth stuff."

When I look up at Bastian, he's still watching me. Then he steps forwards and pulls something out of his pocket, offering it to me. It's the crane I made, the one he enchanted to fly.

"Maybe when she's back it'll be different," he says, carefully tipping the crane into my hand. "Maybe you'll do stuff like this."

For some reason, that feels wrong to imagine. To fantasize that the evening was different, that Elizabeth was in Bastian's place. I gently close my hand around the crane, still a little warm from Bastian's magic, and tuck it into my pocket.

"Maybe," I say, turning away. "See you later."

The next week after our non-date is a bit weird. Bastian is just as kind and cordial as always and we spend the same amount of time together, but something has dropped down between us. He doesn't hug me like he did before and I try not to miss it. I tell myself it's for the best, of course it is, because soon we will have resurrected Elizabeth, and I don't want to have to explain to my girlfriend why I've been flirting with someone else. We both focus on the Black Shuck. I find myself practising drawing conjuring and exorcism circles everywhere, copying diagrams Bastian has shown me by sketching my toe across the carpet while waiting for the kettle to boil or outlining them on the fogged-up mirror after a shower. I am also paying urgent attention in any of my classes that mention hell dimensions.

On Thursday we have our Medieval Witchlore class for third and fourth years with Professor Wallace and the seminar is on exorcisms. I am on the edge of my seat the entire time, taking frantic notes as he talks.

"...Of course, the last big Manchester exorcism was the cathedral hellhound, the Black Shuck, exorcized in 1910," he says, and my stomach clenches. My pen stops on the page and I listen avidly. "Prior to its exorcism, it was considered a haunting, the curse laid on it pulling it through to our world at certain points in the moon cycles. Nowadays, however, it is utterly benign, unable to break through without magical intervention."

"But they *can* break through?" I find myself asking.

"Scared of ghosts, shifter?" Carl calls. "Makes sense. She'd *definitely* be coming back to haunt your arse."

"Shut up," Kira mutters to him, shooting me a look that seems both curious and a little nervous.

"Only if summoned, Lando. Or if they are still operating under a previous curse and haven't been exorcized," Professor Wallace says, smiling at me. He clearly thinks my questions are a sign of renewed academic rigour rather than desperation not to accidentally unleash a hellhound in the city centre. "This one did wreak havoc in the 1800s. Many humans died. But the Merlin Foundation intervened."

"How did they do it?" I ask. "What spells?"

Bastian, who is sitting next to me, stands on my boot under the table. I can tell it's a warning to shut up but I move my foot away and try not to be distracted by the sensation of his knee pressed against mine.

"Sometimes, the oldest ways are the best, products that already have power woven into them. There's a reason that magical blood, holy water and holy fire have such prominent cultural representations," Professor Wallace says, looking at his watch. "That's all our time today. Please remember to check your college emails; there is a compulsory all-college seminar on Monday."

"How compulsory, sir?" Carl asks, deliberately bumping into my shoulder on his way to the door. Bastian glares at the back of his head with enough acid to burn through paper.

"Very, Carl," Professor Wallace says.

"Come on," Bastian mutters to me, taking my arm and jostling me out of the seminar room before I've even had a chance to pull my coat on. "What was that about?"

"Just asking questions," I mumble, gently pulling my arm away to lean against the wall a few metres from the door. Further down the corridor, Carl and his mates are bunched together, glancing back at us and laughing. I try to ignore them. "This is way more dangerous than the others, isn't it?"

"Well, yeah, kind of." Bastian fiddles with the strap on his bag and shoots Carl a vicious glare when his cackling laughter reaches us. "But it's going to be okay."

"What if we set it loose?"

"We won't." Bastian fixes his expression back on me and it softens. In a way that's actually really unhelpful. I have to stare at the drama society's poster for last year's production of *The*

Crucible to stop from blushing. "But you can't go on asking questions like that, you're going to draw attention."

"They'll just think it's academic interest."

Bastian opens his mouth and I'm sure he's about to say no one will believe the student who never speaks up in class has suddenly been imbued with curiosity overnight, but Kira walks past, looking curiously at us both and then down at the book I'm holding about conjuring spells. Maybe he's onto something.

"Better not to risk it," Bastian mutters. "Lunch?"

I think I should probably say no, better to keep my distance, but Kira is lingering and so is Carl, both clearly intent on interception that I don't feel up to facing.

"Sure."

"Did you see the email about the mandatory seminar on Monday?" Bastian asks me when we're sharing a cone of chips in St Ann's Square. "Is that a regular thing they do at Demdike?"

"I've never seen it before." We both checked our emails while waiting for our food. All it says is that it's for everyone and attendance will be taken.

"We could bunk it off," he says.

"For someone so literate you have an interesting interpretation of the word 'mandatory'."

"Fine, we'll be obedient." He bites the straw of his milkshake and grins at me, suddenly so stupidly charming, I have to look down at the bench. I find myself drawing an exorcism circle in the raindrops, joining them up into the right shapes.

"Hey, that's pretty good," he says.

"Yeah, if you have a need of someone to perfectly sketch one and tell you everything about it without actually being able to *use* one, I'm your person," I say sarcastically.

"I find I have a need for exactly that person," he says, and then nudges his shoulder against mine. I suck in my breath. I think he might press against me, to let me feel more of the warmth of his body, but he doesn't. He goes back to drinking his milkshake and watching my nervous fingers. Suddenly, I wonder how it will be when Elizabeth is back. Will I still feel this odd, irritating sense of lost potential when he sits near me like this? Or will these troubling feelings vanish, and I'll be perfectly satisfied with my new friend and my old girlfriend? The idea doesn't comfort me the way that I think it should.

"Only twelve days to go," he says. "Then we're one step closer to the end."

"Yeah." My mouth is a lot drier than I expect it to be and my stomach drops with anticipation. When I think about the wild eyes of the Black Shuck in the picture from the book, it seems way too soon. "Twelve days."

On Monday morning, when I walk down Faraday Street to the mandatory meeting, chased by a blustering breeze that sweeps along the yellow leaves that have fallen in the square, I see a tall, blond-haired woman standing outside college. She's in her forties, smoking a cigarette and wearing a belted tartan coat. I stop in my tracks, my heart racing. It's Elizabeth's mother.

The last time I saw her was the only time I have ever spoken to her, at Manchester Royal Infirmary, after the cave. I was sitting on a hard plastic chair, shivering uncontrollably, my hands torn and bloody from wrenching fallen slate and stones off Elizabeth's body, an ambulance blanket around my shoulders. I saw Dr Toppings as soon as she walked through the automatic doors. I could tell, just from her expression, that she had already been told. She looked like she'd aged ten years from the photos I'd seen on display in Elizabeth's house. She saw me and her ring began to glow, the same kind of pearly colour as Elizabeth's but her magic smelled like witch hazel, making my nose smart and run.

"I'm sorry," I gabbled as she stalked over to me. "I don't know what happened, I shifted and she fell over and hit her head—"

"I should curse every inch of you, shifter," she said. Her voice was so gentle and dangerous, I cowered in my seat, wishing I could disappear. "I should dedicate my life to it, turning you to nothing. It should have been you."

Now she is looking at me with that same expression, her blue eyes, which are so much like Elizabeth's, completely cold.

"What are you doing here?" I blurt out, without meaning to. She looks about as happy to run into me as I am to run into her.

"The miracle is that you are still here, shifter," she says. When it happened, she lobbied hard for my expulsion from college, but Professor Wallace was clear that since it was a "first offence" and hadn't happened on college grounds or even during term time, it had nothing to do with my college performance.

"I never meant—" I stammer out, thinking that saying something must be better than saying nothing. "I didn't know what she had planned to do, it was a secret, she didn't tell me."

"My only child is dead because of you," she says, stuffing her hands into her pockets. "Your intentions mean nothing."

She drops her unfinished cigarette and stamps on it with the heel of her red snakeskin boot, clearly more desperate to get away from me than to absorb more nicotine. I stare down at the stub and wonder if she wishes she could grind me to dust the same way. Then she turns and walks up the stone steps and into college. I watch her go and think I should have listened to Bastian. I should have bunked off. I wonder, if I had told her I was trying to make up for it, that I was trying to bring Elizabeth back, would she have been happy or angrier? I suddenly have an uncomfortable feeling that even if we manage to resurrect Elizabeth, her mother will never see me as anything other than a murderer.

"Hey, Lando, are you okay?" I jump when someone touches my elbow. Bastian is standing next to me, his cheeks flushed with the exertion of walking through the cold wind.

"Of course," I say mechanically. "Let's get this over with."

I keep my eyes peeled for Dr Toppings as Bastian and I walk to the main library, barely listening as he tells me about his research. I imagine those snakeskin boots marching her all the way to Professor Wallace's office to demand my expulsion again. My mind races through all the terrible things she could say – *violent young person, a threat to others, no control, killed my daughter* – then we reach the library door and I see her. She's removed her coat, she's standing in front of a PowerPoint that has the words DANGEROUS MAGIC: THE THREATS OF MAGICAL DISCHARGE on it. I stumble to a dismayed halt, as other students brush past us and find seats.

"Lando?" Bastian frowns at me, then looks at the PowerPoint and Dr Toppings standing talking to Professor Wallace. His eyes widen when he sees the title. "Is that—"

"Elizabeth's mother." I cannot believe that she's chosen to do this, to talk about her own daughter's death in front of four hundred students, but I've clearly underestimated how much she hates me. My breathing is shallow and I feel like I'm going to be sick. "This is about me."

"Come here, come on," Bastian urges, grabbing my arm and guiding me back out into the corridor, out of the flow of students entering the library. I lean against the wall and try to catch my breath, but it's like I can only breathe in and not out. "It's not going to be about you."

"She hates me," I gasp out. "She blames me. She told me it should have been me."

"Shit," Bastian mutters, rubbing my arm up and down. "It's okay, look, follow my breathing."

He takes my hand and presses it against his chest. His hand is warm, his sapphire ring catching the light. I can feel the steady thump of his heartbeat through his T-shirt and he breathes in, holding my gaze, and then out steadily. I mimic him, my own breath stuttering, my heart trying to jump through my ribcage.

"It shouldn't have been you, it shouldn't have been *anyone,* it was an accident," Bastian whispers. The entire world is his hazel eyes, his steady heartbeat and the rise and fall of his chest. "Just breathe; it's going to be okay."

"Oh, you're still hanging with the shifter, Chevret?"

It's like someone has burst the little bubble of safety I feel around Bastian and I'm aware, again, that we're in a public place and Carl bloody Lord is staring at us. He's looking me up and down, a sneer on his lips. I find myself, without meaning to, gripping Bastian's hand. I'm even more surprised when he grips it back.

"Can you piss off, please?" Bastian says coolly.

"Ooh, touchy." Carl smirks, fixing his eyes on where Bastian's hand is holding mine. Then his eyes flicker to Bastian. "I guess you fancy him more now he's a bloke again?"

"Not a bloke," I manage to snap out. Carl leers at me.

"Yeah, but you are in all the ways that matter." The look he gives me is so derisive, so sly and greedy, that suddenly I'm back in first year and he's pushing me against the wall of the library. Then he looks at Bastian. "Right, Chevret?"

Bastian drops my hand. For a horrible second, I'm sure that Bastian agrees with Carl, that somehow Carl has got to him and ruined this for me too, but that's not what happens. Instead, in a single fluid motion, the blue shine of his ring pouring strength and magic into his fist, Bastian punches Carl in the face.

Chapter Twenty-Two

"Bastian!" I exclaim as Carl staggers back, falling to the floor. Students around us start yelling and panicking, and I'm sure I can hear Professor Wallace shouting something in the library.

"Fuck me, that hurt," Bastian gasps, and I get the sense that this might be the first time he has ever punched someone. He shakes out his trembling hand and I try to grab him, to pull him back, but Carl is scrambling to his feet with a particularly ugly look on his face before launching himself at Bastian with a guttural growl. I've never seen a sober fight up close and I'm distantly surprised by the lack of finesse in the whole thing, and how it just seems to be two people with their bodies locked together trying to get out of one another's grip long enough to throw a punch.

"What the hell is happening?" someone yells, and suddenly Kira is there, trying to pull Carl away as I grab the back of Bastian's jacket, dragging him out of reach. Somehow, he's come away with a cut lip and a bruised eyebrow. "Carl, stop it!"

"He started it!" Carl yells, and then he's twisting his fingers;

the particular smell of his magic, which always reminds me of overripe bananas, is pungent as his ring glows pink and a directional blast of heat, sharp and scorching, pushes through the air towards us. "Because he's fucking obsessed with that bloody shifter—"

"Fuck OFF, Lord!" Bastian yells back, and he raises his hands above his head in a quick sequence that I recognize from our night with the boggart. There is a blinding blast of ancient Cornish magic, so bright it's physical, knocking Carl and Kira and me off our feet and sending students screaming into the library and running down the hallway. The air is thick with the scent of bonfires at their peak, and I struggle to my feet, grabbing Bastian's arm and pulling it down.

"Bastian, no!" I yell. I've never touched a witch in the middle of a spell before and something weird happens when I do. My own hands glow, not with Bastian's blue light from his ring, but with a pearly white sheen, the same as I do before I shapeshift. Bastian and I both stare down at my hand, utterly distracted by it.

"Your magic," he whispers. "It's...it's right there."

"Yeah, I...I don't—"

"CHEVRET!" a voice bellows, interrupting my confusion, and we both turn to see Professor Wallace standing at the doorway of the library. Unfortunately, Elizabeth's mother is standing beside him. Her eyes are fixed on my slightly glowing fingers and I quickly let go of Bastian, stuffing my hand into my pockets. "You and Lord, in my office, now! Everyone else, get in the seminar!"

Carl is groaning, cradling his face where Bastian punched him, and Elizabeth's mother immediately steps back into the library.

"Message me," I tell Bastian urgently, as he moves to follow Professor Wallace and Carl. He nods, squeezing my wrist before walking away, running a hand through his hair. The other students are giving me a wide berth, staring at me with terrified eyes as if I'm the one who produced the colossal blast of magic and not Bastian.

"Come with me," Kira says, abruptly grabbing my arm. I'm shocked when she pulls me around the corner to the toilets rather than pushing me into the seminar. It must be serious if Kira Tavi is ducking out of a college-mandated activity. She's breathing hard, her hands trembling as the door closes behind us.

"Is this about peer mentoring?" I ask blandly.

"You need to stop hanging out with Bastian," she says. "He's dangerous."

"What, because he beat up Carl?" I exclaim and then, when someone comes out of a cubicle and looks at us curiously, I drop my voice to a whisper. "I can't believe you're defending that bigot."

"I'm not defending him! Bastian literally just shot a dangerous spell at me!" Kira doesn't seem to care about being overheard. Her voice is getting louder and higher and she's trembling. "He'll be lucky if he isn't thrown out!"

"If he is, it would be a complete overreaction," I say, trying to brazen it out. "It's not a spell designed to hurt anyone; his coven is just different from yours."

"You mean dangerous." Kira pushes her purple glasses up her nose, angrily. "I heard he used to be part of a *Nimue* coven!"

"It's called *Arlodhes an lynn*," I correct, utterly butchering the Cornish but I want her to realize I know more about Bastian than she does. "And so what? You and Elizabeth were part of an Artemis coven, it's not like *they* don't have some dodgy views."

"If you knew anything, you'd know witch communities are diverse; covens that follow life cycles often celebrate and meet together but it doesn't mean we're *identical*," she snaps. "At home, my family follow Tafukt. We celebrate the same seasons, but we *don't* have the same beliefs as Dr Toppings, and unlike a Nimue coven, we *definitely* don't have a reputation for wanting witches to be superpowered!"

That might be her way of telling me she's less homophobic than Elizabeth's mum, but it doesn't exactly endear me to her right now.

"You don't know anything about what Bastian wants!"

"I know that people who do *that* kind of magic are reckless!" Kira points to the closed door. "They shouldn't be trusted!"

"Like shapeshifters, you mean?" I say harshly. "Witches shouldn't be friends with shifters, right? Shouldn't go out with them?"

"You know that's not what I meant." Her brown eyes are flashing angrily. "Honestly, Lando, you act like you're the first bloody shapeshifter to have ever been in a relationship with a witch! You know it's not true, I keep telling you I wasn't against your relationship, what's it going to take for you to hear me?"

"It's going to take you getting out of my life and actually

respecting my privacy," I say coldly. "You keep trying to pull me and Bastian apart. It's none of your business."

"Elizabeth made it my business." She steps closer and I can feel how wound up she is. Her ring is glowing softly and her magic, which I hadn't noticed until now smells like ripe plums, is rising off her skin. "She would want me to look out for you, she worried about you all the time. The last thing she'd want is you hanging out with someone like Bastian Chevret."

I laugh in her face. I can't help it, because it's too absurd to think about what Elizabeth would want in this situation, especially when Kira has no idea how complicated it really is, that Bastian is the only one helping me get Elizabeth back to the land of the living.

"I'm sorry, but that's absolute crap," I say. "Don't tell me what she wanted for me. You sound like an idiot."

Kira's lips purse into a line and her eyes gleam.

"I know a dangerous witch when I see one. I know what happens when a witch loses control of their power," she says. "He's right on the edge. If you're smart, you'll stay away from him."

"Guess I'm not smart, then." I turn to open the door but she pushes her hand against it.

"Has he asked you to do anything?" she asks me urgently. "Any spells?"

I stare at her, thinking, *How does she know?* Then I realize Bastian must have been right on the money about how my extra questions in class would draw suspicion. I decide sarcasm is the way to go.

"Yeah, totally, he's tricked me into a spell that's going to drain all of my magic so he can use it for himself, like a fucking supervillain," I say. "And I'm going along with it because I'm just a lonely, gullible shifter who can't look after themselves, right?"

"That's not what I mean!" she says, almost desperately. "Just...don't do any magic with him!"

"I can't do magic, remember?"

With that, I slam my way out of the bathroom. I can hear the lilting tone of Elizabeth's mother's voice as she gives her seminar from the library, and deliberately walk in the opposite direction. I message Bastian and tell him I'll be waiting for him, and stand outside college, my back pressed against the graffiti on the walls. I stare down at my hand that glowed when Bastian was doing his spell. It looks exactly the same as it did that morning, long fingers, a bit of gingery hair coming down from the wrists, freckles and blunt nails. Tentatively, I take a deep breath and put my hands in the preparatory triangle, then slowly twist them through the heating spell that Bastian's been teaching me – a Neptune's Rise and a Logi's Spear – but nothing happens except that some passers-by look at me curiously. I blush and stuff my hands into my coat pockets.

"Hey." Bastian slumps against the wall next to me. One of his eyes is swelling up, looking puffy and uncomfortable, probably from a rogue elbow of Carl's.

"Are you okay?" Without thinking, I trace my fingers over his cheekbone underneath the swelling. "It looks right grim."

"I'm fine, it was worth it." Bastian smiles, gently batting my hand away. He squeezes my finger for a moment and there's a fluttering in my chest, like a bat has got loose inside my ribcage.

"You didn't have to do it for me," I say, feeling awkward as our hands drop apart. I want to keep touching him, to assure myself he is all in one piece, but I content myself with leaning against the wall beside him, our shoulders pressed together.

"I didn't do it for you, I did it because he's a wanker and it was the right thing to do," Bastian says, his eyes sharp. When he looks at me like this, I feel very…watched. Noticed. It's the first time it's ever been pleasant for me.

"Well, it was still kind of…gallant."

"Gallant?" He smiles.

"Yeah." I flush because it's an absurd word, an old-fashioned one, but it's the best word I have without using the word that's truly in mind: chivalrous. Like a romantic knight in an epic medieval poem. The word gives me a little pulse, deep in my abdomen, but that probably says more about the kind of reading material I find sexy than it does about him.

"Well, gallant or not, it's two weeks of suspension." He sighs heavily.

"What about Carl?"

"Only two days."

"What?" I exclaim. "Why?"

"Because only one of us used 'witchcraft that is inappropriate for an educational context'," Bastian says, smiling wryly. "I've been given a warning too and been told I'll be very closely watched until the end of the year."

"God, it's so hypocritical." I shake my head. "If Carl had known the spell you used, he wouldn't have hesitated."

"He wouldn't have had the power for it." Bastian's voice is dismissive as he looks down at my hands. "Did it stop?"

"Yeah, as soon as I stopped touching you." I berate myself for wording it so gracelessly and blush like a flipping tomato, but Bastian only nods thoughtfully.

"That's weird," he says. "Maybe it means our magic is compatible or something like that? I know some witches work in pairs for certain crafts, partners within covens and stuff. I can look into it."

I've heard of such things but I've never imagined I could be part of them. To be a shifter is to be solitary or only with other shifters, and to be me is to be lonely. Plus, the idea of a shapeshifter sharing magic with a witch in any way at all is so taboo I actually start to sweat a little. From nervousness or anticipation, I can't quite tell. Even between witches such things are considered unusual at best and dangerously misguided at worst.

"You'd want to try that?" I ask awkwardly. "With a shifter?"

"I'd be up for exploring it with a witch, if I found someone who I was genuinely magically compatible with. I think the benefits outweigh the risks." He shrugs. "Why wouldn't I do it with you?"

Because my father would murder the both of us if he found out, I think. I still remember his characterization of powerful witches: *Of course, they would rip the magic out of our blood if they could.* Despite those warnings, ingrained deep in my psyche, I'm not averse to the idea. Quite the opposite. I want to feel the way I felt when I touched Bastian and my hand felt more alive with something new than it ever has.

"Maybe," I say, trying to conceal how shockingly keen I suddenly feel. "Maybe it will help us with the Black Shuck. If you still want to do it?"

I wonder if he's thinking that all of this is a lot of trouble for a potential place at the Merlin Foundation, especially if he's on thin ice at college.

"Totally. We'll go to the cathedral next Tuesday," he says. "We're nearly finished."

"Yeah. We are." I feel weird, suddenly, like when I'm reading a good book and I realize I'm over halfway through and suddenly I try to read slower. "I mean, maybe we could do it next month?"

"No, we want to do the final spell at Samhain, if we can," Bastian says. "Otherwise we'll have to wait until the winter solstice and that's not until the end of December."

I don't have a reason to disagree. If we do this, I get Elizabeth back and everyone will leave me alone. Everyone will know that I didn't do anything wrong, because she'll be here, telling them, telling her mother the truth, and proving that our relationship was real. *Is* real. Then I won't be alone any more, and everything will be the way it was supposed to be. So why do I feel so hesitant?

"Lando?" Bastian presses.

"Sounds good," I say with a smile and a nod.

The twenty-fifth of October comes around much too quickly for my liking, but I wonder if there's ever a good time to conjure a hellhound. I read up on the old ghost stories about the Black Shuck from before it was exorcized. Like Professor Wallace said, it was certainly a menace, a grim portent of death, said to murder anyone who looked it in the face. As the days pass, I get strange flashes while I'm riding the tram or getting dressed, cruel imaginative visions of angry eyes and slavering teeth.

I've not really seen Bastian since the incident at college, but I wonder if that might be because he's buckling down to keep on top of his college work while he's suspended. We've been messaging almost every day but I realize quickly how easy it is to be lonely without him studying beside me in the library or getting a quick coffee with me in between classes.

On the night of the new moon, I follow Bastian's instructions to wait until it's truly dark to catch the ten o'clock tram into town. I huddle inside my peacoat and think about the plaid blue coat that Elizabeth wore last winter. It's suddenly bizarre that the seasons are turning and Elizabeth isn't seeing the leaves fall. It's a lurch of feeling, like I forgot something, but it doesn't stab me between the ribs like it used to. Counsellor Cooper once told me that recovery can be held back by fear; the fear of moving on, of being happy again. Tonight, with my breath steaming the cold window of the tram, the black night rushing by, the seasons themselves are reminding me of it.

The weather is anticipating winter, wet and blustery with a deeper chill in the air than usual. As I walk past the town hall and through St Ann's Square, there are paper pumpkins hung in the trees, their little faces catching the light from the street lamps. It's a particular experience, walking through a wintery city on a weeknight before Halloween. Decorations stand inanimate and unwatched, waiting for human eyes to bring them to life, and there's an eerie aura to the quiet city. The cold weather is keeping everyone at home, tucked up warm.

When I walk into the empty cathedral square, the building glows with titian-orange spotlights illuminating the astonishing gothic facade, turning the pale sandstone rust coloured. The ancient tower looms over the square, its turrets twisting up into the black night, lost from view. This is where the Black Shuck has haunted and hunted for generations, and I shiver, my eyes catching on shadows. Bastian is standing by the huge metal gates in front of the door and when he spots me, he smiles so widely. I try not to notice the pleasurable churn in my chest, despite the rising anxiety in my legs.

"Hey," he says. "It's been ages."

"It's been eight days," I scoff, but that only makes him smile more.

"You counted."

I ignore him and point at his eye.

"This doesn't look too bad."

It's no longer as swollen or red. There is a nauseating yellow tinge to it and a little splurge of brown broken blood vessels that look to still be healing, but it's better than Carl's, which honestly still looks purple as hell.

"Oh, yeah." Bastian looks sheepish. "I have a really good recipe for a bruise paste."

"Handmade?" He nods shyly and I grin. "You just have to be the smartest person, don't you?"

Bastian shrugs but I can tell the compliment has sort of flustered him.

"Are you ready to meet the Black Shuck?" he asks. I can't possibly answer that positively so I nervously nod at the chunky padlock on the cathedral-gated door.

"We're not breaking in here, are we?"

"No, there's a spot down here behind the wall we can use." Bastian holds out his hand expectantly. "Come on, I'll show you."

I slowly withdraw a hand from my pocket and take his. It feels so natural to be pulled along by him and I can't stop myself imagining what we'll look like to anyone who walks past us. A pair in a relationship, maybe. A gay couple on their way home from the village, or two men on a first date. Or in love. That last thought gives me a thrill, deep in my gut, and I can't help squeezing his hand. If he notices he doesn't say anything.

"Here," Bastian says, choosing a shadowy spot on the cathedral grass between two trees, away from the street lights. Hidden by the wall on one side and the cathedral on the other, hopefully no one will see us. He drops my hand and starts to unload everything we need out of his satchel. I bend down and open the library book to the spell Bastian wants to use. He's pulling a jar of something dark and red out of his satchel: the blood necessary for forming a conjuring circle.

"Rank," I mutter. Just looking at it makes me queasy.

"It's only pig's blood." He pulls the lid off it and brings out a paintbrush, beginning to sketch a pentagram on the grass. "There's salt in my bag. Can you do the containment circle?"

I pull out a bottle of sea salt and pour in a circle, just like I've been practising over and over. Conjuring like this requires corresponding shapes, the pig's-blood pentagram inside a pentagon to act as a portal and the salt circle to contain it with the specific markings inside it. Having something to concentrate on quiets the steady thrum of unease running through me. But still, when I'm finished, it hits me again: *Holy hell, are we really doing this?* Bastian has finished the blood pentagram and is standing inside my circle, the book open on the grass in front of him.

"There's a pair of tweezers in my bag," he says. "Can you get them out?"

"And what are these for?" I pull them out of the pocket. They're sharp, long and vicious looking.

"They're for you." Bastian is holding his hands in front of him in the preparatory triangle. "Once I've conjured it and trapped it, you're going to pinch some fur from it."

"I'm going to *pinch* some fur?" I repeat, staring at him. For all we've talked about conjuring the hellhound and making sure we send it back safely, we've not discussed the actual hair part. I suppose I assumed the hellhound would shed, like a golden retriever, or something. But now I have to face interacting with a murderous hellhound rather than just observing one and I don't know if I can do it.

Trepidation rises in my throat. This is exactly the kind of thing Kira warned me about, exactly the kind of thing that Bastian got in trouble for at college. I wonder if it's worth it and then I want to stab myself in the leg with the tweezers, because how can I think that anything wouldn't be worth having Elizabeth back and fixing what I broke? How can I justify being so cowardly when Bastian is standing here, ready to do this, risking himself too and doing all the spellwork? Yet I can't help it; this hellhound has a real body count and my fear is tingling in the soles of my feet. Bastian must see something in my face because his expression softens and he reaches for my arm, stroking it gently.

"Look, I'll try to be as quick as possible," he says. "Just get the hair. Like plucking your eyebrows, but on a bigger scale."

"Do you pluck your eyebrows?"

"No, what?" Bastian blushes and turns back to the books. "Course not."

His fingers find the triangle; he settles his feet wide; his ring glows. He shoots me a final look.

"Ready?"

I'm touched that he's still thinking about me, checking on me. I nod sheepishly. *He's doing all the heavy lifting, the least you can do is watch and pluck,* I tell myself firmly.

"Yeah."

"Good." He rolls his shoulders with a sigh, closing his eyes. There's a moment of beautiful serenity, the hush in the eye of a storm, and then he begins. Bastian looks terrible and wonderful, a witch cloaked in rising blue magic from his ring, smelling like a bonfire, silhouetted against the stark bright stones of the cathedral, its sharp orange lights casting his shadow long and menacing behind him. When Bastian did magic in the library, it felt like standing near an open flame. Today, it feels like the temperature is dropping, a frost descending. I try not to shiver and watch as Bastian's power builds in his fingers and he moves them in a rhythmic sequence between two hand positions. It's simple – only Beelzebub's Horn and the Head of Anubis – but I can tell straight away that the complexity is in the rapid shifting between the two positions that rely on fingers connecting at all times. Still, he doesn't stop, his eyes fixed on the text, his hands keeping perfect time. I'm not sure but I think I hear a distant growl under the earth, almost pulsing in time with his movements. My stomach churns with panic and I hold the tweezers out in front of me like a weapon. *For Elizabeth,* I tell myself. Then I wonder if this is what I really want, but before I can give it too much thought, Bastian pulls his fingers out in a long gesture, stretching an invisible thread between his hands. A rope of shadows is growing between his fingertips, his ring glowing with a cold blue light. It reminds me suddenly of making a bubble with string, the shadow wavering precariously between his trembling hands.

"*Dod gwyllgi,*" Bastian chants. Only really ancient spells use words, so it's a surprise to hear his voice like this, in concert with his magic. My skin prickles. "*Dod gwyllgi, dod gwyllgi—*"

The bubble of magic expands, monstrous and blobby, like a black sack or a picture of an early-stage embryo about to divide. This is it, the space between dimensions, opening for something terrible to come through. It begins to writhe and squirm; there's something inside that is scrabbling to get out. Bastian's hands are shaking as they hold their pinched position, prising open an invisible gate. I look down, seeing frost on my boots. The ground begins to tremble with enormous footsteps. I hear the growl of a beast, far away, coming closer.

"It's coming." Bastian's voice is tense, his whole body taut and shaking.

"Okay." My teeth are chattering but I get the words out. "I'm ready."

The growling rises to roaring and the night darkens until we are trapped in the centre of a black hole. Plunged into impenetrable gloom, all I can hear is our heavy shared breath and rapid, terrified heartbeat. Then I see red eyes, burning and flashing.

"*Laqueum diaboli,*" Bastian whispers and I can see, in the dim, cold light from his ring, that he is moving his hands in a different spell. There is a crack like a whip and a corresponding snarl. Bastian holds his hands in a particular shape – a twisted interlocking of the fingers that I don't know the name of – and in front of him, contained on top of the blood pentagram that has scorched into the grass with black flames, is the Black Shuck itself.

It's weird to me that something so associated with devilry should be so cold, but I'm shaking with the icy waves of wind coming off it as it struggles against invisible bindings. Bastian slowly pushes his hands down, still holding the spell position. As he does, the hound sinks, thrashing and spitting, the weight of Bastian's spell pressing it into the earth.

"Now, Lando," Bastian gasps. There's sweat on his brow despite the cold, and he is panting heavily, his breath misty around him. Cautiously, I step closer to the hound, my boots crunching on the frosty grass. Its wild, fiery eyes twist to glare at me and I pause.

"It can't get out?" I ask, desperate for reassurance of what I know to be true, hating how my voice shakes.

"No." Bastian's voice is curt with effort. "Not unless the salt circle breaks."

"Okay."

For Elizabeth, I tell myself. I hold my breath and reach down with the tweezers but my hands are shaking too much and I drop them. I bend to pick them up but they're frozen to the grass, unmovable, my cold fingers slipping to grip them.

"Shit," I whisper. I look at Bastian, his eyes are wide with worry. I can tell he doesn't have a clue what to do. "It's fine, it's totally fine, I'll just..."

I look at the rippling black fur of the Black Shuck. If Bastian can do frankly ridiculous conjuring, I can surely rip out some hair. Sending a prayer to no one in particular, I dive. I grab the fur, which is thick and oily and so freezing cold it burns, and wrench it away. The hound roars with anger, but I don't hear it. The second I touch it, I know what's going to happen. I have to tell him.

"Bastian, I'm—"

I can't complete the sentence; my throat has closed, my body rigid and out of my control. I can feel it beginning inside me, just like it did on the beach at St Annes and at Boggart Hole Clough. I'm shifting again and tumbling through memories that aren't my own once more.

"Near the cathedral, love," she says. She is peering up through the windscreen of the ambulance as the air-raid sirens wail around us and the sky is lit with red fires and spotlights. "Turn left, here!"

"You asked me to drive, love!" I half laugh, half yell as she throws her arm across me, determined to give me instructions.

"Now! Now!" She laughs loudly, the ring on her finger catching the light of the fire of the city. I take one hand off the steering wheel to grab it, pulling it to my lips and kissing the back of her hand. I wish she hadn't come on shift tonight because I am so worried about something happening when we're out here, working in the raids, but I would worry if she stayed at home too. She won't go to the shelter when I ask. She's only twenty-one and she's a wonder, a marvel.

"There!" She points ahead and I accelerate, hitting the brakes in front of an air-raid warden who is standing in the shadow of the cathedral, desperately trying to direct people away from the terrible fires all around. We throw ourselves out of the ambulance, leaving it running to rush over.

"There's a lass, I've let her have a lie-down in the garden there," the warden bellows. "Lost half an arm. This lad has terrible burns."

"I'll take her!" she calls to me, already heading over to the girl in the grass. I give the lad my attention. The boy's face is blistered, eyes shut either from damage or pain. I wrap him

carefully, wanting to keep the wounds sterile, and help him climb blindly into the back of the ambulance. With the great roar of red fire all around us, I see two figures in the grass by the cathedral. She's waving to me, the signal for the stretcher, and I pull it out of the back, tucking it under my arm. I'm sweating with the heat, brushing dirt out of my eyes. That's when I hear it, the long drone of the falling bomb, and before I can call out, it hits. I watch helplessly as the cathedral tumbles. I cannot move, cannot say anything, as the building falls and swallows the woman I love.

Chapter Twenty-Three

I come around on the cold grass, head ringing, bones aching. I rub the tightness across my chest, feeling breasts again. *Female form,* I think dazedly. My throat is so dry I turn my head and cough, inhaling something grainy and tart. *Salt.*

The salt circle.

Bastian.

Fear jolts through me so fast I scramble up. Bastian is gone and so is the beast. The salt circle is smeared. I must have broken it when I fell, which means the Black Shuck is free and Bastian is in a lot of trouble.

"Bastian?" I yell. No one answers me. "Oh no, oh no, oh no…" I chant as I run stiffly around to the front of the cathedral and see, with a terrified lurch, that the door is open. There's no alarm blaring, which can only mean one thing – Bastian opened it with witchcraft.

I run inside. The light from the open door is sharp and violent on the floor, making the pillars cast long, ominous shadows across the stone. There is a sense of endless space around and all above me, as if the Black Shuck could be hiding in the rafters with the carvings of angels. I cling to the nearest pillar, grateful for the firm, grainy feel of the sandstone against my face. I peer into the threatening darkness, trying to make out shapes, chairs or pews or something, but there's nothing. Then I hear it. A growling, low and persistent, echoing against the columns and carved faces of saints, all around me and nowhere.

"Bastian?" I whisper. All I hear is a wet cough and a horrible low growl. I try to open my eyes wider, standing on my tiptoes, desperate to illuminate more of the darkness, my own gasping breath so loud I can barely hear the forbidding growling. Then I see it. A flash of red eyes, a shadowy, prowling form and, further down, sprawled on the floor by the altar, a wounded man being stalked by a hellhound.

"Leave him alone!" I yell, lurching forward and running straight into a chair. I grasp downward, seize a cloth-bound Bible and lob it at the shadowy beast. It flinches and rolls its red eyes towards me but doesn't stop advancing on Bastian. "Leave him ALONE!"

I throw another Bible, a hymn book, anything I can find. It does nothing and Bastian still isn't moving. Maybe he'll never move again. My heart stutters in my chest at that thought but I have to do something. I try to remember everything I've learned in the weeks we've been researching. Bastian called the Black Shuck, so that's why it can come into the church – he's tethered it to himself – but there are ways to send a demon back. *But I'm useless!* I think desperately. *Can't do fucking magic, can't do anything.* Then I remember Professor Wallace's words in class: *Sometimes, the oldest ways are the best...*

"Magical blood," I whisper. "Holy water!"

I spin around, scouring desperately for what I need, looking past stained glass and marble plaques and gilded crosses until I see it. I twist and run back up the cathedral to the bell tower, my footsteps slapping loudly against the polished marble. I search frantically for anything to cut myself with, a knife, anything sharp, and my eyes fall on an intercessory display, rows of candles that have been neatly trimmed for visitors and a set of wick scissors left beside the matches. I glance at the Black Shuck, and it's far enough away that I risk it. I snatch the wick scissors up, wincing as I set the circular blades around my fingertip, pinching them together until the skin breaks and the blood flows. After all, what's more magical than shapeshifter blood? Panting, I throw myself to the floor in front of the font, hastily using my bloody finger to draw one of the many exorcism circles I've been practising.

"Please work," I whisper frantically. "Please, please, fucking work."

I scramble back to the font and haul the ornate wooden lid with its carved angels off it with a thunderous clang, loud enough to draw the Black Shuck's attention. I look up and see red eyes advancing towards me, dipping in and out of the shafts of light weakly cast across the stone, one minute a hairy, bristling wolf made of shadows and the next, entirely invisible apart from nastily glowing eyes.

My hands are bumbling as I seize the plastic jug left inside the font. There's not a lot of water, maybe just whatever was left over from a baptism, but I know it will have been consecrated.

It'll have to be enough. The Black Shuck has stopped halfway down the aisle, licking its foaming jaw and tilting its head to look at me. It sniffs, scenting my magical blood on the air. Then it looks back to Bastian, as if weighing up who is the more exciting treat.

"Hey, Cujo! Fluffy!" I yell, waving my hand with the bleeding finger. The hound sniffs the air, its growling intensifies. "Come and get me!"

Drops of my blood hit the floor and it gnashes its teeth, before crouching closer to the ground, a hunting stance. *Oh, shit,* I think. *It's actually coming to get me.*

"Here we go, here we go," I chant to myself, grabbing the small jug and scooping some holy water. I squeeze my hand, again and again, so the blood keeps dripping, keeping up the scent. It's sickening to watch the beast inch closer on its belly, teeth so huge, abnormally long and slathering. I try not to think about how much of Bastian's blood it's lapped up.

"Come on, yes, good pupper, good pup, just get in the circle," I mutter, as the Black Shuck's growls send shakes of terror trembling down my limbs. The water in the jug rocks precariously in my ready hand. "Come on, you ugly mutt! COME ON!"

With an indignant, haunting howl, it launches into the air; I see it happening from outside myself – its body crossing the blood circle, my hand throwing the water, its hideous mouth opening, a long purple tongue ready to taste my flesh – and then I'm losing my footing. I'm toppling down, my back is hitting the tiles with a painful smack and I'm waiting for the piercing sting of hideous fangs that never comes. Instead, there's a horrible high-pitched scream and a hissing sound on the other side of the font. The water is burning the Black Shuck, melting and eating away the beastly fur. It's pushing itself from side to side, trying to free itself from my blood circle but it can't because it's *working*. I stare in amazement as it bangs itself against the walls of its invisible cage, horribly writhing, disintegrating, becoming less of a dog and more of a burning shadow. Then it's howling and twisting into nothing but sparks of fire in the air, before disappearing.

It's done. The air is empty; the cathedral is quiet; I can hear cars driving by on the ring road outside. Inside, the silence is oppressive, my heavy breathing too loud and echoey in the vast, open space. I stare hard at the blood circle, not daring to believe the Shuck is really gone, but the finals embers drift to the stone and…nothing happens. *Holy shit, I actually did it!*

My realization forces me to scramble up and stagger back down the aisle to Bastian, legs feeling like jelly. In the illuminated patches of the cathedral floor, I can see ugly dark streaks leading to a pair of blood-flecked jeans. I crumble on the stone flags next to Bastian, dragging his head into my lap. His eyes flutter open.

"Cujo," he chuckles wetly. "Funny."

"Bastian." His T-shirt is dark and damp, ripped with giant gash marks. Suddenly, I see Elizabeth in his place, the way dirt and blood muddied her blond hair. My only thought is, *This can't be happening to me again.* "No, no, no—"

"I'm okay, Lando." Bastian's sluggish hand finds mine,

squeezing it impossibly tight. "Don't panic, I'm not going to die."

"You're not?" I gasp, realizing that I'm panting through tears.

"No, I...I have a healing ring." Bastian winces, trying to pull up his T-shirt. "I just need you to...to put it on the wound..."

I've never been so glad to touch a witch's ring. I fumble to place Bastian's hand against the bloody scrapes of huge claws across his stomach.

"Can I—" Bastian swallows heavily, his eyes rolling sluggishly. "Can I borrow some of your...your magic? I know how to do it, I've been looking into sharing magic, there's...there's a spell I found. It won't work if we're *not* magically compatible but..."

I know I should be terrified of it; I know it's exactly the kind of thing that shifter parents down the ages have warned their children about, sharing magic with a witch, but I'm not. I don't care what my father would think, his disdain and ridicule. All I want is for Bastian to live.

"Try it anyway," I say determinedly.

"Do the Eye of Horus," Bastian whispers. "Around my ring."

I pinch my first finger and my thumb into an eye shape around the huge blue sapphire on Bastian's middle finger. With his other hand, Bastian holds two of his bloody fingers over the eye my fingers make, blinding it. His ring glows blue and I smell it, the rush of wood catching light that accompanies Bastian's magic. Our fingers are welded together, hot and sticky, starting to burn, and then I feel it. It's like the beginning of a shift, the stretching and dragging inside me when my body changes, but instead of flowing through me, it's flowing out of me. It's weirdly uncomfortable, reminding me of the times I've had a period in a female form, and I breathe through it heavily. If this is what magical compatibility feels like, I'm not sure I like it. Then I'm aware that my hair is changing around my head, my shifting power still working on my body even as it is pulled out of me like a rubber band.

"That's enough," Bastian croaks, flopping his hand down, and I wrench my fingers away, rubbing the burning sensation. Bastian spreads his fingers across his wound then twists them into a shape I recognize for sealing. He groans as a blast of blue light sinks into his wounds but, amazingly, I see the wounds closing. *Not permanent,* I remind myself, but I can't help the staggering flood of relief inside me.

"It's okay." I stroke his hair and rub his arm, feeling him tremble all over. "You did it, you're okay."

"We need to go." Bastian is already wincing and trying to stand up. "Someone will notice the door's open."

"Okay, come on." I slip his arm over my shoulder and pull him to his feet. He groans and is leaning against me pretty heavily, but I manage to drag him out of the cathedral and round to the conjuring circle. I sit him on the wall while I pull my backpack on and shove the books back in Bastian's satchel, throwing it over my shoulder. I see the dark clumps of the Black Shuck's hair on the grass and fumble to press them into the glass specimen vial Bastian had ready. Then I rush back to him. He's listing to the side, propping himself up with one hand and looking like he's about to tumble down onto the paving stones.

"You're never going to make it back down to Spinningfields."

I press my hand against his forehead. It's cold and clammy. "Let's get a taxi."

Bastian nods wearily. Clumsily, I do up his denim jacket to cover the bloodstains. Together, we stumble down to the main road and luckily, a taxi driver is sitting idle, singing loudly to Radio 1.

"Hey, mate," I call out. "Could you give us a lift down to Spinningfields?"

"Peak fare, though." The driver nods, looking curiously at Bastian as I manhandle him gently into the back of the cab. "He had a bit too much?"

"Food poisoning," I say, improvising.

"If he throws up in here it's a hundred and fifty quid for cleaning," the driver warns, pulling out into traffic. As he does, Bastian slumps against me, his head dropping into my lap.

"Are you okay?" I whisper, automatically stroking his hair. "It seems like you lost a lot of blood."

"Yeah, I just need a coconut water."

"Coconut water?"

"Yeah, it's…it's good after blood loss."

"For hipsters, maybe."

He laughs and then coughs, looking drowsily up at me.

"Hey." Bastian reaches a clumsy hand up to pull on one of my brown curls. "It's curly. It was straight when you shifted."

"Yeah, I—" I'm trying not to be distracted by his hand in my hair. "Giving you magic made it curl."

"I like it, it's cute." He frowns and puts a heavy, weary hand on my shoulder. "Are you sore? After the shift?"

"No." I smile wryly at him. "Adrenaline's a hell of drug."

"Ha, yeah, I could do with some of that."

"Here we are!" The cabbie calls through the glass. "That's fifteen quid, love."

It's complete highway robbery for a five-minute drive, but Bastian presses his debit card against the card reader and I open the door. Bastian groans as I drag him out and we stagger past the people dressed up and heading to the Ivy and the other fancy bars. They stare at us; a few yell drunkenly, probably noticing the blood, but I ignore them and pull Bastian on. When we reach the door, Bastian manages to punch in the code and we stumble into the lift. In the mirror and the fluorescent lights, we look a total mess. Bastian is too pale and his jeans are covered with blood, his hands grubby with it. I'm not looking too good myself, coated in blood, dirt and salt.

In the time it takes to get to the twentieth floor, I examine my new form. I'm shorter again; Bastian has to stoop to lean against me. My boobs are much smaller than my last female form – I probably won't feel like I need my binders – and my hair is jaw length and a curly, mousy brown. My eyes are wider apart, my nose longer, my chin sharper. Elizabeth's white-gold hoops still shine at my ear lobes.

"Come on," I mutter, heaving Bastian over the threshold. Immediately, René is barking and jumping around our ankles, so excited to see us. Bastian's feet are slowing entirely; he's clearly used all of his energy just getting into the room and he's almost too heavy for me to drag him to the sofa, flopping him down with a huff. "Coconut water?"

"In the fridge," Bastian moans. The sofa is one of those ridiculously long ones, a sectional that wraps around the coffee table and is almost as wide as it is deep. Bastian easily pulls his feet up onto it. René jumps up next to him and starts to lick Bastian's face. "There's some paracetamol on the side too."

"Where's your dad?" I ask.

"Fucked if I know." He gently pushes René away from licking the blood off his trousers. "He writes notes on the fridge."

"Okay." I open the huge fridge, notice with a smirk the giant wheel of goat's cheese with a note that says BASTIAN'S, DO NOT TOUCH among the Tupperware of various pepper- and allspice-scented leftovers all marked with a "B". The kitchen might be immaculate, but it looks like Bastian enjoys cooking. I pull out a carton of coconut water for Bastian and the orange juice bottle for me. "Here."

I toss the coconut water gently to him and he drinks slowly, as if it's taking all his effort to swallow, but he is managing it. While he's drinking, I drain the orange juice, relieved to quench my thirst. When I'm finished, I notice that Bastian is watching me with amusement.

"Thirsty?"

"Shifting always makes me thirsty." I close the fridge. I glance at a note that says LONDON UNTIL 2ND NOVEMBER. "Does your dad know you were suspended?"

"No, and I'm not telling him," Bastian mutters. I scoop up the paracetamol and cross back over to the sofa. I sit gingerly down next to him and pop the paracetamol out of the packet, watching him take them. I'm amazed to see how the colour is beginning to flush back into his cheeks just from drinking the coconut water. René shuffles past Bastian and puts his head on my bloody jeans, looking up at me with those big adorable eyes.

"Well, you're the nicest dog I've met tonight," I say, stroking his ears before turning back to Bastian. "I should sort you out before that spell fades."

"Do you know how?" He looks sceptically between me and his injury.

"Yes, Bastian, I know how to wipe up blood and bandage wounds," I say, pointedly holding up my wrist. My scars are just visible under the edge of my long-sleeved T-shirt, stained on the hem with blood.

"Sorry." Bastian winces. "There's a first-aid box in the cupboard under the sink. There's some skin glue in there and some Steri-Strips, you might need both if it's already failing."

There's a rise of sickness in my throat at the idea of Bastian's wounds reopening, returning to the leaking terrifying gashes they were before, but I nod and retrieve it, sparing a second to quickly wrap a plaster around my sore finger before dampening a clean tea towel under the tap. René follows me into the kitchen, looking balefully up at me when I put the paracetamol back down next to a glass jar of dog bones. I drop him one and he merrily trots back to his basket by the big windows. The view at night is even more astonishing than in the day, the lights of the city yellow pinpricks in the darkness, the reflections shimmering on the canals. On the sofa, Bastian is carefully shrugging off his denim jacket and trying to lift his T-shirt.

"Easy," I say, helping him pull it over his head, trying not to look at his scarred collarbones. He's breathing shallowly as he leans back, gingerly twisting so he can rest back against the sofa cushions. The two slashes across his abdomen have closed, but the dried blood is smeared all across his skin.

"They still look good," I say sceptically. "The spell doesn't look like it's failed…yet."

"Huh." Bastian's face is wearily quizzical. "I guess…I mean, I do have a healing ring…and if I used *your* power it might be strong enough on its own, right?"

"Are you asking me about witch-ring powers?" I say, trying to joke as I open the first-aid box. He doesn't smile, just stares down at his wounds in puzzlement and then lets out a huff of exhaustion.

"I guess just use the Steri-Strips and we'll see how it goes."

"Okay."

I gently wipe away dried blood, trying to avoid the wounds and trying not to notice the dark curls of hair that mat wetly against his stomach above his jeans.

"That's nice," Bastian mutters, leaning his head back and closing his eyes. I feel myself blushing as I pull out some antiseptic wipes.

"This might hurt."

"It's okay, I've had worse." He gestures clumsily to the scars across the top of his chest and shoulders. His many necklaces and charms hide most of it, the splotchy texture of healed skin.

"Is it…from Shasta's car crash?" I ask hesitantly. I've suspected Bastian was there when it happened for a while but we've never discussed it.

"Yeah. The only good thing that can be said for being mauled by a hellhound is being hit by a four-by-four is worse."

"Hold onto that." I tentatively brush the antiseptic wipe over the wounds, as carefully as I possibly can while still getting rid of the grit and blood. Bastian hisses through his teeth as I mutter apologies then tentatively apply Steri-Strips and some long, sticky dressings over the wounds.

"All done." I wipe my hands and pack everything away while Bastian breathes deeply through his nose, a clenched fist pressed to his forehead. I queasily throw the bloody, dirty wipes into the wastepaper bin behind the sofa and am silently thankful it wasn't something much worse.

"That was fast thinking," I say. "With the magical compatibility thing in the cathedral."

"Yeah, finally putting all that reading to practical use." Bastian smiles wanly, then his face takes on a look of worry. "You didn't feel pressured, did you?"

"No, I'm glad you did it," I say. I feel strangely awkward talking about it though. It's supposed to be this massive magical milestone that we passed together, but I don't have words for the quiet anticlimax of it. I've done the unthinkable, something no shapeshifter should do or has done in centuries (if my parents are telling the truth) but I feel utterly unchanged. He might as well have borrowed a pen or my lecture notes. I want to ask Bastian if he feels any different, but his face is already slackening with exhaustion as his shoulders wilt.

"That's a relief." His eyes droop. "You were so amazing, getting rid of it. Was it an exorcism circle?"

"Yeah, my blood and then some holy water. I was shitting myself. I didn't know it would work but it turns out Professor Wallace was right, sometimes the oldest ways are the best."

"Ha." His eye opens and he gives me a slightly wry look. "Good thing you asked that question in class, then."

"Is it too soon for an 'I told you so'?"

"Maybe after I've slept for twenty hours." He yawns, eyes drifting closed again. He really does have the most fantastic eyelashes.

"Do you want to go to your bedroom?"

I look around, trying to assess the distance to the nearest doors and if I can get him there safely.

"No, I don't think I can move and this is wide enough for both of us." He flops a tired hand against the sofa. I stare at him for a second, wondering if I've misheard him.

"For both of us?" I repeat.

"Oh. Um." Bastian opens his eyes and shoots me an apologetic look. "You don't have to stay."

"Do you want me to?"

"I... Yes." Bastian sighs heavily. "I probably need someone here, in case the wounds reopen and...I'd like your company."

"Then you'll have it."

It would have felt beyond cruel to leave him now, on the sofa, barely able to move. A part of me is still in the cathedral, holding his head in my lap, seeing his blood and panicking that he was going to die right in front of me, just like Elizabeth. I reach down and unlace my boots, helping Bastian ease off his trainers too.

"Thank you." I feel Bastian's hand stroking my hair and my breath catches in my throat. I sit back up. He doesn't move his hand away. Instead, he drifts it cautiously around, so slowly that I can pull away if I want, until his thumb is stroking my cheekbone and my jawline, mapping out my new face.

"I always want your company," he whispers.

"Bastian..." I don't want him to stop but I don't know what to do either. *Don't do this if you don't mean it,* I find myself thinking desperately. *Please.*

"I know." He's breathing sharply through his nose, each word costing him. "I know you're not over Elizabeth, I get it, but I almost got eaten by a hellhound tonight, so I feel like I just really need to say...that I think you're beautiful."

My expectations go into free fall. My body is so heavy with crushing disappointment. This is a pretty form; I've got big eyes and nice cheekbones. This skin that barely feels like mine yet, *that's* what he finds beautiful. Not me.

"Yeah," I say hollowly. "This is...a nice form, I guess."

"No." His voice is so fierce and his hand holds my chin, forcing me to look into his eyes. "Not your form, whatever it is, but *you*. All the time. Because whatever your form, you're always sharp and funny and you always give me the same eye roll and the same annoyed look and eat biscuits like a weirdo—"

"Rude," I mutter, and he smiles, rubbing his thumb over my new nose, my different freckles, like he's been looking at them fondly for months.

"You're always you," he goes on. "And nobody else has made me feel..."

"Feel what?" I ask, wondering how I'm still breathing when he's saying all this.

"This." He takes my hand and presses it over his heart, just like he did when I had a panic attack at college. This time, it's no longer slow and calming, but vibrant and frantic. I reckon it could match my own. "Whether you're in a hoodie or daft dungarees, redhead or brunette, whatever, you always make me feel *this*. I think you're...brilliant, Lando."

He rubs a thumb across my lips. They tingle. There's a residue of spellwork in his hands and I can suddenly taste it, that smoky air of the magic inside him leaking out of his pores. Maybe I should have hesitations, but how can I? After everything, we are both here, unexpectedly together, miraculously alive.

"Is it really weird if I say I've been thinking about kissing you for weeks?" he whispers. The relief is unimaginable; it sweeps away every other feeling in its path. Fear, anxiety, even guilt dissolve into his soft brown eyes.

"I thought you were into men," I blurt out, but I have to know, even as I'm leaning towards him, even as his other hand is slipping to my waist. "Are you...?"

"I'm pansexual." His eyes are fixed on my lips. "Is that okay?"

"It's amazing," I say, and I kiss the life out of him.

Chapter Twenty-Four

I'd forgotten this. I'd forgotten how when you first kiss someone, time stretches and bends around the taste of them. I'd forgotten how having someone touch me is a solace, calming the parts of me that ache so deep down they can't be soothed by anything else. It's blinding, the way it runs through me and wipes out all thought in blissful relief. I thought I'd feel weird or sad doing this with someone after Elizabeth, but I don't. All I feel is wanted and safe.

After a long, very delicious time, I'm lying across the giant sofa in just my T-shirt with my head in Bastian's lap, reading to him from *The Witchlore of Bodies* as he passes me Oreos to munch on. I'm reading about the shifter's adventures with their newfound love in 1940s Manchester when I realize something: I am happy.

"I have a confession to make," Bastian says.

"Oh?" I raise my eyebrows suggestively and he tuts, poking my nose.

"I've wanted to be here for a really long time," he says slowly. "With you."

I look up at his beautiful face, the dishevelled hair, the hazel eyes that are full of gentleness, the many necklaces and chains hanging over his bare chest. I smile and reach up, playing with one of his necklaces, a row of shark teeth on a leather cord.

"It was sort of a date, wasn't it?" I say. "The bar?"

"I was nervous enough for it to be," he says ruefully. "But I don't think it was the right time for you. I felt so stupid afterwards."

"You are lots of things, but you are never stupid." I tug on his necklace, pulling him down to meet my lips, oily from the biscuits, his mouth tasting so sweet. This is the wonder of it, the intimacy that comes once the threshold has been crossed. Before, every time he touched me I noticed it; now, I'm so full of his touch and his skin and his body against mine that I don't even notice the closeness. I can relax into it entirely, knowing that any casual kiss or stroke won't be spurned or pushed away. I'd forgotten this too, the happiness being with someone brings, the change from friends to something more.

"So your shifter was an ambulance driver in World War Two?" Bastian asks, twisting his fingers into my curls as I pull the Oreo apart and lick out the middle. Above me, Bastian makes small noises of disgust and I smirk with the predictability of it.

"They're not my shifter, but, yeah, they were. Their father died during the First World War and he was angry that they had taken a male form and fought in the war, so they didn't want to do it again. They took a female form when the Second World War started and then…well, they fell in love with a witch who was also an ambulance driver."

"A shifter and a witch, who'd have thought it?" Bastian says, and I pinch him softly.

"I wonder what she was called, their lover." I stroke the page with the old ink on it, my fingers brushing over the letter "B". *Bella? Becky?*

"They must have kept a young form, to stay with them."

"Yeah, but they felt really seen by her." I smile fondly. "They weren't afraid."

"Which is kind of amazing considering they were basically lesbians in 1940." Bastian shakes his head. "That's a rough time to be gay."

"Yeah." I don't add that I think, sadly, the lover might have died in the bombing of the cathedral. How would I justify it, since I haven't read it yet, only seen it in my vision? I feel a shiver of discomfort at all the things I can't explain to myself. "But sometimes you can't help yourself, can you?"

"You're right." Bastian's voice is distant as he strokes my thigh. "Sometimes you can't help yourself."

We fall asleep like that, wrapped around each other. Elizabeth and I never got to do this and I realize that it's the nicest thing in the world, falling asleep hearing someone's heartbeat in your ear, the sound of their breath like the ocean. Bastian smells like antiseptic and blood but underneath, that unique scent that each person has. His is sweet and musky and utterly delicious. It's the easiest I've fallen asleep since Elizabeth died. Then I dream.

* * *

I'm standing in front of the mound of fresh earth that's marked with a simple cross, too early for a headstone. With trembling hands, I lay a bunch of carnations on the dirt, their petals white against the dark mud, cold with the early January frost. I shiver and feel tears slip down my cheeks.

"I'm sorry," I whisper. "I couldn't get to you, I tried so hard but...I couldn't save you."

I sniff and wipe my cheeks with chilled hands. I remember the people I have lost, my father, my mother, the years of my life that now seem agonizingly stretched.

"I've lived so long and never loved anyone the way I love you," I murmur. "I miss you so much. Don't leave me."

I drop to my knees and press my hands into the cold earth, my tears falling on it like rain, instantly lost. I wish I could dig down into the ground and lie there with her. I do not know how to live without her.

"Lando." Someone is rubbing my back, holding me gently, kissing my shoulders. I'm sobbing into the sofa with all the pain of this loss but it's not just the shifter's loss, it's mine too. *Elizabeth is dead.* I can smell salt and eucalyptus. *Bastian.*

"She died, the witch died," I gasp, turning around and pressing my face into his chest. It's so warm and the scarred skin has a stretched, smooth texture in some places and bumpy in others. I brush my lips against it, comforted. "I saw her grave, the shifter's lover, the one who died in the Second World War—"

"You saw what?" Bastian asks.

I don't answer. I sniff and wince and wrap my arms carefully around his torso, wanting to squeeze him tightly but aware that he's wounded. Bastian strokes my back and kisses my hair. It's so comforting it makes me cry more. Aside from Elizabeth, no one has ever touched me like this. I don't have any memories of my mother or father doing it when I was little and had nightmares. Suddenly, I'm not just crying for everything now, I'm crying for the child I once was, lonely and without comfort. There's one thought, repeating in my mind: *None of it has been fair.* I cry until I'm just hiccupping quietly, my cheeks and nose wet against Bastian's skin, and he kindly doesn't push me away. If anything, he pulls me closer.

"Are you ready to tell me what you've not told me?" Bastian whispers into my hair. The muscles in my back tighten with nervousness, but of course he's worked it out.

"Yes," I sniff.

"They're not normal shifts, are they? Or normal nightmares?"

"No, they're..." I take a great, shuddering sigh and shiver against the cold. "I don't know what they are."

"Tell me." Bastian pulls a heavy, slightly itchy wool blanket over us. Its dark, ruddy colours make me think of big Canadian trees and shiny glaciers, and I feel cosy and safe enough to talk.

"Since I started reading the grimoire, I've been having these... visions," I say hesitantly. "It's like I remember things that happened to the shifter in the diary. Things they don't mention but they all fit together. Every time I've touched an ingredient for the spell I see their life, I feel it's mine. But how could I be getting their memories? What does it even have to do with the spell? We don't even know if the same person who wrote the diary in the grimoire wrote the spell... This is all so weird."

"It is weird," Bastian says. "But it's a weird spell. There's a reason there are no resurrection spells any more. It's a type of transformative power we only see in history; it's volatile. But shifters, you have that power naturally." He kisses my forehead reverentially. "I'm not surprised it's impacting you."

I swallow hard. It has been impacting me, not just the strangeness of it or the way the grimoire has been gradually sliding into my consciousness over time, but the heaviness of carrying thoughts and memories that are not truly mine.

"It is a lot," I confess in a whisper, my eyes stinging.

"I know." He sighs. "I wish I could tell you why it's happening and why you keep shifting, but if I had to guess...I'd say it's because it's a spell that needs a shifter. So the magic is starting to connect to you. In some ways it's positive, I think it means it's more likely to work, but..."

"But it means I might have more shifts ahead of me," I finish for him. *More visions too.* Bastian nods.

"If I knew how to stop it, I would." He runs a finger down my nose. "I don't want you to be in danger."

"I don't want you to be in danger either." I press my hand against the edge of his bandage. He nearly died tonight. I remember how it felt to hold him in the cathedral, the helplessness overwhelming me, staring down at the inevitability of losing another person. The idea of feeling his last breath leave his body, just like I felt it leave Elizabeth's, is unbearable. There are so many things I don't know right now, but I do know I cannot ever do that again.

"Maybe…we could just stop," I whisper, body tense with anticipation. I know what I'm suggesting. *If we stop, I won't ever see Elizabeth again.* When I think that, I hear Counsellor Cooper's voice in my head: *I would encourage you, Lando, not to be scared of it, of…moving on.* Bastian's hand, which has been stroking my hair, pauses.

"Is that what you want?"

I don't know how to answer that. Of course I want Elizabeth not to be dead, but do I want her back if she is different? Do I want her back if it means I can't have Bastian, just like this, warm and soft and holding me so closely? Most importantly, do I want her back if I have to risk Bastian's life again to achieve it?

"What's left for the spell?" I ask, dodging answering.

"Not much. Getting the last ingredient, dirt from her grave, will be easy, and using your blood to open the wizard stone won't be difficult," he says. "'Wizard stone' is nearly always a reference to Merlin and to caves. I've done some research and the only local place that fits is the wizard's cave at Alderley Edge."

"What?" I jerk up, staring down at him, suddenly feeling lurching sickness rising up inside me. I hear her voice inside my head: *Don't leave me, Orla.* "No, I can't go back there. That's where Elizabeth died."

"Wait." Bastian winces as he leans up on his elbows, frowning at me in the darkness. "*This* was the cave you were in?"

"Yes!" Inside my head, I see a repeat of the moment all over again: her body, lying half-in and half-out of the cave, her head caught against a deadly slate, her bloody hair and my bloody fingers.

"Maybe that's why you had a magical discharge, why you shapeshifted," Bastian is saying, pulling me out of my recollections. "If there's a resurrection spell connected to shapeshifter blood cast into that particular stone, then having shapeshifter blood there but not the rest of the spell would have disrupted whatever she was trying to do. You could have been the right ingredient in the right place but with the wrong spell—"

"So you're saying it's my fault?" My voice is sharp, because I already know it was, I just don't want to hear him say it.

"No, Lando, no, I'm not." Bastian cups my face, his eyes earnest. "I'm just saying – magical spaces like that are ancient. There were spells cast into that rock that we have no record of and they're connected to some of the oldest and most volatile magic in the country. If part of our spell is woven into the stone there and it depends on a shifter's presence it could, theoretically, react badly. It's absolutely not your fault."

I don't believe him. All of the technical stuff about the spell might be correct but not this. *My only child is dead because of you,* Elizabeth's mother's voice echoes in my mind. It will never stop being true.

"I don't know if I can do this," I whisper. "I don't know if I can go back there."

"You don't have to." Bastian strokes my cheeks soothingly.

"But if we do this and we do it right, then everyone will know that none of this, her death, any of it, was your fault."

It's what I want, I realize. Not just to have Elizabeth back but to no longer be responsible for her death. The only way to get rid of that guilt is to undo it. I want to give Elizabeth back her life, to turn back time entirely. This is the closest way to get there.

"You're not worried about resurrecting my girlfriend?" I trace a pattern on Bastian's naked shoulder. It feels like we should definitely talk about it. If Elizabeth comes back she will have questions, but at least she will be alive to ask them.

"Listen, we all have to do what we have to do." Bastian's eyes are lit with intensity. He pulls my bare wrist, ghosting a kiss over my scars. I shiver. "I won't be mad if you still have feelings, but that's not important. I remember what it's like to be...haunted."

"Are you talking about Shasta?" I ask.

"Yeah." Bastian sighs and pulls me down so my head is resting on his chest. I brush his charms out of the way so the feathers aren't tickling my nose. I remember what Bastian said at my parents' house, about it being okay for me to wish that the moment of Elizabeth's death was quicker. I imagine Bastian and Shasta in the car on a dark road; I imagine the abruptness of Shasta's life, snatched away.

"After Shasta died, and everything with Mum and Dad just fell apart, I was...well, I went a bit wild. I think it's because I was so angry that the world was moving on without him. But it has to move on." Bastian's voice is distant. "We all have to do what we have to do to move on."

What seemed impossible to me three days ago now seems just very, very difficult. There's hope here, in Bastian's touch and Bastian's words.

"How do you move on?" I whisper. "How did you do it?"

"You just...keep going. It seems weird but, like, I had to get used to the world changing and not hating it for doing that. Reading helped, studying, having a purpose, moving up here and meeting you, it all made a difference, and then I realized I was moving on and it was okay. I wasn't watching the world change without him any more; I was part of it changing. At first I was a bit angry with myself, like I was betraying him..." Bastian's voice breaks and we wait, holding one another in the darkness and silence until he finds the words again. "Then I realized...that's exactly what Shasta would have wanted. That it wasn't about me moving on *from* him, like forgetting him, but moving on *to* something. He'd want me to keep going, keep...living."

"He'd be so proud of you," I say firmly. "I didn't know him, but I'm sure he'd be proud."

"Thanks." Bastian presses his face into my curls, breathing deeply. "I don't know exactly how it happened but one day I realized I was looking forward instead of looking back, and I realized I wanted to keep looking forward. A new future." He swallows and I feel his Adam's apple move as he squeezes me close. "With new people."

"Yeah." I flush coyly, despite everything we've done tonight. "I think...that's what I want too."

I want to do what Bastian's done, to transform myself and create a new future. If he can do it, maybe I can too?

"That's why we need to do the ritual. Then you won't have it hanging over you. No one will blame you any more. You'll be free, and you deserve to be free, Lando. Because you're so amazing. You make me feel..." Bastian's voice becomes thick with emotion. He's holding me too tight; I'm worried that I'm hurting the wounds on his stomach where I'm pressed against him, but he doesn't seem to care. "You know me. You see me, like no one else does."

I think about what the shifter wrote about the woman they loved. *I feel seen.*

"You too." I kiss him on the lips and think to myself that it doesn't matter if I bring back Elizabeth. I want to be with Bastian. When I bring back Elizabeth I'll have undone the worst thing I've ever done, robbing an innocent person of the rest of her life. She'll get to live, and that's all that matters. She doesn't have to live with me. Our futures can be whatever we want them to be; the important thing is that we'll have them. All of our choices, all of our lives, spread out before us. Bastian found his way through his grief and I can find my way through too. "We'll do the rest of the spell on Samhain."

"Okay," Bastian says sleepily. I settle back down against him with a sigh. Everything will be okay, I realize, as long as I'm with him.

CHAPTER TWENTY-FIVE

Over the rest of the week, I basically move into Bastian's flat. He's still serving his two weeks' suspension so whenever I'm not in college I'm in Spinningfields, eating Bastian's amazing home-cooked meals (some so accidentally spicy I cry and Bastian has to kiss me to make it better), and watching TV on the big sofa with René cuddling happily between us. I get used to sleeping in Bastian's bed and waking in his arms. Beryl is absolutely overjoyed by the development, but I think that's just because my new form is female and she likes the idea of me having a boyfriend.

I make liberal use of Bastian's wardrobe, and when I need to go to college on Friday, I leave the flat dressed in a pair of his old jogging bottoms and one of his vintage band T-shirts he says looks "sexy as hell" on me. I walk up through the city in the sunshine, the air smelling like soot and crisp leaves. The world is bright and sharp and lovely, as wintery and fresh as an apple, and all I think about is the fact that Bastian has given me firm instructions to come back to the flat as soon as my class finishes because:

"I can't go more than four hours without kissing you now. It's the new rule."

"The new rule for what?" I grinned up at him as I stepped into the lift.

"Our companionship." He winked at me. "Don't tell me you never got gay vibes off Frodo and Sam."

"I do love a queer reading."

Now, as I'm walking into the common space as light as a cloud, all I can think about is how his lips are a little bit chapped and, actually, it's really sexy. Especially when he kisses me in very soft places. I'm so full of happy butterflies, I don't even notice that I've flopped into one of the nice seats by the big windows. I pull out my headphones and am cheerfully lining up my next Stephen King audiobook when my phone buzzes with a message from BBB. I open it and laugh. It's a photo of René and Bastian on the sofa doing matching puppy-dog eyes. We miss you. I'm about to message him back when someone kicks my boots. I glare up at Carl Lord.

"Where's your boyfriend, shifter? Oh, that's right, suspended." Carl doesn't look so good. Unlike Bastian, he clearly doesn't have a good recipe for bruise paste, and the mark of Bastian's fist has bloomed dark purple and livid green across his nose and is taking its time to heal. I'm weirdly proud of Bastian for it.

"Yeah, because of you," I mutter. Carl grins nastily and sits down on the arm of my leather chair.

"Because he's a *sucker*," Carl says emphatically. "Anyone would have to be to be with you, right?"

I'm sure he thinks this is hilarious wordplay.

"Oh, piss off." I stand up to get away from him. I'm a little surprised when Carl stands up too, crowding into my space. After all, I'm in a female form and he's not stupid enough to think that his popularity will protect him from the consequences if he hits someone who looks like a girl.

"Say it again, shifter." His voice is low, threatening, just like it always used to be when he would corner me, telling me I was fit and he wanted me. I'm not the same person I was then. I've talked down a boggart and survived a drowning and thwarted a hellhound; I've lost someone I loved and found someone new who gives me hope. Carl Lord doesn't get to treat me like I'm nothing. When he sees I'm not backing down, he scowls. Suddenly his ring glows pink and he moves his fingers quickly, producing a sharp blow of heat, a warming spell misdirected again, just like the one he shot at Bastian in their fight. I flinch a little but I don't turn and run; I plant my feet wide. Even if I don't have any magic I can use like he does, I can use my words.

"You think your little ring is going to scare me?" I sneer. The air smells sickly sweet with his magic and his hands are trembling just to hold this small spell. He's always thought he's much more powerful than he is. Having seen Bastian in action, I'm no longer afraid. "I said, piss off!"

Around the room, a hush descends.

"You want to go, shifter? You're finally going to use some of that magic you're pushing into changing your boobs every two days?" He looks around, expecting a laugh. It doesn't come. Maybe people are more scared of me after he and Bastian had their fight, but they're looking at me as if they're expecting me to do something astonishing. It's the first time I've thought that people's prejudice might be helpful.

"Right, because you want to pick a fight with the one person who can't do witchcraft, right? That's what you like, isn't it, Carl? To pick on someone vulnerable?" Carl's eyes twitch and it's that, the signal that actually he's nervous about me speaking up, that gives me the courage to go on. "That's what you were thinking when you tried to hump me every second of the bloody day in first year, wasn't it?"

"You wish, shifter, like I'd ever look at you!" Carl spits. Another wave of pink magic comes off his ring as he moves his fingers in the same blunt movement, but even though the heat stings, I don't grimace. I won't back down, not now.

"You did look at me, you always look at me, you never stop looking at me." I fold my arms across my chest. "If you don't care about me then why don't you just leave me the hell alone?"

"Because—" Carl splutters, his eyes darting to his friends, who are watching impassively, all of their rings quiet, letting it happen. Maybe they've seen this coming for a while. Maybe they've secretly hoped for it. He looks desperately around the silent room but no one stands up for him, just like no one stood up for me. "Because—"

"Because it's fun, right?" I say. Carl looks at me with a panicked expression on his face. "It's fun to feel like you're the most powerful person here, like you're the one everyone respects and you're the one who can make or break people. Well, newsflash, Carl..." I pick up my bag and pull it on my back.

Carl hasn't moved; he's watching me like I'm dangerous, and suddenly I do feel dangerous to him. The truth is powerful. "Being a gropey *wanker* isn't sexy and it doesn't make you less of a patriarchal *dick* just because you only want to shag boys, okay?"

With that, I turn to leave.

"You're a fucking *murderer,* Orlando!"

I feel the rush of a spell coming towards me; I can smell the sugary nastiness of it and I know I can do nothing to stop it. I turn to face it so at least everyone in the common room will see I was defenceless, but suddenly, someone is beside me, moving their fingers, and silvery magic shunts a stack of chairs between me and Carl's spell. Carl's eyes widen. I turn to look at the blond boy who I thought was Carl's boyfriend. His high cheekbones are flushed, and the diamond ring on his finger is shimmering with a silver sheen as his trembling fingers hold the position of Atlas's Grip, glaring at Carl.

"Now everyone knows," he says to Carl, who is too shocked to speak. Then he turns to me. "Thank you," he mutters under his breath. "I thought it was just me."

I realize then that the shifter in the book was right. No one changes the bad things in the world for us. Sometimes, we have to stand up against the bad things, to be honest about how they've hurt us, because maybe other people, people we would never expect, have been hurt too.

"You're welcome," I say, nodding and walking down the stairs. For the first time since I started college here I feel like people are seeing the real Carl Lord. Perhaps they're also seeing the real me too. It's a shock, but now this thought doesn't make me afraid.

I ride on the high of standing up to Carl all day. I take a moment to message Bastian about it.

> Just so you know, I stood up to Carl.
> I told him he was a gropey wanker.

Bastian responds with a video of René doing what Bastian calls "a victory dance". I'm about to walk into Ezra's and buy us both celebratory coffees when someone taps me on the shoulder. I flinch and turn, expecting Carl or one of his crew, maybe wanting to make trouble, but it's only Kira.

"I need to talk to you about something," she says, looking particularly earnest today in a pair of clear-rimmed glasses.

"Don't you think you've said enough already?"

"Fine, don't listen to me, but you need to read this."

Kira reaches into her bag and pulls out a flat blue file. It's got no stickers or cats doodled on it, so I know it doesn't belong to her.

"What is that?" I ask, my throat dry.

"It's Bastian's personal file." Kira shifts awkwardly and looks down at her shoes. "From college."

"You stole his personal file?" I stare between her and it. "Why the hell would you do that?"

I realize it must be something bad for her to take such a risk, for Miss Goody Two-Shoes to actually steal a file, but something inside me rebels against it. I don't want to know. I'm happy; why can't I just stay this way?

"Because you need to know the truth." She pushes it into my chest and walks away. *Oh, no, you don't,* I think wildly. I follow her past the street art peeking out from the alleyways, a riot of reds and blues and faces and eyes, and down into the pedestrian area in Stevenson Square. It's busy as usual; some people are sitting on the brightly painted breeze blocks beside Fred Aldous to vape or drink takeaway coffees, and they stare as I chase Kira, but I don't care.

"Hey, hey!" I catch up to her and grab her shoulder, pressing the folder back against her chest. "You don't get to decide what I need to know! This is a massive violation of his privacy; I won't take it!"

"Then you have to hear it!" Kira's voice is louder than I have ever heard. Her glossy black hair is pulled up into a high ponytail today and it swings furiously as she faces me square on, the file clutched against her chest. "He was kicked out of his last college in London. He did dangerous magic there too."

"You just think it's dangerous because you can't do it!" I exclaim. "You're prejudiced against his coven!"

"No, because he killed another student!" Kira yells back. "A shifter student!"

"That's...that's crazy, don't say shit like that." I shake my head, my stomach churning. My mouth feels slimy. I wonder if I'm going to be sick and instinctively look around for somewhere I can throw up, eyes darting over the mulch of yellow leaves under my feet, the drain stuffed with cigarettes and mud.

"It's not crazy. He did a spell and someone died."

"Oh, and that makes someone a killer, does it?" I choke out, glaring at her. "I knew you felt that way about me, I knew you blamed me for her death—"

"This isn't about Elizabeth!" Kira slaps the file against my hand but I refuse to take it, stepping back. "Read the file."

"No, it's a lie—"

"It's not a lie. It was a really unpredictable ancient spell, something to do with resurrecting the dead."

My ready protests catch in my throat. *Please,* I think to no one in particular. *Please don't let this be true.*

"Look, I'm really proud of you for standing up to Carl." Kira's brown eyes are earnest. "I had no idea he was so awful. I don't want you to be tangled up with someone else like him."

"You're proud of me?" I sneer angrily, my voice raising to a shout. "You think you have the *right* to say that to me while you compare Bastian to *Carl*?"

Just the thought is a kick in the chest. Kira gives me a mournful, almost pitying look that honestly makes me want to scream in her face: *You don't know him like I know him!*

"Look." She flips the file open. I immediately look up to the sky, as if afraid the words are going to jump up and assault my eyes. "Please, Lando, you have to know the truth."

I thought Bastian had told me all the truth he had, the truth about Shasta and his parents, the truth about how he felt about me. Was it possible that he was still keeping something back? Hating myself, I look down. The top page is the most recent.

It's an assessment of Bastian from his last college in London. The words jump in front of my eyes: *Reckless, unfocused, too intelligent for his own good, arrogant in a way that disregards the safety of others.* There's a comment that leaps off the page, striking me right in the breastbone, knocking the wind out of me: *Bastian Chevret befriended Cameron Mackay, knowing that she struggled to fit in due to her shapeshifter status. He preyed upon her social vulnerability to manipulate her in the worst way.* I think about the first day I met Bastian, how quickly he learned from Carl Lord that I was a shifter, and then he didn't leave me alone. A horrible thought leaps in my mind: *Did he single me out because he could manipulate me too?*

"I know he's had a troubled life," Kira says softly. "But someone died, Lando. Cameron Mackay died. I couldn't stand by and let that happen to you."

"It's bullshit." I let the file drop to the ground sloppily, its pages spewing into the wind, but Kira doesn't even move, she just stares at me.

"It's right there," she says. "You read it."

"You made it up." I'm breathing heavily, and I really do think I might be sick if I can't sit down and get control of myself soon. "You're trying to take something away from me because you think I took Elizabeth away from you."

"Elizabeth died. It wasn't your fault. I've never said it is—"

"You don't have to say it!" I yell. "You never *spoke* to me the whole time Elizabeth and I were together! I could feel your witch prejudice from miles away—"

"I didn't speak to you because Elizabeth was terrified that

somehow her mum would find out about you, so she asked me to keep up appearances at school, to pretend like you weren't dating, like you and I didn't know each other." Her eyes are shiny but her voice is harsh. "You assume I'm prejudiced because I'm a witch, but you know nothing about me or my family. My ancestors emigrated from Morocco in the nineteenth century, we weren't even *here* for the witch trials, we have nothing to do with this British prejudice, and *you* are not the first shapeshifter to live in this city, Orlando!"

"If all of that's true, then why are you doing this?" I gesture to the file.

"Because it's what Elizabeth would want me to do," Kira says fervently. "Every day I think to myself, I'm alive and she's not and it's the worst thing, but what does she want me to do?"

"And you think it's this?" I yell. "Taking this away from me?"

"Telling you the truth. Keeping you safe." Kira's eyes are glistening with tears. "I'm not a liar, Lando. Whatever else you think about me. Do you really think I'd lie to you about this?"

I know the answer has to be no, but that means too many terrible things for me to possibly accept.

"Stay away from us," I say, turning to leave.

"No, wait!" Her eyes are frantic and she's reaching into her coat pocket. "There's something else I have to show you—"

I cannot possibly take any more of her revelations.

"No," I say and I run away from her, fast, through Stevenson Square, down towards Piccadilly Gardens, back towards Bastian. To the place where I feel safe.

Chapter Twenty-Six

As I speed walk past the library, I tell myself it has to be a misunderstanding. All of it. If Bastian had tried to do the spell before, he would have told me, wouldn't he? Yet the words in that report keep spinning back to me: *He preyed upon her social vulnerability.* By the time I'm at Bastian's door and he's buzzing me inside, I'm breathing heavily, staring at my form in the lift mirror and wondering why I don't look different. The person I have feelings for might have lied to me about everything. How can I possibly look the same?

Bastian opens the door to the flat. He looks amazing, dressed in a pair of plaid pyjama trousers and a worn T-shirt. His hair is wet as he smiles so broadly, leaning in to kiss me. I can't help running my fingers through it. *They all must be wrong,* I think, inhaling the scent of his coconut conditioner. *Maybe the girl died and he was blamed, just like I was for Elizabeth. Maybe someone bullied him and pinned it on him. Maybe Kira's lying.* There are so many possibilities that I'm certain, in that moment, what I read in that file cannot be true. It just can't be.

"How are you feeling?" I ask, trying to act normally as he

kisses me on the lips. He still tastes the same. How can he possibly be a completely different person, a person who lied to me, and still taste the same?

"Bit less stiff today," Bastian groans, making his way back to the sofa. His recovery has been slow but steady since Tuesday. "Could do with a coffee. How was your last class?"

"Fine," I say, thinking, *After it, I listened to someone say horrible things about you.* I sort of hate myself for even entertaining the possibility of it. How could I think that the person smiling so easily in front of me, looking at me like I'm the centre of the world, could ever hurt anyone? "I'll make you a coffee, don't get up."

It's a worthy act of penance for my failure to throw that file in Kira's face. I approach the behemoth of a coffee machine, all shiny bells and whistles, and carefully check the compartment.

"You're out of beans," I say. I'm surprised by how on edge I feel in a place that has been so comfortable to me all week. It's as if all the terrible things I read and that Kira told me have infected the air in the flat, like a virus I've brought in with me.

"Oh, yeah, I have a subscription; extra beans are under my desk in the bedroom."

"Okay." I drop my backpack on the sofa and hesitantly kiss the top of his head. I feel warm and tender when he smiles at me, basking in the blissful normality of affection between us. I watch him throw the squeaky toy for René and I think that maybe I'm trying to sabotage my own happiness. Maybe Counsellor Cooper was right and I'm afraid of something new. Bastian is perfect and here I am, recklessly risking everything we have on some story from a peer mentor on a power kick. I'm mad at Kira, suddenly, furiously angry with her for trying to ruin it. *She's wrong about him,* I think fiercely. *She doesn't know him like I know him!*

I duck into Bastian's bedroom and instantly smile. Unlike the rest of the house, with its depersonalized decor and futuristic furnishings, Bastian's bedroom feels like the home of a witch. Despite Eric's taste imposing in the furniture and paint, Bastian has statues and little shrines and piles of books teetering everywhere so that the desk is practically inaccessible. I navigate round a structurally unsound stack of library books on conjuring circles and look at the many framed photographs he has cluttering up the surface. His grandparents, cousins, his mum, all scattered among the spell ingredients. I glance fondly at the evidence of our adventures: the bone in its jar, the name of the boggart rolled up in a little scroll, the vial with the black hair of the Black Shuck.

My eyes settle on a picture of Bastian and Shasta together, taken in summertime with Shasta wearing sunglasses and Bastian pulling a silly face. I smile at it, thinking that when I met Bastian I would never have imagined him capable of such a goofy expression. I pick it up, thinking he looks adorable, then I frown. Hiding behind the framed photograph, just peeking out from behind yet another book, there is a jar of dirt. I stare at it. Why would Bastian already have a jar of dirt? We're meant to get the dirt from Elizabeth's grave on the weekend. *Unless he already had dirt from a different grave,* a sly voice in my head says. A voice that sounds sort of like Kira Tavi. *Unless he's been lying to you about the ritual all along.* I pick up the jar of dirt, holding it in my hand. It's grey and dusty. It looks old. He definitely hasn't dug this in the last week.

"Lando?"

Bastian is leaning in the doorway. He sees the jar of dirt in my hand. His face pales, just like it did when the Black Shuck attacked him, and in that horrible ground-shifting moment, I know that everything Kira said was true.

"We don't have our dirt yet." I hold up the dirt and look at Bastian. "Whose grave is this from?"

Bastian swallows.

"Don't lie to me," I say, trying not to plead. There's a sharp pain between my ribs, and if he lies, I will howl.

"Lando—" he starts, but I cut him off.

"Is it true?" I demand. "Did you try the ritual last year with a different shifter?"

"Who told you—"

"Just tell me!" I slam the dirt down on his desk and Bastian flinches, nodding.

"I...yes, I have tried it before, but I didn't...that's not what this is about—"

"Whose grave is this from?" I point at the jar.

"Shasta's," he whispers. I stare at him, waiting for an explanation, but I realize I don't need one. Shasta's name is the piece of the puzzle I need to understand everything the report said. It's the context that was missing, because now I know the one thing, the only thing, that Bastian would do anything for.

"You told me you'd moved on. That you were moving forward. I wanted to move forward too, but this...this was never about moving forward or about me," I say slowly. "This was always about Shasta."

I remember how, when we first read the book, he had muttered to himself, *If this is all of it, why didn't it...?* He was referring to the time he'd tried before. The full sentence inside his mind must have been, *Why didn't it work before with my other shifter?* That first night I asked him if this was the kind of thing he did, weird and dangerous spells. He asked, *Did someone say something?* I was too wrapped up in scoffing at the idea that anyone at college would talk to me to realize that he was worried I'd heard about Cameron Mackay. He was concerned I'd already heard the truth about him.

"You've been hiding this from me since the beginning."

"You don't understand." Bastian's eyes take on a frantic edge. "Back then, all of that, I was different. After Shasta died, I completely lost it. I told you I went a bit wild; I didn't tell you how."

"Tell me now," I say, wondering how I am still managing to get words out.

"I was so angry all the time, I just needed to get him *back*. My family was broken and I was failing in college, looking at all these ancient spells, trying everything, and then one of my nana's friends from our coven, she had an old photocopy of a fragment of the spell. I tracked down the book online, started trying to piece the spell together from the photos on the web page. I didn't care how many classes I missed or anything..."

Arrogant in a way that disregards the safety of others; I remember those words from the report. I wonder, for the first time, if Bastian's confidence that we would manage the boggart and the selkies and the hellhound was actually something else. Maybe he really didn't care what happened to me.

"So you tried it for Shasta, you tried it with another shifter." I nod, feeling a coldness settle inside me. "And she died."

"Cameron," he whispers. "From college. It was an accident."

"How could you not tell me that you'd tried it before, and that someone *died*?" I stare at him. "Unless you didn't care, unless you didn't *care* that you might kill me too? They're saying you targeted her."

"No! Cameron recognized from some of the pages online that they were shifter spells, she thought it might need a shapeshifter! We hadn't seen the whole book online, we didn't know about the blood lock and what was missing, how could we? Cameron and I were on the same course, it wasn't like I sought her out—"

"Like you sought me out," I finish scathingly, and Bastian flinches. I realize that it's true. "Is this the whole reason you came to Manchester?"

"After Cameron died, I...knew I needed to see the spell in person and...I needed to go somewhere else for college," Bastian admits. "Dad told me this was my last chance. So I asked to move here."

"Because your last shifter hadn't been up to snuff, right? Inconveniently *dying* on you?"

"No!" Bastian's face is twisted in sadness. "Cameron encouraged me, she gave me something to concentrate on after Shasta, she was into the idea of the Merlin Foundation too—"

"Was she your girlfriend?" I hate myself for asking, but I do.

"No, Cameron was a study partner, a..." He struggles for the word.

"A companion?" I sneer, and he winces.

"A friend," he finishes. "But once Cameron was gone, I was on my own *again*, but then I came here, I met you—"

"Wow, so I'm not just a replacement ingredient, I'm a replacement FRIEND!" The fact that he keeps saying her name is making me unreasonably upset. I believe him, unhelpfully, that Cameron was just his friend, but for some reason I wish she hadn't been. I remember what Bastian's dad said when I first met him: *Not another Merlin Foundation wannabe, I hope.* He was talking about Cameron, already fashioning me as her potential replacement and warning Bastian. No wonder he didn't want to tell his dad he had been suspended.

"No!"

"So you didn't seek me out because you knew where the book was and you knew you'd need another shapeshifter?" I stare at him, daring him to lie. "You didn't find out my girlfriend was dead and think that would be a way to get me on board?"

"That might be how it started but it's not how it is now." Bastian's voice is suddenly urgent. "Meeting you, getting to know you, it changed everything."

"Then why do you still have this?" I pick up the jar and wave it at him. "With all the other ingredients? *Our* ingredients? For *Elizabeth's* resurrection?"

Bastian grips the edge of the door frame, his fingers white with tension. I already know the answer, but there is a crushing feeling inside of me that desperately needs to hear the truth.

"Oh my god, Bastian, just say it!" I shout.

"Yes, when I moved here, I wanted to do the spell for him," he admits. Even though I expected this, it hits me in the stomach like a kick from a horse. "I felt guilty about his death."

"You said it was a car accident." I stare at him. "Why would you feel guilty?"

"Because I'd gone to a party that night. I was celebrating getting into college with some mates and I got drunk. Shasta picked me up and I was messing around in the car, being a twat," Bastian says, the words tumbling out, heavy with despair and self-recrimination, his face twisted with anger. "It was my fault; Shasta was distracted, he didn't see the truck, he could have swerved so it hit my side and not his. He bled out in the car, right in front of me, there was nothing I could do. I tried everything, every spell, everything I could think of but he...just died before the ambulance arrived. My parents never said it was my fault but if one of them had been there..." He looks at me with pleading eyes and there's a lump in my throat because I can imagine it, sharp as a pin inside my mind, Bastian pumping up and down on Shasta's chest like he did for me on the beach. "It's like my dad said, if magic can't save someone, what's the fucking *point* of it? I needed it all to have a point. I just needed him back, Lando, you know how that feels—"

"Yeah, I do know!" I explode, fighting tears. "Because you got me on board by saying we would use it for Elizabeth! But that was a lie. What else did you lie about? Do you even care about the Merlin Foundation?"

"Yes, I do, it's what Shasta wanted," Bastian whispers hoarsely. "Witchcraft is what held our family together. We wanted to do it together."

"So it's all been about getting your brother back, all of it, so you can do mad witchcraft together in your elitist sodding coven, being the most powerful witches you can fucking be, impressing the Merlin Foundation and using needy *pathetic* shapeshifters to get there." Bitterness is curdling the despair inside me, turning it to hatred. "That's why you saved me from the boggart, that's why you were so angry that I nearly drowned, you needed my *blood* to bring him back—"

"I was angry because I care about you!" Bastian yells. "I was angry because I didn't want you to DIE!"

"Yet! You didn't want me to die *yet*!"

"No! Everything changed when I met you," Bastian says desperately, limping into the room with a wince. "I might have kept the jar for sentimental reasons, but I wasn't lying, I *have* moved on. When I came here, I thought I would just get the spell done and get Shasta back but you changed everything." He steps closer and gently puts his hands on my shoulders. I can't pull away, how can I? All I want to do is to fall into his grip, to be held and make all of this not happen.

"You changed me, Lando. You made me realize there are better ways to be and this wouldn't be what Shasta wanted for me, and I...I started to feel alive again."

"Yeah, so did I," I say harshly, stepping out of the reach of his warm hands. There's a coldness descending inside me, the same way it settled the night I walked into the bathroom and saw those blood flecks fall like rose petals on the green and white rug. It's the coldness of being cut off from everything I care about, of being alone with no one and knowing there's no way back. It hurts more this time than it did last time. *Because you really believed him,* a chilling, sneering voice whispers inside me, the same voice that urged me on in the bathroom. *You pathetic piece of shit.*

"I'm sorry, I'm so sorry, but I wasn't doing it just for the spell any more," Bastian pleads, his eyes wet. "I was doing it for you too. I wanted you to feel better, to move on—"

"And when we did the ritual?" I snap. My hands are shaking but my voice is ice. I don't care if he cries. I won't care. "When you had a pint of my shapeshifter blood and the conjuring circle, whose dirt were you going to use? Who were you going to bring back, Bastian?"

"How can you ask me that?" His eyes have filled with tears. He wants me to trust him, to believe that he has good intentions, but I know in my bones that I don't. It's a horrible feeling. So I tell myself I will feel nothing.

"How can I not?" I snort. "You lied to me."

"Lando—" He reaches out for me but I step back, shaking my head.

"Don't touch me. It's fine. It's like you said, right at the beginning?" I shoot him a glare. "We're both in it for what we want?"

"You know that's not true any more."

"It is for me." I grab the ingredients, pushing them all into my bag. I leave the jar of Shasta's dirt on the desk. "You've been using me to get over your brother and to replace your friend? Well, big shock, I've been using you too. I've been using you for a serotonin boost and to get this spell done, but none of that's *real*." I can see from his stricken face that my words are hitting him hard but I don't care if I hurt him. He's already done much worse to me. "What I have with Elizabeth, that's real. I'm in this for her, and no one else."

I push past him, out into the living room, moving faster than I know he can, desperate to get away somewhere where I can finally let myself cry.

"Wait, Lando, you can't do the spell on your own," Bastian calls. "You don't have the skill, it's not safe—"

"Like I care what you say." I stab the button for the lift.

"It was real," Bastian says urgently, leaning a hand against the wall. He looks like he needs to lie down. Then I ask myself why I care. "Everything I felt for you, everything I feel for you, it's real for me. I know it's real for you too."

"You don't know me." I step into the lift. René tries to follow me and I use my boot to block his path. He tilts his small head at me as if worrying why I'm leaving so soon, and that sad, curious face shatters me completely. "I don't know you either. We're just two people using each other to get what we want, but I don't need you any more. I have everything I need."

"Please don't try to do that ritual alone...please." Bastian slams his hand against the lift doors to stop them from closing. "You could die."

I want to believe he cares, but I can't. After all, I don't.

"Good," I say.

Chapter Twenty-Seven

I hate myself for being one of those clichéd people who cries on the tram, but as soon as I sit down, I weep, turning my face towards the glass and trying not to sniffle too much. The worst thing is how guilty I feel about betraying Elizabeth. It was all for nothing. It wasn't moving on, it was just being played, being preyed upon because I'm a shifter. I wonder bitterly how many times in one life I can make the wrong choices about people; first Carl and now Bastian. Yet despite everything, I can't think of them both in the same sentence. I remember Bastian saying, *I think you're brilliant, Lando,* and I feel a rough, clenching sensation in my chest. For a second, I can't get in enough air, panting and huffing. If this is what actual heartbreak feels like, it's more physical and brutal than I've been led to believe by romcoms. It has much more in common with grief, the wearying woundedness of it that seeped into my bones after Elizabeth's death. All the rest of the way home, I think about the bathroom.

When I put my key in the door at Beryl's, I find her standing on the other side of the door, holding Mr Pebbles like a baby.

He hisses at me and I hastily wipe my eyes.

"There's a friend of yours from college here to see you, pet," Beryl says, gesturing to my bedroom. "I signed them in and let them sit on your bed. Also, I changed your sheets. Mr Pebbles did a piddle on your pillowcase."

"A friend?" My heart races. I wonder if Bastian has jumped into his Mini and scurried round to Chorlton to beat me home off the tram, but when I open the door, it's Kira Tavi sitting on my bed. My disappointment is like ash on my tongue. She is the last person I want to see. She might have had good intentions, but right now, all I can think about is everything she's taken from me. Kira seems to know it, because she holds up her hands placatingly.

"I'm not here to fight again. I just want to show you something." She reaches into the pocket of her duffle coat.

"No, get out."

"I'm not trying to hurt you," she says, her voice quiet. She's holding something in her hands, a photograph, with the picture turned away from me. "Please, just look. Then I'll go, I promise."

I stare at it. I wonder what terrible picture she has to show me. Maybe it's Bastian and Cameron together, proof that they were friends. If that's the case, it can't possibly hurt more, and she'll be gone soon, so I nod wearily.

She hands it to me. It's a black-and-white photo of two women, both standing next to an ambulance, wearing green uniforms and tin helmets. They have their arms around one another in a friendly way. One I recognize from my dream with a painful pang. The same dark skin, the same infectious smile.

The woman my shifter loved. The woman who died in the cathedral bombing.

"How did you—"

Then I catch sight of the ring on the woman's finger, the ring I saw in my dream/vision but didn't truly notice until now. It's the same ring, that distinctive silver setting, as the ring on Kira's finger.

"That's my Great-Aunt Bisan, Bisan Tavi." Kira presses her finger against her face. "My ring used to be hers."

B for Bisan.

"Bisan," I whisper. I move a trembling finger over to the face of the person standing beside her, holding her so fondly with a wide smile and knowing eyes. *Could it possibly be?*

I glance uncomfortably up at Kira, running through every time this term that she has messaged me wanting to "chat" and I've ignored her. Answers about my visions were literally walking around college and I was so scared of what Kira might tell me about Elizabeth that I didn't even consider listening to her. I am once again caught up in a well of self-recrimination against my past short-sightedness – *Lando, you absolute twat* – until I remember that I listened to Kira today and look what it's done to me. My suspicion and anger rise back up like a volcano.

"Why are you showing me this?"

"Because of them." Kira points at the face of Bisan's companion with a determined expression. "My Great-Aunt Bisan was in a relationship with them at a time when it was taboo in our world, and even in the human world. Aunt Bisan chose them, even though they were white and they presented female. Even though she was a witch and they were a shapeshifter."

I can't speak. I stare into their eyes, a different type of emotion pushing through the sadness of my fight with Bastian. A gentle recognition, a warming in my heart that seems to say, *I know you. Hello, again.*

"I told you I'm not against shapeshifter and witch relationships," Kira goes on. "I didn't have it out for you and Elizabeth and I don't have it out for you and Bastian. Telling you Aunt Bisan was in love with a shapeshifter was the only thing I could think of to prove it to you."

I nod soundlessly, but I can't take my eyes off the photo of the shapeshifter, like they're an old friend I've been missing. It's staggering, this beautiful truth that they were real. That they lived.

"What happened to them?" I ask, trying to hide my urgency.

"My aunt died in the Second World War, during a bombing," she says quietly. "Her shapeshifter disappeared after that."

I look down at the photo of my shifter and think, *It's really you.* In their female form, they have brown curly hair, waved in that forties fashion. They have a long face, large eyes and a pointed chin. Their eyebrows are bushy and strong, and give their face such an arresting look. I think I can see all of the stories of their life in their eyes: the protests, the wars, the loss of their parents and the miracle of Bisan's love.

"Did they have a name?" I press, all attempts at casual speedily unravelling. "Or even a last name?"

"Why are you asking?" Kira takes the photo back protectively, and I'm deeply disappointed. I want to hear their name so much, it feels like something essential and hopeful has been snatched away again. "Why do they matter to you? Do you know them?"

I open my mouth. *No,* I think. *But also, yes, better than anyone.* I stare into Kira's quizzical and slightly expectant face and realize, suddenly, I have no reason to keep this secret any more. It's not like she can stop me trying the spell if I want to, and if she wants to get me in trouble for stealing a book, so be it. What do I care? I'm already known as a murderer, why not add thief to the moniker? I reach under my bed and pull out *The Witchlore of Bodies.*

"Because I read their diary," I say, opening it to the first page of the journal. Kira stares at it like it's a live snake. She nervously glances at the closed door.

"This was part of the John Rylands exhibition, did you...?"

"Nick it? Yeah."

"You did?" Kira's dark eyes are boggling. "You *stole* it?"

"So? You stole a personal file," I say quickly. "Besides, we're going to give it back. They don't know it's even gone."

"But there was nothing in the exhibition notes about it having a diary in the back!"

"Shifter blood lock." I shrug. "Opened the diary and revealed a...spell."

I'm hesitant to admit we were looking for the resurrection spell, mainly because I don't want Kira to know all her suspicions about Bastian were correct.

"And your blood unlocked the spell *and* the diary," she murmurs, tentatively touching her finger to the page and then turning pages back until it's open on the revealed portion of the resurrection spell. I'm surprised how sad it makes me to look at it now, and I glance down at my bedspread, eyes stinging. "So this is the resurrection spell he tried to use with his other shifter? He was going to use you like he used her?"

That's an unnecessary kick in the face and I take in a sharp breath.

"Happy you're right about him?" I sneer. "Do you want a gold medal?"

"No, I want to know why you were doing it," she says. Her eyes are intensely focused on me. I wonder how much of my motivations she has already guessed. I'm too emotionally exhausted to lie.

"He told me we were going to do it for Elizabeth; we have all the ingredients." I swallow hard, thinking about Bastian pushing me out of the way of the boggart and pulling me out of the water. Everything he did, every little kindness, was a lie. "But now we're not doing anything together."

Kira looks nervous. "Did you break up?"

"We weren't together," I say, even though I felt like we could have been. *What would it have felt like to call Bastian my boyfriend?* I shake my head bitterly. "No thanks to you."

"I'm really sorry it hurt you." Kira looks down at the book. "But he wasn't being honest with you and…you did need to know."

I close my eyes to control my temper. She's right, of course, but I wonder if there is anyone else in the world I would hate to hear these words from more. Maybe Carl Lord. Or my parents.

But, oddly, Kira seems to care about me more than my parents ever did. That gives me a little bit of needed perspective and I take a slow breath. *Why does it matter if she was the one to tell me?* I snap at myself. *It doesn't stop the fact that he lied to me and used me.*

"None of it matters now." I sigh. "I don't know if it will even work without him."

Which means I'll never get Elizabeth back. When she died, I thought there couldn't possibly be a worse feeling than that, but now there is this. Knowing I've failed her twice, failed her horribly, not just by being unable to undo my catastrophic mistake and bring back the life she is owed, but by unthinkingly giving my heart to someone so undeserving. I couldn't even be faithful to her memory and that thought makes me want to throw up. I blink heavily and turn away, staring at where Mr Pebbles is squatting in one of my cacti, having a piss. I don't even bother to shoo him off. When I look back at Kira she is running her fingers across the spellcraft notations on the page, her brows furrowed.

"I can...help you do it," Kira says slowly. "If you want."

"What?" I stare at her. It's literally the last thing I ever expected to hear from her. "Why?"

"Because I think I can." Kira presses her palm against the spell. It's almost a protective gesture. "I know you don't think much of me, but I'm in the year above you, and my family is powerful. I've probably got the knowledge and strength to do it."

"I thought you said witchcraft like this was reckless. You called Bastian dangerous."

"I still think he is dangerous, because he had the wrong priorities and he was lying to you." Her eyes flash with conviction. "But I probably want the same things you want."

"What do you want?" I ask. Kira looks down at her aunt's ring, rubbing the stone reflectively before she speaks.

"I know you don't believe this but I do actually care about you, and I believe you."

"Believe me?"

"I believe that you didn't mean to hurt Elizabeth. She was a secretive person. I loved her. I knew it came from fear, but if she had told me or told her mum what she was planning to do, I believe we could have stopped it. Whatever happened, I believe that you deserve a chance to correct it," Kira says steadily. My ribs hurt and I rub them, trying to breathe through it. So far, the only person to say that to me has been Bastian, and Bastian turned out to be a liar. "Also, well, you're crap at witchcraft. I'm worried you'll hurt yourself."

Her eyes drift down to my wrist. I feel self-conscious and cover it. She's got me there. My plan at the moment doesn't leave room for an in-between scenario; either I'm successful in the ritual, Elizabeth comes back and I am cleansed of my guilt and have atoned for my colossal fuck-ups, or I'll bleed out in the cave just like I almost did in the bathroom. Kira nods, like she's read all of my dark, destructive thoughts in my eyes.

"You're less likely to mess it up or bring her back wrong if I help," she says practically. "And that's what we want, isn't it?"

I close my eyes briefly, imagining Elizabeth, standing again in the sunshine, wondering where the summer has gone. She'll probably never forgive me for what's happened with Bastian, but what does it really matter? She'll be alive. Even if she never touches me or speaks to me again, it'll be enough that she's breathing. I'll have done the impossible. I'll have turned back the clock on death, and even though it might never make up for what Bastian's done to me, or this time without Elizabeth, it will be something, at least. I may have defeated a boggart, a hellhound and my slimeball bully, but Kira is right, I still can't produce magic. I need her help. Also, I reckon there's a real chance that she will follow me if I don't agree to let her join in, just based on the way she seems to have spied on me pretty consistently since term started.

"Okay, yeah," I say. "You can help me. It needs to be Samhain. Early morning, so people don't see."

"I have class at nine on Monday morning."

"Well, bunk it off."

"I don't do that."

"You will." I open my door for her, trying to look dignified, even as Mr Pebbles runs past me with a hiss. "Meet me at the Alderley Edge Cemetery at seven."

Kira lets out a long, frustrated sigh that does not endear her to me one bit. I look at the door significantly. I'm not above telling her to get the hell out if I have to.

"Okay." Kira stands up and walks out of the door, looking back at me. For a second, her brown eyes are filled with nauseating pity. "I'm sorry he hurt you, Lando."

That, it turns out, is the end of my tether. I slam the door in her face.

* * *

On Sunday night, I dream of Elizabeth. I dream of the long, exhausting seconds after her death when I sat in the catastrophe of my loss, her body still painfully warm against mine, despite the world being entirely upended. Then, my dream changes. The face in front of me is no longer Elizabeth's. It's the tear-streaked face of a dark-haired woman who looks like an older Bisan Tavi, staring at me with all the hatred of a woman broken beyond repair.

"I'm so sorry. I'm so sorry that she died," I weep.

"You are the reason my child is dead." Her voice is so cold but full of magic. I know there is nothing I can do to stop what's coming.

"I swear, I did everything I could to save Bizzy—"

"If she had not been with you, she would not have died!" the woman screams, the ruby ring on her finger glowing intensely, light beginning to pulse out of it in a threatening way.

"I wish it had been me!" I scream back at her desperately.

"It will be you! I will curse you, shapeshifter." Suddenly, her face twists into Elizabeth's mother's face, her hands lifted into the preparatory triangle, twisting her fingers into shapes that I know will ruin me.

I wake up, gasping in the darkness. I can still feel the heat and smell of her magic, fierce as a petrol fire. My heart is still pounding, my brow sweaty. Elizabeth's mother's face and the woman who could have been Bisan Tavi's mother blend together in my mind, a sickening combination on the edge of a vision or a nightmare. I turn on my bedside lamp and see that my phone is alight with messages. They're all from Bastian.

> Lando, I'm so sorry.
> Please don't do the ritual.
> You mean so much to me.

I wipe away a tear with a shaking finger. He's been messaging me all weekend; he even tried to drop round on Saturday afternoon, but I told Beryl not to let him in. She looked absolutely agonized about it and offered to do a heart-healing ceremony with me to open my love chakras, but I turned her down. She told me to have a session with Counsellor Cooper but I wouldn't pick up the phone. Beryl or Counsellor Cooper must have made a call to Paris because I received an email on Sunday morning from my mother. The subject line was simple and infuriatingly unhelpful, two words – Not witches – but the content was surprising. A train ticket to Paris. It is certainly a measure of how bad things feel this weekend that I actually considered it; anything to get away from my inescapable, irrepressible want and despair.

Despite myself, when I look at Bastian's messages, I still wish he was here. I wish he could hold me like he did last week, stroke my back and tell me I'm safe. I hate myself for it, for not longing for Elizabeth and for wanting Bastian instead. Sniffing, I pull out *The Witchlore of Bodies* and flick to the very last pages. If my dream was actually a vision, and the woman I saw cursing me really was Kira's great-grandma, Bisan Tavi's mother, then surely there will be an entry about it. I search desperately for any references to the cursing I saw in my dream but I find nothing, nothing at all. The last words in the diary are about Bisan.

> Without her in my life, I don't know how to go on.
> I need to find a way. Whatever it takes, I will do it.

It's so abrupt, I flip forwards, looking for more. That can't be the end, so bleak and unsatisfying. What if my shifter was cursed and died, just like in my dream? It's such a passive, terrible ending for a person who always took firm control of their life. I don't think I can cope with the loss of my shifter *and* Bastian, so I turn my mind to other explanations. I lean back against the headboard and remember Elizabeth's mother's rage when I saw her at the hospital, her words that live inside me every day: *I should curse every inch of you, shifter.* Is it any surprise, really, after all of that, that my mind created a dream where my shifter was cursed, just like Dr Toppings threatened to do to me? I cling to the hope this is a mere invention of the mind. I want my shifter to have had a different ending. I'm not naive. I know it's likely that they perished, either in the war or some other way. The diary ends in 1941, the same year that Kira told me the shifter disappeared.

Suddenly, I wonder if the shifter from the past is more like me than I thought. Maybe they tried the resurrection spell to bring back Bisan Tavi? Even if they didn't survive that process, tonight that feels like a better ending to me. Isn't striving for love better than helpless and cursed?

My phone buzzes, interrupting my thoughts. It's Bastian again. I look at the clock. It's two in the morning. I'm surprised he's awake.

> I know I lied to you but I didn't lie about
> what I feel for you.

I turn my phone face down and my lamp off, rolling over and burying my tears into my pillow. For some reason, that's the hardest part of all of this, because even if that's true, does it make it any better? All it means is that despite what he thought he felt, he didn't feel it enough to be honest with me. Only Elizabeth, I realize, has ever truly been honest with me. It's time to get her back.

Chapter Twenty-Eight

At seven o'clock on Samhain morning, I am standing with Kira Tavi, looking down on the grave of my dead girlfriend. I've never been here before. I couldn't go to the funeral and I've not really had the heart to come on my own, worried about running into her parents. The headstone is bright white marble, so fresh it looks like it's made of polystyrene. There are all sorts of mementos left around it, drooping balloons and dying flowers turning brown in plastic wrappers and, a clear sign of witch visitors, a row of small semi-precious crystals and gemstones on top of the headstone. ELIZABETH TOPPINGS, BELOVED DAUGHTER. It's weird that it's the only thing people will know about her in the future. Not that she loved history and could do backflips on the trampoline and was obsessed with Percy Pigs. I feel a flash of mourning for all of those lost tiny things and that one day she'll disappear in history, just like my shifter's name. Beside me, Kira pulls a polished rose quartz out of her pocket and leaves it on the top, touching the headstone respectfully.

"No one's ever told me why covens do that," I say.

"It's a superstition, really." Kira looks a bit uncomfortable. "It's meant to...I don't know, mean her magic goes on through other witches."

I nod.

"Well, if we get her back she'll have to redistribute them," I say, trying to joke, but Kira only frowns.

"No, she'll keep them. They are well-wishes for her magic. Obviously."

I glare at her for assuming that everything in witch culture is obvious to a person who isn't even allowed to be part of a coven.

"I should warn you, every time I've touched an ingredient for this spell, I've shifted," I say, pulling a jar for the dirt out of my backpack.

"Well, why don't I get it, then?" She kneels down to scrape up some dirt.

"Oh. Yeah. Right." It's pretty sensible when I think about it, but I don't want to think about it, because then I'm going to think about Bastian pushing me away from a boggart's path, pulling me out of the ocean, holding the summoning spell so steady while I reached for the Black Shuck.

"So your shifts, they've been because of this spell?" Kira asks, taking the jar from me. Looking at it reminds me of Shasta's jar. I imagine Bastian at Shasta's grave collecting it, kneeling in front of a headstone by himself. I feel a pang for him then, lonely and stressed, missing Shasta, searching for a way to get him back. Then I remind myself I don't care because he's a liar.

"Yeah, I think so."

"Interesting." She drops a handful of dirt into the jar with a frown. "Do you have any other magical symptoms? Dreams? Nightmares?"

I nod mechanically. Soon, however, it will all be over, and then I won't care about the dreams or the shifter from long ago. I'll have Elizabeth back.

"What are they about?"

"That's not important." I'm not about to share dreams with Kira Tavi. She'd probably make me journal about it.

"It might be."

I shrug. I can hardly tell her that I've dreamed about her great-aunt's death. I might not like Kira very much but I'm not a dick.

"Do you think it's possible that your great-aunt's shifter could have tried the resurrection spell?" I ask instead.

Kira leans back on her heels and stares at me.

"Why?"

"Because I wonder…if that's how they died." I glance at all the headstones around me. For all we know, they could be buried here, an ivy-covered gravestone with no one left to visit it. "You said they disappeared after your great-aunt died, but I wonder if they used the spell to try and bring her back and died, just like Bastian's friend did."

Kira stares at me and then screws the lid on the jar.

"Can you expand on that?" she asks. That's a question that takes me straight back to the hospital, to sitting in a room with Counsellor Cooper, and I smile drily.

"You really do want to be a counsellor, don't you?"

"Yes," she says, without a hint of irony. "Can you? Expand?"

"Not really. I just wonder if that's why I get the dreams." I fix my eyes on a grubby purple teddy bear that someone's left. I wonder why people think everyone would like things a seven-year-old does when they're dead? "Because the shifter is connected to the spell. Maybe it doesn't work. Maybe it only kills people."

"We don't have to do this, Lando," Kira says, and her voice is so gentle, so pitying, it immediately makes me itchy. I shake my head violently.

"No, we're doing it, I guess I'd just...I'd like to know what the chances of success are."

"I don't know." Kira sighs and stands up, brushing the damp patches on her leggings. "All of the successful resurrections are from pre-Roman times. There's basically no literature on them."

"But we have all the ingredients, we have me, that's a good sign?" I take the jar from her, holding my breath. We both stand and wait tensely for a few seconds, Kira's eyes flicking rapidly up and down me, looking for signs of shifts. Nothing happens. I let out a sigh of relief. Kira nods, as if this confirms a theory, and looks pleased not to be on the end of an uncontrollable shapeshifter throwing magic all over the place.

"Intention is important in sacrificial witchcraft rituals," she says smartly. "So I think it's best to focus on what you want."

What I want are all the things I can't have. I want Elizabeth to never have suggested we go to the cave and I want her to never have died. I want Shasta to never have died and for Bastian to never have lied to me. I want to be normal, like everyone else, and not feel like the person who understands me best in the world is a dead shifter from World War Two. Most of all, I want it all to be over.

"I want to do the spell," I say. "I want to make it right."

We get the bus up to the Edge. The forest is beautiful and it's an aggravatingly stunning morning, the sky periwinkle blue with fluffy white clouds; the light on the autumn trees makes the leaves glow in an ombré of fading colours, lemon to amber to mahogany. Even though she died in summer, there is something about the quality of the air, the surprising heat of the October sun that reminds me of that day. I start to feel anxious. Kira seems to notice as I lengthen my breathing, accidentally thinking about Bastian when he helped me with my panic attacks, stroking my back and telling me to focus on my exhalations.

"It's hard to be here," Kira says astutely. I nod tautly. She is quiet as we smile politely at a single dog walker with a Labrador. We pass The Wizard Tearoom, decorated with pumpkins and autumnal flowers, ghosts made of sheets fluttering gently in a breeze scented with fresh cakes, and I think how much I would like to be here with Bastian, holding hands and walking through the crispy leaves. Then I hate myself for wanting that.

"She loved these woods," Kira says, drawing me out of my thoughts and making me feel even worse for thinking about Bastian when she's clearly remembering Elizabeth. "We used to come and play here when we were kids."

I wonder if this was part of the reason that Kira was so

fidgety in the graveyard. This place isn't just the place where Elizabeth died, it's a place that is full of memories of the two of them together. I feel remorse now for what Kira lost, imagining for the first time that like me, she's been wandering around familiar places being stabbed by memories of someone who is no longer here.

"I don't know why it happened. Bastian thinks it's because this spell was already woven into the stone, a spell that relied on a shapeshifter, and it had some kind of reaction to Elizabeth's spell…" I sigh heavily, realizing that Bastian could have just lied to me. He could have said anything. "I don't know…maybe he was just saying stuff to make me feel better."

"Not this. He's right, if there's a spell in the stone, the spell from the grimoire, it would have reacted. It's entirely unpredictable, that's why shifter blood is never used in modern witchcraft, it's too volatile. He wasn't lying about that, at least."

I throw her a sharp look of annoyance.

"Why did you tell me about him?" I snap. "About his past?"

"Because I worried that he was using you like he used that other shifter." Kira looks at me shrewdly. "Was I right?"

I realize I don't actually know the answer. Bastian said he'd moved on, that he was doing this for me and not Shasta, but I don't know if he was lying about that too. I catch sight of the dark entrance of the cave and I stumble.

Elizabeth is tugging me along, laughing in the summer sun. "Come on! It's a surprise! Hurry up!"

"Are you okay?" Kira touches my arm gently and I instantly miss Bastian's firmer grip, but Bastian's a liar. So I take a deep breath and nod, walking up towards the cave.

"This is an intensely magical spot, I've read about it," Elizabeth says. Above us, the trees whistle gently, full of green leaves; the air smells like hay and pollen, thick and bright.

The entrance of the cave is a black mouth in the grey stone all around it. My feet are hesitant, dragging, wanting to run away rather than keeping walking towards it, but I have to. Kira pulls out a torch and I can't help but roll my eyes, because of course Kira is the kind of person to have an actual camping torch the size of a courgette.

"Come on, then," she says briskly. "The wizard's cave is supposed to be at the back."

She switches the torch on and walks into the cave, ducking under the lip. I stare down at the entrance to the cave, looking for the bloodstained piece of slate that killed Elizabeth. It isn't there. I'm absurdly affronted that something as uncaring as the weather may have washed away all evidence of the thing that crushed her skull and took her from me.

"We need a bit of your blood to open the cave," Kira says. I follow her into the darkness but hang back in the entrance, trying not to think about how this was the last place Elizabeth kissed me. The coldness of the damp, the smell of the moss, it brings it all back. Her hands, her netted fingers for the Web of Wyrd, the pressed finger knuckles together with thumbs upraised for Woden's Power, and the chanting of her voice as the spell began. *Breathe, Lando,* I tell myself.

"Come on, Lando!" Kira calls, and I pull myself out of the past, pushing forward, crouched over. The cave becomes narrow and dark at the back, impossible to stand up in.

"There cannot be another cave back here," I mutter.

"It'll be marked. Check the stone for anything that feels like a rune or a gramarye notation. That's where your hand needs to go."

"Okay."

We run our hands over clefts in the stone, feeling furry moss, slimy crevices and engraved graffiti until finally, when I think my neck is going into a spasm from being crooked at this angle, Kira says, "Here. The notation for Merlin."

I shuffle until we're both crouched like frogs staring at the tiny slot of back wall, Kira's torch casting a glow on the grey stone. I see a rough, familiar symbol etched there. I tilt my head to the side.

"I suppose it could be, at this angle."

"We need to put a little bit of your blood on it," Kira whispers. "If it's real, it will open."

"Do you have a knife or something?"

Kira produces one from the pocket at the front of her dungaree dress. I briefly wonder what else Kira Tavi packed in anticipation of this expedition, but then I stare as she flicks open the shining blade. I've shed a lot of blood to get to this point and, honestly, it's brought me nothing but trouble. *But this is the end,* I reason with myself. *Nearly there.*

"Here goes nothing," I mutter, and press the knife tip into my thumb, just like I did when Bastian and I unlocked the journal in *The Witchlore of Bodies*. I press my bloody thumb against the mark and hold my breath. The torch shakes in Kira's hand.

"Come on," she whispers. "Come on, come on—"

"Should I bleed some more?" I ask, pressing my thumb harder into the surface.

"Maybe wiggle it around a bit—"

"I am wiggling!" I protest, slightly hysterically, wanting to laugh and cry, wanting to run and also to punch something, really hard. Unhelpfully thinking, *God, I wish Bastian was here.* "What else should I do, a little dance?"

Then, suddenly, there is a grinding sound, getting louder and louder, and I pull my thumb away, my heart thundering.

"Is that good?" I ask.

"Either it's working or it's going to collapse on us!" Kira says, her voice getting louder over the monstrous grinding sound. I wince, reminded of the way the cave had rumbled when Elizabeth died, the feeling of magic surging through me and turning the world over. The ground shudders under our feet and the rock begins to split. The back of the cave opens into darkness, and through the dislodged sand and trickle of pebbles falling from the ceiling, I see with a lurch that it's just tall enough for a person to stand inside, a coffin in the earth.

"This is it," Kira whispers, when the grinding finally stops. As Kira flashes her torch around the space, I see there's a pentagram drawn on the floor in salt. My stomach flip-flops queasily and I can't help but think, *It's waiting for me.*

Chapter Twenty-Nine

"Wow." I swallow hard and step inside. I'm beyond relieved that the stone doesn't close behind us, so the dim, weak light of the outside can still reach me, here in the heart of the earth. "So this is Merlin's cave."

"It's not actually Merlin's, you know, humans just have a habit of attributing places associated with historical witchcraft to him. All that poetic *wizard* nonsense. There's very little historical evidence that he was ever here. It doesn't mean it isn't a powerfully magical location, though." As Kira speaks, taking off her bag and starting to bustle, like she walks into ancient magical locations all the time, I wish it was Bastian giving me facts and acting like a know-it-all.

"Yeah, I got that." I pull the ingredients out of my bag, along with the grimoire. Kira quickly moves the book, which is open on the page of the spell, to the top of the pentagram and pulls out a magnifying glass. "What's next?"

"Put the ingredients on the points." Kira kneels with her magnifying glass held over the page of the book. I obey and set the hair, the name, the bone in their places. With each one,

I can't help remembering what it took to get it. *Stop thinking about him,* I scold myself. *He betrayed you.* I watch as Kira sprinkles Elizabeth's earth out of the jar in the centre of the pentagram.

"And now?" I ask nervously. Kira doesn't even look up from the grimoire.

"You're an ingredient. You stand on the last point of the pentagram and..." She hands me back her knife. "You bleed."

"Right, yeah, a pint of blood," I mutter, recalling how Bastian explained it to me when we first read the book together. "From anywhere?"

"From...from your arms." Kira reluctantly looks down at my wrist. I sigh. It feels right, in a way, that this should be how I bring Elizabeth back. After all, this was how I tried to get back to her the first time, by joining her in death. This time, hopefully, she'll be joining me in life. "Be careful, though. Don't do it the same place you did before. We need you to bleed slowly, for the ritual."

"Morbid." I set the knife further up, by the crease of my elbow. "How will we know that we're done?"

"Because the resurrection will happen," Kira says impatiently. "Now, cut yourself and be quiet, I need to concentrate."

"Harsh."

I feel a sudden tremor of fear and doubt crawling up my gut, all the way to my throat. The last time I did something like this, Elizabeth died. Kira might be pretty annoying, but I don't want her to die and I'm scared of what will happen, how Elizabeth will come back – what if we make a mistake and only bring her halfway back, trapped between the living and dead, making everything worse? I feel like I can say none of those things to Kira, who lost her too, but I need something to push me on. Something to get me to do this again, put a blade to my arm and bleed, hoping to see her.

"I know she told you not to talk to me and she was afraid of her mum but...was she happy with me?" I ask abruptly. "Can you just tell me, was she happy?"

"Yes," Kira says, her face softening. "Yes, Lando. She'd never had a relationship before; she'd been too scared of being herself. You made her incredibly happy."

I hover the knife over my arm and, for a second, think about what Counsellor Cooper said. She told me not to be afraid of moving on. For a second, I wonder if that's what I'm doing here. Am I so afraid of moving on that I'd rather risk my life for the chance of going back in time? *Yes,* I think. Absurdly, I hear Bastian's voice in my head: *You deserve to be free from this, Lando.* This is how I get free. So I cut my arms. The pain isn't as bad as last time, and as I watch the blood trickle down my wrists I think wearily, *Here we go again.*

"There are three positions you need to echo for me to get it started while I chant; you'll know it's beginning when you feel it. Then you just need to concentrate on staying alive," she says.

"What are the positions?"

"The Web of Wyrd, Woden's Power and the Touch of Persephone. Echo me, okay? Eyes on me."

I nod and lift my hands into the preparatory triangle as Kira does the same. She moves her fingers into the netted position and I copy, the blood from my arms dripping to the floor. Kira chants as we move to the thumbs upraised for the Woden's Power, and her ring glows red, filling the cave with a deep, disconcerting light. Fire without heat dances along the lines of the pentagram and the shadows leap on the walls and suddenly, all around me, I see alchemical symbols scratched into the ancient stone. I feel a nasty wave of dread.

We move to the Touch of Persephone, a cage-like grip of the right hand on the left wrist, and that's when it starts. It's sort of how it felt when Bastian borrowed some of my magic, but it's more intense. A ripping, wrenching feeling; the core of me is being dragged out through the blood in my arms, the drips of it hissing on the dirt when they land. *I can do this,* I repeat inside my head. *I can do this for Elizabeth.* I try to focus on her, remembering her hair and her voice and the way she smiled, but suddenly I think of Bastian, wounded terribly but still caring enough to ask if my last shift took too much energy. There's a wave of sadness inside me, so overwhelming and deep that it threatens to haul me under. I'm tired now, more tired than after my shift. The magic is pulling more blood out of me than I can bear and I sway, feeling like I might faint. I look dizzily down at the pile of Elizabeth's earth, willing it to blow or rise, *anything,* but nothing is happening.

"It's not working."

I'm a bit frightened when my own voice seems very far away, but I can't find my way back. The world is tilting away from me, or I am falling out of it, I'm not sure which.

"I don't know why, I've never done this before—" Kira's voice is panicked. "You're bleeding too much, I should stop—"

"No, don't stop!" I moan, dropping down to my knees. The earth is weirdly hot underneath me, but we must keep going. I remember what Bastian said about Shasta's death, about needing it all to have a point. If we stop, I'll be dying for nothing. "Keep going!"

"I have to stop!"

I know in my bones that if she stops, I'll drift out of my body the same way my blood is running down my arms. I'll drop into the earth and descend underneath it and there will be nothing left of me.

I want to tell her again to keep going but my voice is gone completely now. Everything is dark and I can't see Kira or the flames or the cave any more. *Maybe this is it,* I think dizzily. *Maybe I'm finally dying.* I'm struck and amazed by how unhappy the thought makes me. It's not Elizabeth's face that's in my mind right now. It's the smell of eucalyptus balm and coconut shampoo, it's the feeling of a scarred collarbone under my fingers. *Bastian.*

Now, I might never see him again.

"No, keep going! It'll be worse if you stop!" Suddenly, there's another voice, this one even further away, but richer, firmer and full of conviction. "I'll help you!"

The second voice joins the chanting, fibrous and strong, and through the ringing in my ears, I recognize it. Through a veil of cloud over my eyes I see a blue light joining in with the red and suddenly the air around me is vibrant and purple, and I can see it and feel it again and I can smell bonfires, the strength of Bastian's magic, roaring all around me. There's breath in my lungs and I begin to feel the cuts on my skin sealing. The grasping, heavy feeling inside my body, pulling me down to the rocks beneath me, finally stops and, gratefully, I feel myself slumping forward. Warm, steady arms catch me.

"It's finished, you're okay, you're okay—" Bastian says. His scent engulfs me, slightly sweaty but still herbal and faintly antiseptic. I blearily look up into his face, illuminated strangely by the purple fire still flickering all around us in the pentagram, barely trusting myself to believe he is really here. *He came back for me,* I think.

"You," I croak.

"Me." Bastian gives me a tremulous, tentative smile. "You too."

"I'm alive."

"You are." Bastian's voice sounds so breathless with relief that I let myself lean on him as I stare blearily around me. Kira is sitting in front of the book, twisting her glowing ring nervously. There's no one else in the cave. It's a crushing moment and I slump a little further against Bastian.

"It didn't work," I whimper in exhaustion. I don't think I have it in me to do it again. "Elizabeth isn't here."

"The spell isn't complete, Orlando," Kira says quietly. She pushes *The Witchlore of Bodies* towards me. "You have to close the book and seal it."

My hands are sluggish. I'm so tired. Despite everything, I find myself looking up at Bastian's face. His arm is tight around my shoulder and he looks down at me, his eyes glowing weirdly violet in the strange light. I am so glad that I get to see him again, that the earth didn't swallow me whole before I said all I needed to say. Bastian smiles at me tightly, as if he knows exactly what I'm thinking.

"Here." He makes the shape of the Eye of Horus over one of my cut arms with his ring hand. "Time to return the favour."

I swallow drily, my tongue and mouth heavy, but I manage to raise a trembling two fingers to blind his hand movement. The effect is immediate. His ring glows, I smell fire, but more than that, I *feel* it. It's soaking up through my fingers, the strength of Bastian's magic. It's like warm water, making me imagine the ocean near my parents' house after the brightest day, crystal clear and shimmering. Then there's the taste of it inside me, smoky and vibrant, and I gasp, energy sweeping through me that I didn't have before, and I wonder if this is the most intimate experience I've ever had, to have this precious, impossible thing shared with me. I stare at Bastian as he pulls his hand away and see his knowing smile. *Why didn't you tell me?* I think desperately. *Why didn't you tell me this was how you felt about me?*

"Are you...sharing magic?" Kira's eyes widen as she stares at my hands, glowing with Bastian's blue magic, Bastian's strength inside them. Her shock and perhaps revulsion makes me want to pull back, but Bastian doesn't let me. He holds on. He's not ashamed of me, I realize. He doesn't have any regrets or fears and, suddenly, neither do I.

"It's okay." Bastian brushes a piece of bloody, sweaty hair away from my face and then kisses the top of my head. The light pressure of his lips peals with the song of his magic inside me, swelling to power, encouraging me to go just this little bit further. "I'm with you."

It is exactly what I need to hear. With trembling, hesitant fingers, I close the book and press the triangle of my hands against its cover. My hands begin to glow. I should have expected it, I realize, as the shift rolls through me, utterly unstoppable. Immediately, memories swallow me and I remember everything.

I remember myself.

I remember the day I was given The Witchlore of Bodies *by my father. I remember my seventeenth birthday and setting my pen to the page.*

I remember my parents, their love and their joy and their fear for my future. I remember defying their expectations, refusing to settle in one resting form.

I remember switching into a female form to march with the Pankhursts, to stare down anti-protestors and face imprisonment along with my sisters.

I remember taking a male form when war broke out, switching into a younger form to go to France, to fight on the battlefields and cower in the trenches. To suffer on a bayonet in no man's land and almost drown in the dirt.

I remember being brought home to St Annes Hospital, the smell of the sea air in my room as I recovered.

I remember my father fading, our terrible, desolate last words to one another. I remember my mother's death from influenza years later and the sensation of my loneliness stretching.

I remember war breaking out again and shifting into a female form to serve, too ashamed of my father's death to face the fighting once again. I remember meeting Bisan and feeling my world light up.

I remember Bisan's death. I remember standing over her grave. I remember her mother coming to find me, I remember her last words to me before the magic hit: "You will forget the long years you have lived, you will forget your wealth, experience and my daughter. You will even forget how to use your own power! You will live only twenty-one years, without craft or coven, over and over, for all eternity, just as long as my daughter lived!"

I remember what I felt right before the magic engulfed me, cursing me to live over and over without remembrance. I remember I felt relieved. The last thought I have is of Bisan, looking into my face and smiling. "I love you, Ariel Lander," she says.

That's when I remember my name. Ariel Lander. Orlando Southerns. I remember who I have always been.

Chapter Thirty

First, I feel the familiar ache associated with the shift. I distantly examine how my body feels, trying to work out what form this is and realize I can do it much quicker than before. The ancient memory of decades of shifts completes the gaps in my knowledge. I feel out the skin of this new male form. Something about it is peculiarly familiar to me, the soft hair and the thin wrists. Then, I hear voices.

"What do you *mean* they're the shifter from the book?"

"Just that, Bastian, they've been living without their memories, without access to their magic, living a different twenty-one years over and over since 1941—"

"They won't remember that, will they?" The voice is urgent, worried, but I feel such safety from it. "That's horrible to remember, never being able to use magic, only living until twenty-one and then dying, over and over?"

"I doubt it, it was part of the curse to forget."

"But...Lando won't forget *these* years, will they? With Elizabeth and...and me? Will they remember who they are now?"

Even with my eyes closed and my mind full of the past, I am

sure that Bastian Chevret is someone I could never forget.

"They'll remember their past self but, yes, they won't forget they've been Orlando in the present."

I can feel someone stroking my hair. It is so pleasant. Immediately, it's chased by other memories, as if I'm watching them on a screen inside my mind. *My mother, stroking my hair back from my face as I dressed for the suffragist march; my father, stroking my hair as I recovered from my trench wound; Bisan, tucking a piece of my hair into my tin helmet before we went out in the ambulance.* My heart is suddenly full with it all. In a lifetime of thinking I had only really been loved by Elizabeth, now I know it is not true. I have been loved, so loved, many times.

"Do you know what their name was before?" Bastian asks.

"Ariel," I whisper, opening my eyes. "My name was Ariel Lander."

I stare at them both, at Kira and Bastian, my mind brimming with the past. It's as if I'm waking up from the most vivid dream and I am remembering all of it, stories of so many different shifts and faces unravelling inside my head. I don't look for Elizabeth because I already know she won't be here. The resurrection was not for her. I also realize that the person I really want to see, the last person I would want to see if I was dying and the first person I want to see when I wake up, is looking down at me, an intense and familiar frown on his face. *You can be sad about Elizabeth's death and be happy about other things, Lando.* It's taken a whole life of restored memories, but now I do think that Counsellor Cooper might actually be a very good counsellor.

"Lando?" Bastian asks tentatively. "Are you okay?"

"You came," I whisper up at him. "How did you know?"

"Just a hunch." Bastian grins.

I chuckle weakly and look between them. Kira, who reminds me of faces from the past, and Bastian, who reminds me of everything I've lived in these short years of being Lando. I turn to Kira. "You look like Bisan's mother."

"I know." Kira tucks her hair behind her ear nervously. That gesture, how powerfully it reminds me of her great-aunt, and for the first time in this life, I feel a rush of fondness for Kira Tavi. "I'm sorry she cursed you."

"That's okay." I sit up slowly. Bastian still has his hand on my back and I'm happy about it. "You...undid it?"

"Not me." Kira shakes her head fondly. "It was my grandfather. Great-Aunt Bisan's brother, Samir Tavi. He was a great witch, Grandfather Samir. He went to your old house and found *The Witchlore of Bodies* after the curse had been done. He wrote the spell to undo it, called it the resurrection spell, locked it to anyone's blood but yours. He didn't even know you had blood locked the diary too. I didn't know until you showed me. Did you do that yourself?"

"Yes." I see myself, or Ariel, creating the blood lock on the diary when my parents died. It's a strange sensation. This morning I would have called it a vision and been unsure of it, but now it's a memory and I am utterly certain I lived it. "But why would Samir do that? His sister died."

I remember now how close the family was, how Bisan talked about her brother so fondly. I also remember the horror of their mother's reaction. I felt it had been justified at the time, or at least, my past self seemed to think it had been.

"Yes, but he knew it wasn't Ariel's fault." Kira winces. "Sorry, I mean your fault. He wrote the spell to restore your memories but then, well, he lost the book."

"He lost it?" Bastian says incredulously.

"He was in the RAF. He hid the book in his parents' house and they were bombed out." Kira nods. "When Grandfather Samir got back, he looked for it, but it was lost. He tried to keep an eye out for children who might emerge, shifter babies orphaned by the war, but there were so many of them..."

"And Ariel was a shifter, always changing appearance," Bastian says slowly.

"It was impossible," Kira says sadly. "He stopped looking but he passed the knowledge down to my dad, and my dad to me. Grandfather Samir loved Bisan so much, he was always so proud of her, and he hated that the person she loved was lost too."

"Why didn't you tell us before?" Bastian asks, holding my shoulders protectively. I'm surprised by how gratified I am that he said "us".

"I never thought any of this would happen. My dad knew the grimoire was in the exhibition, but even with the book we still had no idea where Ariel could be. In all the time I've known Lando, I've never suspected they were Ariel, and once I started to...well, you wouldn't have believed me." Kira shrugs helplessly. "You don't like me, especially after everything with Elizabeth."

I watch Kira twist her ring on her finger, a ring that no longer feels antagonistic or threatening. It only reminds me of Bisan, using her magic to help people in the Blitz. Despite all of my past resentment, I recognize how much Kira has risked to help me today. The Tavi family may have brought a complicated mix of incredible joy and terrible sorrow into my past life, but that pain feels very far away. Not as relevant as Kira's actions, right in front of me.

"Well, when did you suspect?" Bastian demands.

"Too late." Kira's face is suddenly so sad, her eyes glassy, and I know what she means. *She didn't know in time to save Elizabeth.* "Honestly, at the start of this term, I was just trying to look out for you, Lando. I knew it would be what Elizabeth wanted me to do. Then you two started to get...involved." Her eyes fix on Bastian's arm around my shoulder. He tightens it. I wonder if she's thinking about the magic sharing, something practically unheard of between witches and shapeshifters that we performed so casually in front of her. If she is, she pushes past it to carry on. "I worried it might be too soon. I didn't know if you were a good person, Bastian, then after all the magic with Carl, I looked into you."

"You found out about Cameron," he says quietly. Kira looks down at her shoes. Then she looks up at me with pleading in her eyes.

"I told my dad what I thought was happening; he told me that spell just wouldn't work unless you actually *were* Ariel Lander. There was no other way to verify your true identity. He said you might be having dreams of your old memories and stuff, so I tried to...sound you out a bit. See what was going on."

I think of all her snooping this term. Now I can see the barely veiled desperation behind it all, trying to give me guidance without pushing me away. For the first time, I think I might actually appreciate the excessive efforts of Kira Tavi.

"But I didn't start to think it was possible until I showed you the photo and it seemed like you knew Bisan. I knew then that the best thing I could do was at least *try* and get you back to yourself. I'm sorry I didn't realize earlier, if I had... If only Elizabeth had said something, if she'd *told* me..."

"Kira." I take her hand, pressing my thumb to her beautiful, familiar ring. I am engulfed in the scent of her ripe-plum magic. "You couldn't have known."

She takes a deep, steadying breath and squeezes my fingers before pulling her hand away and sniffing loudly.

"But do we know for sure now?" Bastian says, voice still a little nervous. "You're really a...hundred-year-old shapeshifter? You're Ariel Lander?"

"I am." I watch memories play out inside my mind. Familiar and strange, remote but true. The longer my eyes are open, the more distant the memories feel, my body focusing instead on the sensation of dirt under my fingernails and Bastian's warm hand gently stroking up and down my back. "I was. I..." I swallow hard. "Sorry, I'm thirsty."

"Come on, let's go outside," Bastian says. Kira helpfully packs everything back into my backpack for me and Bastian supports me as we make our crouched journey out into the daylight. I press my bloody hand against the rune in the stone and the secret door swings closed. I wait patiently while Kira uses a spell to carefully bury the other ingredients in the mud in front of the door. I marvel at how unafraid I am now, watching the magic in her ring. There's even a tingling in my fingertips, as if I want to join in, possibilities of the future, potential magic itching to be released.

I take a seat on the sparse grass outside the cave, my back resting against the algae-covered rock. The air around me smells miraculous, fresh and wholesome, that particular scent of wet leaves drying in the sun, organic and sweet. Bastian reaches into his satchel and pulls out a coconut water.

"Did you bring that for me?" I unscrew the top.

"Uh-huh." Bastian smiles so shyly that my stomach tips over. "I know you get thirsty and it's good after—"

"After blood loss, I remember. Thanks." I smile and sip it. Kira is turning off her torch and putting it back into her tote bag and kicking salt off her shoes.

"So, Lando's been living twenty-one years, over and over, their magic bound up by the curse, without remembering?" Bastian's hand is resting on my shoulder. I try to resist the urge to lean into it.

"It won't happen any more, your magic is no longer bound." Kira smiles at me. "You'll never remember those lives you've lived and your life as Ariel will probably just become a memory of a memory." That makes sense to me. The memories of my past life are already shrinking inside of me, becoming less mine and more Ariel's. They're still there, if I look for them, but they're not so overwhelming. What matters more, the memories I can grab and taste, are the ones of Elizabeth, of my long, lonely summer, of Bastian and his kisses.

"And Lando will be safe now?" Bastian presses.

"Yes." Kira gives me a nod. "You won't die and start again."

Bastian's sigh of relief travels through my body.

"So I get my whole life?" I swallow the coconut water.

"If you want it, yes."

At that, Bastian looks at me, his eyebrows raised. I remember the last thing I said to him in the lift, that I hoped the spell killed me. Now I have my past life back, memories I didn't know were missing. I ask myself, *Do I want to live more?* I smile at him and nod. Relief splits across his face.

"Thank you for helping me, Kira," I say. She nods thoughtfully and looks out over the forest, her brown eyes suddenly distant.

"My great-grandma had a lot of grief, and people do terrible things when they're full of grief. I told you I knew what happens when a witch loses control of her power. She lost control. I understand it." Bisan's mother was undoubtedly a prodigy witch, the kind that my father would have respected, but I can see in Kira's face how the weight of her great-grandmother's power has burdened her family. Then she turns her attention back to me. "But Ariel Lander made Bisan happy. Grandfather Samir knew that, and I know it too. Besides, it was a war. There was meaningless death everywhere, but Bisan died trying to save someone. I think that makes her a hero."

I think about everything I remember about Bisan Tavi now. It's like knowing the story of a figure from history, or a relative from long ago. I remember her laugh, her smile, her magic. I recall the way she made tea before we went out in the ambulance and the smell of her cigarettes. I smile.

"She was a hero," I tell Kira sincerely. "She really was, and not just to Ariel Lander. To lots of people."

It feels right, I realize, to talk about myself and my past life this way. All of it belongs to Ariel Lander, the person I was. The future, however, that belongs to me.

Kira's eyes fill with tears and she nods.

"Thank you." She sniffs. "Okay. I'm going into college. I'll see you around."

"Okay," I say. "Maybe we can get coffee."

She gives me a long, calculating look and then smiles.

"I'll see you at peer mentoring next week. But, yeah, maybe we could get coffee."

"I'm sorry we didn't get Elizabeth back," I say softly. With more perspective, the veil of my own anger has lifted and I understand what I've really felt around Kira has been a kind of fearful envy, a part of me terribly worried that Kira had a stronger claim on Elizabeth and if that was true, then I would lose something essential. Now I know that people we lose are all treasured uniquely by the people around them; a cacophony of love, not a competition. "You were her best friend. She deserved another chance to live."

Kira shakes her head, eyes sorrowful.

"The curse laid against you, against Ariel Lander, was made by my family and it took something from you. It took you out of the natural order of life and death. You were always owed correction, you were always meant to come back. But Elizabeth's death was natural." Kira's eyes rest fiercely on mine. "She might have been doing magic at the time, Lando, but she fell. It was a traumatic brain bleed. Her death was never yours to undo because you didn't kill her. It wasn't your fault. Her death isn't ours to hold."

I feel Bastian's grip on me tighten. How far have we both come to learn this lesson? Too far, maybe, but in coming all this way, we found one another.

"Thank you." I smile at her. "I know."

Because I do know, now. I finally understand and something that has been pressing against my chest for months has lifted. I think of Bastian telling me that he knew Shasta would want him to move on, to live his life. For the first time, I feel it. Like she has whispered it into my bones, I know with every part of me what Elizabeth would desire for my life. I want to walk in these woods and remember the kisses we shared here. I want to smile about it. I want to laugh when I remember her jokes. I want to think of her with love and fondness every time I open a history book. I want to honour her with my life by living it. Kira smiles back at me, as if she knows too.

"Happy Samhain," she says.

"Happy Samhain." My mind is flooded with memories of all the Samhains I have seen. How wondrous it is, to have this one, here, with Bastian. We both watch her walk away. I admire her cat-patterned leggings. Maybe she'll tell me where she buys them. Maybe we'll be friends. Anything seems possible right now.

Bastian is wrapping bandages around my arms and frowning.

"Your name before…" he says slowly. "Ariel Lander."

"Yeah."

"The boggart's name was Elander."

"I know, weird." I smile and shake my head. "Maybe it was Samir's way of leading me back to my name. Finding the right boggart in the right place with a middle-class taste for goat's cheese."

"Yep." Bastian smirks and gives me a sideways look. "You sound the same."

"I am the same." Bastian nods but he looks unconvinced. He stands up, brushing salt off his knees.

"Do you want to go for a walk?" He offers me his hand but then, looking confused, pulls it back. "Or you can just go home, if you don't want to talk to me again."

"I do want to talk to you," I say honestly. All my fury over Bastian's lie has drained away, like it was iron in my blood that has dripped out onto the dirt floor in Merlin's cave. With my restored memories, I understand how people can, astonishingly and miraculously, live through and with a grief that nearly killed them. I survived Bisan Tavi's death and, breathtakingly, met Elizabeth. Then Bastian. It's perplexing and I didn't understand it before, the sting of Bastian's betrayal and my own lack of awareness of how it feels to finally move on clouding the truth: Bastian changed. People change. That in itself is its own kind of implausible magic.

I stand up, feeling my body move differently. I look down at my hands and think I recognize them. As we fall into step beside one another, walking past the small car park and into the forest, I catch sight of my reflection in a car window. This is a familiar male form: same gingery hair, same pale skin and muddy green eyes. This is the same form I had after Elizabeth's death, the form I met Bastian in. I smile to myself.

Gently, we follow the path out towards the Edge, following the marked track underneath the trees, gourds and carved pumpkins laid against tree roots in bright flashes of orange and white and green for a children's trail.

"Can I... Is it okay if I apologize to you?" Bastian asks nervously. I watch the way he fiddles with his snake-bone charm necklace fondly. We're both holding our hands loosely at our sides and, occasionally, the backs of our hands brush.

"You've done that already."

"You're not angry any more?" Bastian looks at me curiously. I sigh.

"I wish you hadn't lied to me, but I would never have got my life back without you. And...I understand now. I understand how you changed. I believe you, that you didn't mean to use everything we found to bring back Shasta and I know that must have been hard. You love him."

"Yeah, but there are...different types of love." Bastian's eyes flicker to me and then away. "I should have told you about Cameron, all of it."

"You should have," I agree. "I think we would have got through it. It was the lying, the keeping of secrets, that made it all feel malicious."

"If it's any consolation, I'm going to regret it for ever."

"Maybe not that long." I catch his fingers with mine. I don't mean for it to happen, but something warm and bright passes between our skin, a static charge, a hint of our magical exchange.

Bastian jumps but squeezes my fingers back gratefully. "Are you going to lie to me again?"

"No, never." He shakes his head. I believe him. We drop our linked fingers and walk on together, climbing the hill up to the Edge. The incline is slow and steady, the path through the forest and the crunchy, freshly fallen leaves opening up on the clifftop to the bare, rugged space of Alderley Edge. The ancient stone beneath my boots, the stone that Merlin's cave is carved from, feels lively and thrumming with potential. I feel the magical possibility in the air like I never have before. It quickens my blood, my spirit, and I smile with it.

"So, do you remember everything from the past?" Bastian asks as we step up onto the great weathered stones that look over the Cheshire valley.

"Yeah." I nod. "Ariel's memories are all there. I remember times of sadness, of anger, of pain, but it's a faint memory. It doesn't feel like it happened to me."

"You're calling them Ariel's memories. Not yours."

"You know how sometimes you look back on yourself at a younger age and think, 'God, I don't recognize myself'?"

"Oh, yeah, my boy-band phase, aged twelve."

"Well, that's how it feels. I'm happy to have it all back, it's like it's fixed something inside me that was broken." I think briefly of how the love of Ariel's parents, my true parents, heals the wounds of the parents I have lived with in this life. "But it is different. The intensity isn't quite there."

"It might come back."

"It might." I can't imagine it right now, what it would feel like to experience the sadness of my parents' death all over again, to feel the desolation of Bisan Tavi's death, but then I realize that if it happens, I will survive.

"You're not...scared?"

We sit down on the edge of the rock, our legs swinging perilously over the trees far below, their beautifully coloured leaves spread out beneath us in a vivid tapestry.

"No." I am done being scared about things I can't change.

"Well, you marched with suffragettes and fought in a war," Bastian mutters, tapping his fingers against the rock. "Of course you're not scared."

"I'm not scared because you're here."

I gently put my hand on top of his. The truth is thrumming inside me: *I can move on.* The past matters, it makes us, but today the future is wide and waiting. Something that seemed impossible yesterday is now wondrously feasible. I look out over the valley, the patchwork of green farmland and russet blobs of trees, dots of white sheep in fields and, silhouetted against a clear blue autumn sky, the city I have known in peace and ruin. This is the land I was born in, this is my life and body and my world, and it is all stupendously beautiful.

"Do you feel...really old?" He turns his hand over and links his fingers with mine. "I must seem...I don't know, young and daft to you now."

"No." I laugh. "Bastian, I can tell you absolutely that you are one of the cleverest witches I've ever met. Besides, I'm a teenager, I don't *feel* old."

"You don't?"

"No." My jeans feel like they fit badly and I'm thirsty, but I don't feel particularly old or wise. "It's like...it's like I've watched a load of films. I can see it in my head, remember smells and tastes and sounds but...it doesn't feel like I did it."

"And what about people?" Bastian's looking at me very sharply. "Do you remember your feelings for them?"

"Yeah, but not the same way I remember my feelings for Elizabeth. I know that Bisan Tavi was the first person in my whole life to love me for what I am."

"Other people might have done," Bastian says. "In those years you don't remember."

"I doubt it." I shake my head and watch the red tail of a hawk as it hovers, seeking out prey in the valley below. "In all versions of myself, I am always a shifter. I am always different. There aren't many people like Bisan."

"Or like your Elizabeth." Bastian pulls the jar of remaining dirt out of my backpack. "I'm sorry you didn't get her back."

He stares at me as I take the jar and roll it in my hands. It feels heavy, like I've caged something that doesn't belong caged. Elizabeth is dead and it still hurts. It's a sadness inside me that won't leave me, just like Bisan will never leave me. But I know now that I will shape myself around it and I don't need to be afraid of that. I don't need to fight it. Elizabeth belongs where she is; she deserves rest, just like everyone else I have lost. I gently open the lid of the jar and tip it over the Edge, letting it sprinkle down onto the leaves of the trees. Back down into the earth below. As I watch the dusty parts of it catch the breeze, I think that it was never about getting Elizabeth back. It was about finding a way to live with myself. Finally, I feel like I can.

"Elizabeth was kind to me and amazing, and I'll always miss her, just like I miss Bisan and my birth parents," I say, setting the empty jar down behind us. "But trying to bring her back wasn't the right thing to do. Just like trying to bring Shasta back wasn't the right thing for you. It's not moving on."

Bastian's eyes are glassy as he follows the flight path of the bird of prey. He nods slowly.

"Moving on is...so hard." Bastian swallows his tears and turns to look at me. I think I see all the pain and regret he feels in his eyes. "I didn't believe I could do it until I met you. You... you made me believe living properly, living happily was possible, Lando. Shit." He closes his eyes and then opens them. "Should I...should I call you Ariel? Or Lando Ariel? Or Ariel Lando?"

"No." I shake my head. "Ariel was my past. I'm glad to have them back, but Lando is my present."

And what is the future? a voice whispers to me, one that sounds to me like Ariel, as they wrote in the diary. I don't know the answer yet. I know what I hope for, but I wonder if I'm still too scared to ask for it.

"What do you want to do next? I mean, you have all these memories and stuff, does it...does it change things?"

"Yeah, it does." I smirk. "I think I'm going to do much better on my exams now my magic isn't bound up by a curse."

"Probably!" Bastian's laugh carries over the tops of the trees like an air current. "I can still help you, if you want."

"You'll teach me how to summon hellhounds?"

"Maybe not right away." He grins and nods down to my

hands. "Do you want to test it?"

For the first time in this life, I am neither nervous nor self-conscious about the prospect. I reach into my coat pocket and pull out the tiny crane Bastian made me on our first date. It's a little crumpled but I set it on the stone between us. I take a deep breath, but I know it's there, just like I know my old name. The curse is gone; I am returned to myself, every part of me.

I twist my hands, copying what Bastian did in the bar, my skin glowing softly, magic pulsing warm and delightful out of my fingertips. *I've been waiting for you,* I think, my heart rising joyfully with it. There are poignant tears in my eyes, tears of reunion, and my father's words come back to me. I am alive with the truth of them: *We are the bird, we are the river, we are the tempest, we are our own music, all the time, always singing.* Together, Bastian and I watch as the tiny crane takes flight, lifted by pearly magic, more gold and vibrant than either of my parents' magic, but definitely, certainly, *mine.* Bastian holds his hand out for it but it soars above us, swooping on currents made of magic.

"Magic doesn't have to be permanent to mean something," I say softly. Bastian looks down at my glowing hands, the way my shifter magic ripples across the surface of my skin, transforming it so easily, freckles rising and then vanishing.

"It means everything." His eyes are full of awe. Very gently, reverently, he touches my glowing hand. It's instantaneous, the magical bond between us, the shocking, trembling intimacy of it. It takes my breath away and all I can smell is his magic, tasting smoke inside my mouth. From the way Bastian is breathing sharply through his nose, he's feeling similarly overwhelmed.

"You felt like this, after the first time with the Black Shuck," I say quietly. He nods and his eyes are wary.

"Like I had a part of you." He presses his palm flat against mine. It helps somehow, the intensity of the feeling spreading out, becoming a pleasant hum of recognition through my body. "Your magic feels..."

"Right," I finish for him, fumbling for the correct phrasing for having someone else's magic touch me and not being afraid of it. "Safe."

There are other words too that might come later, I hope, in this instinctual, magical dance we have, an unending expanse of the new compatibility between us to be explored.

"You've lived a long time." His voice is suddenly timid. "I mean, you must have... Have you shared magic with a witch before?"

I shake my head. It's one of the ways I can easily differentiate between myself and Ariel. No matter how much they loved Bisan, Ariel would never have shared magic with anyone. Unlike me, Ariel grew up with parents and shapeshifter traditions they wanted to honour. This decision, this incredible rare thing that goes against all societal expectations for shapeshifters and witches, this is entirely on me.

"Just you," I say. I watch as relief and joy battle across Bastian's face before he suppresses them, face closing off into neutrality. He nods and stares down over the trees, his jaw very tense, like he's holding something in. I know I have my own apologies to make.

"I lied to you, when I told you that I was just using you and none of it was real. I'm sorry I did that. I was hurting and it was cruel and completely false. Because my feelings *were* real." I think about the nights we spent in his bed, skin bare, hearts touching, laughing and eating and sharing stories. These memories are edged in gold, more alive to me than any of the others. "It was the most real I have ever been."

Bastian turns to look at me, a determined expression on his face.

"I have to tell you something," he says urgently. He takes a deep breath and, delightfully, I know what's coming. "Bisan Tavi might have been the first person to love you for what you are but she's not the only one. You said your feelings *were* real but I need you to know that mine *are* real. I feel very, very real about you. I don't care that you're, like, really over a hundred years old—"

"Not in this body! Come on, that's unfair, I'm probably going to get ID'd more than you."

"You're a shapeshifter, you utter crumpet," and his face splits into a picture of wild glee. "You can make yourself *look* older."

"Okay, but I only *feel* eighteen—"

"I don't care, I *love* you, Lando," Bastian interrupts me, catching my face in his hands, and I think he's going to kiss me but, instead, he stares at me. Like he's trying to map every freckle on my face before they change again. "This, what's between us, it's the closest I've ever felt to anyone in my entire life."

"Me too."

In my mind there's a feather-light string of beautiful sapphire-blue magic that smells like bonfires and sings through my blood then out through the centre of my chest, connecting me to him. I don't want it to ever go away.

"You said Lando is your present, but I want your future. Do you understand?" Bastian strokes my cheek and I shiver, pleasantly. "I don't care about the past; I want what comes next. I want...to be with you."

I look at him, a slow smile dawning on my face, so wide that my cheeks hurt, and it's not from shifting.

"Do you recognize this form?"

"Yeah, this..." Bastian looks me up and down. "This is the form you had when we first met."

"I think I chose it because that's what I want next, you know? More of those moments with you." I take hold of his hand, the magic in his ring chiming with the magic inside me. I'm not afraid of it any more. In fact, something inside of me is ready for what comes next, magic building, ready to fly free. "This is my way of saying I love you too, Bastian."

"It is?"

"Yeah." I laugh at his disbelief, that beautiful, open smile that I fell in love with first spreading across his face. "Is that okay?"

"It's more than okay! It's the best way anyone has ever said it to anyone." Bastian laughs and he kisses me. If this is kissing with true magical compatibility, I can honestly say I have felt nothing like it in all of my long life. The last part of me that has been holding back stops waiting. His magic and mine twist together, a breathless sense of completion. He tastes of coconut water and bonfires and the future.

"You know I don't need you to be in this form, right?" Bastian gasps heavily, eyes wide with excitement as his hands tangle in my hair. "All I want is for you to be you, Lando."

Bravery, then, is this: someone's eyes, full of acceptance. Someone's hands, cradling me close. Knowing I am wanted, all of me, as I am.

"Okay."

I smile at him and let the magic rise in me again. I shift, feeling so alive, the fantastic ease of it that makes me laugh out loud. Bastian looks at me in amazement. It doesn't feel like tugging and pulling any more, something shocking and unpreventable. Now, it is wild and powerful as it always used to be and it is mine, fully mine, and I am coming home to myself. I am pulsing with all the possibilities of what my form could be, freed from boundaries and expectations. *I am more than my body,* I think joyously. *I am more than my past. I am Orlando.*

I know, whatever my form is next, I am loved.

"Let's find out what that is," I say.

Acknowledgements

I am indebted to my wonderful agents, Philippa Milnes-Smith and Alice Saunders and everyone else at the Soho Agency, and Peter Knapp and Stuti Telidevara at Park, Fine & Brower. Thank you for your patience with me as a debut YA author and for your continuous cheerleading. Greatest of thanks to Sarah Stewart at Usborne and Vanessa Aguirre at Wednesday Books, who fell in love with Lando and are responsible for sharing their story with the world.

To my friends who read this book before it was even a real book, my magical and wonderful queer community in Manchester and across the pond, I am so full of gratitude. Mya, Rachael, Nick, Dell; my fantasy experts and world-building pedants, thanks for it all.

I am grateful also to Dr Kensa Broadhurst for her Cornish language knowledge and to my dearest Dr Aly Edwards, for being both my Canadian expert and for inspiring Bastian. In missing you, he came into being, and it has been a joy to build this world for us to play in.

As for my community of existing Prince readers around the world, thank you so much for sticking with me on this wild journey. We survive, dear friends. I hope Lando and Bastian bring you all the magical joy you deserve.

When I was a teenage writer, I used to eagerly read the backs of my favourite books looking for hints of how these author types possibly got to the incredible point of writing an entire book. If that's you, then I want to offer encouragement. Keep writing, keep reading, and tell the stories that excite *you* the most. The content of your mind, your very existence, matters significantly. Words are a gateway; who knows what yours will lead to?

Lastly my beloved J, my stalwart: still no dragon, forgive me.

About the Author

Emma Hinds is a queer writer living and working in Manchester who is passionate about writing queer fantasy that explores the depth of British magical folklore. She has a Masters degree in Theology and the Arts from the University of St Andrews and is the author of the well-known fan fiction series, *The Heir to the House of Prince*, which currently runs at over a million words and over a million hits. She has published two adult novels, *The Knowing* and *The Quick and the Dead*. *Witchlore* is her first novel for YA readers.

For news about Emma's next YA novel,
follow her on Instagram
@elphreads